Jameson

In the Company of Snipers

Book 22

Irish Winters

WINDY DAYS
PRESS

COPYRIGHT

Jameson; In the Company of Snipers, Book 22

Cover design: Kelli Ann Morgan, Inspire Creative Services
Cover image: Paul Henry Serres Photography, www.paulhenryserres.com
My gorgeous cover model: Francis Brunet
Interior book design: Bob Houston, eBook Formatting
Editor: Linda Clarkson, Black Opal Editing and Proofreading

ISBN Paperback: 978-1-7348097-8-7
ISBN eBook: 978-1-7348097-9-4
Library of Congress Control Number: 2020918414

In the Company of Snipers

You can find Irish Winters

On Facebook:
https://www.facebook.com/author.irishwinters

On Twitter: https://twitter.com/irishwinters1

If you're an e-reader:
For news on upcoming releases, sign up for
Irish Winters' Newsletter at IrishWinters.com.

For more information about all my books, visit
IrishWinters.com.

IN THE COMPANY OF SNIPERS

This series revolves around former Marine scout sniper, Alex Stewart, and his covert surveillance company, The TEAM, home-based out of Alexandria, Virginia. An obsessive patriot and workaholic, he created the company to give former military snipers like him, a chance at returning to civilian life with a decent job, security, and a future.

This is not a serial with each book ending at a cliffhanger. *In the Company of Snipers* is a collection of passionate love stories involving strong women and men who are tough enough to take on the world alone. Each is a stand-alone read, complete in itself.

Spoiler alert: Every story contains adult scenes including sexual situations (some explicit), language, and violence. I don't write sweet romance, so be forewarned.

Book 1, *ALEX*, reveals how The TEAM came to be, as well as how Alex met Kelsey, how they fell in love and fought all odds to stay together. Each of the following books is a complete romance in itself, where, in the course of an active TEAM operation, one agent comes face to face with his or her demons. The men and women I write about are all patriots and warriors, dealing with what they've lived through or mistakes they've made.

It's my hope that you will come to realize along with my heroes...

Love changes everything.

Prologue

Five Years Earlier

USN SEAL Chief Petty Officer Jameson Tenney stopped firing at the cunning band of ISIL soldiers hidden behind boulders and rocks up ahead. He couldn't believe what was taking place behind him. Two happy go-lucky boys, maybe six or seven years old, had appeared out of no-damned-where. Giggling and squealing from the bony back of a stout, three-foot-high, miniature donkey, they spurred it across the desert like a couple mischievous cowboys, away from the firefight Jameson was currently waging, and straight into no man's land, the unforgiving desert.

Jameson and his six-man SEAL team had been inserted into the southern Iraqi desert Al-Hajarah, at zero-three-thirty hours this morning. Best time of day to do business. Undercover on a moonless night. Easy orders. Locate Professors Murdock and Upton, two United Kingdom geologists taken captive by ISIL extremists, preferably before they were beheaded.

The good professors had naively come to Iraq to study its harsh, arid topography, specifically the wadis, ravines, and channels that filled with spring runoff. They believed underground rivers ran deep beneath those wadis, sources that could ultimately be tapped to provide drinking water and irrigation for the poorer, more desolate parts of one of the most backward countries in the world. They also thought they were immune to the current political unrest sweeping that part of the planet.

But after three tours in this godforsaken, ruined land, Jameson knew better. These people didn't want anything from the rest of the world but for civilization to leave them alone. That old saying: *'Give a man a fish and you feed him for a day; teach a man to fish and you feed him for a lifetime,'* didn't apply here. The more dollars and experts the world's talking heads poured into this country, the more the tribal leaders, village elders, and villagers hated them for it. ISIL owned them now. It was past time to leave.

But not yet.

"You're shittin' me," Ensign Pierce Steed, handle Derby, hissed, his head also cranked around at the unbelievable sight. "What the fuck are they doin' way out here?"

"Playing," Jameson breathed into his helmet's headset, his throat as dry as the air in this damned country. "They're just kids. That's what kids do."

"In the middle of a gawddamned war? Now?"

"Looks like it. I'm going after them."

"Damn, LT just called in an airstrike!"

"Understood. But I'll be back before the Warthogs show." *With the kids, by hell.*

Warthogs, aka USAF close ground support, the A-10 Thunderbolt attack aircraft.

"Gawddamn it, Saint. Don't do it."

Saint was the SEAL handle Jameson hadn't chosen and never wanted. He'd been tagged that because of his choirboy looks and his early promotion, what some guys called a miracle. What others considered a pain in the ass.

He blew a worried breath between pursed lips now. It was a damned eerie scene. The two little boys were laughing like pranksters, kicking and slapping sad little Eeyore's sides, making him run on his stiff, stubby legs. The donkey was as tall as he was round. With every smack, puffs of dust lifted off his furry rump and shoulders. The boys bounced, their dirty brown legs spread too wide for them to stay seated much longer. He kept running. They kept laughing. Beyond them, only sand, rocks, dehydration, and certain death, while all hell broke loose behind them.

"We know where they came from?" Petty Officer First Class Jase Yeats, handle Shakespeare, cut in. "Shit. How can they not hear those fuckin' AKs?"

AK-47s. The dirty, inexpensive, but prolific weapon in every poor Iraqi's arsenal.

Jameson had no answers. Only a solution. "Won't take long. Cover me."

"Shit, no!" hissed Derby. "You'll die."

"No, I won't. I'll be careful. Stay here."

"They're just kids, damn it!" Shakespeare bellowed. "Someone else's kids. Not our problem."

Jameson turned a stark stare to his Navy SEAL buddy. Shakespeare was scared, that's why he was ready to turn his back on the latest macabre twist to a day that had already gone horribly wrong. Jameson understood. He was scared, too. The A-10 was late, and ammo was running low. But someone had to save those boys from themselves. If Navy SEALs wouldn't, who would?

Shortly after they'd arrived, the SEAL team had easily located Murdock and Upton. Everything went down like clockwork. The infil. The swift, quiet elimination of the eleven hostiles holding Murdock and Upton. The acquisition of both professors. As well as the quick stabilization of Professor Murdock's knife wounds, both superficial.

But exfil went sideways. The second Commander Boyington ordered, "Go time," more ISIL tough guys appeared out of nowhere. Thirty-plus more. All armed to the teeth and now pounding the hell out of the mudbrick wall the SEALs and their rescued professors had taken cover behind. Even that leftover of a previously bombed-out building couldn't explain where those boys had come from. Seemed AF drone intel had proven wrong again.

Jameson rolled his shoulders, loosening his muscles and nerves, readying his body for a quick sprint through the loose sand from here to there. Once he snagged those two little guys off that donkey's back, Eeyore would be on his own. Jameson was only saving the kids, who, now that he had time to think, might be deaf. There were more maimed, blind, and deaf children in this country than anywhere else he'd been. All these boys wanted was to be free to run and play again. What child didn't?

"Damn it, Saint," Derby groused. "You can't go out there alone."

"Chief Boyington's going to have our heads for this, but… shit!" Shakespeare muttered. "Shit, shit, shit! I'm going with you. Let's get it done, damn it."

Jameson shrugged his fifty-pound pack off his shoulders and to his feet, praying the upgraded tactical gear his parents had sent last month did its job today. His nostrils flared at the acrid stench combat always brought with it. The hard, lean, spring-loaded muscles in his calves, thighs, and buttocks bunched, as he powered away from safety and into trouble. Zigzagging, he aimed for Eeyore, but ended up scaring the little thing. Jameson ran fast; the donkey ran faster. Hot lead hissed around them as they ran, smacking up clods of sand and dirt, spraying confetti death while his SEAL team returned fire. God bless 'em.

Eeyore's running made sense. He, at least, knew how to save his life. Pounding across that sand like a son of a bitch, Jameson closed in on the escape artist, and, with one gloved hand, grabbed the boy nearest Eeyore's head. Hard on his ass, Shakespeare grabbed the other. While they rolled to the ground with their rescues, Eeyore kept going, and that was okay.

Gibberish poured out of both boys' mouths. Total shrieking gibberish. These kids weren't just deaf. Their skinny chests and empty bellies were laced with explosives, and this was a gawddamned trap. No son of a bitchin' kidding.

Jameson looked at Shakespeare.

His best buddy had the same wide-eyed, *'we're fucked'* shock in his eyes. "You're shittin' me. We risked our lives for these little assholes?"

"No, we risked our lives for two kids." Jameson jerked his chin at the ISIL bastards firing from across the wadi. "Those are the assholes."

Without thinking, he ripped the shirt off the panicked kid in his arm. Simple twine, a cell phone, and a small brick of C4. Which meant some asshat right now was dialing this phone's number. What did he have to lose? Jameson tugged his Leatherman Super Tool out of his vest and deftly ran a gloved hand between the boy's heaving chest and the explosive. Automatically, he told the kid to hold still, not like that helped a damned thing. The frightened kid didn't understand. He kept spewing gibberish. The clock kept ticking.

Jameson snipped the damned wires, and—thank God!—nothing happened.

Shakespeare did the same. Like two fuckin' idiots, they shoved off the sand with the terrified boys in their arms and beat feet back to their team, dodging a hail of gunfire, with Boyington screaming *'what the fuck?'* in their headsets all the way. Yeah, they had a butt-reaming coming, but Jameson flat didn't care. He'd done his duty today. And he'd do it again. God and country, man. But God and kids always came first.

That brick wall sure felt good and solid when he slammed his ass against it, though.

"For fuck's sake!" Derby growled. "Why didn't you save the donkey?"

Breathing hard, Jameson licked his lips, a profanity laced answer on the tip of his tongue for the man who hadn't the balls to save anyone. By then, Chief Boyington was running toward them, his face a contorted, red mask of rage, his jaws jacking, and Hell flashing in those fierce black eyes. Satan couldn't have looked meaner.

Jameson passed the boy in his arms off to the Air Force PJ, the medic who'd dropped into this nightmare with them. He'd come to treat the geologists. Guess he was earning his paycheck today. He already had hold of the kid Shakespeare rescued.

When Boyington ground to a full stop, his square head turned, staring into the desert.

Jameson did a double-take. His LT was watching Eeyore. The scared donkey was now running back to the mudbrick wall. Only he'd taken a circuitous route, dodging ISIL gunfire. It was almost funny how his stiff legs propelled him forward with all the grace of, well, an ass. He looked like he was hopping.

Jameson took a step forward. "Come on," he urged the frightened little guy. "Run faster, damn it. Run!" Too late he realized the ISIL fighters weren't aiming at Eeyore, only near him. They were herding him. "Fall back!" Jameson bellowed as—

BOOM! The poor little donkey disappeared into dust and smoke.

Then *BOOM, BOOM, BOOM!* The scared little guy had triggered a daisy-chained line of explosives that were headed straight for the wall and the SEALs. There was no time to run or think. Only duck, cover, and—

BA-BA-BOOM! The world condensed into a slo-mo firestorm of raw fury. Wicked unleashed energy. A crippling wave of intense heat slammed into Jameson. His arms and feet extended straight ahead of him. Pounding kinetic energy blasted him backward into the wall. He hit hard. He couldn't breathe. Couldn't think. But he'd be okay. His tactical vest and helmet were intact. No shrapnel hit him. No pain in his extremities. No pain anywhere. Halleluiah! He'd just survived a gawddamned daisy-chain of improvised explosives. His ears were ringing, but that was no big deal.

As fast as it hit him, the blast wind let go. He collapsed like a scarecrow in the middle of a Nebraska cornfield when the stick got pulled out of its ass. His heart pounded like a mother. Overheated ash and dust swirled around him. Over his team and his buddies. Into his eyes and nose. His ears. His face. God, the pain in his head was screaming. Possible concussion. He was going to have one helluva headache. Again, no big deal. He could live with that. What SEAL hadn't had one? Or two?

He slapped his gloved hands to the ground beside him, searching for the men who'd been standing with him. Had Shakespeare survived? Had Derby and those poor little boys? The Air Force PJ? Boyington? Where was everyone?

The oddest slivers of tumbling, falling stars rained down. They were everywhere. It was almost pretty the way they mingled with the clouds of swirling, inky black ribbons in his eyes, so dark they sucked the light from those stars.

It was Sunday. Mom always fixed a big Sunday dinner. He wished he were there. Not here.

Jameson woke to muffled sounds of anxious, harried people working around him. Stringent antiseptic smells filled his nose. Voices talked, using big, important, medical terms that made no sense. His aching head still hurt. He must've been taken to the nearest FOB, forward operating base. Probably because he'd blacked out. No big deal. They'd give him a quick physical check, then send him back to Boyington for a butt chewing. Jameson couldn't wait.

He cocked his head, listening. A door had closed and the noise ceased. Someone had separated him from the busyness of what sounded like an emergency room, where injured guys and gals were triaged, patched up, then sent home or back to work. Like any hard-assed Navy SEAL, he wanted to get back to work. The quicker, the better.

But the room was too dark, and for some reason, that darkness scared the shit out of him. He wiggled his toes and fingers, stiffened his legs and arms, then slapped his palms to his chest and gut, searching for injuries he didn't find, determined to prove he was still fit for duty. Great. All present and accounted for, still in working order. Really great. Nothing even hurt, well, except for his neck. It was pretty stiff, and a headache still pounded behind his eyes. But that was nothing. If all he ended up with was a concussion, no worries. He'd had more than his share of those. Concussions were part of the job.

A gentle but big, solid hand settled on his shoulder.

Jameson turned to face the person he couldn't see, blinking like crazy because it was that kind of dark in his room. He wiped a quick hand over his face to make sure no blankets covered his head. What the hell?

"How you doing, Jameson?"

Oh. Lieutenant Boyington. "LT. Hey! I'm good," he replied earnestly. "Ready to get back to work. Sure dark in here. Mind turning a light on? Are we in the middle of another sandstorm or something? A black-out?"

"Or something..."

Unease crept up the back of Jameson's neck. Boyington wasn't usually this quiet or this nice. "What's going on, sir?"

"You're at Landstuhl Regional Medical Center."

His mouth went dry. Landstuhl was one step away from being sent home. Not good. "I'm in Germany? Why?"

"You're going back to the States, son."

"Why? I'm not hurt. Honest, I'm… Sweet Baby Jesus, I'm ready to get back in the fight. I'm—"

"You sustained a tertiary blast injury when you hit the wall back there. You're lucky you're alive. The blast caused irreparable damage to your retinas. They detached. The doctors here couldn't reverse the damage. You're… damnit, you're blind."

"I'm… What?" Jameson ran both hands over his face, feeling for bandages or bruises on his cheeks or around his eyes. A wound or a hole. Blood. Something! "I'm not blind. I can't be. I'm just… It's dark, and I'm just… Where the fuck's Shakespeare? Derby? They'll tell you. It's a concussion. No big deal."

"Jameson… Saint… Son... They're…"

The heaviness in those words ripped the world out from under him. "No!" he told his LT with vigor. "They're not… I'm not blind, and they can't be..." *That. No. God, no.*

"They're gone, Jameson. The A-10s arrived right after that daisy chain cut you, Steed, and Yeats down. They were the only fatalities. You're one lucky son of a bitch."

Me, lucky? Them, dead? Does. Not. Compute.

"But the… the donkey." Jameson had no idea why he asked. Nothing made sense. Not this impenetrable darkness. Not the sucking black hole in his chest that had nothing to do with daisy chains or IEDs or A-10s or his eyes or—

"You saved those two kids. That damned donkey, too. That's what's important. Focus on the good you did. I called your parents. They'll be here tonight."

"My mom?" he asked like an idiot.

"And your dad. They took the first flight out of Virginia this morning. Hang tight. They're on their way. They'll be here as soon as they can, and I'm not going anywhere. You need something, you tell me, understand? I'm not leaving until they ship you out."

"But Eeyore," Jameson murmured to himself, the life inside of him somehow so much less than it had been only minutes ago. So much darker. Uncomfortably foreign feeling. As if one of those slimy creatures from the movie *"Aliens"* had crawled into his body and poured acid over everything he'd ever been. Ever wanted to be. A SEAL. A brother. As if all he'd given his heart and soul to, was simply—gone.

Boyington didn't respond. No yay or nay or anything. And Jameson was listening, as hard as he'd ever listened in his life. His life—before.

Something was running down his face. It had better be blood. Not tears. Because he refused to give up or give in. So what if he couldn't see? So what if he'd never see Christmas lights again? So what if there would never be shadows, or sunsets, or first glances, or depth perception, or pretty blondes or redheads or—*son of a fuckin' bitch!* Only inky black darkness that, right then, was suffocating the living shit out of him!

Good God! How could this have happened? To him! With just one explosion—or explosions—he'd gone from being at the top of his game and his team—his SEAL team!—to being nothing. No one. The Navy didn't need blind SEALs. He'd be out-processed on a fuckin' medical. He'd be a has-been. A wannabe.

But if Boyington was right… If he really was blind… Shit!

This wasn't luck. This was another damned war, and Jameson was in the fight of his life. Because nothing—*do you hear me world?*—nothing, kept Jameson Tenney down!

Chapter One

Alex Stewart didn't dare breathe. Couldn't.

It was an early morning in August, and it had been a damned long night. He was remembering how smoothly his second daughter's birth had gone. They'd gotten to the hospital in plenty of time, and Kelsey's labor had amounted to less than an hour, give or take a few excruciating minutes. Lexie hadn't been able to wait to meet her mom.

But the baby boy in Doc Fitz's very capable hands now, had struggled all night and every inch of his way into the world. He was struggling still. Despite the best gynecologist in the business and Doc Fitz's excellent pediatric skills, Bradley Patrick Stewart had arrived blue and in obvious distress. Which was the reason his mother had undergone an emergency cesarean the moment his stats bottomed out.

The little boy was just too big, his mother too small. He'd clawed his way through the birth canal, and had almost made it when, suddenly, just as his big head peaked, he'd stopped breathing.

So had Alex. Life really did stand still sometimes. Hearts quit beating, too. He didn't dare speak. Didn't know what to say, or who to say it to. Certainly didn't want Kelsey to overhear any question that might make her panic or jump to conclusions.

Breathe, he silently commanded his first son. *Want to live, Bradley. Dare to beat the odds, son. You've already fought for the privilege, now stay, damn it. Stay with us. Don't break your mom's heart. She needs you, and God, so do I.*

Tears brimmed Alex's eyes, blurring Doc Fitz's hellbent, yet urgent actions as she cleared the little guy's airway, suctioning away whatever he'd breathed in at the last moment. She'd given Alex a quick second to cut the umbilical cord, before another nurse had attached a belt around Bradley's skinny, unresponsive chest to monitor his stats, or lack of them. After suctioning his airways, Doc Fitz set the nasal bulb aside and held a small oxygen mask to the baby's bluish face.

Lexie had been born screaming, red-faced, and mad as hell. But Bradley was quiet. Too damned quiet.

God, don't do this to your mom!

"Alex, what's wrong?" that weary mom asked tiredly from the birthing bed where her obstetrician was stitching her tummy. "Why isn't he crying? Lexie did. Is Bradley okay?"

Alex looked at Doc Fitz from beneath his lashes, daring her to break the news, and in doing so, break Kelsey's heart. *Are you going to tell her, or does that dastardly deed fall to me?* he wondered, his heart stuck in his throat and pounding too hard. Maybe too loud.

"Alex?"

He hated the tremor in his sweet wife's voice, nearly as much as he hated himself. He'd failed her. If this little boy had come all this way only to die, what kind of man did that make his father? Standing idly by, twiddling his thumbs, not able to do a damned thing to save his son?

"There we go. Upsie daisy. You can do it, little one. I know you can," Doc Fitz soothed calmly, her competent fingers moving surely over Bradley's ribs, the other cupping his head as she lifted him, and—

"Ba-ba-bah!" He cried! His flat chest sucked in and his skinny arms flailed, and he sucked in another big gulp of life. And by hell! He was going to make it!

Tears filled Alex's eyes. His chin hit his chest in utmost humility. *God, thank you.* Only then could he face Kelsey and tell her with confidence, "Bradley wants his mom."

She was tired, but still so damned beautiful, his heart hurt to look at her. Her tender smile told him she knew him too well, that he hadn't hid a thing from her. Not even the disaster that could've been.

"Then bring him to me," she commanded her lowly servant, one arm stretched out and her fingers fluttering. She was a queenly study in sweaty chocolate browns and luscious pinks this morning. Alex wanted to obey, but—

"Not yet," Doc Fitz purred, as if she hadn't performed the greatest miracle of her life. "I'm not finished with this handsome boy yet. Just a couple more tests, Kelsey. I'll be quick."

"Is he breathing okay?" she asked, peering around the nurse who was assisting her OB doctor.

"He's just fine, but he sure gave me a scare when his heart decided to stop for a couple minutes there. Didn't you, big guy?" she asked the now squirming baby boy.

"What caused it?" Alex asked tersely, needing that problem fixed right damned now.

"To be honest, I'm not precisely sure. Birth is hard, even on tough little soldiers, and sometimes babies are in a big hurry to be born. They want out. If he's anything like you, he probably crushed his umbilical cord on his mad dash to freedom. It wasn't wrapped around his neck, and that's a good sign. Thanks to Dr. Brown's decision to perform the C-section right here, Bradley wasn't without oxygen for long. Probably simple hypoxia. His cord got pinched during those last moments of labor just long enough to scare all of us."

She turned to really look at Alex then. "You can breathe now, Dad. You and Kelsey make beautiful babies."

He didn't want to just breathe. He wanted to cry. And roar! He was a dad again! He... they had a son. Kelsey needed this third little boy so bad. Aw, hell. Tears flooded his vision, blurring his view of heaven. He dashed them away. Quickly, damn it.

While Kelsey's doctor finished his work, Dr. McKenna Fitzgerald-Villanueva worked quickly, assessing Bradley, talking to him as if he understood everything she said. His hair was a lighter brown than Lexie and Kelsey's. He blinked up at her with the startling wonder of a newborn. He had so much to look forward to.

McKenna wasn't only an old friend, she was also married to one of Alex's best agents. Even now, Beau Villanueva stood patiently outside Kelsey's door, waiting to be invited in to celebrate the newest addition to The TEAM. Several other agents and their wives waited with him, which was probably the only reason Beau hadn't already barged in. The man had less patience than Alex.

The only one missing in this family Alex called The TEAM was the woman he'd loved first. His mom. Abigail Stewart would've loved being here for the birth of her first grandson.

"There we go," McKenna crooned.

By then, Kelsey's doctor had packed up and excused himself. His nurse had left with him. Bradley's feet had been blackened and printed like the little criminal he was, guilty of scaring his mom and dad like he had. Alex's fingers itched to hold him. He needed the scent of his son in his nose, and he needed to kiss the little beggar. But mostly, he needed to be the one who carried his son across the room and put him in his mother's arms. That was a father's right, not McKenna's.

"May I?" he asked Doc Fitz pointedly.

She looked up at him again, and damned if she didn't see right through him. But he guessed most doctors could tell a smitten fool when they saw one. In a deck of poker cards, Kelsey was the queen of hearts. He was nothing more than her most humble servant.

"Of course," McKenna said as she finished wrapping Bradley, turning him into a snug, blue-and-white-striped papoose. Gingerly, she lifted him from the exam table and transferred him into Alex's arms. "He's all yours, Dad."

With one hit of the scent off that little boy's dark, wet head, more tears sprang to his father's eyes. A son. Alex had a son, his first, Kelsey's third. He almost hated to give this newborn boy to her, afraid of the memories this little man might invoke. But nothing could bring the boys she'd lost, Jackie and Tommy, back, and this wasn't her second chance to be the mother of a son. This was simply, irrevocably, Bradley's time on Earth. Kelsey had to be feeling the same tender emotions Alex was today. She'd be remembering the births of her other boys, the same as he was remembering the day Abby was born.

And just as swiftly, Kelsey would remember how she'd lost them, and where they were buried. Like Jackie and

Tommy, dear sweet Abby was also gone. And this precious moment was just one of those oddly wretched, overwhelmingly joy-filled, spiritual moments in time, when it seemed the family members they'd lost were with them again. Unseen, but just as alive as the wiggling baby in his hands.

It wasn't often Alex thought about his mother, but he felt Abigail Stewart's sweet presence here today. She would adore Kelsey, and she'd be thrilled to be a grandmother again. The grandparents who'd raised Alex, Patrick Bradley and Patricia Rose Southerland Stewart, Paddy and Pat, were here as well, both beaming down on him, Kelsey, and Bradley with love and pride. Probably tearing up, too.

The thought struck Alex hard. Because that meant Sara, his first wife, had to be here as well, and Abby, his first darling daughter, had come with her mom to meet her brother. The thought unnerved him, nearly unmanned him. But Kelsey's arms were stretched open wide, waiting. Smiling. With his nose still flat against the head of the tiny man in his arms, Alex leaned into the woman he adored with his whole heart, and whispered, "Here's your son, Mama."

Of course, tears were streaming down her cheeks by then. Kelsey was a crier, and today, Alex was, too.

"Ohhhh," she mewed, as she too, flattened her nose and lips to their son's damp head, kissing Bradley while she breathed him in the same way Alex had. "I love you, Bradley Patrick, and I love your father so, so much. I can't wait for you to meet your older sister. Lexie is so excited to meet you."

"She was wrong. She thought we were having a baby sister." Lexie had, in fact, insisted lately that all new babies were girls.

"She won't care once she holds him. You'll see. He's got your hair color and your blue eyes. He's going to look just like you."

"All babies have blue eyes," he reminded his sweetheart. "And no kid wants to be as ugly as me."

She shook her head. "No, Alex. Trust me. This boy will grow up to be strong and noble, like you. He's your son. He's… he's beautiful." She kissed Bradley again and again, her lashes spiked with tears, as she sobbed into his perfectly round head. A head that was probably as hard as his dad's.

Alex never argued, just closed his eyes at Kelsey's unrelenting love for him, and let her believe whatever she wanted. That was the one rule of marriage he'd finally learned: Never argue with the woman you love and always trust her intuition. Why not? He'd trusted his gut, why shouldn't she trust hers? Those two inexplicable gifts might just come from the same place.

He pulled up a chair, content to sit with his wife and son for as long as he could. This was the closest he'd ever get to heaven. Why not bask in the glory?

His trusted senior agent, Mark Houston, would run The TEAM for the next two weeks, maybe longer if Alex decided to extend his family leave. Mark was capable. He and his wife Libby were two good friends. They'd understand.

"Would you like to try to nurse him before we invite the horde in?" McKenna asked, from the other side of Kelsey's bed.

"They're still out there?"

"Yes," Alex confirmed. "They've been here all night."

Kelsey smiled through her tears. "Guess they've waited long enough then, huh? Sure, let's see if this little guy's hungry after scaring his daddy to death."

"I wasn't scared," Alex declared, but then added, "much."

He smiled at how easily Kelsey bared her breast and handled this little boy like she knew what she was doing. There was a day not too long ago that she'd been timid and shy, afraid of everything, and so damned modest. Not anymore.

Hungrily, the little guy's prehensile lips searched, then quickly, he latched onto his mama's dusky nipple. Alex's heart swelled with pride. He huffed out a soul cleansing breath, part relief and part job well done. His son knew just what to do with that nipple. Damned straight.

McKenna's cell phone chirped. Lifting it from the pocket of her scrubs, she glanced at the screen and grinned. "It's Beau again. He wants to know if they can come in yet?"

Kelsey drew the blanket up, covering herself and Bradley. "Sure. Let everyone in. Bradley might as well get used to his rowdy uncles and aunts."

"Are you sure?" Alex had to ask. That was his brand-new baby son slurping like a little pig at his wife's breast underneath that blanket. He wasn't even an hour old yet. The whole damned world could wait a minute.

But right on cue, sweet Kelsey exclaimed, "Sure. I want to see Beau blush again."

McKenna chuckled. "Oh, trust me, breastfeeding doesn't embarrass Beau. But your unmarried agents might feel uncomfortable. Let's find out."

Walking briskly to the door, she flung it open, and in they came. Beau led the pack, then Mark Houston and Libby. Gabe

Cartwright and Shelby. Maverick Carson and China. Seth McCray and Devereaux. Lee Hart and Tess. Hunter Christian and Meredith. My hell, they were all there. Even Renner Graves and his wife Tara Shanahan, the former Olympic hopeful, had come to welcome Bradley into the fold. Beckam and Camilla Garner, too.

As predicted, Beau gave his wife a quick peck, then headed straight for Kelsey's bedside. "He's hungry already? That's a real good sign." His dark eyes were bright as he grabbed the only other chair in the room and pulled it alongside Alex, as if it had been reserved for him. "How's it feel being a dad again, Boss?"

"Good," Alex offered easily. Damned good. Perfect, actually. So damned good he had to wipe a quick hand over his face again. Beau had changed dramatically over these past two years, first when he'd met McKenna, second when he'd become a father. If Alex changed as much as Beau had, hell, he'd almost be nice.

"Aww," Ember Dennison cooed, a bulky gift bag in one hand as she came through the door. Here was another hard kick in the gut. She and Rory had suffered miscarriage after miscarriage since they'd married. It was about time they had a baby to show for all their trouble. Yet here she was. Supporting Kelsey and with a gift in her hand, but going home without her own baby in her arms.

She tossed the bag at Alex. "Rory said you're gonna need this."

Alex peered into the bag at the child-sized catcher's mitt, then back into her bright green eyes. She had—*that look*. Was she pregnant? Again? That would make four miscarriages in three years. She'd always handled life differently than most.

Hence the Nebraska Cornhuskers football jersey she wore. But how could she keep trying so hard to get pregnant when it always ended in heartbreak? What was Rory thinking to put her through that?

Come to think of it, that shirt was a little large—

"How's it going, Ember baby?" Zack Lennox asked brightly as he cleared the door right behind her.

She whirled into his arms. "Today's the day!"

"You're finally going to tell everyone?" That cinched it. Zack had the uncanny gift of being able to tell when and if a woman was pregnant.

"Rory and me are having a baby!" she blurted to the room, stamping her feet like a little girl on a sugar-high. "Next month! It's finally happening! I get to be a mom!"

"Ahem," Rory cleared his throat. "*We…* get to be parents. Had to scrape Tyler off the ceiling when we told him last night. He can't wait to be a big brother."

Tyler was their son from Rory's previous marriage.

Damned if Kelsey didn't squeeze Alex's hand when she saw his eyes brimming with tears. Again! He couldn't rein in his emotions for the life of him today. But this was such good news. Ember and Rory deserved to be happy.

"Congratulations," he rasped as the room exploded into coos and ahhs and hearty back-slapping congrats.

But when Rory revealed the bouquet of yellow roses behind his back and laid them across Kelsey's legs with a kindly, "Congratulations, skinny mama," son of a bitch! Alex couldn't get his eyeballs to cease and desist. Manfully, he scrubbed a hand over his face. Again!

A solid thump struck his biceps. Rory was grinning. He'd seen the near-tears, the ass. "Brought the new dad something, too," he said as he handed over a fifth of something gold and expensive.

McCallum Estate Single Malt Whisky. "My God, this had to cost you an arm and a leg."

Rory shrugged both shoulders. "Who cares? I'm celebrating my good news, as much as yours. Isn't every day a man gets to bring his child into the world. My turn's next. Best two reasons to celebrate I know."

Alex broke the seal on that bottle, and magically, a raft of red plastic cups appeared out of nowhere. Everyone but Ember and Kelsey got a sip, but he served Rory two fingers.

Renner Graves had a twinkle in his eye when he raised his cup. "To your wee little one," he said in the thickest Irish brogue Alex had heard in a while. "May Bradley Patrick Stewart be surrounded by sunbeams to warm him every day of his long, illustrious life. We already know he's got a big badassed guardian angel to protect him, so..." Renner raised his cup and offered the Gaelic toast for health and wealth, "*Sláinte is táinte.*"

"Cheers!" Zack roared like a beast. "When are you two having a baby?"

The twinkle in Renner's eye turned into a devilish spark. "We're working on it," he murmured as he turned to Tara and placed a kiss in her hair.

"May the moon brighten all of his night times," Eric Reynolds chimed in quietly, "and God bless all the places he'll wander."

"And may God please bless him to be more like his sweet mother than his ornery dad," Hunter growled. "Congrats, Boss. You too, Ember and Rory. When are you due?"

"September eighteenth," Ember declared, her eyes as bright as crystal emeralds. She looked downright radiant. She glowed, standing there with both hands cupping her belly, which was more apparent now. Yet still so much smaller than Kelsey's had been. Alex hoped that was only because this was Ember's first, while Kelsey had carried four babies to term.

He had to give Ember credit for not allowing multiple miscarriages to stop her. Kelsey had been depressed when they hadn't been able to get pregnant at first, but miscarrying would've been so much harder. He raised a plastic cup, his heart full for honorable, hard-working mothers and fathers everywhere, then waited until the room quieted.

"A thousand lullabies to you both," he said, his heart so damned full, it hurt to breathe. "And more butterfly kisses than you'll ever be able to count."

"Awww," Ember cried as she wrapped him into one of her signature hugs. "I remember," she whispered. "You're thinking of Abby. Love you, Boss."

"Yeah, well…" He endured the affection and wiped his eyes for the last damned time.

"Here, here," Kelsey murmured sleepily.

"Time to go, people," Libby Houston said as she leaned into Kelsey and carefully hugged her and the baby still hidden beneath the covers. "Why don't we let this new family get some rest. I'll bring Lexie by later."

"Aww," Beau groused. "Don't we even get to see him?"

Alex shook his head. Damned if Beau didn't act like a spoiled kid sometimes. Which made sense. He'd had, by far, the most screwed-up childhood of everyone in the room. Maybe his baby sister was here today, too, looking down on him from heaven. AJ, that was her name. AJ for *Almond Joy*.

Her drug addict parents had named her after a candy bar, then killed her with neglect and their screwed-up drug addict lives, when she was just a baby.

"Of course you get to meet him, sweetheart," Kelsey replied as she reached under her blanket. And pop! That strong little guy's lips let go. "Would you like to hold Bradley?"

"Err, ahh, me?" Beau stuttered. "You'd let me hold him? Err, now? But he's only an hour old and—"

"Then don't drop him," Alex grumbled.

"Yes, Beau. Here he is," Kelsey said as she handed Bradley over to the man who'd once been beaten, burned, and abused by the son of a bitch who'd kidnapped him from his real family, then threw him away the day AJ died. Beau hadn't even been seven years old.

Alex watched the transformation take place as the big tough guy beside him gently cupped Bradley's head and butt, then lay him lengthwise on his muscled forearm. Beau's thick neck worked extra hard. He blinked and pinched his lips. There was unbridled adoration in his dark brown eyes, that yes, oh yes, were brimming with big sloppy tears he didn't mind everyone seeing.

"He's so tiny," he breathed.

Alex put a palm in the center of Beau's broad back. "What are you talking about? He's damned near big enough to play tackle football."

The guys in the room laughed. The women were still cooing over Kelsey and Ember.

There was a day Alex had wanted to fire this gentle giant. Back then, Beau'd been as rough as a cob and pissed at the world. He'd fight at the drop of a hat, and he'd threatened to quit more times than Alex had fingers to count on. But little by little and layer by stinking layer, Beau's ugly childhood had been revealed. Damned if Alex didn't find a big kid worth saving and a heart of gold beneath that crusty shell. It hadn't hurt that Beau had been smart enough to fall in love with Doc Fitz. Loving the right woman had a way of changing everything.

"He's so, so tiny," Beau whispered huskily. "He's… he's… God, he's beautiful, Kelsey."

The big guy holding the little guy gulped, and yeah. Alex damned well knew Beau was remembering the sweet little angel that had been the one bright light in his miserable childhood. The veil between heaven and earth was very thin today. Births and deaths worked that way. The people who loved you were never very far away, and today, those spirits were close enough to help a guy remember.

Reverently, Beau closed his eyes and pressed his lips to Bradley's forehead. The little guy never squirmed or fussed, just lay there like a wrinkly, little old man with that funny, quirky newborn baby smile twitching his lips.

Alex caught the affection glowing in McKenna's eyes when her shaggy-haired husband whispered, "Sleep tight, little man. You're safe. You'll never not have guardian angels on your six." If Alex were a betting man, he'd put a hundred on McKenna and Beau making another baby real soon.

Skillfully, Beau handed the sleeping babe back to Kelsey, and manfully, he dashed his knuckles over his eyes and growled at Maverick and Hunter, "Yeah, I cry. So what? Get over it."

But they looked as sappy as he did.

Alex shook his head at the mystery that was his life. He'd planted the seeds of an enterprising covert surveillance company. That was all. He'd hired kick-ass warriors, male and female. But what did he get? The best damn family a guy could ask for.

He slapped Beau's broad, muscular back and muttered, "You're all right."

But then, out of the corner of his eye, Alex caught sight of the gray-haired old man blocking Kelsey's door, standing there, like he belonged. In a heartbeat, he was on his feet, his Irish instantly up, hot, and ready to strike. One hand curled into a fist, his other pressed Kelsey to stay still behind him. "What the hell do you want?"

Chapter Two

Of course, he came into the friendly throng like the slimy snake he was, smiling like he always did, acting as if he cared, which he never had. As if he belonged inside this battle-hardened family where true warriors stood with their wives and their children, no matter how hard life became. As if he were one of the gang and supposed to be here, celebrating. As if he were the least bit welcome.

The truth was a far cry different. This was the bastard who'd deserted his only child the day after that son's mother had died of cancer, and three days before she'd been buried. Imagine the balls it took to do that. A liar and a cheat, Mel Stewart had only ever cared about himself. Figured he'd show up today. The man had always spoiled family events. Birthdays. Christmases. Any day that ended in a Y. Why would this uniquely special morning be any different?

Everything warm and kind inside Alex fell silent. The room chilled as The TEAM closed around Kelsey and Bradley. Instantly, Rory stepped in front of Ember. That brought back the memory of the time he'd confronted Alex the day long ago he'd tossed his chair out his office window. Kelsey had been kidnapped and missing then, and Rory had been one brave son of a bitch to have faced the desperate, feral man Alex had become. Rory was still a brave son of a bitch today. And still standing with Alex.

Alex stared his old man down, daring him to take one more step forward. Just one. He didn't need this showdown today. Surely didn't want it. It'd been a long time coming, but God, not today. Mel Stewart could take his worthless hide back to Hell for all Alex cared.

The ass shrugged, almost coyly. Played dumb, as if he were the harmless, innocent victim here, and his son was the aggressor. So be it. Alex rolled his shoulder, old enough and strong enough to knock the bastard on his ass this time around. Sure as hell ready to make up for every hit he'd taken as a kid.

His inner dragon growled, "I'll ask you one more time. What the hell do you want?"

The coy shrug again. The half-friendly smile. Those damned icy blue eyes. God, it was like looking in a mirror. "Ain't you gonna introduce me?"

"No."

"Heard you was here. Just thought I'd stop by and—"

"You heard? How?"

Both shoulders lifted again. "Called your office. See you're a big man now. I'm proud—"

"You were never proud of me. Stop the bullshit and go."

"Heard you's a new daddy. Congratulations, son."

Shit. Now everyone knew. As if they hadn't already noticed the resemblance. Alex took a deep breath, needing to explain to his wife and TEAM, but needing a helluva lot more patience first. "This is a private room. Back off and get out."

Both Mel's callused palms came forward as if he were simply placating an unreasonable child. "Okay. I'll just wait for you at your place, your home then, and we can—"

Alex bristled at the persistent conniving manipulation. "No. Leave the city. Leave the state. I don't care, just leave."

His old man's fingers trembled as they raked over straggly gray hair, then combed down through a tangled, silvery beard. Dressed in what looked like hand-me-downs, he could've passed for one of Alexandria's many homeless people.

"Son, I—"

"I'm not your son." Alex made each word a bullet. "You gave up that right the day you walked out on me and Gramps and Gram. And your wife! Christ, you left before Mom was even cold." Okay, that was more than he'd meant to share, but maybe it was time everyone knew what a bastard his father was.

Mel's chest puffed up. "I was a Navy SEAL, boy!" he bellowed. "I had a call to action, so I went. I served! You were a Marine. You know how that works. I had no choice, and I was damned proud to—"

"You were never a SEAL."

"Was too!" Mel sputtered. "Got my trident 'fore I went to Moga... err, Mogadishu."

Another lie, not even well delivered.

"Sir," Mark interrupted. "It's time you left."

Mel squared his shoulders and threw out a challenging, "Whatcha gonna do, throw me out? Keep me from seeing my first grandkid? You think you're big enough to do that, buddy?"

First grandkid?

"Yes, sir, that's exactly what I'll do," Mark replied evenly. All by himself, he made two of Mel, but Zack had stepped up to the plate now as well.

"We'd rather escort you peaceably to the nearest exit, sir," he intoned, his voice hard and deep, both muscular arms crossed over a chest that was twice the breadth of Mel's. "But we can do this the hard way if you prefer. Your choice."

These two were the big guys on The TEAM. Both wide-shouldered and built like a pair of equally-yoked oxen, they were former Marines. They'd have no trouble making sure Mel hit the street. Preferably on his ass.

"Just like that? You're not even gonna let me take a peek at my only grandchild? Me, a tired old man. Your flesh and blood?" Mel pointed accusingly at Beau. "You let that beaner hold him."

Everything in Alex hardened into iron at that despicable ethnic slur. Once again, he was ashamed of his old man. Worse, Mel now had three big bruisers on their feet, ready to clean his plow.

Right on cue, Beau turned nasty. "You'd better fuckin' git, old man. Boss said go, you go!"

Before this momentous occasion erupted into an outright brawl, Alex intervened with a weary sigh. "Don't you dare insult my friends, Mel. You made your choice a long time ago. You walked out on everybody who loved you then. You don't get to do it again. You have no son or grandson. Not anymore. The last time I saw you was the day you dropped me at Gramps and Grams'. You left me at the end of their driveway after Mom died, for God's sake. Didn't even have the guts to tell them what happened to her, or why you were leaving me. You just drove away, and now it's too late. There are no more second chances. Don't make this hard by starting a fight. Trust me, my guys will end you, and I'll let them. Go. Just go."

Yet even as he cast his old man out of his life once again, he heard Kelsey's gentle, "Alex?" behind him.

Not ready to face her yet, he fastened his hardest gaze to the one who could hurt her without a second thought. "For the last time, walk away." *Before I make you.*

But damn. Soft, sweet fingers breached his fist, and Kelsey was doing what she did best. Getting through to him. Making him rethink everything he believed and knew to be true.

Alex swallowed hard. He'd hated his dad for years. Mel hadn't been much of a father when he'd been around, which had been damned seldom. But he'd always been a liar and a braggart, one of those mouthy guys who wasted everyone's time talking about how great they were, but who'd never accomplished a damned thing other than ordering their browbeaten wives around and slapping their kids for breathing.

But because of Kelsey—*God, give me strength*—Alex gestured toward his old man and begrudgingly admitted, "TEAM, Mel Stewart, the…" *Asshole.* "… man I haven't seen in thirty damned years."

Mel brightened as if Alex had just conceded the battle. Straightening his grimy button-up shirt, the sly old fox grinned, as if he'd been welcomed with open arms. "Well, howdy. 'Bout time. Pleased to meet y'all."

Not a single agent returned the greeting. Camilla looked like she had something to say, though. Alex was glad she kept it to herself. Beau might be the one who went off half-cocked most often, but Camilla's tongue was as sharp as a razor, and twice as lethal as Beau's. She'd calmed down since she'd married Beckam, and he'd turned into a bigger sap than Connor Maher. But Alex didn't want to remember Bradley's birth by what might take place if Camilla spoke her mind.

She'd been another abused child. Another miracle that began when she fell in love with Beck.

Flustered, Mel ran his fingers through his beard yet again. His nervous tell. "Well, err… Guess maybe I'll just hafta—"

"Wait!" Kelsey called out. "I'm Kelsey, Alex's wife. Scoot over, honey. Let me say hello to my father-in-law."

Son of a bitch! She'd spoiled the whole damned goodbye and good riddance. Yet like the good husband he was, Alex sucked in his nasty temper, *'scooted'* over, and allowed this snake a glimpse of the woman he'd kill his dad for. *Count on it.*

Gritting his teeth, he said, "Kelsey. Sweetheart." *Damn, this was hard.* "Mel Stewart. Mel, my wife." *And if you hurt her feelings even once, I will end you.*

Of course, Mel pulled his Southern gentleman schtick out of his ass and bowed with a flourish. Brushing past Alex, he took her clean, pure hand between his grubby paws. "Nice to finally meet you, Kelsey Stewart," he purred as he placed his dry, filthy lips on her knuckles and kissed her hand. "Always wanted a daughter. Guess I got one now."

You've got nothing…

Alex met Mark's dark eyes over the top of his old man's gray head. The stark stare of brotherhood glowered in his friend's hooded gaze. Alex knew his second in command would take this jackal by the scruff of his skinny neck and toss him out if Alex gave even the slightest nod. But now that Kelsey was involved… He heaved a resigned sigh and signaled Mark to stand down with one curt shake of his head.

"Can I see the little tyke since I'm here?" Mel asked. "What'd you name him?"

Tugging the blanket away from Bradley's face, Kelsey was her usual overly-kind self, a trait Alex hated at the moment. "Of course, you can see him. You're his grandfather. We named him Bradley Patrick, after Alex's grandfather. Just reversed the order of the names."

"You didn't name him after me?" Mel pasted on his conniving crestfallen expression. "Well, darn."

Why the hell would we?

"After *your* father, Mr. Stewart." Her bright eyes sparkled as she soothed the old liar's ruffled feathers. "Think of it this way, by honoring him, we've also honored you."

Like hell. Gramps was a man worth honoring. But Mel was... nothing.

Right on cue, he groused. "Don't seem quite fair, me being his real granddaddy and all, but..." He lifted both shoulders as if he were insulted but would get over it. "Guess it'll have to do."

You bet your ass it will do. You were never a father, and you're not a grandfather now.

"Boss, we're heading out," Rory said, his arm tight around Ember's waist, still standing between her and Mel.

"Thanks for the whisky. That was damned nice."

"I left another fifth on your desk for when you get back. Enjoy these first days with your fam—"

"Whisky?" Mel nearly broke his crepey neck when he dropped Kelsey's hand and twisted around. "You guys been celebrating without me? What kind ya got? Is it the good stuff?"

And wasn't that just the truest picture of good old Grandpa Mel? Ignoring the loveliest lady in the world and the precious grandson he claimed he came to see, at the mere whisper of liquor.

"It's gone," Alex put as much sarcasm into the two words as he could.

"Oh, no, it's not. Look, Alex. There's enough left for one tiny swallow. Pour your dad a drink. I'd love to get to know you better," Kelsey told Mel sincerely.

Damn it to hell! Alex wished Kelsey would go to sleep and stop sabotaging him!

When Mel beamed at her kindness, Alex knew exactly what the old goat was thinking. He'd snagged another hapless sucker.

"Later, Boss," Zack rumbled as he headed out. He, Mark, and Libby were the last to leave. But Mark had stopped at the doorway, his head canted as he listened to whatever Libby was saying. His dark eyes turned expressive. He nodded, then waved Zack off.

Back in the room, Mark carried the chair Beau had vacated to the other side of the bed, and gestured for Libby to take a seat. Which she did, a knowing glimmer in her eyes. Bless her heart. She didn't want Mel there any more than Alex did.

"Why don't you and your old man go down to the cafeteria and catch up, Boss?" Mark offered as he stood behind his wife, his fingers on the back of her chair. "We won't stay long."

"Good idea." Alex set a heavy hand on Mel's shoulder. His ragged coat felt grimy to the touch. Slept in. For the first time, he wondered if his dad truly were homeless. Or if this was just another ruse, another con. He hated putting Kelsey in the position of having to choose his feelings over his dad's.

He should've told her about Mel a long time ago. Wished he had.

"Come on, *Dad.*" Sarcasm had never felt more justified. "Let's go get a cup of coffee." *Then I'm showing you the door, and you'd better stay gone this time.*

"Goodbye for now," Kelsey said tiredly. "See you soon, Mr. Stewart."

"Oh, please call me Mel, Sissy," he all but gushed.

And Alex wanted to puke. Mel used to call Abigail Sissy when he came home drunk.

Kelsey granted him one of her sweetest smiles. "Of course, Mel. Tomorrow then."

"You betcha," he replied, the cunning old toad.

Libby followed up with a polite but measured, "It was nice meeting you, sir."

He tipped a finger to his forehead and the hat he didn't have. "Nice meeting you, too, pretty lady."

Mark said nothing. He didn't have to. He knew the tricks and ploys of absentee, disengaged fathers, who'd never once showed up unless there was something in it for them. Mark had suffered a lifetime of neglect at his dad's hand. When he'd joined the Corps, he'd finally discovered that he wasn't the broken one. John Houston was. Still was today.

Alex turned his back on Mel and bowed his forehead to Kelsey's. "I'll be right back, sweetheart," he promised as he kissed her mouth. "Keep our son warm."

Her lips were soft and sweet as if she hadn't just endured a long night of labor and a C-section. A sigh escaped. "Don't worry about us; we'll be fine. You deserve time with your dad."

"No," he breathed into her face. "I don't deserve what he's doing here, and neither do you or our kids. This is not a family reunion, Kelsey. This is goodbye."

"But he's your father," she whispered, her brown eyes pleading for him to be the better man she knew he could be.

He shook his head, not going down that dead-end road again. He'd been a nice kid and an obedient son before. Too often. Mom, Gramps, and Gram had been kind and considerate, too. More than Mel had ever deserved. It hadn't worked then; it wouldn't now. This guy was one rank cup of cold, bitter coffee, and Alex was only going to spit him out on the curb.

"Stay with her until I get back?" he asked Mark and Libby.

"Sure thing," Mark answered easily. "It's no trouble. JayJay's thrilled Lexie's sleeping over again tonight. They're making s'mores in the microwave right now."

"And JayJay knows the recipe to make pink popcorn," Libby added slyly. "You should see our living room. It's one big tent city full of giggling little girls."

"Lexie?" Mel asked, his head cranking between Libby and Kelsey. "You mean…? I got a baby granddaughter, too?"

Alex snaked an unwilling arm around his dad's neck and all but shoved him out the door. Lifting his other arm over his head, he waved goodbye to the room as he dragged his old man into the hall and said, "No, Mel, you've got distant relatives, and it's time for you to go."

As expected, Mel elbowed out of Alex's stronghold the second Kelsey's door shut behind him. "I've got family, you son of a bitch, and you can't keep me from seeing them."

And enough! Alex bullied his father away from Kelsey's door, down the hall to the elevator. "Don't call Mom a bitch, you asshole! And I can and will keep you away from my family. You walked away from yours. All of us. From Mom!" Alex rolled his shoulders, fighting for a modicum of restraint. "Where the hell have you been all these years? Why are you here now? What do you want?"

Mel stiffened his hairy chin and rolled one shoulder. He thumbed the bulbous end of his nose as if he were some kind of prizefighter. He was—the loser kind.

"I been places, you little fucker. Important places. Not like you ever cared."

By then Alex was glaring down at the bastard. He was bigger, taller, and his shoulders were wider than the man who'd made his childhood hell. He was also meaner than he'd ever been as a nine-year-old. And smarter. "For once we agree. I don't give a shit where you've been, and don't ever call my wife Sissy!"

"Why not? She's pretty enough. She looks like a Sissy."

Pretty enough? "Because that's what you called Mom! Or did you forget her, too? Or is that what you call all your girls? That's it, isn't it? Calling your whores Sissy made it easy to keep track of the one you were with." That actually made perfect sense. Mel had other women. Alex knew that for sure. He'd hid the secret from his mom because by then, she'd been sick and hadn't needed more crap in her life. Cancer and Mel were crap enough.

"I call 'em all Sissy because—"

"You know what? I don't give a shit! How much do you want?" Alex jerked his wallet out of his rear pocket. "Fifty? A hundred? Two? How much will it cost me to get rid of you?"

Mel's brittle gaze zeroed in on the bills in the wallet. His tongue flicked his upper lip like the snake he was. "I don't need your money, boy. Fact, I don't need nuthin' from you. Just stopped by to say hey."

"Hey," Alex spat.

"Fine then." Mel's startling blue eyes fell to the tiled floor between them. "'S just that…"

Everything inside Alex turned to stone. *Here it comes. He's going to tell me he's got cancer. Or two months to live for some vague reason. Or another bullshit story he thinks will force me to take him in. Not happening.*

Mel stuck his hand out. "Never mind. You got a nice little family, son, and Sissy, err, I mean, Kelsey, looks happy. Just wanted to catch up on good old times with my boy."

"I'm not your boy, and we've got no *good old times* to catch up on. Do you even know I was married before? Were you there after my first wife and daughter were killed in a car wreck while I was deployed? Hell, no! Where were you when I buried them, huh? Did you give a shit when Gram died from a broken heart after I buried Sara and Abby? You weren't even there when I buried your own mother. For the love of God! You don't get to just walk back into my life like you belong. You lost that right years ago. The fuckin' day you walked out!" Alex raked a hand over his head. God, he was pissed.

"You're sure a selfish bastard."

"Learned from the best, didn't I?"

"I'm outta here."

"Don't let the door hit your ass on the way out."

Mel shuffled into the waiting elevator, and Alex joined him. The ride down was dead silent, but finally, they were in the hospital lobby. Mel headed straight to the wide glass exit doors, and Alex was damned glad to see him go. Yes, he was a pitiful sight with his head down, and for certain, he'd slept in those wrinkled clothes. The sides of his dirty shoes were broken down and his jeans were worn and tattered. Those clothes and that ratty jacket were probably all he owned.

But Alex truly did not care. Abigail was the one he'd wished could've been here today. Not Mel. She was the one he adored. She'd been a saint, a long-suffering angel who'd made the mistake of falling for a foul-mouthed swabbie out of Norfolk. A sailor who'd done more harm than good to the people he'd declared he loved. Lies. All lies. Good riddance.

Abigail had passed years ago, long before Alex had ever thought of marriage or adulting. Long before Gramps and Gram died. He'd been nine when he'd lost his mom, and the memory still hurt. But he felt nothing for the man he'd lost the next day. Melvin Stewart had only ever been a lousy husband and a worse father. A loser. He shirked responsibility then, still did today.

Not like a motherless nine-year-old kid would've been better off with Mel in his life. Truth was, Alex had done just fine after he'd been dumped at Gramps' farm in West Virginia, three days before Abigail's funeral. But for that brief time with Mel, those couple days it took Abigail to die, that stupid nine-year-old had actually believed he'd be going home to live with his dad. That they'd, somehow, become a real father and son team. A family. That Mel would finally care.

Not so. Mel was there when Abigail died, but he wasn't at the cemetery when Alex and his grandparents went back to Norfolk to lay her to rest. From that moment on, Alex hadn't wasted a minute thinking about his old man. He'd learned the hardest way possible. Mel had nothing to offer anyone. Not a goddamned thing.

Standing at Abigail's grave that blustery winter day had left one of those sucking black holes in that foolish nine-year-old boy's heart. That was the day Alex turned to Gramps for the comfort and fatherly support he'd never gotten from Mel. Was also the day Patrick Bradley Stewart finally had a son he could count on. Alex and Gramps were inseparable from that day forward.

His paternal grandfather was former Navy, like Mel, but he was one of those injured survivors from the WWII battle at Iwo Jima in the Pacific. Unlike Mel, Gramps was the real deal. He might've been a drunk when he'd come home after the war, but he'd never laid a hand on Gram, Abigail, or Alex. Never called them names, never said a mean word to anyone. Never embarrassed or humiliated his grandson like Mel had so often done. Hard-working and truly one of the best from the greatest generation, Gramps was the man who'd taught Alex to play baseball, the slickest way to skin beaver without damaging the pelts, and how to be silent when tracking elusive white-tailed deer. Gramps also taught Alex how to stand up to bullies and how to bank coal stoves in winter. He taught his grandson to be a man, and Alex adored Gramps still today.

Yes, he'd definitely liked the bottle. He was an Irishman and the Irish loved their whisky. But when he drank, he was a cheerful drunk, who'd boisterously declared he'd just needed a nip now and again to chase what he'd called 'the ghosts' away. That was Alex's first experience with post-traumatic stress, aka shell shock, battle fatigue, and soldier's heart. All those worthless euphemisms that didn't do squat to help a guy.

But his mom…? Abigail would forever be the ache in his heart that wouldn't go away.

She'd lived a sad, miserable life of neglect and abuse, broken dreams and lost chances. Yet she'd sat with every light on in their shabby house on Iowa Street, Norfolk, Virginia, waiting for Mel to come home when he'd promised. She'd kept his suppers warm, even bought a bottle of wine now and then to celebrate his shore leave.

But the ass usually never showed. If he did, it was always too little and too late. He'd stumble in after midnight, and he'd stink of cigarette smoke, hard liquor, and another woman's perfume. He'd been loud-mouthed and mean, quick to slap Abigail, just as quick to call her a liar if she challenged him. By then, he would've squandered the rent and grocery money away, and he'd be too tired to do anything around the house but empty that bottle of wine and pass out. And Alex had wished he'd never come home.

To help his mom, he'd gotten a paper route when he'd turned seven. Gramps told him someone had to be the man of the family. So Alex stepped up, never thought twice, and never looked back.

Gramps might've had bad dreams, but his only child was a living nightmare. Which was why Alex knew Mel was pulling a con now. He just didn't know what the old bastard was really after. But he meant to find out. Being the ass he was, Alex watched his useless excuse for a father cross the street and disappear into the parking lot.

Yet his gut was telling him he'd missed something. Telling Kelsey what he'd just done would be difficult enough, but why'd he feel as if he hadn't seen the last of Mel? Because historically, that was how the old bastard worked. He said one thing, then did another. He got your hopes up, then jerked the rug out from under you. Mel was the culmination of more unrealized expectations and childish heartbreaks than Alex could count.

Retrieving his cell from his rear pocket, he watched the parking lot, as he thumbed the senior agent he'd left with Kelsey. He had three: Mark Houston, Harley Mortimer, and David Tao. But of the three, Mark was the natural leader and prone to be in the office more than the other two, which made him Alex's right-hand man.

"Hey, Boss, what's up?"

"Please step into the hall, so the women won't—"

"Already done. Go ahead."

"Need you to check Navy records and verify—"

"The comment about Mel being in Mogadishu? Already pulled his USN record while the girls were chatting. Sorry, Boss, but your old man was never a SEAL, nor was he in Somalia. He was dishonorably discharged with less than two years of service. He spent most of that in the old brig at Norfolk. I'm looking at a long list of assault charges, drunk and disorderly, and petty thefts. Small time stuff. Nothing too violent. Just enough to get him kicked out of the Navy."

"Son of a bitch," Alex hissed, embarrassed that the secret he'd kept close to his chest for so many years was now public knowledge. He'd stopped watching the front door and had come to a full stop at the elevator that would take him back up to Maternity and Delivery. Mel's dishonorable discharge made everything so much worse. No wonder he'd never come home. Those charges would've earned him total forfeiture of pay and allowances.

"No worries, Alex. My dad's convinced farming dirt's more important than getting to know his five granddaughters."

"He still hasn't come for a visit?"

"Don't think he ever will. Libby and I call monthly, but he's never going to change. Honestly, I'm ready to call it quits. It's hard holding a conversation with someone who grunts and growls like you've offended him by calling. JayJay won't talk with him anymore when we call. She says he always hurts her feelings."

Alex looked at the floor, his shoulders heaving with disgust. "At least you and Libby tried."

"Sounds like you did, too."

"Yeah, well…" He rolled the first nine years of misplaced regret and boyish-devotion for a man who'd only cared about himself, off his shoulders. "I need you to trace his whereabouts over the last few years. He's up to something."

"You bet. I'll handle it as soon as I get in the office. Today."

"And find out who the hell volunteered my home address and whereabouts."

"You do remember Mother's back. All Mel had to say was that he was your dad, and she would've been an open book."

"Damn." Alex dug the heel of his free hand into his eye socket behind which a migraine was just starting. Mark was spot on. Mother liked to talk, and she'd always been nosey. He wondered what else Mel knew now, and how he'd found TEAM HQ in the first place. Alex didn't advertise, and unless a person knew where to look, there was no street-side signage that indicated a covert business resided in Alexandria.

Mother, real name Sasha Kennedy, had become another problem all together. She'd taken a lengthy hiatus after her daughter Dempsey's death. But when she'd come back from her South Pacific vacay, she hadn't been the same person. Right out of the gate, she'd told Alex she'd only stay on if he made her a partner. She honestly believed her elite financial status made that promotion from office assistant to deputy director obvious. Alex disagreed. Not only had she hidden her extreme wealth from The TEAM, including her so-called best friend, Ember Dennison, Mother had also hidden the fact that she had a severely handicapped teenage daughter. While Mother had been intimately involved in every other TEAM member's personal tragedies, successes, and lives, she'd kept hers secret.

The revelation about Dempsey had come to light recently. By then, the young woman had been dying, and The TEAM hadn't yet recovered from the depth of Mother's betrayal. Also, she'd never served, and that was a hard stop for Alex. Just because she was good with computers and video games did not make her a better warrior than Mark, Harley, or Ember. They knew what it meant to put their lives on the line. Mother knew how to hack encrypted codes and create successful computer games. Her genius had made her wealthy and Alex appreciated her skillset. But when it came to running The TEAM, Alex demanded loyalty, and Mother had let him down.

"Thanks, Mark. I don't know when I'll be in. I can't leave Kelsey and the kids alone while Mel's hanging around."

"No worries. I'll handle the office. You do what you have to. Just be careful. Libby's got one of her feelings. There's something not right about your old man."

Alex huffed. "You're telling me."

Chapter Three

Tie on straight? Check.

Shoes polished? One could only hope they gleamed like Jameson meant them to.

Teeth brushed and hair cut, not short, high, or tight, just trimmed enough to look professional and befitting this much sought-after job? He ran his fingers over his head, hoping he looked reasonably presentable. Check, check, and double check.

Dark glasses? Oh, yeah. Nearly forgot them.

Hooking his extra-dark, round-framed spectacles over his ears, Jameson Tenney faced the reflection in the bathroom mirror he could no longer see, and imagined he looked *good enough.* That was what Walker Judge had said when he'd told him to haul ass down to King Street and apply in person. That Alex Stewart didn't want perfection, just men and women who were *good enough.* That's precisely what Jameson was.

Finishing up, he tucked his loaded .44 Magnum into the well-worn leather holster beneath his suit jacket, under his left arm. Circumstances might take a man out of the Navy, but they never took the SEAL out of a man. It just didn't work that way.

Ready to be all he could be, Jameson clasped his trusty graphite cane in his right hand, and left his comfort zone behind. The cane transformed with the flick of his wrist, from a compact, barely noticeable, umbrella-length nightstick, into five feet of lightweight freedom. It was also a weapon, not that he'd needed to defend himself lately. Or ever would again. Life was different now that he couldn't see. Not dangerous so much as disadvantageous. Unfortunately—*big sigh*—his rough and tumble days were behind him. And that was just plain—inconvenient.

He strode down the hallway to the building's secure entrance, his stick feeling his way forward. There was no guard at the front door, just a smart lock with network connectivity, that allowed Jameson the freedom of unlocking the entry with one click of the remote entry key fob in his suit jacket pocket.

Out of the building and onto the sidewalk he went, confidently stepping into the promise of another bright, sunny morning he couldn't see, but could surely feel. He lived on the first floor of a small apartment complex in Rosemont, Virginia, a quiet burb west of Alexandria. A quick walk eastward on Braddock Road took him to the nearest metro station. From there, the Blue line, Franconia-Springfield train would take him south, then bring him home again, hopefully with a new job.

The trick now was getting on the right train. But he'd had help for that since he'd first moved to Virginia, after the incident, to be closer to his parents. Metro Agent Jersey Townsend looked out for oddballs like Jameson.

Sure enough. "Yo, Navy!" Jersey bellowed from across the platform, his deep voice a boisterous "glad-to-see-ya!" that Jameson never tired of hearing. "Good luck with your job interview today. Hope you knock 'em dead!"

Probably not the best thing to wish on a former Navy SEAL sniper, but Jersey didn't know that part of Jameson's past, and what did it matter? Jameson's gunslinging days were behind him, but life was still damned good, and he meant to live it.

"Thanks, buddy!" he yelled back, hoping he wasn't bellowing into some poor stranger's ear. "How's Portia this morning?"

"Still waiting for that big old watermelon belly of hers to pop. I'm bringing cigars when it does. You smoke?"

"Hell, yeah. I drink and womanize, too," he called across the crowded platform. "Am I in the right place to board your train or is it running late again?"

Metro stations were noisy places, especially on game days, during rush hours, or when the trains blew through. But always exciting. Yet Jameson could tell Jersey's footsteps from everyone else's when he closed in. At last, his big, warm hand landed on Jameson's shoulder.

"I don't know how you do it, but you're standing right where you should be. I guess you already know that, don't you, Navy? So why do you always ask?"

Jameson shrugged. "Guess because it gives you something to do. Must get boring sitting on your big old black butt all day long."

Jersey's laugh was rich and warm, as friendly as Jameson had come to expect from most everyone he'd met in Alexandria, Virginia. "You got this, boss man. I ain't worried about you. Maybe you oughta be the one bringing me cigars once you're rich, pushing pencils, and flirting with all your secretaries."

Jameson cocked his head, listening as the blue-line approached on time from the northwest. "Keep your fingers crossed that I get this job, and I might just do that. Remind me. When's your interview?"

"Day after tomorrow." The excitement in Jersey's voice reminded Jameson of a little boy on Christmas morning. "After all the school I've been choking down, I'm finally going to intern."

"Which hospital?"

"Not hospital, dummy. I'ma goin' into law, remember? Powers, Brooks, and Haggerty. Smack in the middle of DC."

Jameson smiled. "I remembered. Just making sure you did. You and me, bro. By the end of this week, we're going to be gainfully employed and on our way to the top."

"And famous!"

Jersey, maybe, but Jameson doubted he'd make the front page anytime soon. Fame had never been a goal, even when he'd been sighted. "You have a great day, buddy. Say hi to Portia for me. And stop calling her a watermelon! Be nice to your wife. Women have feelings, Robin."

"Will do, Batman. See you tomorrow."

"Same bat time, same bat channel," Jameson replied as he took five steps forward and boarded the train that would take him to King Street, a six-minute ride away.

He took the vacant seat three rows inside to his right and stood his cane upright between his knees where it wouldn't bump anyone. It was interesting how Jersey had started calling Jameson Batman the first day they'd met. He'd said Jameson looked like a bat the way he'd cocked his head and listened as if he had radar ears. Only it wasn't radar, not at all. It was concentration, focus, and balance. It was an inner determination to succeed, to be in the world, but not of the world. It was the daily decision Jameson made to remain positive in the face of the stark negativity that same world offered.

In the last five years, Jameson had chosen to adapt. Instead of stoking rage for what life had taken, he'd filled his mind with the light of discipline and his body with the calm of the still living. He could've died that day in Iraq. Others had. But he hadn't, so he let their sacrifice become his decision point. Kind of a 'what would Derby and Shakespeare say if they saw me today?' philosophy. Would they be proud because of how he lived or ashamed to call him friend because he'd turned to despair? He'd opted to make them damned proud.

Once the train braked to a slow stop at King Street station, Jameson disembarked quickly to the platform, along with the early morning rush of tourists, vendors, and business types. The TEAM building was located directly west from the station on Diagonal Road, another short walk.

"You can't miss it," Walker had said. Easy for him to say.

"We'll see about that, buddy," Jameson muttered to himself as he made his way down the escalator to the lower level, then went with the flow out the station's east exit, his cane tapping his way forward.

In minutes, he'd crossed the parking area due east, then maneuvered across Diagonal Road. Twenty-three steps from curb to curb put him on the opposite sidewalk, and, hopefully, right where he was supposed to be. Probing his cane forward, Jameson located the massive metal handle of the heavy glass entrance door, shoved it open, and entered the reverent, silent space Walker had told him about. A magnificent mosaic of

America's flag occupied the entire opposing wall. Jameson took a moment to reflect on the symbol he loved but would never see again.

But regret never got a man moving, and he was convinced there was still good work to be done, that he was just the man to do it.

Next stop, the elevator. It was as easy to locate, more so because Walker had described this place thoroughly. Made Jameson smile. Sighted people tended to forget that the *Americans with Disabilities Act* provided wheelchair access to all public places, as well as readily available Braille markers for the visually impaired. But that was okay. Walker had always been sensitive to Jameson's needs after the incident. As expected, he found the Braille-coded button for the floor he needed, and waited anxiously for his chance to prove he was still a productive member of society. To hell with being good enough. He was going to be great!

Once the elevator announced his arrival with a cheery ping, Jameson veered to the right and straight into his newest adventure. He aimed his stick over a carpeted walkway that dissected the circular configuration of work areas Walker had described. The work bay was designed like a wheel, its spokes the aisles between segments where agents' desks were located. He'd been told to speak with a woman named Mother at the customer service desk in the center of the wheel. Interesting name for a secretary.

But damn, this office was quiet. Where was everyone?

Stepping up to the counter, he cleared his throat, shifted his cane to his left hand, and announced, "Jameson Tenney here for an interview with Mr. Alex Stewart."

A much younger sounding voice than he'd anticipated replied, "Hi, Jameson. I'm Mother." She reached over the counter and shook his free hand. "I'm sorry but Alex isn't in today. We'll have to reschedule."

Well, damn. Not again. Jameson had been to more job interviews where, once a prospective employer knew he was handicapped, somehow, mysteriously, the job offer disappeared or the perspective boss came up with some excuse about it being filled, or something just as lame.

"Sure, I understand," he answered stoically, gripping his stick a little tighter. "I'm available at his convenience. What'll work best for Mr. Stewart?"

A hearty back slap bumped Jameson into the edge of the counter. "No need to reschedule this guy. I'm handling appointments today. Glad you made it, Jameson Tenney. Walker thinks a helluva lot of you. I'm Senior Agent Mark Houston, former USMC."

"Yeah, well, Walker's got brain damage," Jameson bantered back. "Nice to meet you, sir. Sure sorry about your disability."

Mark grunted.

"I didn't know you were back from the hospital," Mother told him. "How's Kelsey?"

"She's great. Wish you'd been there."

"Justice couldn't get away this morning or I would've been there."

"Knowing Kelsey, I wouldn't be surprised if she's gone home by then. You might want to call first."

"Of course, I'll call."

Jameson got the distinct impression Mother was annoyed. Also, that Mark was built like a fullback. From the mellow bass coming out of him, he seemed open and easy and big, not someone petty who'd kick a person when they were already down.

Not that Jameson was down. He wasn't. He had a good handle on his disability and his attitude. He'd never let his lack of sight become more than what it was, the loss of two excellent tools. Yes, being blind had been life altering, but so what? He was here today because he needed more than just a job. He needed his life back.

Mark grabbed onto Jameson's hand, adeptly mashing the handle of his cane within their conjoined grip. "Damn glad you made it, Tenney." He let go, but latched onto Jameson's elbow next, directed him around Mother's counter, then a few steps to the right, twelve to be exact, into what sounded like a short hallway. When they came to a halt, a knob to the left turned with the tiniest squeak.

"Six steps straight forward to the chair in front of my desk. Take a load off."

Cues also helped. Jameson strode confidently into Mark's office, his chin up while his stick tapped the layout of his way forward. Table to the right. The back of the wooden chair he'd mentioned was easy to find. Taking a seat, Jameson leaned his walking stick against Mark's desk where he could easily reach it.

"So, Navy SEAL, huh?"

"Yes, sir. Five years in, five years ago. Sorry about that crack about you being disabled, but you were a Marine."

"Still am," Mark admitted easily as he leaned back in his chair on the other side of the desk. Jameson could tell. He heard joints cracking and boot heels pushing over nubby carpet. Outdoor carpet, excellent choice for high-traffic work areas. "Your record shows you earned a helluva lot of awards those five years in."

"Awards don't mean anything. You know that."

"They tell a story though, don't they? Heroism's a hard thing to hide, and you were promoted early. That alone's damned tough."

There was nothing Jameson could say to that. 'Thank you, sir,' or 'So's stupidity,' sure weren't it. So he respectfully sealed his lips and let Mark get on with the interview.

He was leaning onto the top of his desk by then, into Jameson, which was a good sign. Not away from, which would've told an entirely different story. His fingers were interlocked, and he was breathing easy, probably had both elbows on the desk, too. "I've only got one question."

"Yes, sir?" Jameson straightened in his chair and cocked his head, striving to sense if an upcoming bad attempt at humor, maybe a Helen Keller joke, or an easy let down, was headed his way. He'd heard them all before. Probably shouldn't expect anything else, but it'd be nice to fit in again somewhere. The family a guy earned during combat tours was unlike any other, and Walker'd sounded so positive about this place and his new boss. He'd been kicked around a long time. All Jameson wanted was that same chance that Walker had. Redemption, damn it. The handicap did not make the man!

Mark cleared his throat. "When's the best time to take a kill shot?"

Jameson blinked. Maybe this was his lucky day. "Most guys will tell you it's the second your target steps into clear view, sir, but…" He swallowed hard. He had so damned much riding on the line. To have to walk back out this door, past the customer service desk, and get on the elevator with his head still held high, would suck. But his gut had always served him before, so he went with it again. "If you want my honest opinion, best scenario would be never. Optimum outcome would be for that terrorist to drop his weapon, raise both hands, turn himself in, and swear allegiance to something better than ISIL, or whichever asshat's running the current shitshow. That way he could still contribute to his family. He could be a better man and heal his country instead of tearing it apart from the inside. And America's sons and daughters could all come home."

Dead. Silence.

Shit. The answer that sounded damned good when he'd said it, worried Jameson now. He couldn't get a clear sense of Mark's reaction. He'd slowed his breathing. Might even be holding his breath, the dog. Clever trick. Must have been a scout sniper in the Corps. Seconds dragged. But then—

"Shake my hand, you son of a bitch," Mark growled. "You're now working for the best damned employer on the Eastern Seaboard." He didn't hold back, just leaned across his desk, grabbed Jameson's hand, and squeezed the ever-loving shit out of his fingers. Hurt so good!

"I am?" he asked to make sure he'd heard right. "I'm hired? Just like that?"

"Just like that," Mark breathed as he ended the gripping congrats. "One word of advice, don't call anyone around here sir, especially not Alex. He'll rip you a new one if you do. Ember Dennison's out today. She's one of our three technical assistants, but Beau Villanueva's just as good. I'll introduce you when he gets in from the hospital, then to The TEAM when we're through here."

"Someone hurt?"

"Nope, Alex's wife had a baby this morning, their first son together, that's all. He won't be in for a couple weeks, so yell at me for whatever you need." Mark slapped several papers on the desk. "Here are your insurance forms, health, dental, and life. In Braille, so you won't have to rely on someone else to explain things. You're smart enough to figure them out, but my phone number's at the top. Call if you have questions, but don't be shocked when you get to your deductible. Alex covers that, so don't argue with the man. When Beau gets in, he'll get your computer set up, make sure the headset works and your audio's clear. It also converts to Braille, by the way."

"You've already got a computer for me?" Incredible.

"Sure. A tablet and ruggedized laptop, too. You'll need them when you travel. All in Braille." Mark's fingers drummed the desk top, which, now that Jameson was more relaxed, sounded smooth and dense, like granite. "We expect all agents to keep in top military shape. Looks like you're already doing that. Not sure if you've ever HALO jumped before, but—"

"I have. Looking forward to doing it again."

"Great. You'll have full access to the weapons vault upstairs, and you're expected to attend and pass monthly range certification with flying colors. Can you do that?"

"You bet. I still carry," Jameson confessed.

"Don't worry about hitting your marks the first month. We've got specially designed gear and rifles for visually impaired operators, as well as spotters if you need one. You're not dead yet, are you?"

Jameson shook his head, shocked at the confidence this man had in him.

"Breathing once in a while doesn't hurt, you know," Mark teased. "Take a breath, Junior Agent. You're definitely hired. You'll get your signing bonus by mail this week, unless you sign up for direct deposit today. For your information, we've got one of the best physicians onsite, as well as a full gym downstairs, and, occasionally, when David Tao's in town, a genuine Buddhist monk who can teach you how to enhance all your senses."

"I'm already proficient in Krav Maga." *And I can hear your heartbeat. Sometimes, I can detect... more. Someone sneaking up on me. Intense emotions like rage. Lust. Hostility. Deadly intent.* He was also sure he'd just heard a vertebra in Mark's neck pop.

"Seriously? Which version?"

Krav Maga was an Israeli-style of self-defense. Derived from a combination of Aikido, boxing, wrestling, Judo, and Karate, it focused on extreme efficiency of motion. At its core, Krav Maga took the best practices of other techniques and streamlined them into concise, hard-hitting, core fighting maneuvers that expended minimum energy, yet achieved maximum results.

"As you know, there are two versions: civilian and military. I've been studying under Jacob Ben Amin the last two years. He's shown me how hard Israel's military fights, and why they win as often as they do."

"General Ben Amin? Well, good god damn! Maybe you can teach us a thing or two."

"It'd be my pleasure." As he said those words, Jameson meant them with every fiber of his being. At last, his chest heaved. His lungs relaxed enough to fill with the air of this brand-new day and the fantastic opportunity he'd just been granted. Almost made him giddy to think he now worked for the much-maligned Alex Stewart, the guy who'd turned King Street on its ear when he'd become the most successful defense contractor in the States. For some unknown reason, the press hated Alex, and he hated them right back. Working for him was going to be fun.

"One more thing." Mark pushed his chair back, so Jameson did the same and stood, bringing his walking stick centerline of his body.

"Yes?"

"We've got a client who insists she needs a bodyguard tonight. All other agents are on assignment. You feeling lucky?"

"Yes, sir, I mean, Mr. Houston. I am." *I'm damned lucky!*

Mark knuckled Jameson's shoulder. "Stop with the mister crap. We operate on first names around here. I'm just Mark. You're just Jameson. You'll be on your own tonight, but all you need to do is make sure this woman boards her private jet leaving Reagan, precisely at ten. You've been to Reagan before, right?"

Jameson nodded. "That's how I got to Virginia."

"Good. She claims she's got a couple stalkers. Beau will drive you there, but frankly, he doesn't have the patience to deal with someone like her, and you'll be her official escort on the tarmac. She's flying out by private jet; you won't have to navigate the terminal. The jet should be waiting for her when you arrive, so you won't have to deal with her long. Can you handle an easy op?"

"I can," Jameson declared adamantly. *Hell, I'd walk though fire right now for you guys.*

"Good. Her name's Lucy Shade. Have you heard of her?"

"Ahh, yeah." Damn. Who hadn't? Miss Shade was the sole American reporter to be granted an interview with Pops Delaney, the Irish Godfather, straight out of Ireland.

Much to the chagrin of the FBI, he allegedly worked his dirty arms business on the South side of Boston, and was getting away with it. As if that interview hadn't garnered her enough fame and glory all by itself, she'd publicly trashed Delaney's reputation after meeting him, made unverified allegations, and, oh, yes, she fancied herself a celeb and had her greedy sights set on stardom in Hollywood. No wonder she needed a bodyguard.

"Any questions?"

"Nope, I'm good." *Damned good.*

"Well, I've got one for you. I pass your building every morning on my way to work. Can I give you a lift?"

"You'd do that?"

"Sure. No trouble. You're on my way."

"I usually take the metro, but yeah." *Wow.* "I really appreciate the offer."

"Great. Let's introduce you to the gang then."

Mark had no more than opened his door, when the sweetest breath of spring bounced into Jameson's chest, damned near knocked him on his ass. He grabbed onto whoever she was to keep her from falling, then gripped tighter when he detected the distinct hammering of her pulse under his thumbs. His nostrils flared at the lush scent of mellow lavender mingled with peppery pheromones and the sweet tantalizing zing of feminine stress.

"I didn't hurt you, did I, ma'am?" he asked, his head cocked as his senses opened wide to resolve the mystery behind her worry.

"Oh, no. It's my fault. I am so, so sorry," she cried. But then she brushed her fingertips over his chest as if trying to make a boo-boo better. Which was just plain endearing. There was no way this fluff of femininity could've bruised a former SEAL in the first place, not by bumping that soft, warm body into him. "I didn't know you were talking with anyone, Mark. But I... Darn, I'm sorry I'm really late again. But I'm here now, and I'll stay after to make up for not being on time."

Jameson caught the impression of her running her other hand through her hair. Which was long enough he could hear its silky strands flutter over her shoulders and fall down her back like a very quiet waterfall. The gentlest cascade. That's where the lavender scent came from. Her shampoo. The zinging stress and peppery pheromones were all her.

This was when he missed sight the most. Around women. Was she blonde, and how long was her hair? What color were her eyes? Blue or green? Brown like his? Did they sparkle? He'd detected no foreign accent, not like that meant anything. His Navy days had made one thing abundantly clear. It was a great big world out there, most people were good, and women everywhere were be-a-u-ti-ful.

Her fingertips stopped tapping, and for a split second, he enjoyed the scintillating warmth seeping from her light-as-a-feather touch, through his dress shirt, to his skin. The internal firestorm he'd weathered every day since the incident that changed his life, suddenly calmed. Whoever she was, this woman's touch was magic.

An odd sizzle started humming at the base of his spine and quickly tap-danced up each vertebra to the back of his neck, making all those tiny hairs stand up. This woman might sound timid, and her touch was a balm to his whole being, but she was chock full of vibrant electricity that speared straight through him. He was caught on an invisible lure. Hooked. And he didn't even know her name.

"No worries, Maddie. Relax."

Ah, Maddie. How lovely.

"How's Alex's wife? Umm, Kelsey. I really wanted to be there with everyone at the hospital, but something came up, and I... I'm so sorry."

"Kelsey's fine, so are Alex and their son. They named him Bradley Patrick Stewart after Alex's Irish grandfather."

"Aww. How much did he weigh? How long is he?"

Maddie's anxiety over missing her boss's son's birth seemed out of proportion. She was trying too hard, which to Jameson meant she was hiding something.

"He's a big boy, weighed in around ten pounds, I think. Not sure how long he is, but mother and baby are doing great. This guy here is Jameson Tenney, our newest agent. He's decided to work with us, starting today. Since Beau hasn't come in from the hospital yet, and I wouldn't be surprised if he took the rest of the day off, would you mind introducing Jameson to the gang and being his driver tonight? It's for an easy bodyguard op. Just grab one of The TEAM limos and make sure he hooks up with Lucy Shade at her hotel. She flies out at ten, so be there by nine thirty."

"Nine," Jameson interrupted. "I like to be early. Gives me time to familiarize myself with the location."

"Fine, nine it is," Mark agreed. "Then drive Jameson and Shade over to Reagan National and wait until Shade's onboard. Maddie, her network's private jet will be parked near the east hangars. Look for their logo on the tail. In the meantime, show him around the office, get him situated at his desk, and tell him the rules."

"Sure, Mark, but, umm, what rules?"

Jameson was sure Maddie had just tipped her head, that she took everything too seriously. Which was sad, but kind of cute, too. She needed to learn what he'd realized after the incident: *Life was short. If it handed you lemons, by hell, make the best lemonade ever. Drink it up, and never let the burn slow you down.*

"Kidding, Maddie. Just a joke," Mark teased. "Jameson'll need to know where to store any personal weapons, as well as what to wear when he's on active ops."

"Mark, do you have a minute?" Mother called out.

"You bet. Later guys. It's gearing up to be a busy day."

"Copy that," Jameson replied as Mark stepped away.

"Sure, yeah. I guess," Maddie answered tightly.

Jameson offered his hand and said, "Pleased to meet you, Maddie."

Unfortunately, that handshake ended quicker than he would've liked. Tactile contact provided intel. The key was to maintain physical contact long enough to pick up pulse rates, heartbeats, breaths, all those little tells most people didn't realize they gave away. But Maddie had all but tossed his hand back at him after a brief, mostly insincere clasp. All he'd learned was, yes. Stressed.

"Pleased to meet you, too," she said. But her tone said otherwise. She wasn't pleased. Not at all. And that handshake had been more like gripping tense pencils instead of warm fingers. "I'm sorry I ran into you. I was in a hurry, then you were there, and… and…" She stammered. "I wasn't looking where I was going. I'm sorry."

The sorry part he believed. But Maddie seemed as if she'd been in more than just a hurry, almost as if she'd been running from something. Or someone.

"Apology accepted and forgotten," he replied, gesturing for her to walk ahead of him. "Lead on, and I'll follow. Just don't stop too short." He tapped his index finger to his dark glasses in case she hadn't noticed. "Blind man coming through and all that. And never move the furniture. That's not funny."

"I would never! That'd be mean."

Joking about himself always did the trick. Her heartrate settled into a normal rhythm. She stepped to the side of his walking cane and waited on him to join her, which was nice. Despite him telling her to lead, he'd never been much of a follower.

"You're blind?" she asked, a completely different tremor in her very lovely voice.

People often asked the obvious. "Yes. Five years now."

"If you don't mind my asking, how'd it happen?"

"I've never minded honest curiosity. It's what keeps life exciting. Simple answer: improvised explosive device. Iraq."

"How awful!" Another obvious response, although this one had been honestly spoken.

But awful didn't begin to describe the terror of waking up sightless in a strange place. Jameson had learned early during rehabilitation that he could either stay in bed snuggled up with pity and survivor's guilt, or he could throw himself back into the deep end of life, learn how to swim all over again, and continue to contribute… something. Somehow. Man, he hoped The TEAM was that something.

"How long were you in the hospital?"

"A couple weeks," he answered easily. "Landstuhl Regional Medical Center in Germany. It's near Ramstein Air Base. But I wasn't crippled or anything. Most of that time was just spent taking tests and more tests. You know how the military is. If it ain't broken, fix it till it is. In the end, there was nothing to be done that hard work and rehabilitation couldn't resolve. The IED my team encountered blew me backward into a brick wall. I hit my head pretty hard. When I came to, I thought I'd gotten off lucky. Still had all my fingers and toes. I wasn't bleeding anywhere that I could see…" *Which should've been my first clue.* "Actually, I couldn't see anything, but I could feel my helmet. It was still on and wasn't damaged, but…" He tapped his temple. "Both retinas detached from the impact. Everything went black. No big deal. I'm still alive, and I'm doing just fine." *Because I'm no quitter, and I freakin' love lemonade!*

They were inside the circular aisle that led to the work bay before she murmured, "I'm still sorry you lost your sight. That must've been hard, going from being able to see everything to seeing nothing."

"Was. Not is. It happened a long time ago, Maddie, and I've moved on." He turned toward her and changed the subject. "Why were you late? Traffic?" *Or something else? Someone maybe?*

"No. Traffic's not a problem."

Not *a* problem or not *the* problem? Jameson detected the coverup and the twinge of panic behind it. Fear maybe? Or was she just brushing him off?

Reaching out, he grabbed her hand and secured it under his elbow, patting it when she closed her fingers around that pointed joint. "Sorry, but it'd be easier if you directed me where to go while I'm meeting everyone. I might become disoriented. We're going in a circle, right?"

Which Walker had explained thoroughly, but Maddie didn't need to know that. It seemed she needed something to hold onto, and an elbow was, well, an elbow was so damned genderless it couldn't pose a threat to anyone.

He turned toward his new teammates, eager to meet the men and women of The TEAM Walker was so enamored with. At last, Jameson Tenney had a real job and an upcoming mission. All in the same day!

Chapter Four

Maddie licked her bottom lip, flustered at the seemingly innocent, useless assignment she'd been given. But that's what she got for being late. Leftovers. This was her third tardy in two weeks. If Alex knew why she couldn't make it on time, he'd fire her for sure.

Jameson Tenney was a good fit for The TEAM. He already knew former SEAL, Walker Judge, who was on that black op into China, with his wife, Agent Persia Coltrane. Jameson also knew Adam Torrey, another former SEAL. They were still good-naturedly insulting each other like guys did.

Maddie was eternally grateful she'd landed this job as TEAM Protocol Officer, but working with all these handsome guys was nearly more than she could handle some days. They were the deadliest eye-candy. Every last one of them was walking, talking, manly sex on steroids. Not only were they breathtakingly handsome, but they were real men. Not whiny boys. Not pretty white-collar college guys who primped and sent out hundreds of selfies to their adoring, do-nothing fans, either.

Strong, capable, intelligent men comprised a good ninety percent of The TEAM. They worked hard every day, and earnestly strived to serve their country. Sometimes, they even put their lives on the line during missions. Not just anyone could or would do that. These men really were the few and the brave. That much she knew firsthand.

This new junior agent seemed to be another rock-solid warrior. Jameson walked like he knew where he was going despite being unable to see. She'd kept close to him like he'd requested, her hand under his elbow while he'd chatted and joked with everyone, even Beck's wife, Camilla. She'd sure changed since she'd come back from maternity leave and started working fulltime. Beck had changed, too. Both, in good ways. They seemed happy, something Maddie had yet to find. Certainly wasn't in marriage.

"Donuts!" Harley Mortimer bellowed. He cleared the elevator, his arms stacked high with pink bakery cartons, his chin resting on the top one to keep the rest from slipping.

Maddie would've run to help. She loved working with Harley. But she was supposed to stick close to Jameson, so she resisted the urge.

Thankfully, Ember and Rory burst through the fire doors at the opposite end of the work bay, both out of breath, with her giggling, "I win. You owe me a bubble bath."

"How about a glazed confection instead?" Rory asked as he aimed for Harley and took over half the boxes. "TEAM! Ready room!" he called out, walking straight to the Sit Room where Alex held morning staff meetings.

"Are you hungry?" Jameson asked quietly.

Maddie looked up into a handsome, albeit expressionless face. He'd gotten too close, yet he stood there with his head cocked, his round, dark glasses facing her, as if he were intently waiting on an answer. Maybe even listening to her. Really listening. Like he cared. He cocked his head to the other side when she didn't answer right away. He did that a lot, and she could've sworn he was reading her mind. It'd sure be nice to look into his eyes. His glasses were too dark. They told her nothing, not even his eye color. Which might be because his eyeballs had been grotesquely damaged from that roadside bomb, or his eye sockets were empty. Maybe those glasses were a good thing after all.

"No, I'm fine."

"Are you sure? Sounds like a party in there."

The TEAM did sound rowdy, in a good-natured way.

"Do *you* want to join them?" she asked, throwing the decision back on Agent Tenney.

The barest smile shifted over his manly countenance and landed on lush tanned lips that looked tender enough to kiss.

Frightened at that crazy notion, Maddie glanced over her shoulder, afraid someone might've caught the illicit thought that dashed through her mind. But her ex, Nash Coogan wasn't there. Neither were his associates, the loan sharks who'd decided she should pay off his account when they couldn't track him down. They were the reason she'd been late today, and their late night warnings were getting scarier. A sheet of sturdy CDX plywood now covered her front room picture window after a huge rock sailed through it last week. Today, she'd had to buy four brand new tires before work, to replace the four someone had spiked with roofing nails overnight. This morning, there'd been a nasty threat pasted to her windshield: *Last chance, bitch!*

She didn't need a babysitting assignment. She needed a safe place to hide.

"I could be persuaded," Agent Tenney murmured, his tone as sweet and low as melted fudge. "Can you?"

"Can I what?" she asked, her heart hammering like an idiot bird in an out-of-control cuckoo clock. What was it about this blind guy that was getting through her defenses? Did she feel sorry for him? Okay, yes, a little. Which was stupid. He didn't seem to need anyone's help or pity, least of all from her. Mark hadn't been holding his elbow when she'd run into him. She was pretty certain Jameson hadn't really needed her guiding him through the work bay, either. The man might be blind, but she could tell that he sensed more than most people did. Which begged the question, did he feel sorry for her? And why? Had she given something away? Could he tell what a mess her life was in?

He crooked his arm again. "Can you be persuaded to lower your guard long enough to join me for a cup of nasty office coffee and a fat pill?"

"A fat pill?" Instead of linking arms with him, she cupped his elbow, ready to steer him into the Sit Room, make sure he found a chair, get him a cup of coffee and a donut, then leave.

He intercepted her hand and pulled it through his arm, then rested his cane hand over it. Which was almost courtly. Almost nice. "Yes, fat pills. Donuts are nothing but carbs and the grease they're fried in. All those calories are easy to burn off during intense energy days, like when you're humping up mountainsides or running for your life. But sugar is still poison, and it messes with metabolism. I'd like a coffee, though. What do you say, Maddie? Join me?"

That almost sounded like a date. She tugged her arm free and reconnected with his elbow, determined to get through this assignment and put the morning behind her. "I'm sorry, but since I was late today, I've got work to catch up on. I'll get you seated, but ask Harley to call me when you're done partying and ready to continue the tour."

The corners of those lush lips turned up into the biggest, most handsome smile. It transformed Jameson's manly features into little boy glee, and she was star struck. Everything about this man was genuine, from the neat, precise part in his dark hair to the warmth of his hands.

"You're right. Almost forgot. We have a mission tonight. Well, carry on then. I'm at your disposal. But before we get back to work, may I ask your last name?"

"Oh, sure. Sorry. Maddie Bannister." Maiden name. Never Maddie Coogan again. Not. Ever. "Now let's get you set up with a TEAMwear polo, then a weapon."

"I'm already carrying," he informed her smoothly. "Forty-four Magnum. Under my left arm."

"That's quite a big pistol. I never would've guessed. It doesn't show." Of course it didn't. He was a former special operator, hard-muscled and smart, already trained, and nothing like her.

"That's the idea behind concealed carry, isn't it? Never let the bad guy see you coming."

She nodded like a dolt. He couldn't see, so she said, "Yes. Excellent. But rule number one: agents don't carry in the office. From now on, you'll have to store that bad boy in the bottom drawer of your desk. The drawer's been rekeyed and the new key's in your pencil drawer. Or you can put your weapon in the vault upstairs each morning when you get in. Zack keeps all his weapons up there. It's no big deal. You already fit right in."

"I'd like to. I don't make a very good telemarketer, and I suck at insurance sales."

"That's what you've been doing these last five years?"

"Yes, but only to put myself through school. VA benefits only cover so much."

"What field did you go into?"

"Criminal Profiling. You?"

Maddie shrugged, embarrassed to admit. "Accounting. I was just Civil Service, a payroll clerk at Fort McHenry. But I put myself through college, too." Maddie had no idea why she felt she needed to defend her life's decisions.

Jameson seemed not to notice her blabbering. "Thanks for making sure I got paid," he replied smoothly. "You don't have to wear combat boots to serve the warfighter, Maddie. I'm sure you're as proud of the work you did at Fort McHenry, as what the rest of the people here did overseas."

She took a long hard look at him then. They were in the elevator on their way to the third floor. "Yes, sure, I get that, and I am proud. But if I could do things over again, I would've joined one of the services fresh out of high school. I would've been more involved." *I would've truly served. Like you.*

Somehow, her hand was resting on his forearm again, and he was gently patting her fingers. "I'm sure there were good reasons for the decisions you made back then. But every person in the chain of command counts, even logistics tails. How could we have done what needed being done, without someone behind the scenes paying our bills, buying ammo for us to shoot, stocking supplies, and making sure we had enough of those dry-as-shit MREs to choke down?"

She couldn't help the laugh that bubbled out of her throat. Jameson was easy to talk with.

"But I didn't serve," she insisted. "Not like you. Not like I could have." *Not like I wanted to.*

The elevator doors opened. His fingers on hers stopped moving. "My mom used to say nights would be mighty dark without every last one of us little stars. We shine wherever we end up, Maddie. Look at you, Protocol Officer for a bigshot like Alex Stewart. I'd say that's a damned important job. I'll bet he thinks so, too."

"Well, of course, or he wouldn't have created the job description or hired me," she admitted. "He depends on me to organize his meetings with senators and White House staff, the press and the local police. I handle all his transportation needs, too. If he's traveling out of state, I set up his schedule and make his reservations. I know what he likes to eat, which hotels he prefers, and which press reporter to not invite to press releases. I like what I do, and I'm good at it." That should've made her feel better, yet it didn't. No matter how good of a job she did, she could still hear her father's disapproval.

"I'll bet Alex is smart enough to appreciate what you do for him, too."

"Umm, yes. He tells me all the time." *Only I've never believed him before now. You make it sound like I really do good work. As if I'm somebody, too.*

"So which service would you have joined?"

"Marines."

"Why didn't you?"

"I was ready to. Scored high enough on my ASVAB that I could've been a..." She wished she'd kept her big mouth shut.

"Been a what?"

They were paused at the vault. To distract Jameson, Maddie pressed her palm to the pad, then keyed in the double-authentication passcode until the vault hissed open.

"Never mind. Something came up," she said lamely, remembering the day her father had put his foot down and told her not only would she not embarrass him by marching off to war, but if she thought she was so smart, it was time she moved out of his house, got a job, and stood on her own two feet. Which she'd told him she would. *So there.*

As if he'd needed to lash out at her worse than he already had, he'd pointed at the front door and bellowed, "Go to hell, little girl! You're not smart enough to make it out there. It's a big world. You'll never amount to anything. You're just like your mother. You don't have the balls!"

He had that right. She hadn't come with balls, but it'd been good to finally understand why he'd denigrated her throughout her life. He must've wanted a son, but got stuck with a daughter.

Instead of marching straight to the USMC recruiter, she'd panicked and applied at the local grocery store as a bagger. Her dad had ridiculed her so much growing up, that she'd never had much confidence in herself. And because living on the streets those miserable weeks after she'd been forced out of her dad's house had been so, so scary, she'd cut herself short and settled for less. Then, when she'd met Nash, she'd settled for less again and married the first guy who came along. She knew now that the Corps would've snapped her up, no questions asked. But she hadn't known that then. Hence her safe accounting degree. Her college debt. And Nash Coogan, her lying, two-timing ex.

She was one of those stupid, stupid women who married their dads. Nash was her father all over again. Condescending. Critical. Quick to point out her mistakes and flaws. Never listening, always arguing. Oblivious to the sound of her voice. Neither he nor her father had ever shut up long enough to understand that she was no idiot. That she'd always contributed more than her fair share. Not like what she'd said had ever mattered.

"Life hands us lemons sometimes, doesn't it, junior agent?" Jameson asked, his head cocked as if he were still trying to figure her out. He shrugged. "I figured if the new guy in the office was a junior agent, you must be, too."

"I'm not an agent." She glared up at him, intent on a sharper retort. But there she was, speaking with a man without sight, who was still determined to serve. A man who couldn't see, but had somehow gotten to Alexandria and into this office without anything more than a cane. "I'm just admin. Just staff."

"But you can still make good decisions. You're intelligent. I can tell."

The world tilted, just a little. Or maybe those were the tectonic plates along the Eastern Seaboard settling. Whatever, Maddie felt the minute adjustment her perspective had just undergone. She saw herself clearly for the first time since she'd left her selfish father behind. She did have a darned good job, and she loved what she did for a living. She'd worked extra hard in college and aced her accounting degree. But she'd also been smart enough to realize she needed more than ledgers and balance sheets. Accounting wasn't very fulfilling. It paid the bills, but it wasn't her dream job. That was when she'd changed her mind and gone looking for the career she actually loved.

She'd been just as smart when she'd dumped Nash. It'd been scary facing him and telling him she was through. That marriage to him wasn't working for her. He'd torn her apartment apart, but he'd left. Maybe she was brighter than she'd thought after all.

"Guess it's time I mashed those babies and turned them into lemonade then, huh?" she asked quietly.

Jameson made an adorably cute funny face. "Ewww, mashed babies. Not a good visual. No, just no."

He made her smile. "You know what I meant. Puppies, then."

"Not puppies!" He folded both hands over his chest, faking a heart attack. "No, no, no! We never mash puppies or bunnies or babies."

Maddie laughed. There was that tantalizing thought again. Blind or not, this man was kissable, and he was funny. He knew how to clown around, and he actually listened. "Fruit! Lemons are fruit. I'm mashing fruit! Not children or puppies, and who said anything about bunnies?"

Jameson took hold of her hand again and laced his fingers between hers, matching their palms. "Sugarless lemonade, okay? Let me know when it's ready. I'll be your taste-tester. Deal?"

"Deal," she promised, feeling lighthearted on a day that had started so, so badly. Maybe there was hope for her. "But before I show you the vault, let's get you some clothes."

Her mouth dried at the thought. Him. Without clothes. Needing to be dressed. Or undressed.

"I mean, a shirt." Flustered, she added, "Office rule number two: dress code is casual. We aren't invited to many formal affairs, so we wear whatever we want to work. You're only required to wear a TEAM polo on active operations. Wear whatever you want otherwise."

Leading Jameson to the storage room, she entered first so he could follow her voice. "This is where we keep TEAMwear, as in polos, tactical vests, boots, snow gear, scuba gear, skydiving equipment, and…" She took a big breath. "You name it, it's probably in here somewhere. No charge, just take what you need. What size are you?"

She shouldn't have asked. For some reason, the question sounded nosy. Intimate. Especially when he told her his casual shirt size. Of course. He would be extra-large.

Okay, stop, she told herself. *And breathe.* Yes, he's ripped, and he's tall, and he's good-looking as heck, but dayum… extra-large? Really? In all departments? "Grab a few shirts so you have extras at home. You know, in c-c-case you ruin one or t-t-two or... or..."

He'd stopped directly in front of Maddie, facing her, his mouth close enough she could smell the mint on his breath. Her lungs failed, just flat out quit working at this, oh, so close proximity and the heady scent of a strong, handsome male. Jameson wore a crisp white dress shirt under a dark gray business jacket, a combination that right now was working her last quivering nerve. He smelled good enough to lick, of aftershave and dryer sheets. Of clean skin and freshly washed hair.

At the moment, he held his cane in one hand, but his other hand rested on his hip. He'd tossed his jacket out of his way, exposing half of his chest and abdomen. The way he'd tucked his shirt into his slacks. That fact that he wasn't wearing an undershirt. There was something decadently sexy about a good-looking man who dressed professionally. Maybe it was the thought of getting him out of all those properly pressed clothes...

The air vibrated between them.

"Show me," he murmured, his voice gone husky and thick. Like her blood.

"Show you w-w-what?" she whispered, her heart beating in her chest like a kid's pajama-clad feet pounded on Christmas morning when he ran downstairs to see what Santa left.

That same adorable smile quirked Jameson's manly lips, lips she wanted to touch and taste and nibble. "Where do you keep my size shirts?"

'Who needs a shirt?' her new-found wicked imagination asked.

Maddie could only see her wild-eyed reflection in his dark, round lenses. The woman looking back at her was still a timid girl with stage fright and no courage. Yet her fingers clenched, wanting to lift those dark glasses off the expertly carved bridge of this man's perfect nose. To smooth the errant chunk of black hair off a forehead that lined with gentle wrinkles when he smiled. To look into his eyes and truly see him. Were a blind man's eyes still the windows to his soul? She wanted to know.

Yet she wouldn't, so she didn't. Her life was already complicated, and the last thing Jameson needed on his first day at work was trouble. Taking his hand resolutely, she steered him a full step backward and to his right.

"H-here," she said, her voice lost and her throat dry for some reason. "This bin should fit you."

"But I don't want to wear a bin," he told her, his voice so damned low and sweet and adorable that she wanted to faint in his arms.

But this was their place of employment, and this wasn't a hook-up. Okay then. Her lungs started working again. She sucked in a deep breath and muttered, "Smart ass. Bins are in. Didn't you know? It's all the rage. Wear one on your head or go without. Be a has-been. It's all the same to me."

Just as quickly as she'd found her breath, she lost it again.

Jameson had set his cane against the rack and jerked his dress shirt out of his slacks. He'd started unbuttoning it and— *Good God!*

Maddie closed her eyes. Then opened them. Then shut them again. But why not look? He didn't seem embarrassed or shy being bare-chested, and he didn't know she was staring goo-goo-eyed at his physique, and who else would know she was staring at a lean-muscled god with just the right dusting of dark, crisp, chest hairs sprinkled over two manly pecs that begged to be petted and nuzzled and—?

No. Just no. I'd never do something like that! Daring girls reached out and touched half-naked men. Sassy, full of life, courageous, risk-taking girls grabbed onto guys like Jameson. Not her. Not ever. But if she were that kind of woman...

There were no words to describe the capricious winds of fate that had put her with this man in this room today. He'd stripped his dress shirt off, then faced her. The shirt now lay over the bin from which he'd removed one folded black TEAM polo shirt. It hung off the ends of his long, elegant but manly fingers. Trim cuticles and neatly trimmed nails led to strong, tanned arms covered with dark hairs that lay in one direction, as if they'd been combed. Purpled veins that declared this man worked out, ran over his hands and inside his arms. From there, her eyes strayed to his sharply defined biceps, relaxed now, but obviously capable of more than just lying beneath a dress shirt.

A neat trail of dark hairs trailed from his navel to a simple square belt buckle, and for some crazy reason, Maddie licked her lips at the way his slacks fit his thighs, his long legs. She couldn't have quit looking if the earth ended. He was too much. So much. Smooth, tanned muscular shoulders. Matching collarbones that came together in a sexy hollow that begged for her nose or her lips or her—

"Tags?" he asked, his head cocked again in that endearing way she was beginning to like.

For the first time, Maddie wondered if he was listening to the wild thrumming throughout her body. Could he feel her temperature rising from all her deliciously wicked thoughts? Did he know what she was thinking? What he was doing to her? What she wanted to do to him?

Heated waves coursed up her neck and over her cheeks. "N-n-no price tags," she breathed, her voice gone as wispy and limp as a spring breeze.

"Well, then…" He stood there stock still. His magnificent chest as unmoving and solid as stone. Warm stone. Granite she wanted to touch.

He'd done it again. He was studying her in his quiet, psychic way.

Just reach out.
I'm not that kind of girl.
But you want to be…

Shut up.

That terse mental command should've put an end to this crazy, tempting moment. Good grief! She wanted to kiss this man. Jameson was funny and handsome, and he smelled sinfully clean, the kind of clean she wanted to get dirty. Carnally. Primitively. Really dirty.

"I come with a warning label," he murmured. "Should've told you before. Guess I didn't think I'd ever feel this way again."

"Feel w-w-what way?"

"Like kissing a beautiful woman."

OhGodOhGodOhGod.

"But you need to know…"

She could hear his throat muscles work as he swallowed. All that hung between them was that shirt, that darned TEAM shirt. "I'm blind," he murmured.

"S-s-so?" she had to ask. "What does that have to do with anything?"

"The blind develop senses they never knew they had, Maddie. Like I can hear your blood hammering in your veins, and I know your heart's racing. I know when you're looking at me, and I'm pretty sure I can guess what you're thinking."

"Ah, err, umm… I'm thinking that shirt will fit you per-per-perfectly."

"And you're purring."

"I'm married," she blurted.

His head canted to the other side. "Married? That's too bad," he said quietly, yet so quickly she was sure he knew she'd lied.

In seconds, he dragged that TEAM shirt over his shoulders and the peep show was over.

So was Maddie.

Fanning her overheated cheeks, she turned to the door, her body jacked up on hormones and every last one of her lost dreams. Here was a man worth living for.

If only she could.

Chapter Five

"He's not who you think he is, sweetheart," Alex told Kelsey again. "The only reason Mel's here today is because he wants something. You saw how quickly he asked about that whisky. Bastard forgot all about you and Bradley the second he thought he could get some booze."

Bradley had just nursed and was sound asleep in the bassinet at Kelsey's bedside. For now, she and Alex were seated at the window bench overlooking the Potomac. It was late afternoon. She should be sleeping, but she wanted to talk.

"I get that. He's got problems. I just hate letting him leave without doing something for him. He looked so—"

"Conniving?"

"He is that, yes. He's not fooling me." Kelsey leaned toward Alex, resting her elbows on her thighs as she clasped her hands together. "But I can't help thinking that he's sad, too. Maybe he's had a change of heart. We might never see him again. Don't you think everyone deserves a second chance?"

"Not after what he did to Mom, Gramps, and Gram." Alex didn't dare tell her what a blessing never seeing Mel again would mean to him. Saying that would make him sound cold, which he was where Mel was concerned. But he couldn't hurt Kelsey's feelings. So he kept his mouth shut.

"And you," she added softly. "Mel hurt you, too. That's why you've never talked about your past much. I haven't been exactly forthcoming, either. Maybe it's time we were honest with ourselves and each other about those old ghosts. I'll start by telling you about my Uncle Rafe."

Alex's chest heaved with a full intake of air. Mel had spoiled a day that should've been only about Bradley, and now Kelsey was defending him. "I don't want to do this. Not today."

"Then just listen. Please, sweetheart. I need to get this out in the open. I've wanted to talk with you about it for years, just never knew how to start."

Alex licked the corner of his mouth, resigned, willing to do anything for his wife. "Okay. I'm listening."

She'd slipped into the plush royal-blue robe he'd brought from home. Her chocolate brown hair lay soft and shiny on her shoulders. She'd had it trimmed into a blunt cut that bounced more, and that bounce somehow made her look younger. Kelsey had the purest brown eyes of any person he'd ever known. Her cheeks were a healthy, glowing pink, and he couldn't wait for the day she'd be able to make love with him again.

She was his wellspring, his chapel, and the goddess in that chapel, his one true light and the only one on earth he adored. With her at his side, he'd finally reconnected with the God he'd cursed for so many years after he'd lost Sara and Abby. But that was what hard men did. They fought what they didn't understand until, somehow, that same God sent the miracle they needed to heal. Despite her own overwhelming tragedy, Kelsey had taught him how to live again.

He'd also believed in her when she hadn't believed in herself. He'd taken her into his home, provided for her, protected her, and taught Kelsey how to protect herself. How to believe in herself. Eventually, the broken woman she'd been at their first meeting had healed from the double tragedy of losing her two sons. She'd gone back to her church. She'd prayed and grown strong. Yet, it was her simple way of recovering that had eventually saved him from himself. To this day, whenever she mentioned how thankful she was that he'd saved her, he had to smile. He knew better. She was the one who'd done the saving that day at his cabin.

Her lips pursed as she drew in a fortifying breath. "There's a reason Louise never wanted children. I suspect you've already guessed why. But honestly, Alex, I didn't think she'd ever marry after what she went through. But then she met Phillip Timson, and everything changed. He's good for her, and he adores her. She's happier now than she's ever been, even living on that farm in the middle of nowhere."

"Pendleton, Oregon, isn't exactly nowhere."

"Right, but it's very different from Portland, where we spent most of our childhoods." Her gaze strayed to the wall over his head.

"It's okay if you'd rather not tell me," he told her. "I've waited this long, what's another lifetime?"

Her lips furled into a small, sad smile. "My parents were missionaries, Alex. They believed they'd been called to save the world. Called to higher, grander work than just raising their two daughters." She swallowed hard. "I don't think they ever really wanted us. The last time I saw them, I was eleven. Louise was thirteen, a teenager. We were at the airport waving goodbye."

Alex held his breath. He'd long ago surmised that Kelsey and her sister had suffered incest or abuse as children. Didn't make hearing those suspicions were true any easier.

"They were on their way into Egypt that morning. As usual, they left us in the care of my mother's sister's husband, our Uncle Rafe." She rubbed her biceps as if the thought made her flesh crawl. "He came to live with our family after his wife, my Aunt Willa, died. Mom felt bad for him. Said it was our Christian duty to help the homeless and downtrodden, the broken-hearted. Stuff like that."

Alex reached for Kelsey's hand. By then, they were face to face, both leaning into each other. The sun filtering through the blinds at her right cast Kelsey in gentle golden hues. Alex was feeling golden too, but his was more the molten variety than the glowing kind. Knowing what was coming stoked the deepest furnace of his soul. Yet he controlled the bellows that breathed life into the wicked fire in his gut. This was her story. Her history. And there was nothing he could do to right the wrongs done to two unprotected little girls all those years ago.

But God, he hated pedophiles.

Kelsey blew out a quivering breath. "In Cairo, they boarded a smaller plane that was supposed to take them up the Nile River. But it crashed, and, umm, there were no survivors. Mom and Dad came home two weeks later in wooden boxes. Rafe held a very nice joint funeral service, but I honestly don't remember much about that day or where they were buried. I do remember a million chrysanthemums, all different colors, though. Wreaths. Vases full of them. So, so many mums…" She ran her fingers into her hair, combing it back over her shoulder as her eyes glistened. "Mom and Dad were always going somewhere else, Alex. They had a mission, other children to save, other little girls to serve and convert and—"

Ever so gently, he bumped his forehead into hers. "You had no one."

"I had Louise," she declared firmly. "But even that changed once they died and Rafe was stuck with us. I didn't know then, but I realized later, after I'd finished college and was teaching, that they'd left everything they owned to him in the event of their untimely deaths. I guess he thought that made us girls his, too. Like chattel." Her lips pursed into a tight O. "Anyway, yes, Alex. He molested Louise. He'd creep into her room at night and tell her he'd kill me if she didn't, umm, let him. But the day after she turned seventeen, she went crazy. Scared me to death when she started screaming and crying and yelling that she couldn't take it anymore. She packed a stupid plastic grocery bag, Alex, and she ran away. Just like that. She left me."

He waited, his chest hurting for the frightened little girl Kelsey had been then.

"I didn't reconnect with her until after I'd graduated college and was teaching kindergarten. Someone knocked on my apartment door one day after I'd come home from school, and there Louise was. Alive and happy. Crying and telling me how sorry she was that she'd deserted me. She stayed a month with me that time, even introduced me to Phil. Also told me everything Rafe had done to her after our parents died."

"Did he touch you?" Alex asked gently. He damned well needed to know.

Kelsey shook her head, silky dark strands shimmering with that same golden glow. "No. I think he was afraid Louise would go to the police. From then on, he made sure I did my homework and went to college. But I was the mouse in the family; Louise was always the lioness. She used to argue with Rafe, even bossed him around at first. You know how she can be. But when she went silent, I knew something was really, really wrong. She wouldn't talk to me, and I was such a backward kid, I had no way to know what was happening after I went to bed. God…" Kelsey's cheeks puffed with a long shuddering sigh. "I don't hate many people, Alex. Hate is such an ugly emotion to let into your soul. It steals the life and light out of you. But I hate Rafe. Louise hasn't ever been the same bright, vivacious pain in the ass she used to be. If you think she talks a lot now, you should've known her before. I swear Louise could've talked the paint off Phil's big red cattle barn."

"You were fifteen when she left."

Lifting her chin, Kelsey looked Alex square in the eye. "Yes, but Rafe always said I was the dumber sister, which worked out pretty good, all things considered. My being awkward and shy saved me from him."

"But it drove you into Nick's arms." And for that, Alex would gladly wring *Uncle* Rafe's slimy neck. Nick Durrant was the bastard ex-husband, the son of a bitch who'd murdered Kelsey's two tiny sons and then tried to kill her. Who'd very nearly killed Alex to get at Kelsey.

"Yes, but Nick's dead now, and you're here," she breathed. "I look back on everything I've lived through, and I can see how every last one of the people in my life, good or bad, brought me to you. To us." She cast a sideways glance at the bassinet. "To this special day and to our family. We may not have everyone we care about with us right now, Alex, but the ones we've loved are waiting for us. This might sound strange, but I'm excited to meet Sara someday. It'll be good to talk about you with someone who loved you almost as much as I do."

That did it. Alex tugged his wife across the narrow space between them and settled her onto his lap. The world always felt more tolerable with Kelsey in his arms and his nose in her hair. His lungs expanded as he wrapped his arms around her and drew in a deep, satisfying breath of the woman he lived for. "You and Sara together, huh? You'd like her."

"You do realize that you have two daughters and three sons now," she murmured into his neck.

"And two wives."

He felt her lips curl into a smile. "Yes, just two. Those other two women you married never counted."

"No, no they didn't," he breathed. Wives number two and three had been stupid mistakes born of despair and grief after he'd lost Sara and Abby. Neither marriage had lasted a year, and Alex knew he'd been out of his mind, thinking another woman in his bed would fill the holes in his heart. He'd divorced and lost touch with those two, long before he'd met Kelsey.

She'd wrapped one arm around his neck and was fingering the top button of his dress shirt, her fingertips soft and warm on his skin. He'd barely gotten home from work last night when she'd gone into labor. Now he was at the end of a tumultuous day, the proud father of five, and the humble servant of his queen.

"I'll never understand how I got this lucky," he confessed.

"Easy," she breathed. "You were smart enough to marry me."

He settled his palm over her hip, his fingers splayed across the cheek of her lovely ass. "I was that," he whispered as he dipped his head and captured her lips.

"I love you, Alex," she breathed into his mouth.

"And I will love you to the day I die," he promised, mumbling around her lips. Swearing fealty to his queen was easy.

"So tell me about your dad."

Damn it. Were all queens this persistent?

"After dinner," he promised. "First we eat, then story time."

"You're stalling."

He nodded. There was no sense trying to fool the woman who knew him best. "I promise. Tonight, I'll answer all your questions. But first, I'm ordering you a steak and a salad. Chocolate cake for dessert."

"And you," she whispered. "All I really need is you."

Alex dropped his nose into her hair, so damned tired of hiding his tears, but hiding them all the same. He was that guy in the Christmas story, *"It's a Wonderful Life."* He was the richest man on Earth.

Chapter Six

Jameson froze at Maddie's blurted declaration, positive she wasn't any more married than he was. She'd lied, and he wanted to know why. Yet he'd never ask. People lied for many reasons, most frequently, when they were backed into a corner. Asking would only back her into another corner. Confrontation never worked in meaningful relationships; not like he'd had one in a while. But he was hopeful.

People didn't realize that lust was a vibrant, living, two-way connection. Maybe it was just the adrenaline of getting a new job—a blind man's dream job. But he was certain Maddie had also felt the sexual tension simmering between them. He surely had. Felt like a strand of det cord on fire. Hot. So damned hot that he needed a couple minutes to get his body to stand down. Not up, which it was certainly doing now.

He was breathing hard, trying not to. For her sake, he'd put on his TEAM polo, then located his cane and held it centerline, hoping like hell that skinny white stick hid the bad, bad boy now pressing tightly behind his zipper.

But if she wasn't ready or—God forbid—if she were truly married, well… Damn. That'd be too bad. Because finally, Jameson was raring to go and ready to live again. He hadn't told Maddie he'd failed at dating too, because really? What kind of a wimp would that make him?

So he went for nonchalant. "How do I look?"

"Good," she answered, but her vocal cords were still too tight.

He'd pushed her too hard, too quickly. Time to reconsider. "Just good?" he teased. "Damn. Thought maybe I looked stellar or buff in this shirt, or, I don't know, maybe like… Hugh Jackman. Heck, make that Captain America. If I'm gonna dream, I might as well dream big, huh?"

She huffed through her nose, and he was sure she'd just smiled. "Sorry. Still think you should try the bin on for size. It's square like your head."

He lifted his chin to the ceiling and laughed. "Well, thank you, Missus Smarty Pants. You sure know how to keep a guy in line. What's next?"

"The vault."

Oh, yes, he'd almost forgotten. Pointing his elbow at her, he said, "Then lead on. We've still got a diva to get out of town."

"Don't worry. I won't let you miss your first mission."

After a quick, thoroughly delightful visit to a weapons vault that rivalled some of the best private armories Jameson had ever seen, he spent the rest of his day acclimating to the sense of belonging to something bigger and grander than just himself. At last! He was back where he belonged, with brothers and sisters who knew, who'd been there.

Around three pm, someone ordered a dozen pizzas, and that was another thing about this new team he was on. Everyone seemed to look out for everyone else. Most agents came around and introduced themselves, but the stories they told, mostly on each other, brought tears to his eyes. Good tears. Tears of laughter. Tears that made him feel like he was finally home.

Mark came by and talked about completing Alex's ungodly after-action reports. But nothing could dim the tremendous high Jameson was floating on, not even the fact that he was working overtime on his first day on the job. He was a trusted agent and he was alive again. Alive, damn it!

Turned out Maddie was an excellent guide and chauffeur. She made sure he was at Lucy Shade's five-star hotel in Crystal City precisely at nine pm. Which gave Jameson plenty of time to acquaint himself with the comings and goings in the lobby before Miss Shade came down from her room. The lady hadn't asked for an escort, but a bodyguard. If anyone was lying in wait for her, he damned well intended to stand between them and his client.

The only problem to his well thought out plan was that Miss Shade was no lady. She'd huffed and complained the entire ride to Reagan National Airport, and Jameson got it. His egocentric client was annoyed, and he was the subject of the complaint she'd already promised she'd deliver to Alex. Upon meeting her in the lobby, she'd demanded to know who the hell he was. After he'd introduced himself and flashed The TEAM badge Maddie had given him in the weapons vault, Miss Shade had demanded to know why she'd gotten saddled with *'some blind guy with a cane instead of one of Stewart's manly hunks.'* Her words, not Jameson's.

The last time he'd seen himself, he'd been a damned big manly hunk and not too bad looking. His words.

Being a true professional, Jameson had worn his suit jacket over The TEAM polo, just to look a titch more professional. He politely apologized for being less than she'd expected, collapsing his offending cane while he did. Since canes for the visually impaired were a glaring white, and heaven forbid she be seen with *'some blind guy,'* he'd stashed it inside the inner jacket pocket he'd had made for it. He'd promptly promised her The TEAM would provide a better escort next time she was in town. That he'd make sure someone befitting her celebrity was assigned to guard her in the future.

But he was pretty sure she'd been taken aback when he'd offered his elbow and escorted her from the hotel like a sighted person would have. Swiftly and accurately. Which was simple when a person kept their cool, counted steps, and focused all senses on their current surroundings.

Since he'd lived through some of the toughest endurance tests on Earth, namely BUD/S, SEAL Qualification Training, and those damned daisy-chained IEDs, he'd become extremely hyper-alert. As difficult as transitioning from the masses of seeing to the few unseeing had been, lack of sight had opened the world and universe to him. Small things popped out of the steady hum of what he'd once thought was life's monotony. Like the scent of men's aftershave on Miss Shade's left cheek. The way she sniffed and bumped her knuckles to her nose every few minutes. The way the tiny hairs on the back of his neck had stood on end when he'd introduced himself in the lobby. He'd been sure someone had been watching Miss Shade. And she'd very recently snorted coke.

Prior to arriving at the hotel, Maddie had promised Jameson that she'd keep The TEAM limo parked where she let him off, and she was good for her word. In very few minutes, he'd opened Miss Shade's car door for her, closed her in, and took his seat at her left directly behind Maddie, like a good lap dog.

"Yes, yes, I'm finally on my way," Miss Shade complained into her cellphone. "No problems. Just a change of plans. Be ready. This might actually work better. Hey, you, blind guy. How many minutes to Reagan?"

Blind guy? How politically incorrect. Not that Jameson cared about the overly sensitive PC opinions of others. But Maddie did. He felt her hostile glare radiating through the rearview mirror.

"From here, seven minutes, ma'am," he answered.

"How do you know? You got some kind of Braille watch?"

"No ma'am, just instinct. Trust me. We'll be at your Global 8000 in exactly seven minutes."

That pissed her off. "Why should I trust you, and how do you know what kind of jet I fly in?"

"Because TEAM agents study their clients beforehand, ma'am. It's my business to know. Six minutes now."

"You spied on me?"

"I made sure I knew everything I needed to know in order to best protect you. That's all."

"Humph," she huffed at whoever she was talking to. Then said, "I'll be there in ten. Yes. Count on it."

She was wrong. Six minutes later Maddie pulled The TEAM limo alongside what Jameson assumed was an impressive luxury jet on the far east runway at Reagan. He knew the Global 8000 offered a range of seven thousand, nine hundred nautical miles and a top speed of Mach 0.925. It was incredible the accommodations national press outlets provided their super stars these days. Also incredible that Jameson was right about those six minutes. Imagine that.

"Get my things on board," the diva ordered as he gave her a hand out of the limo. "You, driver. Yes, you. Grab my purse. It's too heavy for me."

Maddie hopped to, and Jameson wished he could see the look on her face. He'd been sure to keep his words and expressions guarded. Had Maddie?

"Wait!" Miss Shade ordered. He could almost picture her, standing there with her finger in the air. "You want me to go where?" she asked whoever was still on her cell. "Why should I?"

While she turned her back on her lowly hired help, Jameson stood with Maddie at the bottom of the stairway to the jet, biding his time until Miss Shade was finally ready to board. What a pain in the ass. No wonder she wanted to be a star. She'd fit right in with the current Hollywood trolls.

"You can see the Jefferson Monument from here," Maddie breathed. "It's like a glowing beacon of freedom."

"It's beautiful, isn't it?" Jameson asked, pleased she was there with him.

"Oh, sorry. You can't see it. Anything, I mean… Good grief, I suck."

He tossed his chin at Maddie, smiling at her consternation. "You do not. It's an ordinary question for an extraordinary day. Besides, I can see the monument in my head, and I'll bet it looks the same as the last time I saw it. It's lit up and golden, and its reflection glows in the Tidal Basin, doesn't it?"

"Yes, it does." Maddie had taken a step closer. "How do you do it? Stay positive all the time?"

"Hey! You! Bodyguards! Christ, do I have to do everything?"

Jameson snapped to, facing the client he couldn't seem to please. "Yes, ma'am?"

"I said..." Shade drew out her scorn. "Get my shit on board. Hustle! I don't have all night!"

"Yes, ma'am," he replied as, swiftly, he gestured Maddie to go up the stairs first, then followed with her Highness's bags from the limo trunk. Three heavy suitcases, but no computer bag. Interesting baggage for a reporter. Didn't they all have laptops these days?

Maddie snagged the smallest bag out of his hand, probably cosmetics, when he hit the top step. "Thanks," he murmured, then asked, "Do we get hazard pay for escorting clients like this?"

Her giggle was like a bright light shining in a very dark place. "No, but be sure to put everything she's said tonight in your after-action report. Alex will want to know."

Jameson stood there, wondering which way to turn, and where Shade wanted her bags.

"I'm guessing we should put her stuff in the back. Follow me. It's got to be where her bedroom is."

"Yes, ma'am," came easily to his lips. Maddie was a joy to follow, especially to a bedroom. And she'd blithely provided the cue he'd needed. She'd be a good... friend. She was understanding of his impairment, yet openly curious. He liked that combination.

He was halfway through the jet when the hairs on the back of his neck stood on end again. Jameson cocked his head, sure he'd just heard the slightest tick, followed by the nearly silent clip of a metal striker on metal. "Maddie, wait!"

Too late.

BOOM!

A heated rush of air blasted him off his feet. He rag-dolled a full three hundred sixty degrees backwards. Miss Shade's luggage flew out of his hands. His head hit the floor hard, but Maddie's body hit him harder when she landed on his belly and knocked the breath out of him.

"Jameson!" she screamed as a river of hellfire roared over the top of them.

"I've got you," he said as he closed both arms around her and turned her face into his chest. The jet shuddered like a wet dog and groaned. Electrical conduits popped overhead. Metal screeched. He could smell the alcoholic heat from burning jet fuel. "Are you hurt? Can you walk?"

"It's hard to breathe, but yes. I can move."

Possible broken ribs and shock, he thought as he maneuvered to his feet, pulling Maddie up with him. As quickly as she was upright, he turned her toward the front of the plane and away from the scorching fireball behind him. His hair was burning. He could smell it. Brushing a quick hand over the back of his head, he smothered the heat and told her, "Hurry."

Good girl. She ran, and he ran right behind her. In seconds, they were out the door and stumbling down the steps, holding hands and choking on the thick, roiling smoke engulfing the jet.

"Ouch," Maddie cried as her fingers slipped from his.

She'd fallen. He dropped on the tarmac to her side, needing to get her as far from the conflagration as he could. The heat billowing from the rear of the jet was unbearable, and his skin felt as if it were on fire. "We can't stop yet. Hook your arm around my neck. I'll help."

The instant she obeyed, he regretted the order. The skin on the back of his neck was burned. Not like it would slow him down. Scooping her into his arms, he ran with her, away from the sizzling, popping, booming explosions. In seconds, they were yards from the heat. They were safe and alive. He bowed his head, so damned grateful for that uncanny sixth sense he'd developed since the incident.

"You... okay...?" he asked between great heaving breaths.

She curled under his chin, her entire body quivering. "Y-y-yessss. I think so."

"'S okay. We're alive. That's what counts," he told her as he smoothed a hand over her head.

His fingers tangled with long hair, a plus in his little black book from so, so long ago, back when he'd actually dated. His nostrils detected the slightest hint of lavender mingled with feminine sweat, ash, and smoke. She was a trembling mess. Somehow, that was another plus.

"Good grief! You're smoking," she cried. "The back of your jacket's on fire."

Well, so it was. "Does that mean I'm hot?" he asked, joking to keep her calm while he slouched out of his business jacket, curled it inside out, and smothered whatever flame was there.

"Do you always joke in life and death situations?" she asked, her tone bordering on hysteria.

"Mostly, yes," he answered as he slipped back into his extra warm jacket.

"You're so calm and I'm so—not."

"I've been trained, Maddie. It's what I do."

Another wicked explosion shook the ground, knocking him to his knees. He rolled just in time to grab Maddie and save her head from impacting with the tarmac.

She burrowed under his chin.

He could barely speak. Just held onto the trembling woman in his arms until the intense heat subsided. The vicious dragon breath hovering over them seemed like it came from a living entity intent on roasting them alive.

Jameson rolled to his back when it dissipated. His ears were ringing, and his skull was scrambled from the fall. Now, when he needed to be on his best game, he was compromised. Maddie tilted up from where she'd landed on his chest. She cupped his face between both hands, but if she was talking, he couldn't hear her. Damn this blindness.

He turned his face to the jet, seeing nothing, but straining to hear everything. Something! Only muffled ringing filled his head. Where the hell was his client? Come to think of it, where were Lucy Shade's crew, the flight attendants, and pilot? Jameson hadn't encountered anyone inside the jet. Hadn't they survived? Then who had she spoken with on the drive here? Who'd she tell there was a change of plans?

Gradually, his hearing came back online, thank God. By then, Maddie was sobbing out of control. Her intermittent words didn't make sense. "...all my fault... sorry I dragged you into... after me, not you. Oh, God! I'm not even married! I lied! What have I done?"

Except for that bit about not being married, Jameson didn't have a clue what she was talking about. He pulled her flat against him, and together, they breathed hard at their harrowing escape.

"What's going on?" he asked after a few minutes, needing her to slow down, take a breath, and start over.

"This is all my fault. M-m-my ex. He owes some loan sharks a lot of money. They can't find him, and now I'm supposed to pay his debt. They've threatened me, said his debt was my problem, and that's why I've been late to work. Only I don't have that kind of money, and they won't accept payments, and they want it all at one time, and they threw a brick through my picture window last week, and they slashed all my tires today, and…" Her chest heaved with a great breath after that amazing string of run-ons. "And… and they're going to kill me, and this is all my fault, and now I've dragged you into my mess, and… and…"

"Shush. Quiet Maddie. We'll figure it out. It's okay," he said even as he clamped a hand over her mouth, needing her to be still, so he could hear the argument coming from across the tarmac.

Canting his head, he listened for the human sounds that didn't fit the calamitous scene. Sounded like Miss Shade was screaming. But not for help. Despite the carnage, he distinctly picked up on her uptight, "You let them get away?"

He didn't detect anyone answering. She had to be on her cell. But holy hell. *Let who get away? Maddie and me?*

"But, but, but…" Maddie murmured around his fingertips. By then she was a mess of tears, smoky sweat, and adrenaline. He could feel her blood pounding through her veins.

"Be still," he told her gently, striving to hear the entirety of Shade's vicious rant. "To be honest, I'm really glad you're not married anymore, but something's not right with our client, Maddie. Please—"

"Get away from me! Let me go!"

Jameson clamped both arms tight around her, but someone jerked her away.

"Jameson! He's got me. Help!"

"Let her go!" he roared into the dark, up on his feet now, his senses reaching out to understand what had just happened and who had Maddie.

Until something hard slammed into the side of his head. He fell then. Went down hard.

Chapter Seven

Bradley was a hungry little guy, and for whatever reason, Alex loved watching Kelsey breastfeeding his son. It had been the same when Lexie was born. It was after dinner, and he adored the sublime peek into eternity that childbirth offered. Fatherhood rested like a kingly mantle on Alex's shoulders tonight. He was one lucky son of a bitch, and that little boy was a baby beast. Ten pounds, three ounces. No wonder he'd had a tough time being born. His mama was a tiny thing.

The only one missing tonight was the little girl he adored. Lexie would love this little guy. But she'd had fallen asleep somewhere between helping Mark and Libby's girls making the fudge and the popcorn. Mark had called to say they were keeping her tonight and would bring her over first thing tomorrow morning.

"You're still stalling," Kelsey murmured sleepily.

Man, she was stunningly beautiful tonight. Motherhood fit her like a glove. He was sitting on the edge of the bed, trying hard to wipe the smile off his face. But what a day. Turned out Mel hadn't spoiled a damned thing. He'd tried, but like everything else, he'd failed at that, too.

"Not sure what else there is to say. Pretty much covered everything when Mel showed up earlier."

"Alex…"

He shook his head, more out of love for his wife than disgust with Mel. Drawing in a deep breath, he admitted the obvious. "You already know he wasn't a good husband nor a fit father."

And there Alex stopped, not wanting to go down this memory lane. It never ended well. It was like watching reruns of the Titanic sinking. Everyone always died, and the day he'd lost his mom was still an unfathomable ache he couldn't forget and wouldn't forgive. Maybe Mel hadn't killed her, but he'd sure never cared what cancer had done to her. How she'd wasted away. How her beautiful body had turned skeletal, and how her honey blonde hair had fallen out in handfuls. How she'd cried herself to sleep some nights, and how lovingly Gramps and Gram had taken care of her until they'd had no choice but to transfer her to a hospice home for the dying.

Sucking in a deep breath, Alex released it on a slow sigh. "What do you want to know?"

"Tell me about Abigail. What'd she look like? Why didn't her family take care of her when she got sick? What did she do while you were in school during the day? Is she the one who taught you to love books and how to read?"

"Yes," he admitted quietly. "She taught me to read and how to laugh. Mom and me visited Gramps and Gram quite a bit, you know, because Dad was always deployed—or so he'd said. Gramps built a treehouse up high in the willow outside his guest bedroom. That's where we'd stay while we were there. Mom was blonde and willowy thin. Her parents both died before she'd met Mel. She used to climb out the window with me. Sometimes we'd just sit in that great big tree and talk and laugh. Old willows are jungles all by themselves." Alex paused, once more wrapped up inside his mom's arms, their bare legs dangling happily into thin air. "One summer day, she dragged a wooden chest into my treehouse. Said it was buried treasure, just for me. It was full of books. Used books of adventure, stuff boys liked. She loved to read." *Hell, she loved me.*

He cleared his throat. "Every day that summer, we'd hide out in our tree. I was five, maybe six. She started reading *"Treasure Island."* By the end of the book, I was reading it to her. We didn't live with Gramps and Gram all the time, but Mom made sure we visited every summer. Gram kept their guest room ready for us. Mel never came along, always said he was too busy." *The liar.* "Which was okay. I think those weeks were the best times of our years together, me and Mom. She'd help Gram with chores, and Gramps was always tinkering with something. I helped him build the treehouse, and he made sure I could access it from the wooden ladder he installed down the side of the house, as well as from the guest room window. He thought of everything. Eventually the guest room became my room. By then…" He took a deep breath and slowly let it go. "Mom was gone."

Kelsey's gentle fingers on his wrist pulled him out of the reverie of long-lost times. "I'm so sorry, sweetheart. She's another one I'm looking forward to meeting when it's my time to pass on. Imagine me, Sara, and Abigail sitting on a cloud in heaven, comparing notes about you. I wonder what secrets they'll tell me."

Alex shook his head at the way his wife always focused on the positive side to living and dying. Gramps might have made him a man, but it was Abigail who'd taught him to love, and Kelsey who'd taught him, eventually, to forgive himself.

But love or forgive Mel? There was a tough one. Two things Alex didn't know when or if he'd ever care enough to do.

Rin-n-n-n-g! Talk about being saved by the bell. Tugging his cell out of his rear pocket, he caught Mark's ID on his screen. "Yeah, Stewart."

"Hey, Boss. Sorry to bother you so late, but wanted you to know there's been trouble at Reagan. Lucy Shade's plane blew up. She's safe and already talking with the press, but—"

"Who'd we assign to guard her?"

"Jameson Tenney. Maddie drove him and Shade to Reagan."

"Maddie and Jameson? Were they—?"

"Yes, I have reason to believe they were inside the jet when it blew. I'm at the terminal now, but Boss..." Mark choked. "It's a damned inferno. Airport fire trucks are here. Firemen are all over the place, but they haven't been able to knock it down yet. Son of a bitch won't die."

"What the hell was on that jet?"

"It had just been refueled. Tank was full. Was ready to taxi and had clearance to leave as soon as Shade showed."

Jet fuel could burn for days without proper fire suppression. But not at Reagan. More than any other airport in the States, the crews at Reagan knew how to deal with disaster.

"I'll be right there."

"No, Boss, stay with your family. There's nothing you can do here. I'll keep in touch."

Alex hesitated, something he rarely did. Mark was right. He could handle this. But two TEAM agents had died tonight, one newly hired, the other a damned good Protocol Officer who had no business being on that jet. What the hell had happened?

"I'll be there. See you in ten," Alex told Mark, then turned to his wife and said, "I have to go. Sorry."

Kelsey blinked. "What's wrong?"

"Jet exploded on the tarmac at Reagan with two of my people allegedly on board. Mark's already there, but I need to be there, too."

"Then go. We're fine. Do what you have to do, Alex. Hurry."

He nodded, a hard lump stuck in his chest at the merciless whim of Karma. God, she was a bitch. Give a life. Take two? "I'll call as soon as I know more."

"I know you will. Be safe, sweetheart."

"Take care of the people I love best," he murmured as he dipped his head and kissed her mouth. "I'll be back before you know it."

Chapter Eight

Jameson came to in a thick black fog, disoriented, with blood and ash in his throat. His left side hurt. His neck felt tender as hell, sunburned, blisters and all. He coughed, then choked at the thing wrapped around his head and the knot stuck in his mouth. Slowly, things came back to him. The drive to Reagan... Miss Shade's jet... Explosion... Fire and heat and...

"Maddie!" he yelled. But the rag in his mouth turned his words into worthless mumbles. Another groan close by pierced the fog in his head, clearing his mind. Had to be Maddie. She'd been beside him in the jet. Then on the tarmac. Details came back swifter then. Maddie Bannister. Protocol Officer. His dream job. The TEAM. His first day at work. He and Maddie running for safety. For their lives. Lucy Shade. Her last words... *"You let them get away?"*

Then arguing, closer this time. Not a memory. Jameson stilled, straining to hear, focused on the familiar voices coming from the room next door instead of his memory.

One was full of venom. "You spoiled everything." Her. The diva.

"I had no choice!" the asshat with the oddly familiar brogue said. "That wanker got her out of there so bloody quick, what was I supposed to do, shoot them where anyone could've seen them? Maybe you didn't know, but Reagan's got more security cameras than the feckin' Queen of England's summer palace. And even if I had—"

"Of course I know that, you fool! I needed my escape caught on film, Reagan airport's film, too. But no, you set the charges wrong. They went off early. You thought kidnapping them instead of me was smarter?" Her again. "This is not what I paid for! They were supposed to die in that fire. So was Vlad, my feckin' bodyguard. Can't you do anything right?"

A definite growl. Boots scraped over the concrete floor. Chair legs creaked. Then, "Shite, you're a bitch."

CRACK! Okay, that was definitely flesh against flesh.

"Feck you!" Her Highness shrieked. "You ruined my publicity stunt!"

Say what?

"Yeah, well feck you right back, you worthless blighter!" The Irish stooge.

The chair again. Or another chair. Boots shuffled. A door slammed. Staccato clips against concrete. High heels. It was high time to move.

Jameson fought the restraints at his wrists. Simple plastic ties bound his wrists together, not sturdy Flex Cuffs. Which meant someone hadn't been prepared to take hostages tonight, or whatever he and Maddie were. He wasn't hanging around to find out. With his bound hands in front of him, Jameson dispensed with the rag in his mouth first, then sucked in a breath of damned righteousness.

Most folks would've thought themselves helpless when they came to in a strange place, groggy from being drugged and restrained. Not Jameson. He'd been almost drowned, shot at, tortured, humiliated, and spit on. He'd been made to carry water-logged inflatable boats through pounding surf, or his fellow wannabe SEALs when they'd drag-assed or had been injured. And that was just during BUD/S.

Whoever'd abducted him and Maddie tonight was in for one helluva rude awakening. Yes, he was blind, well, so what? He was still a SEAL. Only now he was a pissed-off, lethal, son of a bitchin', fight-til-you-die SEAL. And they'd hurt Maddie. They would pay.

She hadn't come to yet, but he remembered now that she'd fallen during their mad dash from the fire. In the mayhem, he hadn't asked how badly she'd been hurt. He would. Later. The plastic ties had to go first.

Jameson put his wrists together, both up to his mouth. After he pulled the tie as tight as he could with his teeth, so tight it cut into his skin, he flexed his arms and snapped that son of a bitch off. Odd, but the thing stabbing his side was his pistol. Another mistake the diva and Irishman had made. They'd left him in his jacket with his holstered pistol tucked under his arm. Guess they assumed blind men weren't much of a threat and didn't carry. Guess again.

"Hey," he growled as he removed Maddie's gag, which was half of someone's torn t-shirt. Still had one sleeve. "Are you hurt? Can you breathe?" At least that detail had come back to him. She'd said she couldn't breathe once they'd cleared the jet. He'd thought she might have sustained a broken rib.

"Hmmm," she whined sleepily.

He lifted to one knee, still crouched at her side, but needing to get the lay of the land before anyone returned and interrupted his escape plan. "Come on, Maddie. We've got to leave before they come back, and I could sure use your eyes."

Because, okay, being blind sucked at critical times like this.

"Jameson?"

"Yeah, babe. I'm here. Talk to me. Are you hurt? Can you breathe?"

She sat up, breathing hard and panicked. "I'm fine. Where are we? Oh, God, what happened? Who's they?"

"We've been kidnapped by Lucy Shade and... some Irish guy." His muddled brain couldn't supply the name of that Irishman. "Hold still. Let me get you out of those cuffs." He reached into his pants pocket, but his knife was gone. So were his wallet and everything else. His brand-new badge. Dumbasses had emptied his pockets.

Okay then. Plan B. Since Maddie was still cuffed and wouldn't be able to break those plastic ties... On second thought…"Put your wrists together," he told her. "Hurry."

If a man could do it, so could a woman. Once she complied like he'd asked, he jerked the ties on her wrists tight until she hissed, "That hurts. Whose side are you on?"

"Yours. I need you to focus. You're a strong, capable woman, and I know you can do this. Put your heart and soul into flexing those gorgeous biceps and breaking these restraints. They're just plastic. They'll snap off if you do it right. I promise. You've got this."

"Is that what you did?"

"Yes. You can do it, too. I know you can."

He could hear Maddie breathing through her nostrils, and not once had she said she couldn't. But damn. After three tries, he could smell the blood. Her wrists were bleeding. The ties were too tight, and either she wasn't strong enough, or she didn't believe in herself. Jameson called time-out. Plan B it was.

"Tell me what you see." His heart was hammering by then, but adrenaline did that.

Maddie was shaking plenty, too. "It's dark, but there's light coming under the door. I can see. You lost your glasses. Oh, my gosh, the back of your neck is burned."

"Tell me something I don't know. What can't I see?"

"Okay. Umm, well, we're in a room without windows. Looks like a basement. Smells like somebody's dirty bathroom. Concrete floor. One door directly behind you. Simple hollow core with four-square molding. But no doorknob on this side. A wooden workbench to my right. It's full of holes." She must've looked upward because her voice shifted slightly away from him. "High ceiling. One large vent over the door. Two screws."

"Now you're talking. How big's that vent? On the ceiling or in the wall?"

"The ceiling. Maybe two by two."

That was something he could work with. "Could you fit through the opening if I helped you reach it?" He already knew she could. The moment they'd collided in that explosion, he'd gotten an armful of delicate femininity that just might save their lives tonight. Or today or whenever the hell it was.

"Yes," she said with determination. "I'm small enough. But I don't get it. Why would loan sharks kidnap us? They won't get their money that way."

"That's not who's after us, and this isn't about your ex. Lucy Shade planned this. I heard her and some Irish dipshit talking. This was supposed to be a publicity stunt, where we died in the fire, while her stooge rescued her from whoever allegedly blew up her jet. Then… she said…" Damn, his pounding head made remembering the exact wording difficult. *Think!* "… he'd set the charges wrong, that the jet exploded too early. That he'd thought kidnapping us instead of her was smarter."

Jameson ran a quick hand over his aching head, but stopped short of rubbing his blistered skin. "Shade doesn't know what to do with us. So let's get you up into that vent and out of sight before they come back. I'm relying on you to be extra-quiet moving through the ductwork. This place is old. You might run into spiders or mice or—"

"They're going to kill us, aren't they?"

She needed to know, so he nodded. "Unless we get away. We're supposed to be dead already. We're just loose ends."

"That doesn't make sense. Why would kidnappers still be in a jet they intended to blow up?"

"She needed two dead bodies. That way she could claim she got away from us before the jet exploded. There'd be no one left alive to contradict her story. It'd be big news. She'd be the reporter who escaped wicked kidnappers, the next big star."

He could hear Maddie's heartbeat soar and the sound of her dry swallowing. "You're not coming with me?" she asked.

Jameson came to a full stop. The tone in her question was blatantly plaintive and frightened. She'd never been in combat, much less what they'd lived through today. He could smell her fear. "Babe, I—"

What could he say? That he meant to stay behind and kill Miss Shade and her stooge to give Maddie time to get away? That he meant to die before he let anything happen to her?

That this had been, hands down, one of the best days of his life, and all because he'd met a waifish Protocol Officer who had once upon a time wanted to be a jarhead?

Jameson swallowed hard, needing her to understand. "Hope that vent cover has at least one sharp edge so I can cut those ties off your wrists. But I've..." He cleared his throat. "I've never met anyone like you before, Maddie. You're brave, but you don't know it. And you're strong, you just don't believe in yourself yet. But once we're out of here, I'd like to take you out for coffee or... or something. Whatever you want. I'd just like to get to know you better. Right now is your time to shine, Maddie. My shoulders are too wide to fit through a narrow vent. Get out of here, while I create a distraction. Get help."

The air shifted as she came closer and raised both arms.

He knew what she meant to do. Jameson ducked and let her settle her joined arms around the back of his head, avoiding his burns. She needed something from him before she manned up, and he intended to give it to her.

Especially when she asked, "Do you ever kiss on a first date?"

He licked his lips, so damned hopeful. "Haven't had any dates lately, but yeah, I'd like to."

"This isn't exactly what I'd call a date, but..." She came to him as soft as a sigh, her lips sweet and tender, her kiss a breath of life he hadn't realized how much he'd hungered for until now. Something warm and wonderful unfurled in his chest. Felt a lot like coming home from Iraq had.

There in the dark, Jameson canted his head and kissed Maddie with all his heart. He wrapped her tight inside his arms and held onto the best thing he'd come across in a long, damned time. She was lush, warm, and soft, returning every last lick and fervent kiss, as if she felt the same things he was feeling.

Lives would be changed tonight. People would die. But God, please not her. She tasted like minty toothpaste and hairspray and smoke, like an American woman who enjoyed what his mouth was doing to hers. As precarious as their situation was, it should've been a quick kiss. But he got lost in the warmth of being wanted and held by a gentle woman. Her mouth was sweet and slick, her tongue a luscious treat after tasting ash and dirt. Made a man feel wanted. Felt perfect.

There was no pulling away from her. The plastic ties wouldn't have allowed it if he'd tried. He didn't want this magic to end, but time was a luxury they didn't have. He needed her to live.

Breathing hard with his blood humming like a hornet's nest, he murmured huskily, "Sorry, but it's time to go, babe."

"I like that you call me that."

"I like that you're willing to fight for our lives." Hint, hint.

Her tongue took one last lap around his mouth, and she whispered, "Let's do this."

Reluctantly, he ducked out of her embrace and took a step back. "Work bench?"

"This way," she said as she bumped hips with him. "Straight ahead. Looks heavy. We'll have to drag it."

It was heavy, but with her help, Jameson managed. He worried while they grunted and sweated the sturdy table made of four-by-fours across the concrete floor. "Were you injured? You said you couldn't breathe earlier."

"Just scared. It's not every day a girl ends up in a burning jet."

"I think that was Pops Delaney working with Shade. Had to be him. They argued. She slapped him."

"Delaney's a flat-out killer."

"So's Lucy Shade." Which meant Maddie was in more trouble than he'd thought.

"Do you think there's more than just them two?"

"Might be, so be extra stealthy once you're out of here. Run for your life, Maddie."

"What if my big ass gets stuck in the vent?"

He couldn't help the smile that broke through the gloom of her leaving him behind. "Trust me, you don't have a big ass. One step at a time, Maddie. That's how we get the tough jobs done. You can do this. I have faith."

"Aww, you say the sweetest things."

At last, Jameson positioned the bench at the door, so Maddie could reach the vent. He made quick work of the screws holding the vent in place. Maddie had climbed up on the bench and was at his side by then. Luckily, the screws were long and sharp. He used one to carefully saw the ties off her wrists, and she was ready to go.

Interlocking his fingers, he crouched to boost her up to the ceiling. "Ready?"

Her palms clapped over his shoulders. A dainty booted foot settled into his cupped hands. Her breath warmed his face when she kissed him again and said, "I'll be waiting for you."

"That's the plan," he whispered into her open mouth, loving the smell and taste of her. Wanting to know her better. It'd been ages since he'd felt this way about any woman. How could he let her go?

She made the decision for him. With one little push, she was out of his life and into the vent. "Sure wish I had that bin of yours now," she teased. "Lots of cobwebs up here. I could use a big, square helmet."

"I'll let you borrow it next time," he quipped, wishing it was him up in the vent, not her. Wishing he could see, damn it. Was she sitting there looking down at him? He doubted it. Ductwork wasn't usually large enough to allow much movement but forward travel.

Since the incident, he'd come to believe that everything happened for a reason. Karma had to work that way, else there'd be no balance in the universe. No yin and yang. No reason for mankind to struggle like he did. No challenge for life to go on. But now? Maddie was the one Karma had singled out today, and that kiss might be his last. Just when he'd finally caught his balance.

"Be careful," he told her one last time.

But she was already gone.

Chapter Nine

Alex stood with the fire chief while his men finished fighting the blaze outside Reagan National Airport's private hangars. They ended up using more Class B fire suppressant foam than usual on the aircraft, but at last, the fire was under control. Since airspace over Reagan was restricted, no media helicopters hovered overhead to fan the flames. Which they would have done, if this had happened anywhere else.

What troubled Alex most was that Lucy Shade, an obvious stage name, was nowhere to be found. Yet Vladimir, who the fire chief had claimed was her personal bodyguard, was the person who'd placed the 911 call to report the explosion. He'd claimed two people were still on board. That he'd feared for their lives. Which Alex would soon find out. But if there were bodies in the debris, they'd be burned beyond recognition. DNA and dental records would be useless. To validate what his gut was telling him—that Maddie and Jameson were still alive—he'd requested access to Reagan's security tapes. This portion of the tarmac was within view of several separate cameras. He'd know soon enough.

Also troublesome was Junior Agent Walker Judge's high opinion of former CPO Tenney. Walker had bragged about the mad ninja skills Jameson had developed since he'd lost his sight. For a SEAL to brag up another SEAL was telling.

Walker was as solid an operator as they came. Which meant Jameson was just as good. Alex hadn't yet met him, but upon Walker's recommendation alone, he'd told Mark to hire the visually impaired warrior. Hell, Alex would have done that sight unseen. No pun intended. It just didn't feel right, that a trained special warfare operator of Jameson's caliber, would've been trapped and burned to death in a fire on his first night at work. The entire scene stunk, and Alex meant to get to the rat behind it.

"Where's my limo?" he asked Mark, meaning the vehicle Maddie had driven to Reagan.

"Over there." Mark pointed to the south side of the airfield. "What's left of it. The firemen moved the carcass before I got here."

Alex stared at the smoking wreckage. There'd be no forensic evidence coming from that mess. "Is Mother able to track our people?" She tracked all TEAM agents' cell phones when they were on active ops.

"No, which means they were frisked before they were abducted and their phones destroyed, or..." Mark let the obvious—*or they were dead on the scene*—go unsaid.

Turning his head, Alex glared at the glowing, smoking wreckage of what had been a luxury jet, not willing to accept defeat just because some reporter said so. Sparks still flared orange inside the burned fuselage, and the entire tail assembly lay detached, twisted, and charred on the runway. He had no doubt there'd been an explosion aft, possibly in the cargo hold. Which declared a bomb, at least that something explosive had blown the tail off. The cockpit was intact, but was a burned, hollowed-out shell. The portable stairs lay melted on the tarmac.

Maddie and Jameson were NOT on that jet. They WERE alive. Alex damned well knew it. "We know where the pilot is?"

"From what the fire chief told me, her crew hadn't arrived yet. Check this out," Mark muttered as he handed his cell over. "Online video of the conference Lucy Shade held immediately after her jet blew."

Wasn't that just like every fame-hungry reporter? Worry about her media exposure and rep more than the people who might've died on her damned corporate jet? God, he hated self-serving reporters.

Alex took the phone and thumbed replay. It was her all right. Dressed in black slacks and a flashy orange, yellow, and red flowing blouse that wrapped around her tiny waist. A twitchy African American male, the width and breadth of Mark, stood at her side, but he kept looking over his shoulder as if someone off-screen was talking to him or worried him. "Is that Vladimir?"

"She didn't introduce him, but I assume so, yes."

Miss Shade didn't act nervous at all as she glanced at the man beside her and fluttered her long, gold painted fingernails over her well-endowed cleavage. "Again," she said, her voice breathless and fake, "I have my excellent bodyguard to thank for saving my life tonight. If Vladimir hadn't been here, those two awful people would've had their way with me, and I—"

"So you believe your kidnappers were aboard your private jet when it exploded?" another reporter interrupted.

"Yesssss..." she hissed. fanning her face with all ten gaudy fingers. "I don't know what would've happened without Vlad. Why, I could've been killed or... or worse. And

I know this will sound awful, but I'm glad they're d-d-dead, and I'm not."

"She's lying," Alex said flatly. If there was one thing he'd learned to recognize at an early age, it was a liar. "Why would kidnappers run into the plane they meant to blow up? And why blow it up to begin with?"

"*If* anyone was onboard," Mark replied. "We still don't know that for certain. Wait. It gets better."

Sure enough. Someone in her audience asked if she knew the perpetrators or if she could describe them. She shook her head adamantly. "Once my handsome bodyguard came to my rescue, they ran for their lives. I was so scared; I didn't get a good enough look. Sorry. Next question?"

"She's sure pouring it on about Vlad," Mark commented.

"Then why'd she contract with me to guard her ass tonight?"

"I've already had Mother pull her contract. A copy's on my phone if you need it."

"She's not making sense. If Vladimir reported two people onboard when the jet exploded, then who ran away from it? Were they her abductors or not? How many people are we looking for?"

Someone else asked Miss Shade, "When exactly did the assailants attack? Were they both males? Were they armed? Why weren't you already inside the plane if you were cleared for take-off?"

"Oh yes, they were both carrying great big AK-14s," she declared, her head bobbing as if she knew what she was talking about, when it was obvious she didn't. "Them, I saw because they were pointed straight at me. I was so, so scared. Next question."

Alex rolled the cramp out of his shoulder. *AK-14s? What an ass.*

"She's avoiding most questions," Mark noted.

Another reporter: "Miss Shade, the hotel you were staying at earlier today just released their security footage, which shows your departure this evening. Is this the man who tried to abduct you and ran away, or is he one of the two people who died in the fire?"

The mega-screen behind her filled with time-stamped footage of Junior Agent Jameson Tenney standing in the hotel lobby, his chin up, his shoulders back, and his head canted. He was a good-looking, dark-haired young man, wearing a TEAM polo under a suit jacket, most likely to conceal his weapon. The round-framed, dark glasses perched on his nose and the white cane perfectly aligned in front of him identified him as visually impaired.

An older woman with salt-and-pepper hair and one of those fluffy, yappy dogs in her arms, entered the hotel's revolving doors behind Jameson. She'd no more than cleared the entrance when he stepped back and out of her path, then nodded deferentially at her. To look at his reaction, Alex wouldn't have guessed he was blind. She nodded at Jameson, then stopped, and they chatted for less than a minute. He smiled broadly at something she'd said, then reached forward and patted Fluffy's cute little head as if he knew precisely where it was. After she headed for the elevator, Jameson resumed his watch.

Alex was damned proud of the caliber of man he was looking at. Clean-shaven. Straight as an arrow. Square shoulders. On duty and on time despite what, to some, would've been a debilitating impairment. Looked like

Jameson hadn't let that ugly incident in Iraq slow him down or define him at all.

Exactly four minutes later, Miss Shade stalked across the lobby. Her body language spelled rage in flashing neon capital letters. When at last she jerked to a full stop, she stabbed a finger into Jameson's chest, her jaws jacking like a damned troll. He stood there, taking her abuse with his head cocked as if he were trying to understand her anger.

"Is there audio?" Alex asked Mark as he watched his newly hired agent maintain his cool in the face of one of America's *finest* reporters.

"No. Just video. Have no idea what she was mad about. He was early and waiting in the lobby as she'd requested."

"Oh, my God!" Shade had squealed during her private news show. "That's him. Wait. There was a woman with him. Why isn't there a clip of her?"

"Dig a little deeper, Mark. I want the woman with the dog. Find her. Speak with her," Alex ordered as he handed the cell back. "Shade just accused my agents of a federal crime. I'll have her lying ass for this. But if they're dead…" *I'll have her head.*

Which may never happen, as quickly as her fellow reporters had fired more probing questions at her than she could handle.

"You're kidding? Your kidnapper was blind?"

"Where's his AK-14?" That was asked with blatant sarcasm.

"There's no such thing as an AK-14. Did you mean AR-15, AK-47, or M16? Which was it?"

"I can only tell you what the police told me," she yelled over them. "I promise to meet with you once I know more. Thanks for coming!"

"Which will be a cold day in Hell," Alex groused.

"She's bitten off more than she can chew," Mark added, "and she knows it. She seems to be making this crap up as she goes."

"So who's running this shit show, Shade or Vladimir?"

"My guess is Shade. He might be built, but he acts like he's scared of her."

"You think she lured Jameson and Maddie to their deaths?"

"No, Boss. I interviewed Jameson. He's smarter than that. I'll give you ten-to-one-odds that he and Maddie weren't on the jet when it blew. Miss Shade is about to become the sensational news story of the year," Mark drawled. "I can see the headline now. Lucy Meets Bitter End."

Alex grunted. He had a different headline in mind. *Lucy Shade Found Guilty of Attempted Murder.*

"Call everyone in who's not out of town. Finding Maddie and Jameson is our only active operation as of right now. Mother needs to be ready to pull local traffic cams and satellite imagery the minute I can access airport security videos. I want eyes in the sky and boots on the ground. Call Harley. I need his dogs."

"Mother's already on standby. Your helo pilot as well. Harley can't make it, he's on call at the emergency vet tonight, but he'll bring Boris and Karloff as soon as he can get away. Don't worry, Boss. Once we know where to look, we'll find Maddie and Jameson."

Boris and Karloff were two of Harley's best tracking dogs.

Alex raked his fingers over his head, impatient as always and antsy as hell. Finding Maddie and Jameson wasn't the problem. Finding them alive was.

Chapter Ten

Go, get help, humph, Maddie thought as she crawled steadily through the ceiling ductwork. *What am I, just some brainless woman who can't do anything but run away like a scaredy cat?*

In twenty feet or so, the ceiling level ductwork turned into floor level ductwork that emptied into an old-fashioned kitchen with worn, linoleum-tiled flooring, dirt encrusted walls, and an empty square space where a stove had been. Men's voices came from the next room. A dim overhead light was on. A dozen or so fast food bags and empty beer bottles littered the counters.

Pressing both palms to the grated vent, she pushed, but then cringed when one side of it held tight while the other creaked open a scant few inches. She hadn't anticipated the vent wouldn't pop off like they did in movies. By then her hands were shaking. When no one came running to see what the noise was, she steeled her wits and tried again. Then again.

Good grief, the screw holding the vent in place on the left wouldn't give. But Jameson had said this was her time to shine, and one little screw wasn't going to stop her. Gripping the free side of the grate with both hands, she bent it outward at a ninety-degree angle, then extricated her ass and legs and scrambled to her feet. Her throat was drier than dirt by then, and her heart pounded, but she could do this.

Looking over her shoulder as she worked, Maddie bent the vent cover back into place, then lifted to her feet and flattened her back against the wall to keep from shaking. The way out lay directly across the floor from her. But some guy in the other room was growling a terse string of angry Gaelic that sent an icy shiver up her spine. Other loud male voices followed, their tones more agreeable. Mr. Tense-and-Gaelic had to be the boss, maybe Pops Delaney?

Maddie didn't intend to stick around to find out. She could get herself killed, and she just plain didn't have that kind of nerve. Jameson was the covert operator, not her. She was just admin. But tonight, he needed her help, and he was going to get it. Any minute now...

He'd create a distraction, and then she'd run and then...

A better idea sprang to mind. If he could create distractions, so could she.

Ducking quickly across the open kitchen doorway to the next room, she made it to the back door and was outside in seconds, her lungs pumping for air and her heart racing from too much adrenaline. She could do this. She could save Jameson. Wouldn't he be surprised?

But she had to act fast. What to do, what to do? Several trucks and assorted cars were parked in the dirt outside the kitchen exit, under a dim yard light stuck way up high on a telephone pole. It gave her just enough light to see without being seen. Maddie prowled those vehicles carefully and quietly, looking for keys. She didn't spend much time in any of them, afraid the dome lights might give her away. Finally. Bingo. Not only a set of keys, but a lighter, an unopened pack of cigarettes, and a ball cap. Those things might all come in handy, but she only took the keys and lighter.

More quick prowling earned her a loaded pistol hidden inside the driver's side door pocket of a topless SUV, a tire iron from the open bed of a pickup, and a deadly looking knife in a nice leather sheath from the cab of the same truck. Until she'd joined The TEAM, she'd never shot a gun. But since all TEAM members had to certify at a nearby range, she'd learned plenty. Would've been better if she'd found an extra, loaded magazine to go with the pistol, but the gun would do for now. She racked the slide and chambered a round, prepared to be all she could be.

With heart-pumping speed, she retraced her steps and stabbed tires. All of them. Her dealings with Nash's loan sharks had taught her well. Why flatten one when four ruined tires sent a scarier message?

Okay then. The night was warm and she was sweating up a storm. Before she went any further, she sheathed the knife and secured it in the waistband at her back. Setting the tire iron and pistol on the dirt beside her boot, she wrapped her hair into a long ponytail, tied it off with a couple strands of loose hair, and shoved it over her shoulder and out of the way. She pulled out the lighter. What these guys needed was a nice big bonfire, and...

Oh, look. A barn. If burning that down didn't get them out of the house long enough for her to rescue Jameson, it would certainly raise an alarm among the neighbors and bring the fire department.

Keeping an eye on the rear door of the house, she skittered between the parked vehicles to the old barn with her assorted weapons. She hesitated just inside the open barn door until her eyes adjusted to the lack of light. The interior was dark, really dark. This had to be how Jameson felt every day, feeling his way around a pitch-black world.

At last, she could make out the wide, barren, wooden floor, a couple empty stalls to her right, and a big mound of hay piled against the back wall. No horses or cows, though. No farm equipment, either. Just a big empty barn and...

Whoa. A shiny limousine had been backed into the far-right corner behind the stalls. *Well, well, well.* Want to bet that belonged to Lucy Shade? Which begged the question: where was that maniac?

Maddie hid the heavy tire iron in the hay now that she had a killer knife and a loaded pistol. Stepping lightly and quickly toward the limo, she second-guessed herself all the way, wondering if stabbing all those tires had been a smart idea. The men inside the house needed to see just the burning barn when they ran out and investigated the fire. She expected they'd all vacate the house, because that was what people did when someone yelled fire. It'd give her the time she needed to sneak back inside and break Jameson out.

But even if she made it all the way back inside the farmhouse and to Jameson, there was no guarantee she could get him out alive. And if even a single one of those men noticed the flat tires first... If someone stayed inside the house instead of running toward the fire...? *Good grief.* Actual covert operations were scary, dangerous things.

Finally at the limo, Maddie licked her lips at all the ways rescuing Jameson could go wrong. But she was determined. That counted for something, didn't it?

Biting her lower lip, she smoothed her fingertips over the sleek hood on her way to the driver's door handle. So far, so good. The door opened without setting off an alarm. Which she hadn't remembered until she'd sprung the latch, and by then, it would've been too late.

Focus, Maddie! Settle down. You can do this. Save Jameson. Save the day.

She leaned one knee on the driver's seat, weighing her options. Darn, this was a long vehicle, but she knew she could drive it. A key fob with no keys lay on the center console. Well, that was stupid. Decision made.

Thinking like a real covert operator now—she wished— she climbed in and fastened her seatbelt securely. Then, with her eyes closed, she risked everything and pressed her index finger to the button that relied on the low-frequency signal coming from the fob to start the engine. It purred to life. Oh, my gosh, without any of the noises her much cheaper, economy car made.

She opened her eyes and blew out a low, congratulatory breath of *'I did it!'* This time, she made sure the headlights didn't come on. Parking lights, either. But by then, she'd also thought twice about leaving the tire iron behind. Sometimes, more really was just that, and what woman didn't need a heavy-duty weapon when face to face with ruthless killers?

Braking to a slow, soundless stop at the barn door, she put the car in park, unfastened her seatbelt, and quickly retraced her steps. She'd been smart not throwing the tire iron willy-nilly. It was out of sight and under the hay, but it had to be close by. She'd just delved both arms up to her elbows into the dusty pile when—a great big hand grabbed her ankle. *Good Grief!* Maddie scurried backward, but she was caught.

"Let me go!" she nearly screamed, she was so scared.

Whoever he was, the guy held on tight. His hand was so big that it shackled her entire ankle, making getaway impossible. And it was black. Dark, dark black. Like ink. And big. But his voice was weak when he asked for, "H-h-help."

"Who are you? One of those k-k-killers?" There was no way she'd help one of Pops Delaney's men.

"Vlad..." he groaned.

"What are you doing out here?" She truly wished her voice would stop quavering.

"Shot. She… she shot me," he wheezed.

"Who? Lucy Shade?"

"Yeah. She's insane."

Maddie sucked up her courage and crawled back to the man under the hay. She brushed it off his long arm, then off his shoulder and face. He was a big African American with a funny name for a Black guy. But the gooey, bloody hole in his side, under that long arm in the sleeve of a dirty white dress shirt, was telling. Maddie knew what to do. Back when she'd been homeless, she'd been smart enough to duck into an American Red Cross class in emergency first-aid. She'd been hungry and cold that wintry evening, and she'd only gone in because she'd heard on the street they served hot coffee and donuts after class, and the class was free.

Despite the fact she hadn't showered in days and her clothes were wrinkled and dirty, and she had no doubt she'd smelled, she'd learned a lot that night. She'd even made a couple friends who'd told her about the women's shelter in Roanoke. Hop, skip, and jump a couple months forward, and she was tossing greasy fast food into tiny bags, going home to a warm bed in her very own small but affordable apartment, and attending night classes at the local community college.

Now was the time to put that first-aid class to use. Maddie turned back to face the farmhouse, her one chance to save

Jameson gone and another man to rescue. What to do now? Rescue two guys? Two big men? She could almost hear Jameson telling her, *"Well, yeah! One step at a time, Maddie. That's how we get the tough jobs done. You can do this. I have faith."*

"I sure hope you're right." Before she could move him, she needed to patch the hole in Mr. Vlad's side. With what? There was nothing clean enough in this barn except—her clothes. Even they were sweaty and smelled of smoke. But okay, then. Another decision made.

She unbuttoned what had once been her own crisp white shirt and laid it on Mr. Vlad's wide chest. Turning her back on him, she slipped out of her white padded bra. It was the cleanest thing around. It would have to do. Still facing away, she put her shirt back on and buttoned up.

Again, she called up other details from that long ago first-aid class. Mr. Vlad groaned a lot more this time, but after she'd cut her bra into small squares, Maddie used her fingertips to push just enough of it into his ugly bullet wound to stop most of the leakage. By the time she was through, she was desperate for a good long cry. Her nerves were shot, and she wasn't sure anything she'd done would save either Mr. Vlad or Jameson. But plugging the hole wasn't good enough. That much she knew. For Mr. Vlad to live, she had to make sure those bits of bra didn't pop out.

He reached out and patted her arm, then stroked it almost affectionately, as if telling her, *'Good girl.'*

"You'll live now," she told him in case he didn't know. "But I need to cut your shirt off to use it for a bandage. I won't cut you, I promise. Hold very, very still."

His chest heaved and he stroked her arm again. He certainly seemed to have a lot of faith in her. *Glad someone did.*

"Well, okay then." She blew a loose strand of hair out of her face. "Let's do this."

Breathing through pursed lips to slow her rising panic, Maddie lifted the fabric away from his chest, then slipped the blade of her knife into his shirt. Pop, pop, pop went those tiny shirt buttons as she made quick work of removing as much of the cotton material as she could reach. The blade was extra sharp, so she was extra careful. At last, she had enough material. She cut the pieces into long strips, then tied them into one long bandage.

He'd need real medical care soon, and he'd get it. She'd make sure of that. Okay then. If a blind man who couldn't see his hand in front of his face had faith in a scaredy-cat woman with wide-opened eyes, she could get Mr. Vlad to safety. Then, she'd come back, start the barn on fire, and rescue Jameson.

It took a bit getting Mr. Vlad upright and sitting, but he seemed as eager to get away from Shade and her murderous friends as Maddie was. He assisted as much as he could in getting his shirt wrapped around his chest, then tied off to hold her makeshift bandage in place.

"OhGodOhGodOhGod, that was really scary," she muttered to herself, wishing her heart beat would slow down. *But I did it, by heck. I just saved this guy's life.* Getting him on his feet took more effort. Maddie knew she was hurting him, but he seemed made of the same stuff as Jameson. Pure determination. She just wished he'd hurry a little faster.

Jameson needed her, too, and any minute now, he'd create a diversion. She needed to be ready to jump into action then.

Mr. Vlad stumbled along until, at last, she had him flat on his back in the limo's spacious rear seat. Maddie folded his long legs inside, then carefully, silently, closed the door. In seconds, she was behind the wheel again, and they were on their way.

Maddie drove extra slowly out of the barn, along the long, dirt driveway, away from the farmhouse, until finally, she hit pavement. Less than a half-mile down the road, she veered to the left onto another dirt path that obviously hadn't been used, it was so full of weeds. The path took her through dusty brush, thick grass, and short, spindly trees. *Sumac,* she thought as she steered a hard right and came to a gentle stop. At last the long, elegant car was out of sight from the road.

Mr. Vlad was either asleep, unconscious, or dead by then, but, short of leaving Jameson behind, she'd done all she could. Scared to death he might already be dead, she ran like the wind, backtracking with her meager arsenal to burn the barn down. The night was dark, but there was just enough ambient light to keep her headed in the right direction. Past all those flat tires and into the deep, dark shadowy barn she raced, her pulse a pounding, throbbing beast in her chest, making it harder and harder to catch a breath. Finally, at the haystack piled at the far wall, with the tire iron at her side, she dropped to her knees and prayed this crazy plan worked.

A single *BOOM* from the house snapped her head up. God, she hoped that was Jameson's signal. There was no longer a choice. She had to act now! As if he were standing right there beside her, his other encouraging words flashed to mind. *I like that you're willing to fight for our lives.*

"I'm sure trying," she told him, her heart pounding so hard that her chest felt ready to explode. She flicked the lighter's igniter wheel, but her fingers were trembling, and she was breathing too hard, and she blew the tiny flame out the second it sprang to life.

"OhGodOhGodOhGod, help me." She'd just managed another spark when—

BLAM, BLAM, BOOM! Jameson was in trouble!

Hurry, hurry, hurry! Into the hay went that little, orange spark and—

WHOOSH!

"Oh, crap!" The entire pile of hay ignited into one huge, hungry fireball. Without taking a breath, it leaped straight up into the wooden timbers of the loft overhead, its wicked tendrils jumping from one rafter to another as if they were in a race. Another hissing whoosh sent sparks flying in all directions. She'd created a monster fireworks show that had morphed from a tiny spark into an out-of-control inferno. Even now, long, crackling tongues of fire licked at the roof overhead. The single, tiny flame from a gas station convenience store was igniting every speck of wood it touched. And some it didn't.

Scared for her life and crab-crawling backward as fast as she could, Maddie scrambled out of the burning barn and made it between two parked cars just as the farmhouse door burst open.

Right on cue, some guy bellowed, "Fire!"

Good grief! She was on fire, too! Her pants were smoking. She patted her thighs and legs, smothering whatever sparks had gotten into the fabric, then she rolled to her knees for a fast getaway. She'd known fumes and dust were incendiary and could explode, seeing the power it held was another thing all together. She had no idea this old barn would burn that fast or so hot. Her face felt sunburned, and that lightning quick ignition had literally sucked the oxygen out of her lungs.

But it was done. No one had yet spotted the flat tires. Most of the guys were running around, looking for hoses. Mission accomplished. One man down. One to rescue. Maddie Bannister, the woman her father had never believed in, had, in fact, never heard or actually seen—not even once—through all her seventeen years living in his house, would rescue the man she cared about. Jameson said he'd wanted a date, well, tonight was that night.

"I'm c-c-coming," she told him over the roar of the flames behind her, "and you'd better be ready to go when I g-g-get there."

Chapter Eleven

Jameson turned himself into a radar dish, his senses unfurled like solar panels into the universe of sight and sound, soaking up every last nuance radiating off the men standing outside his door. They were here to kill him. He'd heard them coming, had even startled them with a shot from his pistol. Sure, it brought a shitload of trouble his way, but that was okay. He'd anticipated three shots, but had been surprised when one of those blasts came from a shotgun. That hollow core door was now splintered, and he knew he'd probably die in the next few minutes. But Maddie would live. She was all that mattered.

He'd been here before. Trapped. Outnumbered and outgunned. But he was a different man now. The tiniest smile flickered across his lips. As Walker Judge would say, he had mad ninja skills. But all Jameson really had were two ears that knew how to listen better and quicker reflexes that he'd honed to strike true. Like a pool player knew how to angle his shots for maximum results, Jameson knew how to sense and anticipate movement, adjust momentum, and counterattack. It didn't hurt that Lucy Shade had probably told these guys that he was just some '*blind guy.*' Big, tough guys weren't afraid of blind guys. But they should be.

He waited for Delaney's men behind the concrete wall to the left of the none-existent door. He was ready, had counted the three sets of heavy boots that pounded down the stairs. He knew these guys were operating with plenty of light, while he was consigned to total darkness. But they weren't quiet, and he wasn't stupid. He could smell them and the beer they'd been drinking. He knew precisely how close they were to breaching the already shattered doorway. A bow wave of body odor, cigarette stink, and cheap aftershave had preceded them. The closer they came, the stronger the stench. They meant to assassinate him. He meant to let them think they could.

His nostrils flared as the acrid scent of fire and ash drifted into the basement. Before this standoff, he'd heard some guy yell, "Fire!" Either one of Delaney's men was an idiot and had started the blaze that had taken everyone outside, or someone else was on the property. Hopefully, The TEAM. It'd be a shame to die on his first day of work.

For now, Jameson stood stock-still with his body angled sideways and his head cocked. The guys outside his door would soon charge in and kill him, but not before he took out one or two of them. Three'd be better. It was the guys outside the farmhouse who were the problem. Whether he killed these goons or not, by the time the rest of Delaney's men came running, he'd be out of ammo. So he waited and listened as those boots advanced. One cautious step after another until—

He jumped into their view and fired quick successive shots through the bullet-ridden door. Jameson heard one killer groan. To his right, a big body connected with a wet splat on what sounded like a damned hard wall. Something grated like leather against granite until it hit the floor. Relying on nothing but sheer instinct, Jameson charged through the splintered hollow core, brought his fist up, and punched the only killer standing in the throat. He'd aimed, hopefully, for the guy's face, but blind men couldn't be choosers. He took what he got.

Number Three gurgled and went down like a bag of wet concrete mix.

By then, Jameson was sure he'd eliminated Numbers Two and Three. But Number One had climbed to his feet again and was coming up behind Jameson. He was the jerk with the shotgun. Jumping sideways to avoid what would be a life-ending shot, Jameson crouched into a squat and swept his dominant leg forward. Contact. The guy went down with a profanity laced curse. Which was all Jameson needed to know, precise location and distance. Like he'd been trained, he sent another well-placed kick. This time, he connected with the killer's face. He heard the guy's nose crunch and the spin as the shotgun flew. Jameson picked it out of the air on its downward arc. Spinning the butt end of the weapon into his chest, he pointed the barrel where Number One crouched. Jameson fired. The battle was won. Three assholes down. Righteous kills, all of them. Now for the others.

Quickly, he scavenged what the dead men had brought to the fight. Two pistols and a high-capacity, double-barreled, bullpup pump action, twelve-gauge shotgun. He jerked the nylon ammo bag of shotgun shells from the guy he'd killed last. Slick with blood, but still a sweet reward. When he was through, he had a total of six loaded mags for the pistols and a nearly full fourteen-round magazine for the shotgun. Backing into the nearest corner, he sank to his ass on the floor and swiftly reloaded all weapons. The shotgun would be his first line of defense. It went across his knees. The pistols and their specific mags went into a straight line he could reach without wasting time fumbling. He was ready.

Until he heard a lighter tread coming down the stairs and headed his way. Step by cautious step. Ever so slowly. Could that be Lucy Shade? Jameson didn't want to kill a woman, even though she was behind the kidnapping. Taking a deep breath, he stood and waited for a clue that would tell him who he was up against.

His nose flared at the lovely scent he'd thought he'd never smell again. "Maddie?" he asked as he stepped forward. "What are you doing down here? You're supposed to be gone."

She nearly bowled him over. "I couldn't leave you! I came back to save you," she said breathlessly, burrowing into his side and under his arm. "C-come on, Jameson! We have to g-g-go right now."

Damn. She'd seen the bodies and gore. Might even have seen him kill that last guy. He curled her inside his arm, confused as to why she was there, yet so damned relieved she was alive. His senses surged out from him like a hearing-seeing-feeling sonar wave. Instant data poured back. More heavy footsteps in the yard, coming his way. The thwack-thwack-thwack of a helo flying high overhead and, unfortunately, away. It would've been better if that helo was The TEAM coming to his rescue, but he suspected it was more likely Lucy Shade and Pops Delany getting away. *Shit.*

"It's too late. We can't leave now. They're coming."

"Hurry," she cried, slipping one slender hand into his. "We can still make it. I have a car."

"Where?"

"Down the road with Mr. Vlad."

"Who's Mr. Vlad?"

"The other guy I saved. Come on, Jameson. We can make it."

Other guy? "Wrong, Maddie. We're out of time." He pulled her back into the corner, then positioned her behind him, as more of Delaney's killers thundered down what sounded like a narrow flight of stairs. Thirteen steps to that staircase. A truly unlucky number, considering the incident had happened on the thirteenth of May, five years ago. This night just kept going from bad to worse.

Angry roars went up when the other six spotted their dead friends. Jameson focused on the vibration of all those soundwaves to locate his first two targets. A double-gauge came in handy when faced with mob violence, and the one in his hands could dispense fourteen rapid rounds. He cocked the lever and prepared to get ugly.

"Drop your weapons," he ordered Delaney's men.

"Aye, and then you shoot us in the face." Sweet Baby Jesus. The top dog himself was here with his guys. "Face it, boyo. Me and my boys have you and your little girlfriend outnumbered. You'll never get out of here alive."

"Pops Delaney," Jameson stated for the record. "I'm taking you in for kidnapping, racketeering, money laundering, extortion, tax fraud, and a shitload of other federal crimes. Hands up or die. Your choice."

The air in the stuffy basement crackled with tension and bloodlust. It'd been a long time since he'd last smelled it. That time, in Iraq.

"Who's he kidding? He's that blind guy," one of Pops' guys snickered. "Look at him. Look at his feckin eyes. He can't see us to shoot us."

"Last chance, assholes," Jameson threatened.

"Aye, and the one with him's just a wee girl," another added. "Look at her, hiding behind her boyfriend like a scared rabbit."

"I like bunnies and little girls," a deeply sinister voice whispered salaciously.

"I'm no little girl!" Maddie yelled as she stepped around Jameson and—

BLAM!

She had a gun? Judging by the gangster's uproar, she'd just shot Pops Delaney. Sweet baby Jesus!

Jameson fired one round from his shotgun, hoping to quell the upcoming slaughter. But vengeance was a hard beast to rein in once unleashed. When Delaney's gang commenced shooting, Jameson was all that stood between them and Maddie. He unloaded round after round of hell until there was no one firing back at him.

By then, he'd trapped Maddie behind him. She might've gotten off that first shot, but beginner's luck had no place in a gunfight. Only skill. Only quick thinking and faster shooting.

The stink in the basement swelled up like noxious poison in Jameson's nose. He could only imagine what was going through Maddie's mind. But another vehicle had rumbled into the yard, and more heavily bodied men in boots were already on the ground. This wasn't Tombstone, Arizona, nor was it a gunfight at the O.K. Corral. This basement was a kill box.

Like hell.

Chapter Twelve

Maddie held her breath as the farmhouse backdoor creaked open. Her mouth was as dry as a desert, and she was shaking like a leaf, but there were no words for what she'd just seen this warrior in action accomplish. It was as if he could see. Every time he'd aimed and fired, he'd taken out one of Delaney's men. Every shot had been on target, but now more killers were on their way into the house. They'd be down here soon. There was no way out. Not even through the vent. She wouldn't leave Jameson behind this time.

Wearily, she pressed her forehead to the center of his sweat-soaked back. The intimacy of their shared dilemma, their concern for each other, and the very real possibility they could die in the next few minutes, had stitched them together like matching mittens. He being the more adept right, her the clumsy, unreliable left.

Her nostrils flared at the salty scent of the man she meant to die for. Or live for, that'd be even better. But they were outnumbered again. How long could a blind man fight off all these monsters? How long could she?

His free hand reached behind him and found her biceps. "Hang in there, babe," he said with a firm squeeze.

"I know. One step at a time," she breathed. "That's how we get the tough jobs done."

"That's right. Whatever you do, stay behind me." He ended the moment with another squeeze, then dropped to a knee and reloaded the stubby rifle in his hand.

She'd never seen anything like it before. Couldn't be more than twenty inches long. And he was jamming shotgun shells into a magazine? "What kind of shotgun is that?"

"High capacity. You want to use it this time?"

"No," she replied quickly. "I'm afraid I might—"

"Kill everything that moves? That's the point, Maddie. Don't forget who was behind the jet blowing up around us or our abduction. Shade and Delaney started this. The only way out is when we end it."

When, not if… Licking her too dry lips, she swallowed hard. "I know but… h-h-he's dead."

"And we're not, and that's the way it's going to stay. Whoever those guys are who just arrived, they're in the room overhead."

"It's a kitchen. This is an old farmhouse."

"Let me guess, you started the fire."

She nodded, then spoke up with a hearty, "Yes. I had a plan. But then everyone started shooting."

He shook his head, his eyes on the floor. "That was me, Maddie. I thought it was our plan. I create a distraction while you run for help, remember? Wish you'd stuck to it."

"Well, err…" He was right. This was her fault.

The oddest, most welcome, "Clear!" sounded upstairs.

Jameson cocked his head like he did when he was listening extra hard, which Maddie realized was most of the time. His free arm snaked around her. "Don't move," he whispered. "And don't shoot until we know for sure who we're up against."

"Well, yeah…" Did he think she was an idiot? "But that sounds like the FBI up there. That's what they always say. Clear."

"But we don't know for certain yet. We hold," he murmured, his body warm and solid, the only thing holding her together. "I'm glad you came back."

"Oh, sure. I'm insubordinate. Never would've made a good Marine."

"But you applied good tactical strategy, and you implemented a solid rescue plan. Tell me what else you did."

"I slashed their tires. All of them. I stole the limo I found in the barn. I think it was Shade's, and I stashed it down the road behind some bushes. I saved a guy. Mr. Vlad. He was in the barn, and Shade shot him, and I used my—"

"Did he live?" Jameson grinned when he asked.

But Maddie's eyes filled with tears. "Of course he lived, but I should've listened to you. I'm sorry. You're the expert. Alex will be angry. He'll say I screwed the pooch."

"No, he won't, Maddie. He doesn't come across like that kind of guy. And even if he's angry, it's more important you think for yourself than blindly follow orders. I learned that the hard way. Things turn out better when you use your head and trust your instincts. Always follow your gut." Jameson breathed, his face turned toward the ceiling again, his unseeing eyes blinking as if he'd heard something he didn't like. "And that guy you saved would be dead if not for you, right?"

"Yes," she admitted. "He's not part of this mess we're in."

"Then why'd Shade shoot him? Shhhhh… Listen."

"To what?" she whispered.

"Irish brogue. That's not the FBI upstairs, babe. Hurry. Reload."

"I can't. I don't have another magazine, and I've only got five shots left in this one."

Without looking at her, of course, he handed over another pistol, grip first. An extra magazine came next. "Ready now?"

"Y-y-yes," she stuttered as she slipped her secondary pistol into her waistband. "H-how many this time?"

"Nine or ten. Big guys. All of them. That'll be good for us. Big guys make wider targets. Take your shirt off. Cover your mouth and eyes with it. Try not to breathe."

He'd no sooner said that when a smoking canister rolled down the steps. Fighting her fear, Maddie ripped her shirt off, just like he'd ordered. She'd be half-naked, but hopefully, she'd stay alive. She barely had enough time to wad it into a fluffy ball and slap it over her mouth, before tear gas filled the small, stuffy room.

Even with her makeshift mask, she choked and reached for Jameson, but he was gone. Tenney had the grace of a dancer and the stone-cold accuracy of a killer. He'd moved with lightning reflexes, like one of those crazy-fast parkour athletes who ran up walls and bounced off ceilings. He wasn't anywhere, but then he was everywhere. Shooting. Forcing her face first to the floor. Holding a hard hand in the middle of her back while he fired over her head, again and again. Each time, the kickback radiated down his arm to her body.

Maddie panicked. There was too much noise and mayhem, but not enough air! She couldn't think! Couldn't see. So much smoke! Her eyes and nose stung and watered. She couldn't catch a decent breath because of the excess fluid in her throat. Didn't want to breathe when she did. Her lungs quit working. Her bare breasts, now pressed flat to the rough concrete floor, hurt. She was dying!

Suddenly, the noise stopped. Jameson lifted her into his arms, and he was carrying her upstairs. But she was a miserable snotty mess. Worse, she hadn't fired a single shot to help him, and she was half-dressed. And oh, yes. She was still the loser her dad always said she was.

"Stop feeling sorry for yourself," Jameson chided as he settled her on his knee with one arm around her. "Your dad's an idiot."

"But, but, but…" she sputtered, embarrassed she might've said that last part out loud.

"Losers quit, and that's not what you did tonight, Maddie," he said as he poured water over her face. "Sounds to me like he's the real loser and a bully. Your dad quit on you, didn't he?"

The rush of cool water instantly soothed, but didn't completely wash the effects of the tear gas away. She was still choking and snotting, but she could see they were at the kitchen sink, and Jameson was scooping water from the running faucet over her face Something warm and wonderful blossomed in her chest for the first time ever, and it wasn't tear gas.

"Yes," she admitted weakly, wishing she had a blanket or something to cover up with. "Every day of my life."

"Asshole," Jameson muttered. "Real men don't denigrate children. Any children! They build them up, and they teach them how to have confidence in this shitty world. To stand tall and walk proud. They provide positive reinforcement, and they always have their kid's back. They're proud of them every single damned day."

Not all men. "W-was your dad? Proud of you? Every day?"

"You bet. Want to meet him? He and Mom are expecting me for dinner this Sunday. They'll adore you. Come with me."

Maddie shook her head, feeling embarrassed and vulnerable. Exposed and naked and, well, snotty. Yet the sensation of Jameson leaning over her was so, so nice. Even there in the dark, with her eyes burning and watering too much for her to see, she could feel the capable, strong male leaning over her. Sheltering her. That all by itself was a really nice, really new feeling. It'd be better to have her shirt back, and she wished she didn't look this awful. But then, what difference did it make? He couldn't see her. "My hair. I must look like—"

"Like an angel," Jameson murmured. "Maddie, are you…? My God, you are."

He cocked his head more sharply then. He had one hand on her bare shoulder, the other on her rib cage. She hadn't had time to tell him how she'd stopped Mr. Vlad's gunshot wound from bleeding. That she'd lost track of her shirt in the scary confusion downstairs. That she was naked from the waist up. But he knew now.

"Y-y-you can't see me, can you?"

"Oh, yes, I can," he whispered as one big, manly, wet hand smoothed over her bare shoulder. His other was behind her, his fingers splayed against her bare back. "Where's your shirt, babe?"

"Somewhere downstairs," she whispered. "You said take it off, but then I lost it, and I had to cut up my bra to save Mr. Vlad, and I don't know where my guns are, either. Dad was right. I'm such a loser." Her eyes welled with bitter tears.

"No, Maddie. Your dad was dead damned wrong," Jameson breathed. His deep voice had dropped an octave into bedroom range. "You're strong and smart. And you're beautiful."

"No, I'm not. I'm noth—"

"Shush. Who knows better, me or your dad?"

Was that a trick question? "Y-y-you…?"

"Right again. Let me tell you what I know about you that your old man doesn't and never will. You're four feet, eleven inches tall and maybe a hundred pounds soaking wet. Long silky hair. Still don't know the color of it, but I'm working on that. More importantly, you're braver than any woman I've ever met. You're resourceful. You know how to think for yourself."

"Blonde. I'm blonde, and I'm half-naked."

"Oh, yes you are," he rumbled with something akin to delight in his tone. "What color are your eyes?"

"L-light b-b-blue."

"God, you're perfect," he moaned.

Darn, this was embarrassing. He knew she was bare to him, yet he couldn't see her. Any of her. How pitiful was that? To look more womanly, she needed her padded bra. But it was gone, and Jameson was still here, but he couldn't see, so what did it matter? Yet it did, damn it. She wanted Jameson to really look at her with his eyes, the way he seemed able to see her with his ears.

But he *was* smiling. "You're so damned beautiful, Maddie," he breathed.

By then, he'd leaned farther into her face. She could smell his breath and their combined sweaty, tear-gassed bodies. Okay, maybe seeing wasn't believing after all. The air around them went still. She could hear how ragged his breathing had turned. His heart was probably pounding as hard as hers was, too. The intensity etched on his face was almost feral. Good grief, she wanted him.

Blinking furiously through watery eyes, Maddie saw it coming. Wanted it with every beat of her quivering, timid body. Like a man on a mission, Jameson closed the distance between them. One big, warm, wonderfully damp hand settled completely over her breast. All of it. Possessing it. Loving her. And she was lost in the most sublime sensation of her life.

His thumb rubbed her nipple, hardening the bud and sending sparks straight to her quivering core. His other hand was holding the back of her head, cupping her gently when— it happened. He covered her mouth with the most delicious kiss.

Her body ignited, and Maddie lost control. Both her hands cupped his jaw, holding him tight and right where she wanted him to stay for a long time. Slanting her head, she opened her mouth wider, needing this connection, this very affirmative man in her arms, so damned much. Her body seemed to have a will of its own, bucking into his. All her life she'd been nothing, but then Jameson came along and, wham. She'd become visible, and she really was strong, and she knew what she wanted, and it was him. She was starving. Every last fiber in her body and every bit of her soul was so darned hungry.

Too quickly, he growled, tipped back on his haunches, and broke the steamy connection. He was wiping his face, but licking his lips, too. "We will definitely continue this conversation later," he muttered huskily while he shrugged out of his wrinkled jacket. "Here. Cover up."

For whatever reason, those words didn't crush her like they would've if they'd come from her dad or her ex. Maddie wiggled into the luscious scents Jameson had left behind in his jacket. The warmth. Her favorite scent of over-heated masculine spice.

"You're shivering." The worry in his tone was so tender and precious that she wanted to cry.

"I think because I'm… I'm happy," she whispered. "And now I'm wrapped up inside of you, and I… I…" *I don't know how to tell you the boost in confidence you've just given me.*

"I didn't know you weren't wearing your bra. Honest." His cheeks ballooned as he blew out a ragged breath. "Or I never would've told you to take your shirt off."

Maddie shrugged. "It's okay. No one could see me through all that smoke, and it wouldn't have mattered if they did. I had to stop Mr. Vlad's bleeding, so I used what I had on me, and that was my bra, and it worked."

A smile broke through the confused worry lining Jameson's handsome face. Those adorable laugh lines crowding his dark eyes stretched into rays of pure sunshine. He ran the back of his hand over his forehead, wiping a portion of sweat away. "Works for me, too."

"I like how you converse," she offered timidly. Daring to feel sensual and sexy for the first time ever. She'd never be rockstar sexy, but she could tease. Him. Just him.

"There's lots more where that came from," he growled playfully. "Now, where's our ride out of here?" A broad smile crinkled his handsome face. Jameson had the most amazing laugh lines. At the corners of his eyes. Across his forehead. Bracketing the sides of his mouth. Those lush lips…

Maddie licked the inside of her mouth where he'd just been, savoring the taste of him and the wonder of this most excellent minute of her life. She'd found something tonight. When she'd first been introduced, she hadn't wanted to play TEAM guide to another former solider. They were the ones who got to go on adventures. She was the one they all left behind, while they went off and saved the world. But now she felt as if she were part of a whole new world, and it was perfect.

Reaching out, she took his hand and interlocked her fingers with his. "It's a little ways down the road, Jameson. Come on. Pull me up, and I'll show you."

Chapter Thirteen

"We're at their location, Boss, but Maddie and Jameson aren't here. Pops Delaney is though. What's left of him. As well as quite a few of his guys. You should see all these bodies. Pretty sure this is Jameson's work."

Alex squeezed the bridge of his nose between his index finger and thumb, fighting a migraine that wouldn't let up until he was sure Maddie and Jameson were safe. It was the middle of a long, damned night and he was in his office. After reviewing Reagan's security footage, he now knew who'd abducted them. Pops Delaney, a thug and a gunrunner. He'd been there all along, had watched from the shadows when Jameson and Maddie ran from the jet. He and another guy had overcome them, then stuffed them into the back of a black SUV.

And now he was dead, the rat bastard. His death would incite a scramble inside and outside his gang for dominance. More than one hit team would be gunning for Jameson once this information hit the press. Hell, they probably already knew.

Adam cleared his throat. "You still with me?"

"Shade isn't there, is she?" Alex knew damned well she wasn't, but a man could wish.

"No sign she ever was. Hunter and Eric are scouring the immediate area, but this is Virginia, and the farmhouse where

Delaney stashed Maddie and Jameson is a leftover relic from the past century."

Which meant it was overgrown and forgotten, the perfect place for a mob boss to conduct business. Delaney was one of the top kingpins on the East Coast. His gang was ruthless, daring, and growing. Alex had watched them run over weak-kneed governors and crooked mayors, circuit court judges and the FBI's best. They seemed untouchable.

But he knew different. The director of the FBI's one and only psychic team, Tucker Chase, had a man inside the Irish gang. Which was why Delaney had come to Boston. His men had recently fallen to one FBI sting after another. Whoever Tucker's guy was, he'd been supplying inside details of hits, takeovers, and other mob plans for months. Delaney's rep had been on the line for just as long. His people were restless. They didn't feel safe, the poor thieving, murderous scoundrels. Word on the street was it was only a matter of time before someone took him out. And now Jameson had unknowingly lit the match that would inflame Boston, the Eastern Seaboard, the District, and quiet, quaint Olde Town Alexandria with it.

The cost of doing business had just grown exponentially higher for every law-abiding businessman and woman. A new boss always wanted to rule the police. The single-owner neighborhood mom and pop shops and restaurants. Successful enterprises. The world...

"Say again?" Adam asked whoever was reporting back to him. "Copy that. Boss, you still there?"

"Here."

"Hunter found something. Might be our missing people. There's no reason for me to stay here. Already gave an initial statement to the sheriff. His coroner's onsite and an FBI forensic team is on the way. I'm going to catch up with Hunt."

"Keep in touch."

"Copy that."

Alex had barely disconnected the call when his other problem, Mother, opened his door without knocking and stalked in. Today she wore a no-nonsense silvery gray business suit, black heels, and a white silk blouse, its collar tucked smartly under the lapels of the suit. She settled into the chair in front of his desk, leaned forward, and, with one hand, pushed his nameplate aside. She crossed her arms and interlocked her fingers without breaking eye contact.

She'd changed since she'd returned after her daughter's death. He'd thought her long hiatus would've helped her come to terms with losing Dempsey. But she'd come back to The TEAM with a tough, flinty edge. Reminded him of the hard ass he'd been after he'd lost Sara and Abby.

Mother was clearly still in pain, and a child's death would take the rest of her life to process. That didn't entitle her to a partnership, though. He didn't appreciate the leverage she'd assumed she had, that she'd only stay if he made her his partner. Bottom line, he had Ember, Beau, and Maddie Bannister working technical support, and each of them brought positive energy to The TEAM, not tit-for-tat. They were straight with him, and they minded their business, a trait Mother didn't seem to think mattered.

But it sure as hell did. He waited while she stared him down. As if her glare came close to intimidating a Devil Dog? Not hardly. When she didn't speak up and spit it out, he charged. "What do you have for me?"

"Information."

His head throbbed at her continual cat-and-mouse game. "I don't have time for this," he growled. "Support my TEAM or pack your desk and leave."

"I know where Jameson and Maddie are."

"And you didn't lead with that?"

"I wanted to discuss my offer first."

"I have people missing, possibly injured or dead, and you want to talk business? Get the fuck out!"

Her back stiffened, well, so the hell did his. Good people didn't hold back when their teammates' lives were on the line. They threw in and they gave all.

"Where are they?" he growled.

"Face it, Alex," she snapped. "You need a partner and that person is me. You're not a businessman. You want to be out there looking for your people, not sitting behind a desk twiddling your fingers. And Mark—"

"Did you tell Mel Stewart where I was today? Did you break protocol and share my wife's secure location with someone you didn't know or investigate? Without checking with me first?"

"Of course! He said he was your father. For Christ's sake, Alex. He looks just like you."

And that was the last straw. There was a time Alex thought Mother worked miracles. Not anymore.

A sharp knock at the door interrupted the nasty retort on his lips. Mark popped his head in and advised, "Your helo's on its way, Boss. ETA to Adam's location in twenty minutes, once you're in the air. Car's running to get you to the helo pad."

"Thanks, Mark. Don't go anywhere. You were saying?" Alex asked Sasha Kennedy, the woman he'd thought he'd known and trusted since the day he'd hung his shingle on King Street.

But she'd changed since she'd lost Dempsey. Her usually soft blue eyes were hard as flint today. "I only want what's best for this business."

He didn't have time to argue. "We'll continue this conversation later."

"I won't be here." She was on her feet, and her temper was up.

How Alex saw through her bravado just then, he didn't understand. Yet he did. She was him all those hard days and months after he'd lost his family. After the accident, back when he'd struggled like hell to focus on making it through one damned day after another without them. Making everything worse for Mother, he and Kelsey had just welcomed a son, while Ember and Rory were pregnant and due soon. Had she kept that secret from Sasha? Was that what was really going on here? Unrelenting grief in the face of another's joy? Jealousy because her baby was gone, and Ember was finally carrying hers to full term? That Kelsey and Alex had the exquisite happiness Mother wanted? Short answer—maybe.

Mark was waiting, but Sasha was ready to walk away from the best friends, quite possible the only friends, she'd ever had. Alex couldn't let that happen. "Please stay," he said more gently. "Take a time-out, Sasha. Wait until this catastrophe is over. I don't want to lose you."

That honest admission broke her steely-eyed stare. Her nostrils flared with a huff. "That's decent of you. I'll consider it. Th-thanks."

He had to ask, "Where's Justice? I haven't seen him once since you've been—"

"He's gone. Don't ask."

Another piece of the puzzle settled into place. Justice had stood by Mother throughout Dempsey's illness and death. If she'd cut him off the same way she was alienating The TEAM, Alex knew damned well that the know-it-all, gossiping woman he'd nicknamed Mother was so riddled with grief that she was no longer herself. Bitterness had replaced her nosy, sunny disposition. She was drowning. She needed a lifeline. Something to hold onto.

Alex let that lifeline be him. Tipping his head to her, he said, "Life can be a real son of a bitch sometimes, Sasha. But look around. We're all still here for you. We always were." He bit back reminding her that they weren't the ones who'd betrayed her.

Her eyes glistened. She swallowed hard. And aww, hell. Alex did what he should've done the first morning she'd come back to work. He rounded his desk and pulled her into one arm. "You're not alone, damn it. Stay with me, Sasha. Let me take care of this problem, then we'll talk. Over coffee. For as long as you need."

"I'll stay until you get back," she whispered.

That would have to do. He squeezed her tight, then let her go.

"I tracked the GPS locator in Lucy Shade's limo," she admitted quietly. "I'll send you the coordinates."

"I knew you could do it," he told her sincerely.

Mark held the door as Alex ran for The TEAM's underground parking. He had a helo to catch, and a lying reporter to hunt down. But he wasn't giving up on Mother. Hell, no.

Chapter Fourteen

Jameson couldn't get over how much Maddie accomplished during the short time between when she'd left him in the basement and when she'd returned. She wasn't the shrinking violet she thought she was. It was high time she realized that, and kicked her old man's negativity to the curb. She'd proven him wrong tonight. Yet somehow, she still allowed his shadow to hover over her and slap her down.

Even now after they'd driven through more weeds and bushes than a limo should be able to traverse. He'd gone back into the house and retrieved that high-capacity, double-barreled, bullpup pump action, twelve-gauge shotgun, as well as the two extra pistols he'd confiscated from his first attackers. No sense leaving good weaponry behind. They went in the limo's trunk. His Magnum went back under his arm.

But damn. Maddie was a beast behind the wheel, cussing every bump they lurched over and every sapling she mashed under the limo's grill. "Damn you, trees, get out of my way. Shit, I didn't see that rut! Sorry! This is all my fault. I thought I knew the way back to the road, but I got us lost and—hang on!"

"Relax," he murmured even as he held onto the suicide handle over the window while she performed a sharp left turn.

"Whew. That was a big tree stump. H-how's Mr. Vlad?"

Jameson had no way to know. He couldn't see *Mr. Vlad* to begin with, nor could he reach all the way to the rear seat where the man whose first name was probably Vladimir lay. The guy hadn't said a word since Jameson and Maddie had climbed into the limo and taken off into the dark. A paved road would sure be a nice change.

"Good grief! Did you see that deer? It nearly hit us!"

"Sure didn't." Jameson couldn't help the smile that cracked his face. His blindness seemed to be as much of an adjustment for Maddie as it had been for him. Well, almost…

Right on cue, "I'm so, so sorry! You can't see and I can but—"

"It's okay. Pull over, and I'll be glad to check on him."

"Pull over, oh, that's real funny. Like there are shoulders and curbs out here in the sticks. How about I just stop?" She stepped on the brakes and they came to a full stop.

"That'll work. Don't go anywhere," he teased as he climbed to his feet and kicked his way through the thick grasses to the rear door. Jameson enjoyed the easy banter with Maddie.

"How are you doing?" he asked the quiet man after he opened the door and leaned inside. "I know you probably aren't strong enough to speak, Vlad, but reach for my hand if you're feeling good enough to keep going."

He squeezed good and hard, as if telling Jameson he was hanging in there.

"Sorry about the rough ride. As soon as we hit asphalt, we'll get you to a hospital."

An older style flip cell phone slid into his palm.

"Wow, thanks. Maddie, I've got a phone!" Jameson called out while he thumbed his new boss's number.

A woman answered, "TEAM headquarters, how may I help you?"

Thank God! "Alex Stewart. I know it's late, but I need to talk to—"

"Jameson? Is Maddie with you?"

"Yeah," he replied as he sank to the seat opposite Vlad. "Is this Mom? Great! Maddie! I've got Mom—"

"Mother," the woman snapped.

"I've got *Mom* on the phone," he insisted.

"Not Mom. Mother!" *Ewww, the snark.* Mother, who would from this day forward be known as Mom, was testy tonight.

"What phone?" Maddie asked.

"Vlad had a cell. I'm online with the office, and someone is actually there. Can you believe that?"

"I wish I'd known he had a phone!" Maddie yelled over her shoulder.

"Alex is already in transit, Jameson," Mother interrupted primly. "We know right where you are. Stay put."

"Yes, Mom!" he replied with exuberant relish.

"I said don't call me that."

He pretended he didn't hear her. "We've got a man who needs rapid evac. He's been shot, but he's stable at the moment. What's Alex's ETA?"

"He's coming to you by chopper," she replied tersely. "Is there somewhere close he can land?"

"I have no idea. We're in some pretty dense brush, I think. But I can't see, remember? Mom? Are you still there?"

"Damn you," she hissed. "Never mind. I'm switching to satellite topography. Okay, no. The closest LZ is a couple miles due west of your location, and you're right. Your vehicle is in dense trees and undergrowth. Why aren't you guys on a road?"

"Because we're taking the scenic route." He wasn't about to cast any blame on Maddie. Wing men didn't do that.

"Never mind. One way or the other, Alex is still coming. He'll touchdown in five, then make his way to you. I'll contact first responders. Anyone else hurt?"

"No, we're good," Jameson breathed as he sank his weary, worn-out ass into the plush leather seat of Lucy Shade's stolen limo. "Damned good now that I'm talking with you. It's sure nice to hear your friendly voice, Mom. Us kids really needed that. It's been a helluva long day and night."

The connection went dead. Jameson stuffed the phone into his front jeans pocket, semi-pleased that he'd made an impression on Alex's grouchy secretary, if only because he'd called her Mom.

In seconds, Maddie was climbing in the other side door, then into his arms. "We made it," she cried. "I can't believe we're still alive."

Vlad grunted when Jameson closed an arm around her, then settled her onto his lap, where, oddly, it seemed like she'd always belonged. But that was just adrenaline talking. She was scared and reaching out for the only safe port in a storm, and he was lucky to be that port. At least that was what Jameson told himself. He couldn't be that kind of lucky, could he?

Yet even as he gave her a way out of the feelings he admittedly had for her, she snuggled under his chin and whispered, "You saved me."

His head dipped automatically into the top of her head and he buried his nose in her hair. "No, babe. You saved me."

When Mr. Vlad grunted again, Jameson had a feeling he could see too much.

But when Maddie lifted her chin, Jameson knew right where her mouth was and that her lips were so, so close... Too close. He couldn't resist, just shut his unseeing eyes and kissed her with all his heart. Adrenaline, maybe, but she needed this connection and, by hell, he did, too. He dipped her back into the crook of his arm and cupped her fragile jaw while he deepened the kiss.

Maddie opened wide, angling her head as she braced his jaw between both hands and licked her way inside his mouth. He should've held back, maybe held her back. But Jameson wanted this. He really liked this woman, and he wanted her to know it. Besides, the tiny moaning sounds coming from the back of her throat were turning him on. Right here. In front of Vlad.

That reality snapped Jameson back to his senses. A quick kiss was one thing. Going all out and all over Maddie, in front of an audience, was another. He growled as he ended the heated kiss, his heart pounding like a beast. Her kisses were powerful enough to make him think of things like a future and forever. Two things he'd shelved once his life had turned into counting steps and anticipating running into strangers, table edges, or curbs. His life was orderly because it had to be.

But Maddie... He squeezed his eyes shut, feeling like a hypocrite. Here he'd been telling her to believe in herself. Maybe he should take his own advice.

Her silky palm on his cheek brought Jameson out of his reverie. "Where'd you go?" she whispered.

"I'm still right here. Can't you feel me?"

"Yes, but…" Her fingertips smoothed up his jawline and into his hair, melting the last of his defenses. "For a minute there, it seemed like you were somewhere else."

Ahh, she was picking up on his cues awfully quick. See? Smart.

"I'm just tired," he lied. There'd be time for truth later when they were alone.

Her hand didn't move away as he expected. Instead, she cupped the back of his head and settled her cheek on his shoulder. "We're safe, Jameson. We're really safe."

Man, how he wanted to agree, but he whispered, "Shush," instead. The inner spidey senses that ran like tiny livewires through his nervous system were tingling. Telling him they weren't alone, and they weren't safe. Not yet. Someone was outside the perimeter of this monster vehicle. Too damned close.

"Babe, sit tight," he said as he leaned forward and grabbed one of the pistols he'd midnight requisitioned back at the farmhouse. "I'm just going to—"

Too late. Some asshat flung the rear limo door open.

Jameson aimed his weapon for a headshot. "Back off or you'll die," he ordered.

"Shit, man, is that any way to treat a buddy?"

"Adam? Thank God!" Jameson pointed his weapon at the ceiling and thumbed the safety.

"Yeah. Me, Hunter, and Eric been looking for you. Hunter's the one who finally spotted this limo."

The door on Jameson's left jerked open to a surly, "Jesus Christ, you two are a freakin' lot of trouble. You left one helluva mess back at the farm, Tenney."

Jameson was grinning by then. He didn't know who that guy was, but he sounded as good as Adam.

"One casualty," Jameson changed the subject. "Vlad Somebody. Haven't had a chance to get more information. He can't talk because of his—"

"Get that spotlight out of my eyes, Reynolds," Maddie ordered. "I'm not hurt and I'm not Vlad."

"Got him, Maddie," yet another deep, confident male voice replied. "Give me some room, Adam. Let me look at... Damn, who bandaged this guy?"

"She did," Jameson said at the same time Maddie said, "I had to. He was dying."

"Good job, Mad Dog," that same male operator, Reynolds, replied enthusiastically. "What'd you use for plugs in that bullet hole?"

"My bra," she answered, her tone gone timid again. Any other operator would've made those two words sound like a brag, but she made it sound like an apology. That had to change.

"Mad Dog, huh?" Jameson asked. "I like it. That's who you'll be from now on, Mad Dog Bannister."

"No!" she squealed, pushing farther away from him. But he could tell she was smiling, and that Reynolds guy knew how to talk to her. His praise made Maddie feel like one of the guys.

Jameson pulled her back into his side. "Come here, you. I hear Alex is on his way. First responders, too."

"No worries," Adam replied. "Eric Reynolds is former USMC medic. He'll take care of Vlad until they show."

"Here's something to snack on and four bottled waters." The man named Hunter passed the goods to Jameson and made sure he had a hold on them. "You need help with an IV drip, Eric?"

"That'd be good. Vlad's got a strong pulse, but he's dehydrated. Let's get one started. No telling how long the EMTs will take. This place isn't easy to get to."

While the three operators worked on Vlad, Jameson eased back into the seat, with Mad Dog settled against him, her back to his side. She leaned her head onto the arm he'd circled around her neck and shoulder. Her entire body expanded with a beautifully feminine sigh. And Jameson knew what he wanted, make that *who* he wanted, in the rest of his life. In his bed. Who cared that they'd only just met? He wanted the brave, timid kitten in his arms, the one whose purring echoed in his heart. She might be tiny, but her old man was dead damned wrong. She *was* fierce.

And Jameson was damned proud of her.

Chapter Fifteen

Alex landed precisely when and where he expected to. There was no humping through weeds and shrubbery for him. He fast-roped into the scene, then secured his gloves and gear while the rope disappeared into the dark overhead. He'd brought a collapsible stretcher with him, but didn't intend to use it unless the EMTs failed to show. Then he'd hike out with his men.

"Hey, Boss," Adam called out from the open limo door. "Eric has our man ready to travel. Jameson and Maddie are good to go, as well."

"Where are they?"

Adam nodded toward the dimly lit rear seat. "Inside rehydrating. Eating. Resting. Stuff like that. It's been a helluva first day at work for Jameson."

At the opposite limo door, Alex leaned in to look over the pair of grimy, weary employees, one sitting on his newly hired agent's lap. Maddie didn't seem inclined to move, and Jameson Tenney didn't seem inclined to let her go. And Alex was pretty sure Maddie was wearing Jameson's suit jacket.

Damn they looked cozy. He had one arm around her shoulder, his other hand rested on her knee. They were exhausted, their faces smudged with soot and sweat, and a hundred-mile stare in Jameson's eyes. His head was cocked as if he were listening. At least Maddie had the grace to smile sheepishly when she saw her boss.

"Junior Agent Tenney," Alex said as he offered his hand, which Jameson seemed to know right where to reach out and grab hold. The young man had a solid grip. He didn't look directly at Alex; just in the right direction. "I know who abducted you two. Already have Reagan's security footage. Lucy Shade's behind this, and she was working with Pops Delaney, whom you terminated back at the farmhouse. Fill me in. What don't I know?"

"Pleased to meet you, Mr. Stewart," Jameson said as he straightened on the seat. "This was a publicity stunt. Shade wanted it to look as if she'd escaped two kidnappers—us—who were supposed to burn to death when her jet exploded. She needed her escape caught on film, but something went wrong."

"It went damned right if you ask me," Adam growled. "You lived."

Jameson reached out for a knuckle bump, which Adam obliged. "Yeah, bro, no kidding. Don't know why, but Delaney didn't shoot us on the tarmac. Brought us out here to kill us."

"Reagan's a high-profile airport. Too many cameras. What else?" Alex demanded.

"Well, Mr. Stewart, when I came to, she and Pops were arguing. I'm pretty sure she slapped him. They were nasty to each other. When they stomped off, I knew we didn't have much time left. Maddie crawled through the ductwork, made it outside, and…" He turned into the side of her head, close enough to kiss her as he said, "I wasn't there, so I'll let her tell you what happened next."

Alex liked that willingness to share the spotlight.

Maddie cleared her throat and sat up straighter on Jameson's thighs, her fingers interlocked on her lap. Alex couldn't detect the hint of a blouse or TEAM polo beneath the jacket she wore. This was the craziest debrief he'd ever held.

"Boss, I, umm…" Lifting one hand, she coughed politely into her curled fingers. "I kind of changed Jameson's plan once I made it outside. I was just supposed to run and get help, but I had another idea when I saw Delaney's men's cars and all those tires and the barn and all that hay—"

"You set the fire."

Her head bobbed. "Not at first. I was going to, but that's when I found Mr. Vlad buried in the hay. He said Miss Shade shot him, and he was hurt pretty bad, and he was bleeding, but he couldn't breathe, so I kinda had to—"

"She fabricated the perfect bandage, Boss," Eric declared from where he was kneeling by the man in question. "Saved his life."

Alex look over at Vladimir, who had just given Maddie a weak thumbs-up with his IV-taped hand.

"Boss, this is Mr. Vlad," she said quietly. "I couldn't just leave him. I took a first-aid class a long time ago, and I remembered how to plug bullet holes and make bandages with whatever was on hand."

Man, she was nervous, and Alex knew it was because of him. She'd always been skittish. "Settle down, Maddie," he said calmly. "Take a breath. You did good. Might have to promote you to junior agent."

As expected, she shook her pretty blonde head. "No, no, no. This was the scariest night of my life. Well-l-l…" She looked to Jameson. "Almost."

"She didn't want to bother you, Mr. Stewart, but she's got a couple loan sharks pestering her," he volunteered. "That's why she's been late to work. Mind if I take care of them for her?"

"Jameson!" she hissed.

"Stop calling me Mr. Stewart, and we've got a deal."

"Yes, err, umm—"

"Boss or Alex," Hunter supplied the missing title. "Never sir. He'll roast your nuts over a slow flame for that."

"I want in on that loan shark action, Jameson," Adam said as he reached into the limo and cuffed Maddie's biceps gently. "Should have told me you were having trouble, Mad Dog. I like shark meat."

She almost smiled, but Alex could tell she hadn't wanted her dirty laundry outed. He'd talk with her in private about that loan shark. See what else he could do for her.

"Mad Dog, huh?" Alex lifted a brow. "How'd you come to have Miss Shade's limo?"

Maddie reminded him so much of Kelsey way back when. Timid, yet strong. Unskilled, yet willing to take on the monsters in her world. Afraid to ask for help, but obviously smitten with the young man holding onto her. Did Jameson Tenney have any idea what a treasure she was? Alex doubted it.

Her tongue made a quick pass over her bottom lip. "Well, Boss, it was parked in the barn, so first, I helped Mr. Vlad to his feet, and I drove him to a safe location, then—"

"After she punched holes in all Delaney's guys' tires," Jameson interjected.

"Well, yes, I thought that was smart, and then I ran back to burn the barn down. W-w-wow. That fire went so, so fast. It got big in a hurry."

"Old barns burn the hottest," Alex told her. "Dust and dry timber make an explosive combination."

"You're telling me," she breathed. "My pants were smoking. I almost didn't make it out of there alive."

Alex couldn't help it. He grinned. "You've had a busy night, Ms. Bannister."

"You have no idea. Once I got Mr. Vlad—"

"His name's Vladimir Morozov. He's an—"

"He's an undercover FBI agent?" Jameson asked, his head now canted to the opposite shoulder.

"Yes. He works in their psychic unit. How'd you know?"

"Jameson has mad ninja skills," Maddie declared, her pretty, light-blue eyes so wide with innocence and honest affection for the guy at her side, that it was hard to look at her and not see Kelsey. Had she ever looked so frightened, yet strong at the same time as Maddie did now? Absolutely.

"I can see that," Alex admitted quietly.

"Wait. The FBI really has a psychic unit?" Jameson asked, dumbfounded. "Since when?"

"Since a year ago," Alex admitted. "A couple of my agents now work in that unit. Listen, the EMTs are running late. How about we get Vladimir back to civilization? Looks like you two could use a hot meal and a couple days off."

Jameson shook his head. "Not me. I'm good, and I'll be at work tomorrow."

"You're a former SEAL," Alex told him sternly, "which means you're dumb as a box of rocks and you don't know when to quit. But you work for me now. Two days R&R. That's an order."

Junior Agent Tenney had the good sense to stand down. He looked pretty damned content there with Maddie on his lap and in his arms. She was smiling, and it was happening again. Two people in the right place at the wrong time. Fighting together to survive. Beating the odds. Falling head over heels into who knew what.

"How many bodies did you leave back at that farmhouse?" Alex asked Jameson.

The thing about this young man was he was hard to read. He didn't blink and his feelings didn't show, well, except for the tenderness that softened his lips whenever Maddie spoke.

"I'm not sure—"

"Twenty-three," Adam announced proudly.

Alex cocked his head. "You mean to tell me that Jameson took them out all by himself?"

Again, Jameson gave nothing away as he replied evenly, "I didn't realize there were so many. I knew I ended the first three who came for me, then the six after Maddie showed up. I had to. It was totally self-defense and I used deadly force to protect Maddie. Luckily, I acquired a high-capacity, twelve-gauge shotgun after the first go-round, so I was prepared. But I lost track of the body count after reinforcements arrived. There were too many, and, oh yeah, Maddie ended Delaney."

"Way to go, Mad Dog!" Hunter crowed.

"Damn fine shooting, lady," Eric added.

Adam's long arm reached in as he ruffled her hair. "That's my girl!"

But the news stopped Alex's heart. He turned to his meek, demure Protocol Officer. "*You* shot Pops Delaney? The godfather of all Irish gangs on the East Coast?"

Her blonde locks bobbed as she nodded, and he'd made her nervous again. "Y-y-yes, I…" Her fingers twisted in her lap. "He… His guys were big and ugly, and he was going to kill Jameson, and I… He made me mad, Boss." She ended that rambling, timid rant with a definite note of anger. "I couldn't miss. There were so many of them, and he acted like he was God, but he isn't! Err, wasn't."

Alex had to smile. The untouchable goon from Ireland had been brought down by a five-foot-nothing woman he'd pissed off. "Good job, Maddie. Sounds like Jameson finished what you started."

"Yeah. I guess." And she'd fallen back into whatever trap in her past that made her afraid to be the woman she was. Yup. Maddie was Kelsey all over again.

Something cold and sinister crept up the back of Alex's neck. "Where's Shade?"

"She wasn't onsite when we arrived at the farmhouse," Adam answered.

"Didn't see any sign she was ever there," Hunter added.

"Except for Vlad and her limo," Maddie breathed.

"How about you two?" Alex asked Maddie and Jameson. "Did either of you actually see her?" The instant the question rolled off his tongue, he knew better.

"Umm, Boss," Maddie piped up. "I never heard or saw her, but Jameson can't see and—"

"You know what I meant."

"I heard her though," Jameson answered. "Like I said, Miss Shade argued with Delaney about how it was his fault her plans went wrong. She slapped him. He slapped her back. They said a lot of hateful things to each other."

"Find her," Alex growled.

"Will do," Adam and Hunter answered at the same time.

"And you two…"

"Yes, Boss?" It was uncanny how Jameson Tenney could aim those unseeing eyes at Alex and look right through him.

"Forget the R&R. You're going into protective custody until we locate Shade. Eric, once you release Agent Morozov to the EMTs, get Maddie and Jameson to a safe house."

"Will do."

"But Boss…" Jameson protested.

Alex ended the discussion with a steely glare that, oddly, worked on Jameson as much as it did his sighted agents. "Shade's behind this, and I don't take chances. If all she wanted was publicity, she's damned sure going to get it. But if something else is going on here, I'd rather be safe than sorry."

Jameson's whole damned face lit up, like the sunrise creeping over the East horizon. Maddie's chin lifted. She'd changed. It was easy to see. The poor woman was in love.

"But no foolishness," Alex scolded.

"Who, me?" Jameson answered, the sly dog.

"We'd never. Promise, Boss," Maddie said more seriously. Just like Kelsey. So serious and no doubt as honest as Kelsey, too. Damn. Did she have any idea what she was getting herself into with a spec operator like Jameson? Probably not.

Alex turned on his heel, pissed that he couldn't control his agents, and just as pissed that, a few years back, his wife had looked at him the exact same way Maddie had just looked at

Jameson. That Kelsey still looked at him that way today. And he understood, he truly did. *Son of a bitch!* He'd even hugged Mother tonight, and he'd only done that because he'd recognized himself in her pain. Because that broken something inside of him was suddenly fixed, and it had to do with the little boy he'd been able to give Kelsey, and the little girl she'd given him. When the hell had he gotten so damned sensitive?

His world was changing. Alex just hadn't expected to change with it.

Chapter Sixteen

By the time Jameson hit the front steps of the safe house in Arlington, Virginia, he was dog-tired, without glasses or cane. It was nearly time to go to work—if he'd been allowed to. Which he wasn't. Maddie had stuck by his side, so he'd kept one hand on her shoulder as she'd led him inside to the kitchen, where she left him sitting on a stool at the breakfast bar. Then, she hurried down the hall and returned with his jacket on her fingertips. "I'll get this dry-cleaned for you, but I changed into a clean shirt and—"

He reached out and fumbled for the jacket. "No, you won't," he answered as he folded it over his arm. "I might never wash this thing. Why erase a perfectly good memory?"

"Ah… err… Omelet?" she asked amidst a clatter of pans and lids, an obvious attempt to change the subject.

He'd embarrassed her. He could tell. "You don't have to cook for me."

"If she doesn't, I will," a hearty voice said behind him, as an arm reached over his shoulder and grabbed his hand. "Harley Mortimer, at your service. Sorry I didn't make it to the scene tonight, Junior Agent Tenney. Had an emergency delivery. Couldn't get away."

That explained Maddie's sudden need to distance herself. She was back in Protocol Officer mode, but he was still in holding, kissing, I-want-to-know-you-a-whole-lot-better mode.

"Good to meet you," Jameson replied, shaking that callused hand and wondering why a covert operator would be making an emergency delivery. "Pizza or baby?"

Harley cuffed Jameson's back. "Ha, good one. No, I was the on-call vet for the emergency animal clinic in Arlington tonight. Spent an hour on my hands and knees, waiting for the last in a twelve pup litter. He was stuck. Had to take him by forceps."

"You're a veterinarian?"

"Was. This was my last night. Something had to give."

"It's about time," Eric said as he cleared the front entrance, then bolted a noisy series of locks. Jameson counted three. "Holding down two full-time jobs is stupid."

"Yeah, it was," Harley admitted, as he fell into the seat at Jameson's left. Stringent scents of disinfectant and soap drifted between them.

"Honestly, I loved what I was doing, but I missed my wife and my twin boys more. Judy's been patient, but I didn't want her raising the monsters alone. And no way was I quitting The TEAM. You need help, darlin'?"

"With omelets?" Maddie asked. "No, thank you. I'm sure I can handle breaking a few eggs. Eric, would you like breakfast?"

"Sure, thanks," he replied, his gear dropping to the floor. "Got something for you, Jameson. Hold out your hand."

A long collapsible cane bumped into his waiting palm. "You got me a new cane?"

"Harley picked it up when he bought groceries. Just figured you'd like knowing it was here."

"Thanks," Jameson told his benefactors.

"Adam tells me you're pretty good without it."

"When I have to be," he admitted. "But in unfamiliar places, it comes in handy. So you and Harley got stuck babysitting."

Eric offered a throaty chuckle. He had one of those no-holds-barred kind of voices that belied a love for life, as if he could throw back a cold one, then belly laugh with the best of them. "This'll be easy duty. Guarding a Navy SEAL. Pretty lady fixing breakfast. Doesn't sound like work to me."

"No triplets keeping you up at night, either," Harley added. He was the one who sounded tired.

"My girls never bother me," Eric purred, his voice mellow and tender. "Shea's got help with childcare, remember. Plus her mother's in town this week. Five women in my house. Figured they didn't need me hanging around, getting in their way."

"Those babies love their daddy," Maddie added wistfully. "I saw that look in your eye when Shea popped into the office with your birthday cake the other day. She and those triplets have you wrapped around their little fingers."

Eric plopped down at Jameson's right. "Yeah, well..." he grumbled in that quiet way of men who adored their wives and children. "What can I say? I'm a helluva lucky guy."

Jameson smiled to himself, content to be sitting among men who felt more like old friends than new acquaintances.

After a quick breakfast, Harley steered him through a tour of the safe house. "Once you about face from the kitchen, stick to your left, and you've got a clear shot past the sofa and chairs to the hall. Two rooms on each side, but the first on your right's the safe room. Had a couple houses explode a few years back. Had to install better protection. Here's how it works."

Harley led Jameson forward, then, as if he were dealing with one of his twin boys, he took Jameson's hand and placed it on a cool glass pad beside a doorjamb. "Mother's already got your palm print on record."

The door hissed open. Hmm. Pneumatic locks. "Is this a vault?"

"Yup. The entire room's secure, exactly like a bank vault. You've got trouble? You get inside. To close the door, just say 'shut'. It's a smart room and will lock you up safe where nothing can get at you, not even a tank. Plenty of food and water in there and a straight line to Alex. All you've got to do is sit tight until reinforcements arrive. And trust me, once we know a safe house is under attack, it's all hands onboard. The cavalry will be here within minutes."

"Independent air?" Jameson asked. This place was an amazing work of art.

"Yup, plus anything else you need. Bunk beds. Cold beer. Root beer. Decent food."

Maddie came to mind, but Jameson kept that delectable thought to himself.

Two doors down, Harley stopped at the room at the far end of the hall. "This is yours for the duration. Each room comes with its own bathroom and ventilation system, a laptop if you want one. There's a burner phone beside the laptop if you need it. I'm bushed. You need anything else?"

"If I do, I don't know it. Just a shower and a few hours of sleep would be great." *A certain woman's company wouldn't hurt, but you don't need to know that.*

A warm palm slapped his back. "Then you're in the right place. Sleep all day tomorrow, err, today if you can. We'll talk more once everyone's rested. I'm bushed. Later."

And that was that. Jameson cocked his head, listening for Maddie. But she and Eric were back in the kitchen, doing dishes and chatting. Which was the way this mission should end. Her, debriefing an experienced TEAM member. Him, going to bed, getting some well-deserved shut-eye, and minding his business. He took a deep breath and accepted the way this day was ending. Him. Alone. Again.

The bedroom was your basic square design, nothing tricky here. He spent a few minutes longer showering, thankful to get the smell of battle off his skin and out of his hair. But along with it went those lovely feminine hints of lavender and Maddie. She'd certainly been a nice surprise.

By the time he toweled dry and ran his fingers through his hair enough for a quick comb, it hit him. His first day on the job had worn him out. Feeling his way across the room, he found the desk, then the laptop, and right beside it, the phone. He rang home.

"Jameson? What's wrong? My goodness, it's only six am."

"I'm good, Mom," he led with to alleviate her perpetual worry for him. "Wow, it's that late, err, early? Sorry. I lost track of time."

"No, you're fine. I'm usually up by five, you know that. But something's going on. I can tell. What is it?"

"Nothing's wrong, Mom. I'm good. Well, except I have to miss dinner this Sunday, but for a good reason. I got that job."

"Wonderful! I know how much you wanted this one." His mom's smile radiated straight over the connection. "But

Dad'll be disappointed. We didn't realize you'd be working Sundays."

"I'm not, technically. Well, yeah, I guess I am, since I'm already on a mission. Maybe next week for sure." She'd understand that. As a SEAL, he'd been on many missions he couldn't talk about.

"Already? My goodness. Didn't you just interview yesterday morning?"

"I did, but Adam and Walker put in a good word for me, and my boss sent me right out on a job, but Mom..." There was so much Jameson couldn't say, so he told her what he could. "I met a girl."

Chapter Seventeen

Maddie watched Jameson's back as he disappeared down the hall with Harley. She couldn't help feeling disappointed. He hadn't looked her way or said good night or goodbye or... anything. Just walked away without a backward glance. Which made sense. He was the one who couldn't see, but he should've known she wanted one last word with him. Maybe a kiss. He could've at least turned in her direction and cocked his head in the way she was beginning to adore.

Although now that she'd spent time with Eric, cleaning the kitchen and storing the groceries Harley had been kind enough to bring, she understood. This was a job, not a hook-up, and they were all adults with their own, very separate lives. Jameson Tenney was former US Navy, a SEAL, one of the most elite special operators in the military. He'd seen and done things most civilians would never understand. He, Eric, and Harley had that whole band-of-brothers thing going on, something she'd never be a part of. She was just a civilian. A wannabe.

Eric had gone on and on about the effects of adrenaline on a person during combat, how it jazzed up a man's body and hormones, and turned him into a beast. How even for the best guys, that steady chemical overload still made the craziest emotions—like lust—feel more like love, when they were merely the after-effects of hyper-awareness, stress, worry, fear, and... yeah. Adrenaline. If his one-sided conversation wasn't an indirect warning to back off on the romance with Jameson, nothing was.

Swallowing her foolish yearnings, Maddie filled the dishwasher cup with liquid detergent, closed the appliance's door, and started the wash cycle. By then, Harley and Jameson were nowhere in sight, and Eric had just shut his bedroom door. He'd turned the security system on. The lights were muted, and the house was quiet, full of exhausted, sleeping men. And her. Wide awake. Darn it.

She walked to her room, the first on the left, opposite the safe room. Jameson's room was at the far end, between Harley's and Eric's. Where she definitely wasn't brave enough to go. Those darned guys had secured Jameson there intentionally. Not like it mattered. He was probably sound asleep by now. Probably so tired, he couldn't think straight. Might not have given her a second thought when his head hit the pillow. Alex only stocked these safe houses with the best, and that pillow beneath Jameson's head would be just the right kind of soft. Once he laid down...

OhGodOhGodOhGod. The last thing she should be thinking of was him on his back on that bed and her straddling his hips and...

No. Just no. He's a man, and you already know how men are. How many heartbreaks do you need before you get it? Men don't want real women. They want obedient daughters and slaves, someone to clean up behind them and do what they're told. Someone to sit adoringly at their side while they snore their brains out, fart, burp, expect dinner made and read,y and... Where was I going with this?

She paused, her fingertips on the knob that would open her door and put another layer of solid wood between Jameson and her. Wooden doors were good fire protection. She knew that. Every home should be built as safe as this one. But she couldn't take her eyes off the one at the end of the hall.

Most of her life, she'd been alone, first under the thumb of her self-absorbed father, then with her gambling addict husband. For those few months after she'd kicked Nash Coogan out, the loneliness had been a welcome relief from the merry-go-round of lies, lies, and more lies she'd been living with. That was when this TEAM Protocol Officer job came up. As scared as she'd been the day she'd marched into the interview with Senior Agent Mark Houston, she'd impressed him. He'd said so. He'd also been blunt about how difficult working with former military might be for a civilian who'd never served active duty.

But truth was, everyone on The TEAM, even the man she answered directly to and worked most closely with, Alex Stewart, had gone out of their way to welcome her. Because of his vote of confidence in her, she'd learned the ropes quickly. The TEAM became her one safe place where no one lied to her. Where no one talked behind her back or twisted the truth to suit their agendas, either. She was respected. She'd made friends. Camilla and Beckam even had her over for dinner one night. Alex and his wife included her on the invitation to join them at the hospital for their baby boy's birth. How unique and great was that? Being part of The TEAM was fun.

Yet here she was, alone again. Wondering. Working with Jameson tonight had built a fire inside she didn't want to lose. Its roaring flame had died down, but she'd banked those precious embers, hoping for closer contact. The taste of his mouth was still alive on her tongue. No matter what she ate or drank, the heat of his lips still burned, and the sting of his five o'clock shadow had left the nicest abrasions on her chin and around her mouth.

She could still feel his tense, ropey muscles around her when she closed her eyes. He'd left a mark where no one else could see it, where she still felt it. In her soul. Yet it needed fuel to survive, and that precious fuel lay down the hall, so close and yet so darned far away.

He'd called her brave today. And strong. Yet there she stood, trembling with cowardice born of years of being denigrated and scorned. Of never being good enough, smart enough, or, her all-time favorite put-down, *pretty enough*. But what if…?

Good grief. Her fingers lifted to her lips. What if she took those few steps to Jameson's door? What if she opened it and…. Was she brave or was she still her dad's lackey? Did her confidence depend on the man who'd thrown her out of his house before she was old enough to vote, or the man who simply wanted to take her out for coffee? A date. All Jameson asked for was a date.

What if, indeed…

Her heart beat with nervous excitement. Could she do this? Be brave and strong just a little while longer? After all she'd done tonight, could she walk those few steps down the hall and open that man's door? Go to him? Be with him?

The thought of intentionally defying TEAM rules went against all Maddie was. After what Alex had done for her, she hated to betray him. She wanted to serve, she did. But for once in her life, she also wanted something that was just hers. To take those few steps, she'd have to be wrong to be right. It'd be the biggest, most daring risk of her life to walk between Eric and Harley's doors, but—

That solid door between them opened, and…

OhGodOhGodOhGod. There he was, his head cocked, but facing her as if he knew right where she was standing and deliberating and chewing her fingernails. He'd changed into running pants, The TEAM logo stamped in bright gold on the cuff of one pant leg. But no shirt. His wet, tousled dark hair gleamed in the dim light from the kitchen behind her, making him look boyishly handsome even as his body declared he was all man.

"Maddie?" he whispered, his face turned in her direction, but his eyes seeing nothing.

Didn't matter. Her pulse raced at the sight of all that bare, masculine skin. "Jameson?"

He waved her to come to him, and she did. Quickly, without hesitation. Her doubts fled the second she reached his door, and he pulled her inside his room. So did all thought. The door closed noiselessly, and she was lost in the warm steel of his arms. He pressed her back to the wall as his mouth covered hers and swallowed her baseless worries and fears. They were chest to chest, belly to belly, and thigh to thigh. Both breathing hard.

For the first time in her life, Maddie was exactly what and where she wanted to be. Breathless. With every lick of his tongue, he fed the fire she'd kept sequestered for right darned now. Just for him.

Her fingers seemed to adore his body. Of their own volition, they smoothed eagerly over the sleek, sculpted muscles of his chest. She gasped in his mouth when all ten digits tingled at the dusting of crisp, coarse hairs on that rock-solid plane. Her thumbs searched for the flat nubs of his nipples, found and teased them until he shivered. Then, over the smooth rounded bulges of his shoulders, and onto those massive corded biceps. Jameson wasn't like Mark or Zack, all pumped and heavily-muscled. He was cut out of leaner, smoother granite that quivered under her touch. A mighty stallion full of eager energy. Right at her fingertips.

By the time her trembling fingers ended their exploration, those carefully banked embers were a roaring fire in her ears, and heat, not blood, pumped through her veins.

She moaned in his hot mouth. Just once. And Jameson took over.

One hand turned into a gentle bracelet around her wrist as he married her wrists together over her head. Holding her taut and still, he kissed his way over her lips and cheeks. Which wasn't very fair. He'd showered and changed and smelled delicious, but she'd only washed her hands before fixing omelets. For sure, her hair smelled of smoke and sweat, her underwear, too.

Yet with every heated breath over her skin, and with each sweet, tender kiss, he turned her from lowly wait staff into a princess. Maybe even a queen.

Silly, foolish tears stung her eyes when his free hand pulled her borrowed TEAM shirt out of her pants and began a slow exploration of her bare tummy. The tips of his fingers moved up her centerline to her breasts. The difference between this sleek, sure champion and the imposter at his fingertips grew too much. She was drowning in so many sweet, lovely sensations she'd never known before. This whole thing was a mistake.

Yet just as she was about to beg him to stop, Jameson breathed into her neck, "You have a habit of holding your breath when you're tense, did you know that?"

Her head bobbed even as tears spilled over.

"What's wrong?"

"I'm scared."

"Of me?"

"No. Of what I want you to do to me. With me." Even with her eyes closed she could feel him smile. "Don't laugh," she murmured, afraid to look at the man she knew couldn't see her. Yet Jameson had a way of seeing so much more than the sharpest TEAM operator.

The warm, wet heat from his lips moved up her neck to the curl of her ear where he whispered, "Let's take this party to my bed, so you can relax. I'd never hurt you. I hope you know that, babe."

There was that pretty word again. *Babe.* Maybe other guys meant it to objectify their women, but when Jameson said it, she felt protected and special. "I do."

"Whenever you want me to stop, tell me, Mad Dog. You're my best partner yet. We're in this together. Let's turn that frowny face upside down."

Okay, that made her smile. *Mad Dog?* How could she not grin at the ridiculous handle Adam had given her? *Frowny face? Really?*

"I've just..." She gulped, not sure what she needed to say next. She wasn't a virgin. Nash had fumbled that first in the dirty back room of a cheap bar one night. But this thing with Jameson...? He could hurt her worse than Nash or her dad ever had. Because, somehow over these last hours, he'd crawled under her skin and embedded himself in her heart.

She was such a sucker for nice guys, and that's precisely who he was.

Without waiting for her to finish her thought, Jameson let Maddie's wrists loose at the same time he slipped one arm under her knees, the other around her shoulders. "I know what you need," he said very quietly as he lifted her against him.

"What's that?" She tried to sound tougher than she was, but his body was warm and seductive. So big and so much broader than hers. He was a door. She was just a shadow behind that door.

"A good night's sleep. You're a morning person. I can tell."

"What I need is a shower," blurted out of her. She hooked one arm over his neck. But when he flinched, she cringed at her mistake. "Oh, no, I forgot. Your neck is burned. Let me see."

"I forgot you have mad doctor skills," he teased. "Shower, here we come."

"I shouldn't have told Alex you have mad ninja skills, huh?" She laid her cheek on his shoulder and rubbed her nose into his neck. Whatever he'd splashed on after he'd shaved, it was her new favorite scent.

He shrugged as he angled her through the bathroom door. "I'm pretty sure he's already heard that. As long as we're both a little crazy at something, I'm good. Come into my parlor, said the spider to the ladybug."

"It's supposed to be fly."

"But you're not a fly, are you? Flies swarm by the millions on dead animals and smelly stuff like manure. But ladybugs are bright and rare and precious. They protect things, like roses from aphids." He'd set her on the bathroom counter and under the light by then. His fingers were splayed on the sides of her head, the rough pads of his thumbs smoothing over her cheekbones. "You're precious and rare, Maddie, but I get the distinct impression no one's ever told you that before."

Jameson struck her stupid and mute. She was peering up at him. He was looking down at her, his gaze dark and not seeing, yet seeing inside of her nonetheless. Of course, no one had ever said something so sweet before. Dad wanted a slave and a son; Nash, a gofer.

"Your eyes are beautiful. They're brown, like coffee," she murmured, thrilled she could finally see that startling clear color up close. Brown, but nonresponsive to light. His black pupils didn't dilate. Didn't matter. She smoothed her palm, lovingly cupping his jaw, staring into that void. Sure that he knew she was looking at him. Into his soul. Somehow, Jameson had turned what others might've perceived as a debilitating handicap, into an asset and a skill. He was charming and kind and polite to a fault. Resourceful and confident. What more could any woman want?

"I see you," she told him breathlessly.

He pressed a moist kiss to her forehead and whispered, "I'd give a million bucks to be able to see you, Maddie Bannister. You're an unexpected bonus after a hard day's work." Another warm kiss melted over one eyelid as he breathed, "A breath of springtime in, what has been for me, a long, dark winter." He kissed her other eyelid. "I don't know what I would've done without you and your sight tonight."

By then, she was clinging to his wrists, both eyes closed and her nose working overtime. Ah, she loved the smell of this man's skin after a shower. Squeaky clean. Slightly spicy. All him.

"You're perfect, Maddie. Just the way you are. Right now. Right here," he breathed into her ear. "Tell me what you want."

"You," she whispered. "After..." Something. She'd forgotten what, but it was important.

"Okay then. First-aid, then shower, then me. Us. Sound good?"

Oh, yeah. His neck was burned, and she was going to take care of that. She nodded like a dolt, her brain offline, but every other atom in her body was humming and loving the magnetic connection with this gentle man.

Feeling his way across the room to the floor to ceiling cupboard between the counter and shower, he pulled a first-aid kit off the middle shelf and set it beside her thigh. "Might be some burn cream or gel in here. See what we've got, Mad Dog. I'm yours to command." He said that with a flourish and the same soft, sweet smile tweaking his lips, the same smile he'd used on her when she'd nearly run over him coming out of Mark's office this morning, err, yesterday morning.

"Good grief," she breathed. "I almost forgot what I was going to do."

They really were strangers. For now.

Chapter Eighteen

He licked his bottom lip when Maddie slipped off the counter and rifled through the first-aid supplies. She was worried. He could smell it. And still tense. But not afraid of him, more concerned about being with him and breaking TEAM rules. Well, too bad. Rules were made to be broken. Every SEAL knew that.

His blood was thrumming, had been since he'd sensed her standing alone in the hall, probably on her way to bed. Which struck him as damned good timing on his part. He'd purposefully waited until Harley and Eric had gone into their rooms and closed their doors before he'd ventured after Maddie. He'd felt herded tonight from the way Harley had gotten him out of the kitchen and away from her so quickly, leaving her with Eric. Jameson understood. These two guys were protective, and that was good. It was nice to know she had honest-to-goodness badassed warriors on her side. But she wasn't theirs to protect, was she?

Not anymore. He was here now, and so what if he'd only been here one day? He understood why Harley and Eric stood by Maddie. They'd just met, then gone through one helluva first operation together. But every warrior also knew how twenty-four hours in a firefight could comprise a year's worth of solid intel about the people fighting at your side. He and Maddie had clicked. He'd felt it the second she'd brushed her fingers over his shirt in Mark's office, back when she'd plowed into him and nearly knocked him on his ass.

The thought of their first encounter brought a smile to his face. Her. Knocking him on his ass. She'd done precisely that, hadn't she? And she didn't even know it. Probably didn't know she was beautiful, either.

"Ah ha. Found it," she muttered to herself.

The thing about Maddie was the way she filled his darkness. She glowed with the kind of light only a blind man could see. That otherworldly glow came from her innocence and her kindness. Her heart. Despite the losers in her life, she was still true to the sweet woman she was. Her old man and her ex might've hurt her feelings, but they hadn't irreparably damaged the woman she intrinsically was inside of herself. Maddie was better than either of those lowlifes.

Made Jameson wonder where her mother was, and if she'd ever known her. His mom had always been his anchor, through girlfriends who'd turned into Dear John letters, through dozens of deployments, and ultimately, through convalescence and acceptance. His mom had been his sounding board and his best advocate. Dad, too, though his ways were more philosophical than hands-on. But that was their magic. Where Karen Tenney went to bat at the slightest hint that someone dared cheat her son out of the care he deserved, Jules tended to stay out of Jameson's way and let him figure things out.

"Can you tip your head down so I can reach your neck better?" Maddie asked.

"Yes, ma'am. That far enough?" He would've stood on his head if she'd asked.

"Perfect," she answered, her breath cool on that burned flesh. Coo,l but warm at the same time. He shivered. This injury wasn't severe, more like a bad sunburn. But the woman nursing him was fast becoming his favorite addiction.

Spreading his knees, Jameson took possession of her hips. He angled her between his legs, which meant she had to lean over his shoulder to smooth what felt like cool Aloe Vera gel with lidocaine on the back of his neck. *Ahh, instant relief.* Also meant her slender body bumped every nerve between them. His already hard cock. His taut belly. His throbbing chest.

Closing his eyes, he breathed deeply, enjoying the scintillating scents that came with Maddie, as he tucked his thumbs into the creases between her abdomen and thighs. She was a soft handful, and his nose craved the scent of her. She thought she was dirty. Not yet. He intended to scrub this luscious body clean, then get her dirty again and again. Rinse. Repeat. Devour.

But she needed to hurry it up and stop teasing. Because every touch of her fingertips on his neck, and every soft sound coming out of her throat was turning him on. It was getting harder to hold back. He needed to imprint her and fill her in every sense of the word. He needed her to know she was his, if she'd have him. With his body, his manhood, his friggin' soul—the rest of his life.

It'd been so long since he'd had a woman beneath him, much less one as unique and delightful as Maddie. Once he started, would he be able to stop kissing, tasting, eating her?

Jameson wasn't sure.

"There," she breathed. Her breast brushed over his shoulder as she eased back, lighting him up yet more than he already was. Did she have any idea what she was doing to him?

Probably not.

"Shower?" he asked, his voice gone dangerously low and hoarse, every nerve strung tight. His body hard.

Maddie had leaned away and was looking down at him now. Holding back. Not breaking free from his hold, but not yet confident enough to admit to her feelings.

Jameson faced her, not seeing, but believing. If it took forever, he meant to hold this position until she took over and took what she wanted from him.

Use me, he pleaded mentally with the nervous woman between his hands. *Be brave. Be fierce. I can take it. So can you.*

"I, ahh…"

"You what, Maddie?" he asked quietly, not wanting to scare her. Men could be such pigs, but that was the last thing he wanted to be with her. She'd been used enough. Tonight was all about her.

Her body softened then. Relaxed enough that she bowed and wrapped her arms around his head. That put his nose between her breasts. Jameson started to shake. The harder he got, the harder it was to just sit there and wait.

"Join me?" she asked tentatively.

"Absolutely," he growled, lifting to his feet with her circled inside his arms.

With two long strides, he was inside the shower stall and set her on the marble bench that ran the length of the wall opposite the generous shower head. Adeptly, he turned both spigots to get the perfect temperature. The spray ended at her bare feet. Turning toward her, he bent over and pulled his pants off. Her breath hitched, and he was afraid he'd gone too far, too fast—or something. Until she murmured, "You're gorgeous. Are you sure you want to do this with someone like—?"

That did it. He pulled her up off the bench and into his arms. "Take your clothes off," he ordered with mock fierceness. "I want to do everything *with* you, not just with *someone like you*. Just you and me, babe." His own words made him laugh. "Did I just sound like a song from the seventies?"

"Yes," she breathed, her voice gone sultry and needy. "Undress me. I want you to do it this f-first time."

"Yes, ma'am," he growled as he made quick work of her pants zipper and her shirt. The lusty new perfume mingling with the steamy shower spray sent a riot of need up his spine. He peeled her out of her pants and shirt, but saved the panties for later, when he hoped he'd have more control.

By then, her hands were carefully exploring the muscles on his shoulders and back. But the soft, pert globes in his hands were gifts from heaven. They deserved exquisite care, to be tasted and tempted into diamond hard peaks, until she arched her sex into him and offered her all.

Kneeling at the feet of his goddess, Jameson took his time, breathing in the pheromone laden steam as he thumbed her nipples into hard tips. She writhed at his touch, rubbing one knee into the other. He knew what she needed. Breathing hard, he covered one lush breast with his mouth, then suckled, drawing her nipple in deep, making her tremble.

"Jameson," she hissed, her spine stiffened now. Beginning to bow. He didn't need to see to know she was close to exploding. And how sweet was that? With just his mouth, he'd brought her to the edge.

But not yet. Still nursing at her breast, he slid one hand down her belly and beneath her panties to the warm, slick heart of her. One finger. Then two. And he'd found paradise. Her panties fell to her feet.

She hissed, "Jameson… m-more."

"Yes, ma'am," he mumbled around her breast, going all out and all in. The fierce urgency in her tone nearly did him in, but he knew what to do. Curling his fingers, he pleasured that secret spot she probably didn't know she had.

Her fingernails dug into his shoulders. "I'm… I'm…"

"Then come," he breathed into the sweet, soft valley between her breasts. "Come for me, babe. I won't let you fall. Trust me. I'll never let you go. I'm here with you all the way."

With one last gasp, she flew, her head flung back and her body wound as tight as a spring. Up on her toes, she arched backward as her most intimate muscles squeezed the fuck out of his fingers.

Sweet Baby Jesus, he nearly came with her, and he wasn't even inside of her body yet. Not like he wanted to be, not if he would've found even one damned condom in this allegedly, totally equipped safehouse. Guess that was part of what made it safe, damn that conniving bastard Alex Stewart.

"Good grief," Maddie purred breathlessly as both of her feet settled back to earth.

Jameson detached his lips from her breast then, and turned his face up to her, blinking into the shower spray. "You okay?"

"You… you didn't," she breathed down on him.

He shook his head. "Tonight is about you, Maddie, not me." If only he could get his cock to stand down. The damned rowdy thing was making him a liar the way it jutted straight out, poking her for attention. There was no way to hide what his body wanted. She had eyes. She could see.

He lifted to his feet, blocking the view, but making everything worse. Now his randy cock was doing its usual happy dance all over her belly, ready to hump her like the horn dog that it—he—was. Err, that he *could* be. Like now, with this lush, ripe woman in his hands, pressed against his naked body.

"I'm safe," she whispered. "We can, you know. Do it again if you still want to."

"Still want to? Oh, hell yes, I want to do it with you all night." His head, his other head, canted nearly onto his shoulder. He should've asked before. "Does that mean you're on birth control?" *Please say yes.*

"There was no way I was going to have a baby with my ex. He's a pig."

And I'm a pig, too, but thank God! "Of course, I still want to, but are you positive this is what you want?" Jameson asked, needing her to be sure.

Her nose touched the tip of his as her breath whispered into his lips. "I want to do everything with you. Please don't stop now."

No way could he stop the Tenney train roaring up the tracks of his spine. But he had to slow it down, because tonight truly was all about Maddie. She deserved a faithful, loyal lover. He wanted that gentle man to be him, tonight and every night hereafter.

The fire dancing between them created a magic bubble where time slowed. Maybe even stopped. He had his hands all over her luscious ass and down the backs of her thighs as he lifted her off her feet and backed her into the corner of the stall, under the warm spray.

She seemed just as eager to get at him, and he let her. With her mouth, her fingers. Her body... God. It was happening... Her body clamped around him as she chased another release. The slow burn at the base of his spine turned into a raging bull at the sensation of her orgasm. A volcano that curled into... her.

He breached her soft, warm folds just as his hellbent body erupted. Into her. Into the whole damned universe. He was Adam, and she was Eve, and this was the beginning of a new kind of life without end. With Maddie. Only Maddie. He knew it then. This wasn't the last time. It was just the first of many more comings to come. He'd just met her, but he loved her.

Jameson bowed his forehead into her neck, panting as hard as the steam from a freight train, his legs shaking, but damned if he was ready to let her go. Not now. Never.

His dad had always told him that he'd know when he met the right woman. That all the others were just question marks in his book of life. That the real woman would be an exclamation point. And here she was, the exclamation point that felt more like a match that had been lit, bringing him life and light and love. Yet he didn't dare say the profound L word. There'd be plenty of time for that later. Because there would be hundreds and hundreds of laters. She was his, and, judging by the way she had just taken him into her body, he was hers.

Unmanly tears filled his eyes, and Jameson needed, wanted her to see the real him. Easing away from her neck, he faced her and told her, "I don't usually do this, but I'm crying, babe. I'm crying like a little kid in the best candy store ever."

Her breath hitched like he knew it would. "Oh, no. Did I hurt you?"

He had to smile at how she always assumed fault. "No, but you get me, and this is the first time any woman has ever seen me for who I am. I'm sightless, yet here you are, loving me." He hadn't meant for that word to pop out like it had.

But Maddie didn't deny it. Instead, she cupped his jaw and ran a thumb under his eyes. "I'm crying too. You've made me happy. It's almost like you really care about me."

"I do." He tilted his neck and his face down to where they were still connected. "I wouldn't be here if I didn't care one helluva lot about you."

"I think I…" She stalled.

"Say it, babe. It's me, remember? You can tell me anything."

Like the warrior she truly was beneath that timid shell, she squeezed him with all those wonderful feminine muscles, sending the last of his brainpower into the netherworld below his waist.

"I think I love you, Jameson Tenney," she said with sultry, sexy conviction. "I know it's too early, and we just met and, you probably have lots of girlfriends, but I—"

"Only one. You. Shut up and kiss me," he ordered around her silly, flapping lips. With every last beat of his heart, he delved into her warm, wet mouth, licking her into a silence that turned to moaning and groaning, until he took hold of the situation. They came together that time, both soaring with a hiss and a growl, then falling back to earth like the brightest, best Fourth of July fireworks ever.

Utterly spent and completely boneless, he took her down to the tiled shower floor with him while the water rained down over them. There was nothing more to hide, but there was something to say.

"I wish I were brave like you," he told her honestly.

That earned him an unladylike snort. "Me? I'm not brave."

"Yeah, you are. You had the balls to tell me you loved me. I wanted to, but I didn't want to scare you, so I didn't say it. But I'm telling you now. I love you, Maddie Bannister. Think I fell for you the second you charged through Mark's door and straight into my arms."

"That was just yesterday morning," she breathed, sitting on his lap, their legs spread straight in front of them, her toes pointing North, his pointing East.

He pulled her naked self against him, content to sit there and hold her until the warm water ran out. It was his turn to be brave, and maybe a little foolish. "Marry me."

She twisted on his lap. "Really?" Surprise and a hint of shock ruled her voice. "You want...? Are you sure you want...?"

"You," he breathed. "Yes, I'm sure. Never been more sure. I'm a SEAL, Maddie. I know what I want, and I go after what I want, and I want you. Not just for tonight or next week or the rest of the year. I want all of you. For the rest of my life."

He could tell she was shaking her head and looking down at herself, maybe wringing her hands. "Too soon?" he asked.

"No, just..." And now she was rubbing her face and slicking back her hair. The direction of her body had changed. She'd curled her long legs to the side. She was that scared little girl again, going back into her shell.

He backed off. "No worries. How about we date for as long as you want, then? We could actually take time to get to know each other. You could ask me questions. I'll tell you about Mom and Dad. You tell me whatever you want."

"It's just that… I've only been divorced seven months, two days, and thirteen hours."

"Wow, that long."

"Stop laughing at me."

"I'm not laughing at you, babe." Yet he was. Laughing inside. Enjoying the easy comradery he'd found with this woman. Today had to be the best day of his life.

She leaned into him with a sigh. "We just washed that burn gel off. Guess we'll have to do that again."

There, see? She did it again. Made him smile. Turned him down, yet still made him the happiest guy on earth.

Chapter Nineteen

Alex stopped short, not believing what he'd just seen. Kelsey was home, on her feet, and waiting on Mel when she should've been in bed, resting. What the hell was Mel doing here, at his kitchen table? Had that bastard just slapped Kelsey's ass?

"I'm home," Alex declared, shutting the garage door behind him more forcefully than he'd intended. "Why aren't you still in the hospital?" he asked his wife.

"I hate hospitals, you know that. Besides, Libby will be right back. She's spending the night, but her girls wanted to help too, so she ran to get them. I'll be fine. You'll see."

"Daddy!" Lexie squealed, her feet pounding a path straight into his open arms. "I got a grandpa, and he's right here!"

Well, isn't that just dandy...

Biting his tongue, Alex dropped to one knee and caught his fairy princess up in his arms. The scent of her baby shampoo was like crack. He took a deep breath of the luscious life and love and laughter that always surrounded his baby girl. There truly was nothing better for a tired old man to come home to than his family.

It was mid-morning. He'd stopped by the hospital to visit Kelsey, which was why he'd hurried home when he'd discovered she'd checked herself out. Kelsey shouldn't be on her feet so soon after a C-section, and she sure as hell shouldn't be waiting on Mel. Damn it. Alex had also missed another milestone in Lexie's life, the moment she'd met her new baby brother. No doubt Mel had the privilege of seeing what only Alex should've been privy to. He was dying to know how Lexie had reacted, and what she'd said, but he wasn't about to ask Kelsey. Not now. Not in front of—*him.*

But he'd also stopped to speak with Agent Morozov prior to his emergency surgery, about his dealings with Shade, damn it. Because of that urgent side trip, he now knew Shade had orchestrated Pops Delany's death.

Kelsey looked over her shoulder from the coffee maker, her exhaustion written loud and clear all over her pretty face. "Your father was waiting at the security gate when Libby drove up. Isn't that nice? He's tired, Alex."

Like I give a shit... There wasn't much Alex could say out loud that wouldn't frighten his daughter or discourage his wife, so he reined in the thunder rankling in his gut that seeing Mel sitting with his wife and child caused.

Crossing into the kitchen, he put one arm around his weary wife's shoulders and pressed a kiss to her temple. "Where's Bradley?" he asked. Then winced at how curt he sounded despite his best intentions.

Kelsey's brown eyes were wide with concern. "He's in our room. Don't worry, sweetheart. I've got the baby monitor right there on the table. I'll hear him if he makes a peep."

"That's not what I'm worried about. You know that."

"Um, your father and I were just sitting down for a cup of coffee. Would you like to join us?"

She already knew the answer, yet there was pleading in her tone, as if he'd interrupted something. Or maybe she just wanted him to sit down and be civil to the bastard who'd walked out on Abigail so long ago and who would do it again, this time to Kelsey and the little girl who thought he was her grandpa. Like hell. Alex wasn't about to let Mel hurt this family, too.

"No thanks," was the best he could offer. Mel had no business being here, acting like he belonged inside the Stewart family that Alex had built. He didn't. Never would. End of that fucked-up story.

And now Alex was cursing, not out loud, but still… Eager to make amends to his wife through his daughter, he turned his nose into Lexie's soft, sweet cheek and told his wife, "You never need to explain where the baby monitor is, sweetheart. You're Bradley's mom, the best mother in the world. But you need to be in bed." Then to Lexie he asked, "Want to go see your baby brother? Maybe put Mommy to bed with him?"

"Shhhhh, Daddy. He's sleeping," Lexie reminded him like a big sister would. "Baby boys need lots of sleep because they've got lots of growing up to do, but someday, Bradley's gonna be just like you."

"And me," Mel piped up.

Alex rolled his eyes, annoyed that Mel would butt into a private conversation between a father, who actually worshipped his children, and his only living daughter.

"Yes, I'll go with you two," Kelsey interrupted quickly. "Mel, please, help yourself to anything you want. Libby left an entire turkey dinner in the refrigerator. The microwave's over there. Warm up a plate. I'll be right back."

The bastard had the nerve to grin at Alex like he was the king of this house and Alex was just a lackey.

"Don't get too comfortable," he warned the cocky old fart at his table. *Because I'll be back too, and then you and me are going for a one-way ride...*

Briskly, Kelsey led Alex down the hall, past the saferoom where Lexie's toys lay strewn on the carpet. "Sweetheart, I thought I asked you to pick up your playroom?" Kelsey's brows lifted.

Alex set Lexie to her feet. She was a strong-willed little girl. She could handle whatever her mom was going to dish out. But when her pink cherub lips pinched into the cutest damned pout, Alex had to look away before he smiled or worse, laughed out loud. Her terrible twos had never manifested, but her fearsome threes were making up for that lost childhood phase.

"Uh uh, Mama," she said quite clearly as she crossed her arms over her chest. "I don't want to, and you can't make me."

"Are you sassing me?" Kelsey asked.

Alex wished Mel wasn't sitting back there with his feet up and listening. Probably laughing his ass off.

Lexie whined, "But I wanna go see Bradley with Daddy, and then I'll do my chores after I give him another kiss. Pleeeease?"

"No, sweetheart. You've had enough chances, but each time, you've ignored me. Please go sit in the time-out corner while me and Daddy have a talk." Chores and discipline were a hard rule with Kelsey. She was sure children were ruined if raised without structure and love. Real love, the hard kind, not the soft kind that turned children into demanding, entitled monsters who thought they deserved participation trophies for showing up.

"Mommy, no!" Alex's pride and joy stomped her little foot. "I promise I'll do my chores, but only after I get to kiss Baby Bradley again!"

The battle lines were drawn. Alex kept his mouth shut.

Kelsey cocked her head, pointing to the little navy-blue chair in the far corner of the high-tech safe room Alex had built for his family, which Lexie believed was her playroom. "Now, young lady," she said firmly and without a tinge of anger. "You know the rules."

"Awww…" Lexie cried, real tears this time, the little scoundrel. "Fine then, Mama. I'm going to pick up my toys."

"You're too late, sweetheart. I should only have to ask you once to be a good girl. Time-out. Move it." Again, Kelsey pointed to the corner.

With attitude, Lexie marched to the chair that was just her size, picked it up, and tossed it across the room at her mother. "I don't wanna follow no rules no more!"

There it was, Lexie's last full measure.

"Who do you think you are, young lady?" Kelsey asked quietly, as immoveable as the Rock of Gibraltar. That was the thing about her. She never raised her voice to her daughter, yet she never gave in, either.

For some reason that innocuous question floored Lexie. Her mouth dropped open. She came to a full stop where she stood. Those flashing eyes of hers scanned first Kelsey, then Alex. She blinked like she didn't know what just happened. Her entire countenance changed from naughty to incredibly sad. Her bottom lip quivered. With real anguish this time, she cried, "I Lexie, Mama. Don't you remember me? Did you forget? I Lexie!"

Alex looked up at the ceiling, trying hard not to laugh while his eyes brimmed with stinging tears of love. How could anyone forget his Lexie Rose?

"Chair," he told his daughter, the one who would be the death of him someday. God, she was a rascal. How could Kelsey resist this precocious little angel they'd created? So what if she came with horns? She was so damned cute.

"Okay, Daddy," she mumbled through her tears. "I'll be a good girl now."

If Kelsey hadn't been standing there, he knew damned well he'd have been on his knees hugging that sassy, smarty-pants. Worse, he'd have forgiven Lexie, helped her do her chore, maybe even have done it for her. They'd both be kissing Bradley by now, maybe enjoying a root beer float with the cute little bendy straws Lexie liked. But he wasn't, because Kelsey was the strong parent, not him. He was the slave. A total fool for the women he adored.

"We won't be long," Kelsey warned her daughter sternly. "If you have everything picked up by the time we get back, I have a surprise for you."

"Okay!" Lexie cried with gusto. Man, she could turn those tears on and off at the drop of a hat. Which made Alex an even bigger fool.

Two doors down, he entered his sanctuary with Kelsey one step ahead. "You should be in bed," he told her.

"I will as soon as Libby gets back. Promise."

The moment he closed their bedroom door, she spun on her heels. "Can't you see what's going on with your dad, Alex?"

"Other than he's lying to you, no. Mel's a con artist, sweetheart. He's only here because—"

"Because he's an old man, Alex. He's got nowhere else to go, and he's got dementia. Maybe Alzheimer's."

"He's what?"

Kelsey fell into Alex's arms, her fingertips softly patting his collarbones under his suit jacket. "He's nearly seventy-five, honey. He was much older than your mother when they married. I looked up their marriage certificate online when he told me that, because, well..." She shrugged. "I don't trust him any more than you do."

"But he slapped your ass. I saw him hit you." Any other guy would've already died for that. Why not good old Mel? Seemed fair.

She tossed her head as if that mortal sin were nothing, and over Alex's hands on her shoulders tumbled all that dark chocolate hair. There wasn't a part of his wife that Alex wasn't addicted to, and the glimmer off those dark brown tangles reminded him how he was wrapped around her little finger.

"Oh, for goodness sake. Old men do stuff like that all the time. It means nothing. They just forget who they're with, and sometimes, even what day it is. When somebody comes along who reminds them of someone else, like their wife or girlfriend or mother, they lose touch with reality, and sometimes, they behave inappropriately toward that person. He didn't mean anything when he grabbed my butt. Trust me. I've seen this kind of thing happen with some of the older guys who wander into Raymond's Place. He needs help, Alex. Our help. I can't just toss him into the street because you're still mad at him."

Raymond's Place was the home for runaway teenagers that Kelsey managed across the Potomac River in Washington, DC. Originally intended as a safe haven just for teenagers, she'd taken in more than a few homeless vets over the years. Quite a few of them worked for her now.

"Other old guys have slapped your butt? And you didn't tell me?" That needed to stop.

"Oh, for Pete's sake, knock it off. It means nothing. Especially not from elderly men who have nowhere to go and no one to watch out for them."

Her overly kind perspective of his old man set Alex back. "Are you sure he's sick?"

"I'm no doctor, but yes, sweetheart. Mel isn't the same person who left you and your mom. He might act tough, but I'll bet he's just a shadow of the man he used to be. The older he gets, the more help he'll need. McKenna said she'd stop by and give him a quick assessment this afternoon. There are ten signs that'll tell us what we need to know. She gave me the name of a geriatrician who'll see Mel today. I already made an appointment. It's at three o'clock. If you take him, I'll call McKenna and tell her there's no need to stop by."

"Today?" Well, damn. Alex lifted his fist to his lips, his course for the day already set in stone, plotted, and ruined. "I guess that means you want me to take Mel to see this doctor, this geriatrician."

Of course. Kelsey had just had a C-section. She should be in their bed, sleeping with that little boy she'd delivered yesterday moring, while Lexie hovered and fussed about. Not traipsing across town, dragging an ornery old cuss who might get handsy with her between here and there, to a doctor's appointment.

"I think he'll feel more comfortable with his son at his side instead of a woman he barely knows, don't you? I know you're tired, but this is important."

Damn it. Kelsey was formidable when she set her mind to any task. But talk about having the rug pulled out from under his feet. This was not how Alex saw this morning going. He'd been up the night before last with Kelsey, then all last night with his TEAM. He was tired, and now he was pissed. But never at Kelsey.

"Whisper and Smoke should be inside the house with you," he told his dearly beloved. They were his former Army EOD canines. His guard dogs. The beefy four-legged fellows that adored Kelsey and Lexie, would die for them. Would kill for them, too.

"I've already fed them. The boys are fine. Will you go with your dad?"

"Yes, sweetheart," Alex replied reluctantly, pressing his lips to the center of her forehead, behind which was a very intelligent brain. So much for reining in the thunder. He closed his eyes, his migraine starting up all over again. Usually, the moment he came through his garage door and into his kitchen, it backed off. But seeing Mel at the table had brought everything crashing back. And now this…

"Libby brought a complete turkey dinner over for us. She knows how much you like stuffing, gravy, and cranberries."

"So I heard."

"She made pecan and pumpkin pies, too," Kelsey wheedled.

Alex looked down into the deep brown eyes of the woman he adored. He prided himself on having very few weaknesses, but Kelsey was his greatest. So was pecan pie. "With whipped cream?"

"Whipped cream with nutmeg…" She said with plenty of sexual innuendo.

His stomach growled and his body hardened. "Breakfast first, then I might indulge."

Kelsey could read him like a book. "You can't indulge for two more months, sweetheart, but I'd let you have all the pie you want today."

"You will, huh?" God, he loved this woman. "I almost laughed out loud back there," he confessed. "That little girl of yours gets smarter every day. She's just like you."

"Uh uh. She's more like her dad."

"No, Kelsey. She's you all over again, and someday, she's going to bring some guy home, and I'm going to have to kick his ass."

"I can see the fight now," Kelsey breathed into the hollow of his neck. "Who do you think will win, Lexie or you?"

He had to laugh even as his mouth descended over Kelsey's. "I have a feeling I've already lost." And didn't that make him the winner?

Chapter Twenty

Maddie slipped out from under Jameson's arm, out of his room, and back into hers. She showered and dressed, combed her long hair out, and twisted it while it was still wet into a loose chignon. Morning was long gone, but these men would need food and she meant to serve. In the kitchen, she made a large pot of coffee, then decided they needed breakfast again instead of lunch. It was early afternoon, but she knew these guys. So, she whipped up a batch of easy bake cinnamon rolls and put them in the oven, then lined up two pounds of bacon on the side-by-side built-in griddles. She whipped up two dozen eggs and had everything smelling good and herself looking perfectly innocent and normal, by the time Harley yawned his way to the coffee pot.

"You're my kind of girl," he mumbled as he poured a cup, his sandy colored hair sticking out at every angle but smooth. "Mmmm, is that bacon? You sure know a way to a man's heart, darlin'."

Harley slipped into a Texas accent every so often. He'd served at Fort Hood after he'd joined the Army. Was a professional dog handler, then. But he raised Malinois and German Shepherds now, even trained them to be service dogs for other veterans. And he adored his wife, Judy. She brought their twin boys into the office whenever she came into Alexandria. Little A and Georgie, one redheaded like his mom, the other Harley's mini-me. Both had their dad's rangy build.

Watching him interact with his boys always teased the green-eyed monster inside Maddie. What would it have been like to have had a father like Harley? Or Alex or Mark or Eric or—sheesh, just about any TEAM male, for that matter? They were all so in love with their wives and children, and it showed. It was hard to be around them and not feel sorry for the parental love she'd missed in her own childhood. It wasn't their fault, so she shook that pleasant/unpleasant reminder off. But if she were ever to marry—

Not. Going. There.

The only one she avoided at TEAM HQ was Junior Agent Tripp McCain. Thank goodness he'd been assigned to the Seattle office and would finish training in Alexandria by the end of the month. The man was former Army, amber-eyed, blond with straight hair, and as handsome as the other guys. He was tall and big-boned, muscular in the way of Mark and Zack, and he had a way of commanding attention when he entered the room. But talk about cold and unfriendly. Maddie avoided him, hadn't any idea why Alex hired Tripp, or how the other agents could stand to speak with him. Yet they did. Which separated her as a civilian from those who'd served. The few times she'd spoken with Tripp, he'd stared at her as if she were an annoying fly buzzing too close for comfort. He didn't even have to wave her off to get her to leave. If anyone was a fly in the TEAM ointment, it was Tripp McCain.

Eric showed five minutes later, smelling of manly shower gel and deodorant with a whiff of fabric softener. Like her, he was wearing a clean TEAM polo over black jeans from the supplies stocked in each bedroom closet. She might not be an operator, but she was on the job, and she wanted him to know she took it seriously.

"You talk to Alex yet?" Eric asked Harley.

"Yup. Called him soon as I woke."

"You told him you're staying?"

"You bet." Harley lifted his cup and gulped a hearty swallow. "Figured he already suspected I might be leaving. Wanted to burst that bubble before he fired me."

"What are you guys talking about?" Maddie asked, her hands inside two protective mittens as she lifted the extra-large baking sheet out of the oven. "You're thinking of leaving us?" That would be just plain awful. Harley was the heart of the office. Everyone liked the good-natured jokester.

"No, ma'am, not The TEAM. Never. But I did tender my notice to the veterinarian I worked under. I loved what I was doing, and animals will always be part of who I am, but holding down two hard-charging jobs was burning me out. Missed my wife and kids. Was always running out on them, and something had to give. I sure as heck wasn't quitting the job I love best."

Eric's nose twitched. "Is that cinnamon I smell?"

"Cinnamon rolls," Maddie said, blushing at how he always made her feel like she belonged. "They're almost ready to eat. How many do you want?"

"All of them?" he teased, his dark brown eyes sparkling like a babbling brook of coffee.

"Hey, Porky, now hold on. That just ain't happening," Harley drawled. Of all the agents, he was the biggest kidder.

"I'll arm wrestle you for them."

"Pshaww, no way. You're a heavyweight, I'm just..." Harley yawned. "...about to whup your big, hairy butt. Step on up, wise guy." He was bouncing on his feet on one side of the breakfast bar by then, his elbow planted on the counter and fluttering his fingers, egging Eric on. "Come on, don't be scared. You want all them cinnamon rolls, you're gonna have to go through me. Let's see what you got."

"Guys, stop." Maddie giggled. "No fighting in my kitchen. 'Sides, they're my cinnamon rolls, and I get to decide who gets one. So sit down and be quiet. Jameson is still sleeping."

Harley's brows lifted. "Just one?" he asked as if that were cruel and inhumane punishment.

Ah, she loved all these guys. But mostly, the comatose man down the hall, the one who'd been sound asleep on his belly when she'd left his room.

Eric's cell beeped a cheery tune. He turned into the open area between the kitchen and hallway and settled onto one of the extra-large recliners that bracketed the leather sofa. "Hey, Shea. How's things at home?"

Maddie tried not to eavesdrop, but she couldn't help picking up the word Alzheimer's in the conversation between Eric and his wife. None of her business. She set the warming trays on the bar, then placed the platters of scrambled eggs, bacon, and cinnamon rolls on the trays. She'd already set out plates and utensils. The men could serve themselves.

Harley's cell chimed next, and there was Maddie, in the same room as two very capable covert agents and, as always, still alone and not quite belonging. Slicing three mega-rolls out of the twelve, she stashed them in the microwave for Jameson, where hopefully, no one else would find them.

She quelled the urge to sneak back into his room and snuggle back under the covers with him. But what if what happened in his bedroom was just one of those crazy things like Eric said happened after intense combat or life and death situations? She'd die of embarrassment if Jameson didn't want anything to do with her today. Office romances were the ultimate mistakes only losers made, and she'd made everything worse by sleeping with a man she'd just met. What was she thinking?

Determined not to fall head over heels for the man she was pretty sure she'd already fallen for, she took a petite serving of scrambled eggs and one tiny slice of bacon. Worried what everyone might think now, she left the sweet, spicy smelling cinnamon rolls for the men. Her father had always berated her for her love of chocolates and sweet rolls, so she'd avoided them with a stoicism born from too many snarky putdowns.

But then she thought of what Jameson had said. *I wish I were brave like you. Your dad wasn't right, he was dead damned wrong.*

"Am I brave?" she asked herself quietly, as she moved those fluffy eggs around her plate. "I was yesterday, kind of. And last night. Why shouldn't I eat a cinnamon roll, too? I made them."

"So take one," a husky male voice breathed into the crook of her neck, sending shivers up her back and over her shoulders.

"Jameson!" she nearly squealed as her arm reached up and circled his head, holding him in that warm, ticklish spot. He wasn't avoiding her after all.

"Take two if you want them, babe," he whispered huskily. "Life is short. Fill it with gooey cinnamon rolls and sweet lemonade and every damned delicious thing you want. Eat up, Maddie. Live now."

She couldn't restrain her whole body from reacting on impulse. Spinning around on her stool, she pulled him into a hug that ended in a kiss she didn't care if the whole world saw. Jameson Tenney loved her, and she loved him, and damn it, she was eating a cinnamon roll. The whole thing. Then she was dragging Jameson back to her room and eating the best dessert. Him.

"I saved some for you," she told him between panting breaths.

"Already got what I want," he murmured into her mouth, his arms around her shoulders. Which told her he wasn't afraid if the whole world knew that he loved her, either.

"Umm, guys," Agent-in-Charge Eric Reynolds growled from the other room. "When the hell did this happen?"

For once, Maddie wanted to laugh and sing and dance, maybe scream. Okay, so he'd caught her kissing a TEAM agent. So what? She was so happy she could cry. "Yesterday. Last night." She didn't dare tell him she'd been with Jameson since early this morning.

By then, Jameson had turned their bodies to face Eric. "It was a really, really loooong day," he added without a hint of remorse.

"Don't you believe in love at first sight, Eric?" Maddie added.

"Well, yeah," he answered slowly. "Just…" He ran a hand over his head, ruffling his dark brown hair. "You two just met. One day. Don't you want to—?"

"Slow down? Take it easy? No, Eric, I don't," Jameson replied evenly. "Been looking for this woman for too many years already. She's mine. I won her fair and square. You can't have her."

Maddie giggled. He made it sound as if she were a prize. The honest, open affection in every breath and touch of his filled her like warm water filling a bubble bath. More than anything, she wanted to slide under the bubbles and get lost in this man.

"I'm married, smart ass," Eric shot back. "That's not what I meant."

A silly tear sparkled at the corner of her eye, but she dashed it away before Eric saw that, too. Maybe this was too soon. She'd be a fool not to admit that. But Jameson did something to her, and she liked it, needed it. He filled her up, not only with his body, but with confidence she never knew she had. He was everything she'd been missing in her life, and she *was* brave, darn it. Brave enough to break out of the mold she'd been squeezed into as a little girl, and to just be her.

"Hate to break this party up," Harley interrupted. "But I talked with Alex earlier, and you guys need to know that Taylor and Maverick found Lucy Shade, even spoke to her."

Jameson was facing Harley by then. "I assume those are two more agents. Where'd they find her?"

"Yes. Taylor Armstrong and Maverick Carson. Boston."

Jameson cocked his head. "Former USMC General Michael Armstrong's son?"

"One and the same."

"My God. Lucy Shade is Pops Delaney's daughter, isn't she?" Jameson breathed. "Tell me I'm wrong."

"I have no idea how you know that," Harley muttered, "but you're spot on."

"Because it makes sense. She used a word on him when they were fighting in the farmhouse," Jameson replied. "*Feck. She said, 'So was Vlad, my feckin' bodyguard.'* He didn't catch it, but it struck me as an odd curse word for an American woman, which at least means she comes from strong Irish roots. That must be why she didn't take my weapon when we were abducted. She wanted me to take out Delaney. Tell me I'm wrong."

"Mr. Vlad," Maddie whispered. "He must've found out who she was. That's why she shot him."

"Right," Harley replied. "Alex also spoke with Agent Morozov last night, or rather, early this morning, before he went into surgery. According to Vladimir, Shade went into this charade with the sole purpose to destroy her old man. She'd convinced Pops this was all a publicity stunt, while she'd already paid several of his men to betray him and plant the bomb aboard her jet. Once you two were dead, they would've turned on him and killed him. Made it look like you all died in the fire. Everything she did was to that end."

"So the media circus she held last night was what, a smokescreen?" Eric asked.

"More like her attempt to spin what actually happened to her advantage."

"Tell her to bring it on," Jameson declared angrily, his chin up. "I'm not afraid of that snake."

"You might want to think twice about that," Harley cautioned. "According to Taylor and Maverick, she's already taken over Pops' business in Boston. Also made it clear she's gunning for you, darlin'."

"Me?" Maddie squeaked. "Why me? I'm not even an agent."

"Yes, but you killed her old man."

"How would she know that?"

Jameson kept Maddie sheltered under his arm. "I have a feeling Shade knows everything that went down inside that farmhouse."

"Right again. Cameras were hidden everywhere, even in the basement," Eric confirmed.

"B-b-ut... but..." Maddie stuttered. "But if she wanted to kill her dad, and now he's dead, why's she still coming after me?"

"Because now that she's taken over his empire, she has to act the part of the bereaved daughter. If she wants to be the boss, she needs to make a strong statement to her competition and her allies. Looks like she wants an eye for an eye," Jameson explained patiently.

"It's 101 mobster mentality," Harley added. "Weak kingpins don't rule. Ruthless, cold-blooded killers do. Terror and decisive revenge are all other mob bosses will respect."

"But won't she go to jail for m-murder?" Maddie asked, the fear in her voice ratcheting higher, making her voice squeaky.

"Not if she's already taken over her father's mob unchallenged," Jameson said. "She would've ordered one of his boys to do the hit."

"To prove his allegiance to her," Eric added darkly.

"Then have that guy snuffed. There'd be no trail leading back to her. That's what gangsters do," Harley said.

"Because now..." Maddie breathed, "they're her boys." Things just kept going from bad to worse.

Jameson's arm snaked tighter around her waist. "There's no way she can get to us here, right, Eric? Harley?"

"Never," Eric declared. He'd taken the ultimate alpha stance, boots planted wide apart and his hands on his hips. "There've been a couple breached safe houses in the past, but Alex stepped up his design. Even if Shade shows up in an Abrams tank, there's no way she'd get inside."

"There's more," Harley growled. "Someone tried to kill Agent Morozov after he came out of recovery this morning and was transferred into a private room. Mark was there. He got a shot off, but the shooter got away."

"Good grief! Is Vlad okay?" Maddie asked.

"He's fine. He told Mark that Shade had him take a wrapped gift into the back room of her jet before you guys arrived at the airport last night. He believes now it was the bomb that nearly killed you two. Trust me, Mark's no dummy. He and Hunter expected the mob would come after Morozov. They were ready."

"And now the mob's coming after me. Wow, this is right out of *'The Godfather'* movies," Maddie murmured. "You guys ever watch them? Don't mobs always get their m-m-man? Or woman?"

"Not this time," Jameson replied, each word a promise spoken against her temple.

There was nothing more to say. She, Maddie Bannister, had gone from being an ordinary protocol officer for the best boss on the East Coast, to a mob boss's target, in just one day. What was next, a bloody horse head in her bed?

"Guys, I think Maddie would feel better with her own holster and pistol. Do you have any extras?" Jameson asked.

"I should've thought of that," Harley replied. "You betcha. One SIG Sauer nine-mil, coming right up, darlin'.

Would you prefer a double shoulder or a belt holster? Maybe a single that loops under your arm?"

"A single," she said, then added, "I think. Never owned one before."

He'd walked to the weapons cabinet across the room and pulled a lightweight nylon holster out. "Try this on for size. How's it fit? Don't want it tight. It's got to feel comfortable if you're going to wear it all day. Here's a pistol that'll fit it."

She adjusted the holster strap under her arm as he handed the pistol over, grip first. The weapon felt cold but solid and comfortable in her palm. "This is a nine-mil? I thought it'd be a lot heavier."

"It feels good then?"

"Better than the one I stole last night. It was too small. Hurt my hand when I fired it."

"You ever had hunter-safety training? Ever shoot before?"

"Yes," she admitted. "I always go to the range with the guys when they certify. I might not be an agent, but I'm finally hitting most of my targets."

"You're kidding?" Jameson muttered. "I thought you were a professional markswoman the way you took out Pops with just one shot."

Her mouth stretched into an automatic grimace. "Uh uh. That was my first time shooting a p-p-person."

"Talk about beginner's luck," he breathed, combing a hand over his head. "You sure had me fooled."

"Ember's admin staff, too, Maddie, but she's also queen of the range," Eric added, then turned to Jameson and explained, "She's former Navy and an excellent shot, also runs TEAM certifications at the local gun range. You miss your targets, she'll be all over your ass."

"Good to know," Jameson replied.

"You're looking real good, Bannister," Harley said with a lopsided grin, a funny sparkle in his hazel eyes as if he was proud of her.

"Thanks. I think."

"It's loaded, darlin'. Never touch the trigger unless you're ready to kill someone and always watch your backstop. Don't fire into crowds like those idiots do on TV and in movies. Those are fairytales; shooting a weapon is real. It's about life and death. If you're not in danger of dying, you've got no reason to unholster your piece."

"Best time to kill is never," Jameson added quietly. "That's something you can't take back."

Maddie crossed the room to him, shaking from the responsibility weighing in the holster under her left arm. Like she'd told Jameson before, this was all her fault. Maybe those loan sharks weren't after her, but she'd brought the wrath of Lucy Delaney down on these guys, and they were her friends. It would kill her if anything happened to them.

Sitting, she leaned into Jameson's side and let him wrap his arms around her shoulders.

"I'm here, babe," he whispered in her hair. "Breathe. Just breathe."

Maddie wished she could, but Lucy Delaney had singled her out. That distinction alone was mind-numbing. Lucy had put her own father in a deadly situation that had cost his life. Now, she was coming after Maddie. Icy fingers whispered over the back of her neck at the thought that a vicious crime boss—err, godmother?—knew her name. There had to be something she could do.

Chapter Twenty-One

Alex couldn't believe it. Didn't want to. But Kelsey was right, and Dr. Denton had just confirmed everything she'd said. Mel really was sick. Not sick, as in about to die sick, but sickly enough he couldn't live on his own from now on. He definitely had Alzheimer's.

And now Alex knew more about the insidious disease than he'd ever expected he'd need to know. As in how it interrupted the communication process in a person's brain by killing the neurons, thus destroying the delicate synapsis where messages were passed between the brain to the nerves that controlled its victims' bodies and minds. It was Mother Nature's ultimate hacker, a devilish worm bent on reducing even the brightest, most capable men and women, into blithering, forgetful vegetables. There was no cure, only meds that delayed the inevitable.

Mel's memory was shot. He hadn't been able to solve the simplest problems that Dr. Denton posed. Could barely tie his shoes. It was then that Alex noticed the grimy button-up shirt he wore was buttoned wrong. He kept asking when Sissy was going to have her baby. Alex stopped correcting him after the third time. There was no sense getting mad anymore. Mel wouldn't remember that, either.

He'd already forgotten Lexie, which broke Alex's heart in a way he couldn't explain and didn't want to analyze. Yes, Mel had cataracts, and he'd always had poor judgement, but that didn't explain why he struggled to sit upright once he'd climbed onto the exam table. He wasn't drunk. Doc Denton explained then how Alzheimer's also caused problems with a person's spatial relationships, as in how far the floor beneath Mel really was and how near the wall that he kept leaning toward for support, wasn't.

Denton put a firm hand on Mel's shoulder to keep him from falling off the table. Which caused an unlikely acid dump in Alex's gut. He should've been the one to reach for his father. Like the never-ending mantra stuck inside his head, he should've been there.

But son of a bitch. His old man really was sick. He'd have to live with Alex, Kelsey, and their kids. He'd be part of their immediate family from now on, not how Alex saw their golden years going. Not that he and Kelsey were in their golden years, but he had dreams, damn it. He'd planned for a brighter future than nursing his old man. They were supposed to travel. He'd always wanted to show Kelsey the world.

But worse…? Alex had thrown this old fart out of his life and into the street just a day ago. Had never wanted to see him again. Still didn't. His heart hadn't changed, not one whit, not where Mel was concerned. But because of Patrick Bradley Stewart? More because Alex had always strived to follow in Gramps' footsteps, he wouldn't dishonor the kindly gentleman's memory now by turning his only son away. Who knew? Maybe Alex would come to like Mel someday. Yeah, that wasn't going to happen. He might've gotten a little sensitive lately, but he wasn't an idiot. Neither was he that forgiving.

"How do you explain his knowing how to locate me after all these years? My landline's not listed, and I never told him about my TEAM." *Or my wife or my life.*

Dr. Denton wore compassion well. "Alzheimer's moments of clarity will prove the most challenging. Your father is clearly in the middle stage of the disease. He knows something's wrong. He may even get combative at the slightest conversation or comment. Sometimes, he'll remember important details, like how to find his only son or tie his shoes. Other times, he won't have a clue who you are or where he is. Eventually, he'll forget everyone who's important to him."

"That's a damned short list," Alex grumbled. Mel had long forgotten the people who'd been most important, but Alex doubted Mel would ever forget himself. His failing memory might explain why he'd called Kelsey Sissy, though. Might also explain why he'd claimed he'd been a SEAL. Or it might not. That was the nightmare when dealing with a habitual liar and a con. How did one know when to believe them? Guess when Alzheimer's moved in.

While Alex talked with Doc Denton, Mel sat on the end of that table looking around the exam room and kicking his feet like a five-year-old waiting for a treat just because he was in a doctor's office. His illness explained his ratty clothes and broken-down shoes. The fact that he hadn't showered recently. Or shaved regularly. Or used a toothbrush.

The steady flood of geriatric knowledge now slapping Alex in the face, and all that it meant for his future, curdled his blood. Because of Mel, everything had changed in the wink of an old man's wandering eye. From now on, Alex would be the go-to guy for Mel's care. He sure as hell wasn't going to saddle Kelsey with it. That meant his father's feeding, bathing, and God, more intimate personal care than Alex wanted to think about, would be his responsibility now. He'd be the father; Mel would be the child. *Son of a bitch. What an ugly kid.*

"I'll mail you and your wife a list of homecare businesses that are reasonably priced," Denton continued quietly. "When things deteriorate, and they will, you'll have to move him into a nursing home. I'd advise you to start looking for one now. There are waiting lists. He's a big guy, and there's no way to know how fast this disease will progress. He could wake up one morning and unintentionally hurt your wife or children. I don't recommend you take that chance."

"I won't." Alex's cheeks ballooned with a measured exhalation, half of him pissed that his dad had shown up only when he'd needed something, the other half pissed he'd never given so much as a thin dime to Gramps after he'd dumped Alex on him, then disappeared from everyone's life.

All right then. Plan B. Clear a temporary bedroom. Set another place at the table. Get Mel a decent set of new clothes, shoes, and a shaving kit. Set him up with a live-in nurse. Figure things out from there.

"There are medications that may help you regain some of your memory," Doc Denton told Mel.

Of course, Mel, who knew absolutely nothing about everything, waved that smart suggestion off. "Don't use drugs. Never have. Not going to start now."

If true, that at least, was good to know. But he would take whatever medication Denton prescribed. Alex would make damned sure of that.

"It would be smart if you discussed this life change with your lawyer, Alex. Take care of what details you can, now. Powers of attorney. Living wills. Trusts and estates. Probate issues."

Alex grunted. "That'll be easy. He doesn't own anything."

"Yes, I do!" Mel declared, his chest stuck out again, like the braggart he was.

Again... there was no sense debating with a fool.

"Please stay in touch, Alex," Denton said with a distinct undertone of sadness. "I know how hard this is going to be for you. My wife's mother suffered with Alzheimer's for years. Don't be afraid to ask for help when life gets too tough. There are plenty of good resources for patients and caregivers. I'd like to see him next week if that'll work for both of you. Make an appointment at the front desk on your way out."

For years? Alex ran a hand over his head, the sudden yoke of caretaker for his elderly, belligerent father heavier than he'd expected. Guess that was part of the figuring-things-out stage. Which, until today, was something he'd always been good at. Making quick adjustments at the last moment. Plotting a sure azimuth in wicked, stormy weather. Only the monumental task before him now, felt more like a son of a bitchin' category four hurricane than just a simple change of direction.

"You bet," he replied with a sigh. "Come on, Mel. Let's go."

"Why, sure!" Mel exclaimed, as Denton helped him down off the table. "See ya later, asshole."

"Next week," Denton replied calmly.

"Thanks, Doc," Alex said as he shook the patient, understanding guy's hand. "Sorry about my dad—"

"Call me," Denton interrupted sternly. "Don't think you have to go through this alone. It's going to get harder. Reach out. I will always be here to help you and your family."

"Thanks. I will."

At the front desk, Alex made the next appointment while Mel flirted with some young thing in the waiting area, like the old letch he was. The ride back to Kelsey was quiet. Alex had a lot on his mind. He still had to deal with Mother's demand to be made partner, and he'd soon be losing Ember to a couple months of maternity leave. She wouldn't be there to provide solid technical support. Beau Villanueva had proven to be a top-notch techie, but he didn't mix well with Mother. Like that was a surprise. Beau didn't appreciate being bossed, and bossing was what she did best.

The op with Jameson Tenney and Maddie had ended with them being secured at a nearby safe house. But Lucy Delaney—God, he hated that name—was still out there somewhere. She'd disappeared after Taylor and Maverick had tracked her down and confronted her. He'd sicced whatever TEAM agents were available on finding her, but so far, no luck. Eric had already phoned in a timely Sit Rep. All things at the safehouse were good. That, at least, was something.

Best news was Harley's earlier call to say he'd officially quit his veterinarian job as of last night, and he was staying with The TEAM. The possibility of him leaving for greener pastures had worried Alex for months, had also contributed to his daily migraines. Losing Harley would've hurt like a son of a bitch. The TEAM was great in that it had created a family out of some of America's best, sometimes most-wounded, warriors. But losing any member of that tightly knit family sucked. Harley wasn't just an employee, he was a friend. And Alex needed every last one of the friends he had left.

"Let me out up ahead, shithead," Mel grumbled, pointing somewhere off to his right. "By that there store over there. The one with red and green stripes."

"Why? Are you hungry?"

"None of your business. I don't butt into yours. Stay outta mine."

There was no sense arguing with a man whose mind was slowly being eaten away. "Kelsey's waiting for you," Alex reminded his father, striving to be gentle.

"She is? You think Sissy's there by now, too?"

Not that again. "Maybe," Alex breathed as he maneuvered his vehicle through the entrance leading to the gated community where he'd built his version of a stone castle for his queen.

"Well, giddy-up, then. What's taking you so long. Move it, you damn dummy!"

Alex bowed his head, once again back in time, being treated like shit by a man who'd never taken a breath without poisoning it with put-downs and name-calling. "No cursing in front of my wife and kids, Dad. You're the one who needs help, not us."

Mel had gotten hold of an extra fast food napkin from the console. He was doing one of those middle-stage tells, shredding the napkin without knowing what he was doing. And Doc Denton had said this stage could last years? *God, help me.*

Alex felt as if he'd been sucked into an oozing tar pit from which there was no escape.

"Yeah, well, I don't need nuthin' from you, not from anyone," Mel groused. "Let me out. By that there store over there. See it? The one with red and green stripes."

The only thing within range that resembled anything close to a fast food store was the guard shack straight ahead.

"Kelsey's waiting for you," Alex reminded his father again.

"She is? You think Sissy's there by now, too?"

"Maybe," Alex answered, certain he'd just entered the seventh level of Dante's Hell.

"Well, giddy-up, then. What's taking you so long? Move it, you damn dummy!"

God, help me to not kill him before we get home. Or after. Or ever. God, just please help me, damn it.

Chapter Twenty-Two

Jameson heard the stealthy footfall outside the safe house a split second before Eric's cell rang. Jameson was in the corner of the couch under the window opposite the intruder. Until that cell interrupted, he'd been discussing what happened the previous night with Eric and Harley, as well as what supplies came with the safe house. Sounded like Alex had thought of everything. Except how to make Maddie believe in herself.

She'd excused herself from the conversation, said she was tired, and had gone back to bed. He didn't blame her. Yesterday had been a son of a gun. As brave and ferocious as she'd been last night, she'd reverted to her timid, self-effacing alter ego today.

"Guys," he breathed, pointing to direct their attention. "Someone's out there. North side. Six feet to the left of that window—"

"Already got eyes on him. Single male. Can't be more than twenty-years-old. Checking the meter," Harley murmured from the same location. "There's another kid across the street. They're going from house to house. No problem."

"You've got eyes on him?"

"I do. Windows are lined with UV blocking solar tint. I can see out; he can't see in. His company's mini-truck's parked on the curb."

"Relax," Eric assured. "All windows are bulletproof, and the walls are lined with reinforced steel. Besides, no one knows where we are."

Jameson's sixth sense flared. That prickly feeling he was missing something persisted. "Something's still not right," he growled as he pushed off the couch, moving quickly to Maddie's room. He didn't need his cane to get around in close areas like this house, but skimmed his fingertips along the hallway wall as he went.

Eric was instantly on his feet. "Fan out," he ordered as he headed the other way. In the kitchen, he called, "Only vehicle on the street is the meter reader's truck. There's another parked a few doors north of us. Same logo."

Harley was checking the bedrooms. "Clear," he called from his room, then another "Clear," from Eric's.

Jameson cocked his head, listening earnestly for the sound of breathing as he opened her bedroom. "Maddie?" he asked as he stepped quietly inside, leaving the door open behind him. He knew the moment he said her name. "She's not here," he called out. "Window's open."

That brought Eric and Harley into her room. Harley went straight to the window. "No, no, no. Damn it. That woman's smart. She jury-rigged a bypass to the security strip."

"Why would she do that?" Eric asked.

"She did the same kind of thing last night," Jameson replied, his heart pounding as he realized how fervently she accepted responsibility. "Once she found the overhead vent, we had a plan for her to run get help while I created a distraction. But after she cleared the farmhouse, she changed her mind. She said she couldn't just run away and leave, that she had to save me. That was when she found Agent Morozov, worked her magic on him, saved his life, then started the fire that drew everyone out of the farmhouse."

"That fire is how Adam, Eric, and Hunter found you," Harley said.

"And Morozov wouldn't be alive today if she hadn't changed the plan like she did," Eric added.

Jameson turned in the direction of his new teammates' voices. "She always wanted to be a jarhead. She wants to serve. That's what she's doing now."

"By running away?" Harley asked.

"She's not running away. Not Maddie. She's doing what every damned SEAL I've ever known would do. She's going after Lucy Delaney." He cocked his head, listening to the purr of a light-duty truck engine turning over. "How many trucks did you say, Eric? Two? Want to bet there are others canvassing the neighborhood, and she's inside one of them right now, on her way to Boston?"

"But we don't know where Delaney is in Boston," Harley muttered. "Or if she's still there."

"I'm having a serious talk with that woman when we catch up with her," Eric growled, then turned his head and said into his cell, "Boss. Damn it. Hate to have to tell you this, but Maddie fled protective custody about an hour ago. She said she was tired and was going to take a nap, but she bypassed the window security tape, and Jameson thinks she's headed to Boston to go after Lucy Delaney."

Everyone in the safehouse could hear Alex's explosive, "What?!" followed by a string of vehement expletives, some so anatomically impossible they were laughable. Then a terse, "Is she armed?"

"Yes," Eric reported evenly. "Nine-millimeter SIG, standard TEAM firepower. Two mags, courtesy of us wanting her to be able to protect herself."

Jameson ran both hands over his head, wishing he were telepathic and could reach out and touch Maddie, wherever she was.

"Son of a bitch," Alex hissed, his tone as sharp as before. "I... I can't get away. Not right now. Son of a goddamned bitch! First Pops Delaney. Now Lucy Delaney. What the hell is Maddie thinking? She's my Protocol Officer, not one of my snipers!"

"Understood. Never mind. We'll take care of it," Eric promised. "No worries. Already got a plan. We'll find her."

Dead silence hung between their pissed-off leader and his agents—for a couple seconds. Until Alex growled, "You're damned right you'll find her. You lost her. Do it."

"Copy that," Eric answered smartly.

But Alex had already disconnected.

"Hey, guys..." Harley muttered, a boatload of hesitance in his tone. "Alex told me something else when I talked to him earlier this morning. It's private. He wouldn't want me sharing details about his personal life, but there's something else going on right now. I think you two need to know. It's why he can't get away."

"Does it have to do with his father?" Eric asked. "Because you weren't there when his old man showed up in Kelsey's room at the hospital, and that guy's not right in the head. I really thought Alex was going to knock him on his ass the second he saw him. There's bad blood between them."

"Wish I had been there," Harley murmured. Sounded like he'd scratched his head. "Should've quit my second job sooner. Alex needed me, but…" He blew out a deep breath. "Damn. I should've been there." Said every guilty survivor ever…

It was obvious that sharing a confidence was hard for Harley. Jameson reached out to him and settled a palm over his shoulder. Instant data poured into him. Harley was taller than him, which put him over six feet tall, but with a rangy build. Solid, but nervous. And exhausted. That came through loud and clear in the tone of his voice.

Jameson cocked his head and said quietly, "You don't have to tell us anything. If Alex needs an assist on the home front, we'll handle that as soon as we find Maddie."

"He… he just found out his old man has Alzheimer's," Harley blurted, "at least that's what Kelsey thinks. That's where he probably is right now. Man hasn't slept in over forty-eight hours, but he had to take his dad to a specialist, and… shit." There went Harley's hand again, over his head and down his neck. Every muscle in that shoulder felt strung as tight as a rod.

"I should've guessed," Eric muttered. He must've sunk down onto Maddie's bed. His voice came from there. "Thought Alex was going to knock him out when his old man showed up out of the blue. Never seen the boss that ready to fight before."

"Mel's never been part of Alex's life and, yeah. He can't leave his family right now," Harley said. "He's super pissed his dad even showed up. Hadn't seen him in years. The old guy's a loser, and Kelsey's got the new baby, and—"

"Alzheimer's is life changing for the entire family," Eric added somberly. "And now Alex has one more emergency to take care of."

"And it's killing him," Jameson surmised from the little time he'd spent with his tightly strung boss. "So let's do this, guys. Best defense is a good offense. Let's wrap this up before the sun sets today. Alex has the resources. Let's use the fuck out of them and go get Maddie, so he doesn't have to deal with this disaster, too."

Harley's entire body seemed to relax. "Good idea. Only where do we start?"

Jameson turned to face Eric. "She needed a ride out of here without being seen. I'll bet she's inside one of the utility trucks that were in the neighborhood."

"I'll call Mother," Eric said. "She can contact the power company and have them track those vehicles. At least find out where they are now."

"She'll need to ask those drivers to check their vehicles to see if they've picked up a passenger they don't know about. Tell her to tell them to be nice. Maddie will be scared. She's only doing this to help."

"We should go to the airport," Harley said. "Head her off at the pass."

"Good thinking," Jameson said. "Maddie's smart. She'll trade vehicles the first chance she gets. Might already have done that. Let's get to Reagan, guys."

And when I get her back, I'm never letting her go.

Chapter Twenty-Three

Alex stood over his sleeping wife with his cell still in his hand after the latest bad news from Eric, loving her with every fiber of his warrior's heart and wishing he didn't have to leave her again. Especially not today. Not with Mel so close at hand.

But the need to join his TEAM in the field was a fire breathing monster prowling under Alex's skin, demanding to be set free to get the job done. For years, he'd lived for his TEAM, buried too many of them, but always stood by them. When operations turned to shit, as they sometimes did, he'd stopped heaven and earth to rescue them, called in any and every favor he'd ever earned to get to them in time, and he would've died for them. They were his livelihood and his friends, the epitome of everything his Devil Dog soul stood for. If he were bleeding right now, he knew damned well he'd bleed red, white, and blue. He loved his country and his TEAM. He loved all he'd ever given, and he'd live every second of it again.

But this gentle woman lying there with crimped dark chocolate curls spilling over her pillow...

This goddess with the pretty little elfin princess sleeping in one arm and her sound asleep son—their son—in the other...

They were his real reasons for breathing and living. They were his whole heart.

Alex swallowed hard at the father and son reunion he'd never expected he'd have to face, and the quandary he'd never planned for. He'd always thought he'd meet his Maker at the end of a bloody gunfight, with that legendary round of hot lead he'd never heard coming, imbedded in his head or his heart. Guess not. But he hadn't seen his TEAM ending like this, hadn't seen it ending at all. And this abrupt change of plans wasn't a hot round to his temporal lobe. Yet it would end him just the same. As fast as things were unraveling with Mel, ending The TEAM this way might be easier in the long run. This time around, his old man really was killing him.

The time for service to country had finally come to an end. From here until who knew when, his life as CEO of one of America's greatest teams was finished. A man couldn't run a successful enterprise without pumping most of his time into it. Entrepreneurship took dedication, sweat, and long hours in the office, on Capitol Hill, and networking. No more. Taking care of his sickly, aging parent would take everything. The TEAM was done. Over. God, it was hard, letting go and moving on. All those upcoming goodbyes...

Mel now lay sound asleep in the guest bedroom below in Alex's basement. He'd installed his father there after they'd come home from visiting Doc Denton, after Mel took what had to be his first hot shower in days, maybe weeks. After Alex insisted he take the prescription the local drugstore had delivered while they'd been en route. Even that had been weird, more proof that Mel's mental faculties were declining.

He'd stoutly refused to do anything Alex requested, yet then he'd showered and, as docile as a lamb, he'd taken the two white pills Alex offered. Mel tossed them back with a tall glass of orange juice. But after he'd finished, just when Alex thought maybe this cohabitation might be doable, he'd swiped the back of his hand across his mouth, sneered, and spat, "You can't make me do anything, shithead."

Ordinarily, those would've been fighting words. But now, they were just more proof of how quickly Mel was slipping into dementia, and how bad things were going to be for Alex and his family. If Mel's reaction was just the middle stage of Alzheimer's... Shit, Alex didn't want to face the final stage. But he refused to push this familial responsibility, as distasteful as it was going to be, off on Kelsey. Yes, she'd surely take an active part in caring for Mel, but Alex wouldn't expose her to his father's twisted concept of civility.

What an awful thing to watch someone lose their mind, even someone as irresponsible and thoughtless as Mel had always been. Seemed like things were only going to get worse, and damn it. Mel would not treat Alex's family the way he'd been treated growing up. He had to stand between them and the abuse Mel was sure to dish out. Shifting from active operations to the more passive, laid back battle at home...

Son of a bitch. It was like watching The TEAM die, only at a distance. Too far away to be actively engaged. Too far away to run into battle and save anyone. Anyone except his deadbeat father.

Alex still held his cell in his hand, fighting the compulsion to run, to be with his TEAM. Wishing he could. Didn't that make him the biggest chicken shit? To want to run into a war he knew he could win, but run away from the one he didn't want to face. What made one battle better or greater than another? He honestly didn't know. Alex only knew he adored Kelsey, and that she'd stuck by him through an awful lot of shitty times. He couldn't dump his old man on her. Wouldn't. It wasn't her war.

"Did you say Pops Delaney?" Mel murmured quietly behind Alex.

Startled, he glared over his shoulder and quickly closed his bedroom door, denying his father a look at the treasures that lay within. "What are you doing prowling around? What do you want now?"

Mel's red, bulbous nose twitched as he scratched, then thumbed the end of it with his thumb, like he thought he was a prizefighter entering the ring. Which in a way, he was.

Alex's entire body stiffened. He'd been on the receiving end of that hand more times than he cared to recall. But if Mel tried any of that shit now, he'd be in a damned nursing home by sunset. *Just try me.*

"Well, err, the thing is, err…Pops and me go way back. Maybe I can help, son."

"Like hell you can help, and stop calling me *son*. You burned that bridge a long time ago."

Mel blinked like he didn't understand, and honestly, Alex didn't expect him to. What could he possibly understand now? It was too damned late in so many ways.

"Well, okay. Guess I, umm, could do that, *Alex*." Sounded like that word got stuck in his throat. Mel had actually called him by his first name. Honestly, Alex was shocked he'd remembered it. "But I might could help if what you're up against has anything to do with Pops Delaney. Just saying…" The old fart ran a wrinkled hand over his now clean-shaven chin. That was new. He'd shaved his beard off. And he hadn't cut himself.

Alex put Mel to the test. "What the fuck do you know about Delaney?"

"That he's a sneaky, lying son of a bitch. He runs guns outta Boston Harbor, sells them to the highest bidders, don't matter if they're American or not."

"Everyone knows that."

"That he holds court every Tuesday at noon at the Black Irish Rose Tavern on Boston Harbor. That's when and where he dishes out orders and rewards. Hangings if someone's got it coming. The rare promotion when earned."

The thought came without deliberation or reason. What if that medicine was working? What if Mel really knew something—helpful? What if he was telling the truth?

"Prove it," Alex dared him. "Give me one reason to believe you."

The bastard reached inside his brand-new white t-shirt and tugged out a medal on a ball-chain. "This here's his token. No one gets in to see Pops without it." He slipped the chain up over his head and handed it over. "Go on. Take it. You're my kid. I ain't got much, but it's yours now."

Alex stared at the medallion swinging at the end of Mel's gnarled finger. An inch square enameled green shamrock on one side, script etched in black on the other. "What's it say?" he asked instead of accepting the thing that had all the makings of a peace offering.

"*Bráithreachas*," Mel whispered. "It's Gaelic. Means brotherhood."

That word rang a long-forgotten bell, a memory of Gramps and Mel arguing like two Bighorn rams butting heads. Of Gramps bellowing that strange Irish word, cursing Mel to go to hell with it. Yelling it at the bastard whose liquor and friends had always meant more to him than his sickly wife and wee one. That he needed to crawl back to Hell, leave before he brought more death home with him. Of Mel yelling back at Gramps that he could burn in that Hell for all Mel cared. That some things were more important than a stupid, scrawny kid and a lying wife.

Alex reached out and snagged the damned medallion. He was that stupid scrawny kid and the bell this medallion had rung had long been silent. "How did you get this? The truth, Mel. For once in your life, tell me the son of a bitchin' truth."

"You sound just like your grandpa when you say that. Son of a bitch was always his favorite—"

"The truth!" God, for once! Could he be straightforward and honest? Could he answer the damned question?

"Okay, well, umm… Yeah. I ran with Pops back in the day. I was his second lieutenant," Mel replied, his voice as steady as Alex had never heard before. "I was the one he conferred with when the coppers were breathing down our necks. I did what he needed getting done."

Coppers? Was this just a distorted memory from some old gangster movie?

"You were his hired gun? His enforcer?" No way in hell.

Mel nodded, a thin bead of sweat now dotting the space above his upper lip. He was breathing hard. Had all the signs of a man confessing his sins—if anyone was stupid enough to believe him.

"I'm not falling for a word of it. Pops is dead. Want to guess who offed him? One of my people, Mel, and now his deranged daughter's put a hit on that person. She set the whole fuckin' charade up, now she set my TEAM up. So tell me again what a big man you were when you hung with that cold-blooded bastard, Delaney. Go on. Brag some more. I need another good goddamned fairytale shoved up my ass."

Shrugging, Mel spread his arms, his palms splayed as if he were an open book. Which he damned well was not. "Then tell me what you want me to do. You're my son. My only kid. I know I messed up with Abigail and you, but I can't go back in time and change nothing. All I can do is be a better man today and tomorrow. The next day. How can I convince you I'm serious? What do you need? Maybe I really can help."

"No. You. Can't," Alex breathed, his anger so old and so deep, that to turn his back on it now felt like he was being disloyal to Gramps and Gram and his mom. He'd nursed his rage and contempt for too many years to simply turn the other cheek and let bygones be bygones.

"Not even if it helps?" Mel asked, almost plaintively. As if he cared. Which would be the first damned time in fuckin' forever.

"How long were you in the Navy?" Alex bit out.

His old man blinked, then looked down. "I, ahh…"

Exactly, you bastard. Lie to me like you always have. It's what you do. Alex waited for the half-truths that would surely come. But he wouldn't wait long. He had a wife and children to fix dinner for. They couldn't snack on turkey leftovers forever. And he needed to check in with Eric and Harley. He'd have to transition from fulltime manager of a successful enterprise to fulltime husband and father and… shit! To the caretaker of a lying son of a bitch he didn't even like!

Mel's chin tipped back up, and he stared Alex down, damned near eye to eye. "Not quite two years. Dishonorable discharge, but I guess you already know that."

"I know everything about you."

"Not about the *Bráithreachas*, you don't. Listen, I've made a lot of mistakes, I know that. I'll admit to every one of them, but give me a chance to help. One last chance." He cast his gaze to the door closed to him. "Do it for them."

Alex stood there outside his bedroom, his nostrils flared to detect the con, his heart frozen where all things Mel were concerned. But for the first time, he wondered if there wasn't more to that fight between Gramps and Mel than he recalled. Nine-year-old grandsons who adored their hero-veteran-grandfathers were still just nine years old. By then Mel had racked up so many zeroes, it was hard to accept anything he said as true or decent. But if he'd really worked for Pops Delaney, some of his lies and cons made sense.

At last Alex asked, "What is it you think you can do for me?"

Mel shifted his bare feet and licked his bottom lip, then swallowed and licked it again. "Didn't mean to eavesdrop, honest, but I heard you say something about Lucy Shade, and you didn't sound too pleased when you said it. That wouldn't be Lucy Delaney, Pops' little girl, would it?"

"One and the same."

"Well, damn. Umm, she's a real piece of work. But I can get you in to see her."

"I don't just want to see her. I've got a rogue agent on her way to kill Miss Shade, Lucy Delaney, or whatever she's son of a bitchin' calling herself today. I need to know precisely where Delaney is, and how to get to her before all hell breaks loose. I want my crosshairs in the center of her forehead, *Dad*. Can you do that for me? Can you wrap her up in a bow and mail her to me for Christmas like you did all the paychecks you sent Mom, but that she never received?"

Even as he poured a lifetime of hurt and sarcasm into that poisonous attack, Alex knew he'd hit below the belt.

Mel's Adam's apple bobbed along with his head. "I can," he muttered as he avoided the final question. "Yeah, I can do that. I can get you into the Black Rose. Trust me."

Alex growled, wishing like hell he could trust his old man. But what then? Even if he believed all these new lies, should he dare travel all the way to Boston, only to put his TEAM at risk and be disappointed again? Christ, how many lies did it take before a son truly stopped hoping and believing?! Apparently one Goddamned more.

"My private helo's on standby," he told his father with contempt. "If you're lying… If any of my TEAM suffers because of you, so help me God, I'll push you out of that helo and into the Atlantic on the flight home."

Damned if Mel didn't brighten at the threat. "Well, good. Then let's get going."

Alex held his breath, fully expecting to be called a worthless little runt, or something just as mean and belittling. But the insult didn't come. Mel's blue, blue eyes stared back at him. There were no fine tremors to his fingers like there'd been at the doctor's office. His hands were steady. Could anything he'd just said be true?

Sucking in his impatience, Alex rolled his shoulder in yet another useless attempt to get his latest migraine to back off. One of these days, he'd have to succumb to Kelsey's plea for him to see her chiropractor. But not now.

Staring at his old man, he lifted his cell, thumb-dialed the agent who lived closest to him, and put the phone to his ear.

"Well, hey!" China Carson, Maverick's wife, answered brightly. "How's that brand-new little baby boy of yours? Kiri's dying to meet him. I am, too."

"He's good. I need a favor, and I'm sorry I'm calling when Maverick's running an op for me but—"

"Is Kelsey all right? What do you need, Alex? Tell me. I'm five minutes away. Kiri and I can be there in three."

Alex swallowed hard. "Kelsey's fine, but something came up, and I have to leave. I don't want her alone."

"On my way," China said as she disconnected the call.

"Are we good?" Mel asked, his tone rife with concern.

"No," Alex snapped. "We're not good, and if you're lying to me this time, I'm through."

"I'm not."

"Then prove it!"

Chapter Twenty-Four

Jameson was thrilled to be on the ground in Boston, hopefully before Maddie's flight touched down. The express flight had made good time, landed five minutes earlier than the flight that left just prior to this one. Maddie hadn't been on either, and he hoped that meant he and his buddies had gotten ahead of the shitstorm headed her way.

With no bags to claim, he, Eric, and Harley traversed the concourse at Logan International quickly. Eric had clapped a hand onto Jameson's shoulder once they'd cleared the Jetway, ensuring he wouldn't need his cane to maneuver the crowds. He kept it collapsed and tucked under one arm. From out of nowhere, Harley acquired a decent set of dark glasses for him. Round with wire frames. Lightweight. Almost perfect.

Jameson felt like himself again. He'd dressed in TEAM black today, hoped Harley and Eric had, too. The second the express flight landed, that familiar spike of adrenaline before combat hit his bloodstream and amped up his senses. He was a SEAL again, two brothers at his side. This was who he was. This, he could do.

Once outside the airport's front entry, Jameson pointed his cane at the sidewalk, letting it extend to full length. The sounds of the busy metropolitan city wrapped around him. Harried passengers rushed by, seagulls screeched overhead, and a far-off train horn blared. The deep blast of a tugboat bellowed from nearby Boston Harbor. He lifted his head and his nostrils flared, scenting the briny Atlantic to the East, the bittersweet aromas of coffee, chocolate, and cinnamon from the barista just inside the terminal behind him, and the greasy call of fresh fish and chips on the air. The stringent sting of an over-indulgent splash of someone's aftershave. Cotton candy and popcorn.

His stomach growled. The last time he'd eaten was earlier, with Maddie. She'd saved some cinnamon rolls for him, then rewarmed them in the microwave. He'd thought then how adorably sweet she was to think of him. But now he worried what lay beneath all that sweetness.

That she'd struck out on her own declared she might just own a set of brass balls beneath that gentle demeanor. Might also mean she was still trying to prove herself to her father. And to herself. While her motivations mattered, it bothered Jameson more that she'd ditched him. It was bad enough she hadn't trusted Eric and Harley to let them in on her plan. But he'd assumed Maddie's declaration of love automatically entailed trust and honest communication with him.

Instead, she'd betrayed him, as well as her teammates. Bottom line: teams didn't work without the skillsets of trust and communication. Team members coordinated ideas and plans, everything they did, said, or thought. They revolved around each other. Trusted each other. Had to. There was no 'I' in team for a time-proven reason. The lone wolf was as much a menace to successful missions as the predatory object of those missions. Maddie had a lot to learn.

Eric had been on his cell the moment they'd landed, talking with Mother, aka Mom, while still aboard the express out of Reagan to Logan Airport. She'd supplied an address, although she hadn't been sure Lucy Delaney would be there. With time as short as it was, that was where they were headed now.

Eric waved down a cab. As he climbed inside, Jameson collapsed his cane, then spent the short trip keeping his ears open. He could only hope Maddie's plane was late. Or that she'd had a change of heart and come to her senses, had at least re-evaluated her rash decision to take on Lucy by herself.

They arrived at the address within twenty minutes, and the taxi left them on concrete that wasn't sidewalk. Jameson paused a few seconds to get his bearings. Heavy machinery rumbled nearby, vibrating the ground beneath his feet. The air was brisk, full of salt, sea, diesel fumes, and commerce. Full of sound and the capitalistic heartbeat of America, the world of container storage. Of semi-trucks coming and going. Of train engines pushing and pulling. Of dock workers calling out orders and foul language.

The steady rumbles were heavy-duty front-end loaders, forklifts, and massive industrial cranes, each assigned to maneuver containers from here to wherever they were destined. Pushers that moved stacks of containers along railroad tracks, for transport or for safekeeping until their carriers arrived. These were the southern docks of the Port of Boston, and he was standing inside the high-tech container facility once known as Castle Island. Given the amount of time it took the taxi to travel here, and the lack of scenting anything the least bit edible on the breeze, he told Eric and Harley, "We're at Conley Terminal in South Boston."

"Right on," Harley replied. "Don't know how you knew that, but keep your ears on. We do this together. We get in, get Maddie, get out."

By ears, Harley meant the wireless headset Jameson had secured over his head. Listening and interpreting audible data was his gift. Without asking or talking, he turned with his head up, his nose in the wind, and his new team at his side. Maddie was here. He'd never be able to explain how he knew, and it wasn't because he could scent her like dogs scented missing humans. But he'd never been more positive. Somehow, she'd arrived before them.

"She's already here," he told his teammates with confidence.

A heavy hand cupped his elbow. "Then you lead," Eric breathed, "and we'll follow."

He'd no more than uttered that order when his phone chirped. Harley's buzzed at the same time. Both men asked, "Yes, Boss?"

Jameson had lost his cell after Delaney's jet exploded, and he hadn't thought to grab the burner from the safehouse before they'd charged out to rescue Maddie. He cocked his head now, listened, and prepared for the worst. Cell phones ringing in harmony always spelled trouble.

He just didn't expect Alex's voice in stereo, bellowing, "Wait for me!"

"What the hell?" Harley muttered. "Where are you, Boss?"

Jameson sensed the direction of the shockwave rolling toward them. "He's right there." He almost told his teammates to, "Duck."

OhGodOhGodOhGod. Jameson is here? Eric and Harley, too? How'd they do that? How'd they know where I'd be? I didn't even know where I was going until I called Nash's loan shark.

Which had been the luckiest guess of Maddie's life. She'd snagged the burner phone back at the safe house, and then, after she'd snuck inside the power company truck that had been parked fortuitously on the curb outside the safe house, she'd finally called the number that wicked loan shark had nailed to the middle of her front door, like an eviction notice. Which seemed like another good sign at the time, him answering his phone as quickly as he had.

But now that she stood in the shadow alongside the Black Irish Rose Tavern, avoiding eye contact with everyone and keeping her head down, she wasn't so sure of anything. Planning a strategy back inside the safe house was easier than implementing it out here where anything could go wrong. She'd used every last bit of her savings to rent passage on the private plane that brought her to an airstrip outside South Boston. There she'd called a cab to get her to this exact business on the Harbor.

The grimy denim jacket she wore now, she'd stolen on her way past a row of disgusting, smelly forklifts. It was too large and smelled so strongly of body odor that it watered her eyes. The ball cap she'd picked up from the ground didn't fit any better. But the jacket concealed her nine, and the dirty cap made her anonymous, just one of the guys. One of the short guys.

She'd never met Nash's loan shark in person, but when he'd first called, demanding she pay off Nash's debt, he'd sounded just as she'd expected, cold and ruthless. What she hadn't expected was that he'd also be Irish. That made her think. Maybe Pops Delaney owned every loan shark on the East Coast, and bingo. She'd been right, at least that Pops had owned this guy. When she'd informed Mr. Shark that his boss was recently deceased, that she'd seen him die with her own eyes, he'd called her a liar and hung up. But he'd quickly called back, said he'd checked and confirmed her story. He'd been ready to listen then.

"So what do you want, Missy?" he'd asked. Guess he hadn't known Delaney's daughter was even in the picture, or that Lucy Shade, the uppity news celeb, was really Lucy Delaney, Pops only daughter, and the heiress to his empire. Or that she was headed to Boston to take control of his gang. And him, Mr. Bigshot Shark. Guilt by association made him one of Lucy's targets, and that was how Maddie had fed him her lie. He needed to get on Lucy's good side. Him sending his new boss a quick chunk of change might make things easier for him. *Never hurts to grease the hand that feeds you, right?*

All Maddie wanted in return for the privilege of ending her ex's affiliation with the underworld, was the address in Boston, to make that deposit. After a couple more terse minutes of dishonest negotiation as to who had the better hand, during which Mr. Shark threatened to slice all of her fingers off, then her toes, one by bloody one, until she paid him—or else. Not like she wanted to know what 'or else' meant, but somehow, she'd stood firm. Demanded he tell her where Pops Delaney lived or worked in Boston, that she would only hand over the money—yes, all thirty-thousand dollars Nash owed, plus fifteen thousand more in interest—to the woman in charge today, not to one of her lackeys.

Not that Maddie had that kind of cash, but she wasn't going to visit Miss Delaney to hand over money anyway. No. She was here to kill the woman who'd tried to murder Jameson Tenney too many times.

Maddie was at peace with her decision because, like Lucy Shade, she was her father's daughter, and she would always be just that. Nothing more. She wasn't a Marine, never would be. But she'd worked alongside enough of them these past few months, former soldiers and SEALs as well, to know they'd chosen the path less traveled. That in doing so, they made a difference every day. They were the brave and daring heroes America needed. Not her.

This was just her way of honoring the men and women who'd put their lives at risk for her. They'd served; she hadn't. But she would serve them now. She owed the people she worked with more than she'd ever owed Nash or her old man, and she meant to keep Jameson alive. He deserved a better hand than what life had dealt him. She meant for him to have a chance at that better future and more. Just not with her. She was no good for him. A loser like her would only hold him back.

But now that he was here, and marching straight at her as if he'd scented her like bloodhounds scented criminals... Good grief, he looked good. And hot. His chin was set in grim determination, his eyes hidden behind those dark glasses. His head was up, his stride powerful and confident. To look at him, no one would ever know he was blind. He was a soldier in charge, and he moved without his cane or a lick of hesitation. As if somehow, he knew there were no obstacles in his way. As if there wouldn't dare be anything between him and her. He was a hard man, ready for war. Somehow the mountainous stacks of shipping containers behind him only made him look more fierce. Larger than life.

Harley and Eric cut imposing sights, but Jameson had them beat. Her heart squeezed out a dozen sets of jumping jacks that pounded like thunder beneath her breastbone. "What the heck am I doing here," she murmured to herself. "He's the warrior. He's trained. I'm just..." Just what? So in love with that man that it hurt to see him looking so mean? So focused? So ready to kill in order to protect her?

And now I've put him in danger.

She forced herself not to wave at him and give herself away. She was nothing, but Jameson Tenney was someone. The world would miss him.

Not if she could help it.

Chapter Twenty-Five

"Keep up!" Alex ordered the old man slacking behind him. Until they'd run between the two-mile-wide stacks of shipping containers along the dock at Conley Terminal, Mel had been lucid and actively engaged. But now he was tired. His pace had slowed and was looking around like he didn't know where he was. Despite his good intentions, if that was truly what he'd had back at the house, he looked bewildered now.

"Son of a bitch," Alex hissed at himself. Eric, Harley, and Jameson were just up ahead, and here he was, dragging his sickly, deadbeat father behind him, like some idiot nine-year-old who wasn't smart enough to give up on the old fart. Or admit that Mel might not be helpful anymore.

Alex slowed, still moving forward but with more measured steps.

Mel was panting and sweating, obviously suffering from his age and the disease. "It's here. We're close, I can tell," he wheezed. "I can find it. Just give me a minute, will ya?"

That, at least, sounded semi-coherent. "It's okay," Alex replied evenly. "Catch your breath. My men are just up ahead. We'll connect with them and take it from there. You can rest then."

"Damn it. I don't wanna rest, but nothing around here looks familiar, boy," Mel grumbled, scanning the docks ahead and behind himself, as if he'd misplaced the Black Irish Rose Tavern, the alleged home base for Delaney's gang, and all those supposed promotions and demotions Mel had bragged about.

"When was the last time you were here?"

"Umm…"

"You've been here before, right?" Alex shook his head, annoyed that he might've fallen for yet another of Mel's cons.

By then, Eric and the guys were walking toward him. Jameson Tenney lagged behind, then came to an abrupt stop. As if he'd heard something, he turned to his right and cocked his head. Must've been the long row of containers grinding along a railway track at Alex's left.

Mel sputtered and pointed. "There! See? Told you it was here."

Sure enough. The Black Irish Rose Tavern sat between two massive warehouses, tucked between their wide-open concrete docks, nearly hidden from view. The simple red-brick building sported a lattice-work, Kelly-green awning over neon signs that invited the hardworking dockworkers in for a pint of Guinness and Harp, or a bottle of Jameson, Teeling, or Bushmills.

Jameson took off running toward the tavern just as—

Son of a bitch! Was Maddie holding a pistol, her arms extended in a proper firing position, just outside the warehouse corner nearest Jameson? Could he get to her in time to stop her?

"Maddie! Stop!" he yelled.

She'd just turned and looked over her shoulder when—

BA-BOOM! A mighty ball of fire and heat ripped sideways through the tavern, sending a hail of bricks, burning debris, and shrapnel, out toward the Harbor and up into the sky.

Holy shit! The ground shuddered, knocking Alex to his knees. If that wasn't enough, the rat-a-tat rapid fire of machine guns peppered the air, coming from the warehouse Maddie had been aiming into.

Scrambling to his feet, Alex told his father to stay put, then took off running. By then, Jameson already had Maddie covered. She lay prostrate beneath him. Was he hit? Was she hurt? Alex couldn't see through the dense billowing smoke that now obscured the entire dock.

He cast a quick glance back at Mel. God, no. Mel was bleeding and—what the hell? He had a pistol in his right hand. Alex ran back to his dad.

"She shot me, boy. That little bitch shot me. It's over," he whispered as if he were breathing his last. "Don't cry for me."

"Shut up and stay down," Alex growled as he assessed the tiny trace of blood on the outside of Mel's upper thigh. It was nothing more than a graze the length of a pinkie finger. Lexie's pinkie finger! This damned situation was out of control. He didn't have time for a drama queen. "Talk to me," he ordered into his cell.

"One shooter, near as I can tell from here," Harley replied evenly. "Too much smoke to be sure."

"Where are you?"

"On my belly to your far right. Beside the forklift. Got my scope on some guy standing just inside the open warehouse door. He might be who Maddie was after."

Yeah, well might and is were two different damned things. "Eyes on, Harley. Identify that bastard, and take him out."

"Copy that."

Men were running away from both warehouses by then. An overhead PA system dominated the air with booming instructions on where to seek safety. Sirens screamed from every direction. But the blowback from that burning tavern brought the unmistakable aroma of charred flesh with it.

"Anyone know how many people were in the tavern?" Alex asked his TEAM, his vision tearing from the dense gray clouds billowing his way.

"All Pops' boys I imagine," Mel groused where he lay. "That's how I'd clean house if I were Lucy. Invite them in for drinks. Tell 'em a bunch of lies. Get 'em drunk, then step outside and blow 'em to hell. All of 'em. All at once. Make it look like an accident."

Alex stared down at the old man he never, ever knew. Aghast, and damned ashamed that they shared the same blood.

"First responders are in transit," Eric reported, dragging Alex back to the present fiasco. "They'll be here soon."

"Good. Where's the damned bomber?"

"Not sure yet. Got my eye on some guy in black inside the warehouse. Just inside, left of the door. He's armed. Two pistols. Tactical vest. One short-stock rifle. Thought he was one of ours at first, but he's not."

"Harley's already on him."

"Yup. Same guy I'm watching," Harley added.

"Anyone else?" Alex demanded to know.

"Not as far as I can—"

"Yes, Boss! Lucy Delaney's on the second level." That was Jameson. "I heard high heels on wooden stairs just before the explosion. She's somewhere upfront, over the warehouse doors. I can't see. Can someone tell me if there's a window up there? Maybe a vent she can see through? She's the one who fired that MAC 10."

Now how the hell did he know all that?

"Good call," Alex told his newest agent. "There's a five foot long louvered vent near the peak of the warehouse roof. You sure you heard heels? Not something else?" There was no way Alex could've deciphered the sound of high heels in this chaos.

"Heels, Boss. Stilettos. Just like she wore back at the hotel and farmhouse."

Okay then. Alex believed. Jameson might be every bit as good as Walker had said.

MAC 10s, aka Military Armament Corporation, model number tens, were machine guns, similar to Uzis. Both were, generally speaking, illegal in the States, and subject to specific NFA rules, aka National Firearms Act. Them being here made perfect sense. MAC 10s were the weapon of choice that, until yesterday, Pops had been pushing on the black market. They were also why Tucker Chase had an agent inside Delaney's gang. One of his psychics, not Vladimir Morozov.

"Guys," Alex muttered, pissed at himself for his lack of full disclosure. "Tuck's got a man inside. Don't know who, but he might be who you're both tracking. Are you certain Lucy Delaney's up top, Jameson? I don't want to take out Tucker's man."

"Yes, Boss. Positive. She wears enough rose-scented perfume to gag a pig."

"And you can smell that? From out here? Through all this smoke?"

"No, not anymore. But before the explosion, yes," Jameson explained. "Guess it's a gift."

Alex shook his head as his sweet wife's words came back to him. Kelsey always said when one door closed, another opened. Guess Jameson was the winning prize behind this particular door.

"Yup, that's her," Mel breathed, his eyes closed and a silly smile on his face. "Always thought she was better than everyone else. Entitled, you know? Rich little bitch. Loved roses."

"Who blew the damned tavern?" Alex muttered.

"She did," Mel answered. "Lucy's a nasty, spiteful little thing. Spoiled rotten. Greedy as shit but smart as sin, and she's good with Semtex. You ought to see what she can do with C4."

"You know her?" Alex had to ask. Could things get any more bizarre?

"Sure. She's your younger cousin. Pops is my older brother. Always hated the fucker."

Alex couldn't believe what his ears were hearing. "My cousin?! Gramps had two sons? I have an uncle? When were you going to tell me that?"

"Never," Mel replied as he folded his hands and interlocked his fingers over his belly. "The less you and your mother knew about my brother and me and his illegal crap, the better."

"Son of a bitch! Did Gramps know he was running guns?"

Mel turned and stared into Alex's face, icy cold blues drilling into blues just as hard and just as frigid. "Why do you think he kicked me out? Told me to never come back? He knew. He sure as hell knew."

Suddenly, there wasn't enough air in the world. Alex sat back on his ass, his equilibrium blown to hell with all these revelations, and no longer sure who was the bigger liar in the family. He didn't have time for his family bullshit. Not now. The unnamed man in black had just walked to the center of the wide-open warehouse doorway and pointed a black-gloved hand straight up, as if signaling Alex and his team of Lucy's location.

"Who the hell is that guy?" Harley asked. "What's his name? Anyone know?"

"I have no idea, but he just saved Maddie's life," Jameson replied, his voice laced with pain. Real pain. Not Mel's whiny version.

Alex snapped out of his fog. "Are you hit?"

"Maddie's safe. She's not hurt."

"I asked if you're hurt!"

"Nothing serious. Just a scratch."

Which was what every damned spec ops guy ever said, didn't matter if they'd lost a limb, an eye, or... shit. Jameson was blind, yet still working as hard, maybe harder, than everyone else.

"Son of a bitch! Move in," Alex ordered. "She's armed. Take her ass out, Goddamnit!"

His damned cell rang!

"What?" he snarled into the phone.

"Please hold your position, Alex," the cocky director of the FBI's one and only psychic team, Tucker Chase, ordered calmly. "Tell your men to stand down. Don't you dare shoot my guy."

Alex hated working with the FBI, but Tucker and his psychics? They weren't so bad. Had actually been helpful once or twice. Just annoying.

"Belay that order!" he told Eric, Harley, and Jameson. "Son of a bitch, Tuck, which one is yours? Lucy Delaney or the lone man still inside the warehouse?" At this point, he honestly didn't know who was who.

"The cocky son of a bitch standing at the open door is mine. He's now looking square at your man on the ground, whose body is spread over… What's her name?" he asked someone else. Had to be chatting with the psychic agent Alex now had in his crosshairs.

Tuck came back with, "Maddie Bannister. Your man's protecting your protocol officer and she's scared shitless. Jameson Tenney—he's the lucky bastard on the ground with his body on top of hers. Don't worry. Delaney got off a few rounds, and Tenney's hit, but he's a former SEAL. He's tough. He'll be okay. The other round hit that old guy with you. Is that… My hell, that's your father?"

Tuck never waited for an answer, not like Alex would've provided one. "You never told me your dad was in town. Bottom line, both Tenney and your old man aren't seriously injured. Eric Reynolds and Harley Mortimer are with you, too. Sure wish you'd promote Zack Lennox. He's long overdue to be senior agent."

"Shut up," Alex snapped. Tuck always did talk too much, and now that he was FBI director over the psychic team, he seemed to think he knew too damned much as well. "What do you need?"

Delaney opened fire again and—

BOOM! BOOM! BOOM! Jameson Tenney fired three answering shots in lightning quick succession.

The wooden louvers above the open warehouse bay cracked outward. The new boss of the Irish mob tumbled through them. Like a bag of cement with arms and legs extended, Lucy Shade fell face first to the concrete dock a good forty feet below. Her weapon shattered on impact.

Jameson Tenney, the one and only blind TEAM agent, had just taken out the mass murderer no one else could see. Made a man wonder what else he could do.

Tuck's man strolled forward and looked down at her, his weapon poised to deliver a double tap if needed. Which it wasn't. The human skull wasn't much different than a melon when it impacted concrete from that altitude. Lucy Delaney expired on contact. *Good riddance.*

"You know she also set charges inside that warehouse, don't you?" Tucker purred through Alex's phone's earpiece. "She planned to blow the entire place, leave no evidence of her old man's legacy behind. She wanted a fresh start. New crew. Apparently, new inventory, too."

"I know now," Alex groused. "Has your man secured the detonator? Or do we need to call in EOD?"

"Nah. My guy already disarmed the device. One more thing. That warehouse is stacked to the rafters with illegal hardware. Machine guns. Rifles. LAWs. Tactical helmets and vests, NVGs, you name it. And enough ammo to supply every household on the East Coast with a dozen boxes. I'll let you know when or if any of that goes on FBI auction."

Which Alex doubted. The Bureau would be wise to add this stash to their inventory instead of auctioning it off to John Q. Public. Might save the taxpayer a couple million. Not that the Bureau was that kind of smart.

"Anything else?"

"Think about what I said. Zack's a good man. You don't want to lose him."

"Not worried about Zack leaving me, Tuck," Alex replied with venom. "Just remember, two of your men are on loan from my TEAM. The day they come back to me, you'll lose Eden, possibly Isaiah, too. So back off."

Tucker chuffed. "Good working with you again."

"Copy that," Alex replied tersely, switching off that irksome call and turning back to his TEAM.

By then, the local police had arrived on scene. Several vehicles full of agents from the Massachusetts Port Authority, too. A couple fire engines and a raft of radio and television reporters. A damned local news helicopter.

Alex pushed to his feet while Eric and Harley ran to assist Jameson and Maddie. The show might be over, but the circus was just beginning.

Chapter Twenty-Six

"Why the fuck are you here?" Jameson growled down at Maddie, damned angry with her for charging into trouble without thinking things through. Without bringing him! Yet at the same time, thankful she wasn't the one lying twenty feet away with her face poured over concrete.

"This was all my f-f-fault," she stuttered. "I killed her dad."

"So? Pops Delaney had it coming. He meant to kill us, remember?" How could she forget who'd abducted them?

"Yessss, but..."

Jameson's cock went hard at the soft, sweet whisper of her tongue sliding over her lips and the way she smacked her lips... and shit. It was impossible to stay angry with this woman. He'd lost his glasses in the mad dash to get to her and... Damn! He'd give anything to be able to see her, to really look into her eyes. Yet he couldn't let her off easy. He'd just killed the woman bent on killing Maddie, and the resounding adrenaline dump after taking a life was a hard beast to rein in.

"You wanted to be a Marine, well, listen up, Mad Dog. Team members don't leave each other behind, and they sure as fuck don't go off half-cocked on a revenge killing! You hear me, Bannister?!"

He waited for an answer, but when she said nothing, he let her have it. "If I was Alex, I'd fire your ass. And you're supposed to be his Protocol Officer?! Shit. I'd have you peeling potatoes until—"

"I'm not Mad Dog!" she yelled back at him, her body shaking. "I'm just me! You're just like my dad! Stop trying to make me someone I'm not!"

That shut him up. Was that what he'd been doing? Was he as bad as her father? He opened his mouth to say something, shut it, then opened it again, not sure what to tell her now.

Maddie solved that dilemma when she leaned up and crashed into his wide open, ornery mouth, her fingers clutching his ears and his cheeks, her tongue doing amazing laps inside his mouth and over his teeth and... salt. He tasted salty tears. She was crying.

Sweet Baby Jesus. He forgot what he was going to say. Forgot what he was thinking and where he was. Only knew that she'd scared the crap out of him, and now, he'd made her cry. Her tears, more than anything, hurt his heart. He wanted to kiss her better, inhale every last one of her fears, and spank her ass, all at the same time. But she was safe and contrite, soft, and so damned warm...

"I'm sorry," she sobbed into his mouth. "But I couldn't let her hurt you again. I made you a target by shooting her dad, and she knew who you were, and that we got away, and she said she was gunning for me, and I figured you'd never let her—"

"Shush," he murmured around her prehensile, loquacious tongue. "You're alive. She's not. That's what matters. But you've got to stop trying to rescue me. I'm trained for this shit. You're not."

Her chest heaved with a long draw of air. This woman could string more run-on sentences together than anyone he'd ever heard. But she'd come here to save her brothers. She'd purposefully put herself in harm's way to protect men who were bigger, heavier, and meaner than her. That was no small thing.

"Alex is going to kill me," she whined as she ended the best kiss of Jameson's life. Salty and sweet, but earnest as hell. How could he stay angry after she'd risked her life to protect his? That was why she was here. She hadn't left him and the guys behind. She'd charged straight to the frontline like a damned SEAL would have. Like the Marine she'd always wanted to be. To protect and serve. That had to stop.

Jameson bowed his sweaty forehead to hers. "There's no room for rogue agents on jobs like ours, Maddie," he explained more patiently. "Alex can't take a chance on freelancers, and you're not a trained operator, babe. But you sure as hell stepped in a steaming pile of shit by coming after Delaney on your own. So, face him head on, and get ready to get your ass reamed." Somehow, saying that to a woman felt like sexual harassment.

Jameson rolled to his side to catch his breath and ease that stabbing wound in his other side. Felt like a knife was stuck there, though he knew better. He'd been shot before. Nothing serious. Lifting gingerly to his feet, he pulled Maddie along with him. She hadn't yet seen his injury, so it couldn't have been bleeding too bad. He hoped. Biting his lip at the black shadows dancing at his already dark peripheral, he tucked her under his good arm and prepared to weather the oncoming shitstorm with her. He had no sense of where Alex was in all the chaos of first responders and yakkity reporters ahead, but he knew he'd soon find out.

Maddie's hand fell naturally to his chest while they stood there, both breathing hard and both sweating buckets. Both shaky and holding each other up. His heart was still pumped full of the instinctual fight or flight compulsion, but her entire body felt as if he had an arm around a fluttering hummingbird.

"Any reporters come at us, we say 'no comment,' and we walk away, understood?" he warned her. "Agents have no authority to comment on covert operations, ever. Just like in the military. Alex is the boss. He's the only one who talks to the press."

"Okay, yeah. Only Alex. Got it," Maddie breathed. She was young, naïve, and inexperienced as hell. Good intentioned, but in dire need of some hardcore military training. If she wanted to be a Marine, so be it. He'd make damned sure she got that training.

Jameson sensed Eric's approach first, then Harley's. Eric's footfall was a firm and steady tread on the concrete. Harley had more of a casual, rolling gait.

"Guys," he greeted them before they said a word.

One of them whistled softly, but it was Harley who said, "Darlin', what the hell were you thinking coming all the way to Boston by yourself?"

"That you guys deserved better than being shot in cold blood!" she bit out, sounding tougher than she was, but shivering as if she were freezing.

"There you go, babe," Jameson whispered against her temple as he rubbed her biceps. "If you're going to be a bad ass, don't ever back down."

"And Marines don't cry," Eric added gently from her immediate left. "It'll only make your DI meaner. Alex isn't going to fire you, but he might make you scrub toilets with a toothbrush for a week."

"Your toothbrush," Harley added.

Jameson grinned at the nerve of these guys to tease her, until Maddie asked, "W-w-what's a DI?" Man, even her voice was shaking.

"Enough," he told the guys, squeezing her so she'd know he might be mad, but he'd always and forever have her six. "She doesn't need all of us ganging up on her. One asshole's enough."

Her pulse was pounding. She was close to tears again, he could tell. The guys must've noticed the same thing. Eric stepped to her side, brushed Jameson's arm out of his way and put a hand on her trembling shoulder. Harley bumped elbows with Jameson. They were now a united front against the tsunami about to blast over them.

"A DI's a drill sergeant," Eric muttered. "A drill instructor. They're all assholes, Maddie. Like Alex."

Jameson damn near smiled at that description until said asshole in charge barked a wicked, "Sit Rep, goddamnit! Now!"

"Yes, Boss," Jameson answered calmly, even as his body snapped to attention, and his unseeing eyes snapped forward. "Earlier today, we received actionable intel that Lucy Delaney had settled into Pops' usual hideout, The Black Irish Rose Tavern, here on Boston Harbor." Which was not precisely truthful, but this was what warriors did. They always covered their brothers' and sisters' backs.

He took a quick breath and continued. "We suspected she intended to clean house and tie up all loose ends, which meant Miss Bannister and me. She'd already told Agents Taylor Armstrong and Maverick Carson she was gunning for us, Miss Bannister in particular. Because of that death threat, Maddie took the initiative to come to Boston and surveil the area ahead of us. Shortly after we arrived—"

"Cut the bullshit!" Alex hissed. Damn, he sounded nasty. He had that whole back of the throat, I-will-kill-the-next-liar thing down to a fine art. If Jameson hadn't known his boss was human, he would've sworn he'd just run smack into a pissed-off tiger.

"Let me remind you what *you* said." Alex must've zeroed in on Eric. "'*No worries. Already got a plan. We'll find her.*' Sound familiar?"

Whoa, Jameson was impressed with the steaming shitload of wicked sarcasm Alex had just heaped on Eric. Alex was making him feel all warm and tingly inside. Felt like he was back on active duty. Bring. It. On!

"We did find her, Boss, and we executed our infil perfectly," Eric responded evenly.

"But you know how plans go, Boss," Harley drawled, his voice loose and his tone casual, as if Alex didn't worry him at all. "Nothing on the drawing boards at HQ ever works out for troops in the field. Murphy's rule or something. Shit's gonna happen. Sure would've been nice if we'd known Tucker Chase had one of his mind readers inside. Thing's mighta gone smoother if we'd had that intel a little sooner, don't you think?"

Ouch. Jameson couldn't help it. He winced. Had Harley just fired a round over Alex's bow? Must have. Because Alex made an odd, distressed sound, again at the back of his throat, like he might've swallowed wrong.

"We understand. You've got a helluva lot on your plate right now, what with Kelsey having an emergency C-section and a new baby boy and all," Harley went on, "but we wouldn't be in this predicament now if we'd known the whole picture before hell broke loose, would we?" Whoa, he had some balls to take on his boss like he did.

Damned if Alex didn't snap, "You're right. Won't happen again. And you…" There was that feral growl again. He must have Maddie in his sights now.

She froze, and Jameson prepared to go to war with his boss on what might end up being his last day of working for the guy. Jameson's spine stiffened, and his fingers curled into knotted fists. His body and soul went hard. He might've lost his sight, but he hadn't lost his nerve. He could take this son of a bitch down, easy.

Until Alex pulled Maddie out from under his arm and muttered, "I could've lost you, damn it. What were you thinking?"

Jameson held back, his head cocked in case she might still need him. Didn't sound like it, though. Her tears must've done the trick. Alex didn't lay into her after that initial snarl.

"I couldn't let her h-h-hurt my guys," she hiccupped.

My guys. Jameson liked the sound of that. Maddie *was* a team player. Just needed a few pointers on how to play the game better next time.

"Good job. Just don't do it again. Promise?"

She must've nodded. Jameson had the impression Alex held her in his arms. That had to stop.

"Excuse me, Mr. Stewart," a gruff baritone interrupted. "Special Agent Harper Kincaid at your service. Director Chase asked me to offer FBI assistance to you and your team. Understand you've got two injured."

"Yes, the older gentleman on the ground over there. Damn. The one flirting with the female medic," Alex huffed. "Can't take the old fart anywhere."

Maddie came back into Jameson's side then. The injured side. *Ouch.* He couldn't help it. He shuddered. The adrenaline had worn off and the damned thing was beginning to hurt like a mother.

"And this man," Alex muttered. "Jameson? You think you can make it to the wagon?"

"You're hurt," Maddie hissed, "and you didn't tell me? Where? Oh, good grief! Your side's bleeding! Jameson!"

"I'm good," he assured her even as Alex bellowed, "Medic!"

"I've got you, dumbass," Eric cajoled as he slid a strong, gentle hand under Jameson's arm and around his ribs.

"Jameson! Don't you dare black out!" That squeal was all Maddie, and man, she sounded better angry than scared. But she was safe now, and that mattered most. She had a team of stout warriors who would forever fly cover over her. The boss wasn't as big a hardass as he wanted everyone to believe and… and…

The chaotic, smoke-filled scene of first responders and nosy reporters faded into a whirling vortex of peace and calm. Jameson went limp. His face ended up pressed against Maddie's lush, warm breasts. Lavender. He smelled flowery lavender and sweet, salty, feminine perspiration. The scents he wanted to bathe in the rest of his life. Those were her arms around him. Her fingers smoothing over his forehead and cheeks. Just Maddie's. She was going to be okay.

With a sigh, he let go.

Chapter Twenty-Seven

Maddie kept one hand intertwined with Jameson's. They'd been taken to a local Boston emergency room, and were waiting to leave. The bullet hole had gone clean through his side, only causing minimal damage to a single rib. After the very kind ER physician administered a local anesthetic, the nurse had irrigated the wound, and the doctor then stitched and bandaged. The nurse had already removed Jameson's IV. He had ten days' worth of antibiotics and pain pills sitting on the nightstand pending his release. Alex and his father were arguing two cubicles away. They hadn't stopped since they'd arrived.

Eric and Harley were still back at Conley Terminal, giving statements to local authorities and doing whatever real TEAM agents did after catastrophes and murders. A Boston police officer had just left Jameson's bedside after he'd gotten Maddie's and Jameson's statements. Mostly Jameson's. He was the hero of the hour, the blind agent of one of America's best covert security companies, and the man who'd ended Lucy Delaney's short reign of terror.

Maddie had been asked to leave Jameson's cubicle while he'd talked with the officer. She'd taken a seat in the ER lobby, tapping her nervous fingertips on her knees, waiting to get the 'all clear' to join him again. That was when she'd discovered the other side of Jameson Tenney. The Technicolor version. His story had been on every screen in the lobby, and all had been turned up to hear the latest.

The press loved him, hence their back-to-back coverage of the explosion at Conley Terminal on Boston Harbor, the bloody events earlier in the evening at the farmhouse in Virginia, his tours of duty, and well, pretty much his entire life story.

Maddie hadn't realized she'd been in the company of a true war hero. But because of all the media coverage, she now knew precisely how he'd lost his sight. Yes, there had been a roadside bomb. What he hadn't mentioned was that injury had occurred after he and his buddy rescued two little boys.

She'd leaned into the story then, her elbow on her knee, her chin cupped in the heel of her hand. It turned out, those boys were unwanted cast-offs, because both had down syndrome. They never knew they'd been pawns of ISIL that day, released into the desert, the sole intent for them to distract the SEAL team. To lure soft-hearted American warriors into the open.

Somehow, the news outlet had pictures of the boys. Both brown-skinned, dark-eyed, adorable urchins who'd since been adopted. But the boys hadn't known they'd been chased by two SEALs hellbent on saving their little asses that day. The rescue had gone down quickly. Jameson and his buddy had saved those boys. All four were back undercover before the donkey had decided he wanted to be saved, too. That was when grubby, sad, little *Eeyore* had turned back around and headed for the SEALs. He was nearly to the wall they'd taken cover behind, when his hooves triggered a deadly daisy-chain of expertly hidden improvised explosive devices.

The boys were safe by then, both in the care of an Air Force PJ, whoever that was. But two SEALs died that day. One went home blind. That special operator was newly promoted USN Chief Petty Officer Jameson Tenney, whom the press declared was one-of-a-kind, an exceptional sailor. The deployment into Iraq that had cost Jameson his sight, went down mere weeks after he'd gotten 'frocked,' whatever that meant. The reporter on screen said he'd accomplished in five years what it took most sailors to accomplish in ten or more.

Maddie didn't understand what E-5 exams, meritorious promotions, or EP waivers were. She only knew the humble man who'd run straight into trouble to rescue her today, had done it before. That he seemed to have no qualms about risking his life to save others. Yet he'd never once mentioned that trait or drawn attention to himself. And he had a lot to brag about.

Talk about a hero.

It was close to twenty-four-hours since she and Jameson had made love at the safe house. The night before that, she'd rescued Mr. Vlad, then survived a gunfight with Pops Delaney's guys, when she'd gone back inside the farmhouse intent on rescuing Jameson. Turned out, he'd rescued her in more ways than he could ever know. She was light years beyond simple exhaustion, but what a couple of busy days. Thankfully, the press hadn't cornered her yet. She hoped they never did. Her life story was dull compared to Jameson Tenney's.

Because, right on schedule, as usual, Maddie doubted herself again. She'd made a huge mistake going alone to Boston, but she'd done it with the purest intentions. Only, she hadn't. Not entirely, had she? She'd done it to save Jameson, but she'd also gone rogue, as Jameson had accused her of doing, mostly to prove her dad wrong.

Good grief, there seemed no way to close that long chapter in her life and move on without dragging her dad's abuse behind her every step of the way. Everywhere she went, there he was. The moment she'd thought she'd finally left him behind, she devolved back into the weakling she'd been under his thumb. With every tentative step she'd taken on that dock, her dad had been in her head, criticizing, name-calling, and berating.

It had to end. She just didn't know how to exorcise the vicious voice in her head that had always put her down. Why did people do that? Demean their children and call them names they'd remember for the rest of their lives? It was so hurtful.

"Hey, you," Jameson purred as he squeezed her fingers. "You're thinking too hard. I can tell."

She swallowed, then admitted, "I'm not cut out to be an agent."

"Yes, you are." He winced as he pulled himself up higher on the already tilted bed. "You're brave and you're honest. You care about people and you're willing to learn."

He made it sound simple.

Maddie adjusted his pillow so he'd be more comfortable. He was a handsome disheveled mess with his dark hair mussed, and a full day's worth of scruff shadowing his chin and jaw and down his neck. He'd lost his glasses during the showdown on the docks, and the day would never come that he'd be able to gaze longingly into her eyes, like romance heroes did with their damsels in distress. Their *Cinderellas* or their *Sleeping Beauties*. Their princesses.

Yet Jameson had always looked straight into her since they'd met. And he called her babe. Maybe that didn't count to all the overconfident business women in the world. Maybe they took it as an insult. But to Maddie, the way Jameson said babe was a one-eighty change from the names she'd heard all her life. When he cocked his head, she knew he was truly listening, not just waiting for her to shut up so he could talk, or talking over her. He got her just the way she was. Kind of broken, but trying so gosh darned hard to be the strong woman she wanted to be. She knew he cared. That he truly loved her. Crazy man wanted to marry her after knowing her for just one day. Who did that?

Apparently, former Navy SEALs.

"I went rogue," she reminded him. "I split when I should've stayed. I make trouble wherever I go."

"Bullshit!" Alex snapped as he flung the cubicle curtain aside and stalked to the foot of the bed. "Heard you've always wanted to be a Marine, Junior Agent."

She nearly snapped to attention. *Junior Agent?* "Yes, I did. I mean, I do. But I'm not a—"

"Junior Agent? Yes, you are. I can't recruit you into the Corps, but I can give you the next best thing. My TEAM. My rules."

Her head bobbed so hard, her back teeth were grinding.

"Is that a yes?"

"Y-y-yes," she answered accordingly. But her throat was dry. She squeaked instead of sounding confident. And she'd done it again. She'd said what she'd thought Alex wanted to hear. Not anymore. "I mean, err, n-n-no."

"Breathe," Jameson murmured, squeezing her fingers again. "You've got this, babe."

He was right. Her dad had been cruel and heartless. But Jameson was always on her side, and she could do this. She could stand up for herself. It was time.

With a deep breath, Maddie smiled, then laughed as she embraced the darnedest feeling of being free at last. She grabbed Alex's hand and told him, "Thanks, Boss, but I don't want to be a junior agent. I don't have nerves of steel, and I don't want to ever smell tear gas again or get shot at or have to kill anyone. I'd rather just be your Protocol Officer and take care of you. That all by itself sounds pretentious enough, me being any kind of officer. I've never served my country like you guys have, but I like working with you and for you. I like supporting the warfighter behind the wings, and I love everyone in this brave company of snipers. Can't I just be who I already am? That's all I want. To serve you and your guys. Your TEAM."

He had the nerve to smile like he'd already known everything she was going to tell him. "Everyone who marries into, or is a part of, a military family serves," he said extra gently. "Husbands, wives, children, and friends. Hell, even pets. Combat is never about what lies ahead, Maddie. It's always about the people we leave behind. What's this I hear about a loan shark?"

How embarrassing. "Yes, my ex... he left and..." What else was there to say? Good grief, she'd made a lot of bad choices in her life.

"Stop worrying. Those lucky bastards were inside the Black Rose when it blew. They won't be bothering you again. You've also got a new picture window, courtesy of Adam and

Walker. A clean living room, too. Take a week off. Come back refreshed and ready to work. You're needed here, Maddie. Sure hope you know that."

Jameson had taken possession of her entire hand, and he was squeezing it, letting her know he was there for her. Like he had been since this scary, exhilarating, crazy operation began.

"Deal?" Alex asked.

"Deal. Thank you."

"And you…" He turned on Jameson. "You're quite an asset to my TEAM. Mark tells me you're an expert in Krav Maga."

"I'm a student," Jameson clarified, his head cocked as if he were trying to figure Alex out.

Good luck with that.

"You took Delaney's top assassins out inside that farmhouse. I'd say that makes you more than just a student."

The sexiest blush crept up Jameson's neck and spread over his cheeks. He cleared his throat, then said, "I've learned a lot since the incident. And yes, studying Krav Maga has opened doors for me."

"I see that," Alex murmured with something akin to respect. "You've earned a week off. Be in my office the following Monday. Until then…" Alex tossed the curtain aside and stalked out.

Jameson still had Maddie's hand curled inside of his. He lifted her knuckles to his lips and asked, "Did you hear what he said about everyone who marries into military families?"

"I did," she whispered, remembering his proposal. But she'd been married before. It hadn't been much different than living under her dad's thumb, well, except for the sex part.

Even that she could've lived without. Until Jameson kissed her. He was different, more giving than taking. He tasted good and he smelled like heaven, even now when they were both grimy and sweat-stained. She'd orgasmed for the first time ever in his arms. She wanted to do that again. Did she dare believe she could ever be good enough for a man of his caliber?

"Are we going to your place or mine?"

Sucking in a trembling breath, she told him, "Yours, please." *To your bed, into your heart, anywhere... with you.*

He closed his eyes, a dreamy smile on his lips. "Good answer. Let's get out of here."

Chapter Twenty-Eight

There was something good and right when a man brought the woman he planned to marry, home to his apartment, no matter how humble the place was. Didn't matter that she'd already said no, and that she needed more time. Jameson was no quitter.

It was well after midnight by the time The TEAM's helicopter had touched down at Reagan National, after flying in from Boston. Mark and Harley both had someone waiting for them, probably their wives. Jameson ordered an Uber driver. But Alex and his father stayed onboard. Guess he lived near the Shenandoahs and flew back and forth by TEAM chopper every day. As Jameson's mom would've said had she been there, "Well, la-di-da, aren't we fancy?"

"Uh, Jameson?" Maddie asked from the doorway to his humble abode, where she'd come to a full stop instead of entering.

"Yes?" He was still holding her hand, waiting for her to join him. Hoping the apartment wasn't too spartan or messy. He'd been rushed and focused on his upcoming interview the last time he'd been home. But along with his blindness had also come a touch of obsessive-compulsive disorder. *Most of the time* he put things precisely where they belonged. His place couldn't look too bad. What didn't she like?

"Umm, lights?"

Oh, that. Smiling to himself, he flicked the switch on the wall and instant—nothing. But he was used to the dark. "I don't buy many lightbulbs. Did it come on? Can you see better now?"

"Wow. Very nice," she said as she stepped across the threshold and into his tidy world. "Who's your decorator?"

"Mom. Sometimes Dad." Jameson closed the door and locked it. "They come up from Williamsburg at least once a month to check on me. I do okay on necessities, but Mom's the interior decorator. She made sure the walls aren't bare, and that my towels are all the same color. Dad's a professor at William and Mary. I'm their only child, so they can be a little overprotective."

"He's a professor? Really?"

Founded by King William III and Queen Mary II of England in 1693, William and Mary was one of the oldest universities in the United States, second only to Harvard.

"Sure. He teaches American History. It's no big deal. You'll like him."

"My dad owns a bar."

"Oh, yeah?" Jameson asked as he made his way into his kitchen. "Where?"

"Brentwood. Crabby Rocks, that's the name of it. Don't guess you've ever been there. Me either. It's a rough neighborhood."

"Can I get you anything to drink? Coffee maybe? A beer?" he asked, not wanting her to dwell on comparisons that didn't matter. "That's all I've got unless you want ice water."

"Oh, no, you don't." Maddie was at his elbow by then, hip-checking him. "I'll get drinks and fix us something to eat. You're the one with stitches. Go sit down."

"Works for me," Jameson breathed as he granted her control of his kitchen.

The sofa was a welcome relief after one helluva nerve racking operation. He tipped his head back and let the weariness of one damned long day ease out of him. His first two days working for Alex had left him bone-tired, and whatever the ER doc used to deaden the stitching had worn the last of his defenses down. He didn't want to zone out before Maddie made it back into his arms. But he was fading fast.

"You never mention your mother." He made that quiet statement, there in his oyster shell of a bachelor's apartment, where the only feminine touches until tonight, were his mom's. She'd always been there for him.

"That's because she deserted me when I was three. I have no memory of her."

"I'm sorry." He couldn't imagine growing up without a mom. What kind of woman deserted her only daughter? "What's your dad's name?"

"Rick. Richard Bannister." By the sound of cupboards and drawers opening coming from his kitchen, Maddie was doing more than just filling two glasses of water.

"And your mother's?"

"Christina, only it's spelled K-r-y-s-t-y-n-a."

"Who was she before she married?"

"I don't know. Why? Are you going to look her up?" Maddie snorted. "I don't even know if she's still alive. Don't know if I care."

"Why would you say something like that?"

A glass or bottle landed a little too loudly on the kitchen counter. "Because if she were, or if she'd ever cared, she would've reached out to me. Don't you think?"

Jameson made a mental note to look into Krystyna Bannister. "Never mind, babe. It's none of my business. What are you fixing?"

"A midnight snack," she piped up, her voice even now that he'd dropped the subject. "Ham-and-cheese sandwiches. Want yours toasted?"

"I'm a guy. Whatever you want to fix, I'll eat," he replied as the delicious aromas drifted into the living room. Wasn't that the most heavenly smell? The woman he loved making a meal for the two of them? A homemade meal. Not fast food or take-out.

Jameson didn't mean to fall asleep. But suddenly he was waking up, and Maddie was murmuring somewhere over the top of him, "Hey, you. I'm going to take a shower. Want to join me?"

"Sure." Guess he'd missed that midnight snack. Knew he needed a shower. Wanted to jump her bones in the worst way. But...

The next thing he knew, he was flat on his back in his bed, undressed down to his boxers, with the loveliest smelling body snuggled under his arm. Maddie's freshly showered, damp head rested on his chest, and her sweet breath was in his face.

"I'm tired," she told him. "Let's just get some sleep."

Thank God. Jameson closed his eyes and let the drama of the last forty-eight plus hours fade.

Sometime later, he woke with a start, blinking at the welcome warmth of Maddie in his bed. She'd stayed. Man, she smelled good. Squeaky clean and feminine. Sound asleep under his arm. Her hand on his chest.

Jameson eased out of his boxers. Once they were on the floor, he skimmed one hand down her back and found her seductively naked beneath the sheet. Despite the tenderness in his side where he'd been wounded, everything inside of him sprang to attention. Jameson turned his forehead to hers. With his free hand, he cupped her cheek, then threaded his fingers into her long, lush hair. She'd showered, smelled like his shampoo and body wash. Somehow his spicy scent on her stoked the fire in his gut to an urgent crescendo of raw, animalistic need.

Tipping forward, he pressed a fervent kiss to the tip of her pert nose, then let his fingers and thumb roam over her face, mapping the fine contours of her brows, the smooth satin expanse of her forehead, and the exquisite luxury of her plush lips. A pronounced philtrum, the sexy eye-catching indentation between the end of her nose and her upper lip, drew the two peaks of that lip into a perfect cupid bow. So damned dainty and delicate. Made a man wonder what she saw in an animal like him. He was just some guy. She was so much better.

Maddie moaned in her sleep at his careful exploration. Closing his eyes, he brushed a kiss over her lips, needing her to wake up, yet understanding if she didn't. He could wait. A lesser man might've taken what she wasn't yet ready to relinquish while she slept, might've taken advantage of her while she was vulnerable. Not Jameson. Petting was one thing, but the art of making love required two hearts beating as one. Never coercion. Whatever Maddie needed or wanted, he would do. When she was ready. When she wanted him as much as he wanted her.

Her lips parted with a sigh, so he teased her chin and mouth with tiny nibbles and licks and tastes, his body primed and his heart opened wide. "Babe," he breathed into her. "Did I wake you?" *Sorry, not sorry.*

"Hmm," she murmured, rolling flat onto her back. "I was dreaming about you. About us."

"Good dreams?"

"Oh, yesss…" she purred. "Very good dreams."

Jameson changed positions, sliding over her body, his hard angles against her soft curves, his manhood pressed hot and heavy on her belly. His knees between her thighs. Gently, he commenced peppering her chin and throat with kisses and suckles, then drifted to her collarbones and the warm hollow where they joined. He nuzzled his way down between her breasts, then swallowed the diamond hard nipple that begged for his mouth. Everything about her was enticing as hell.

Maddie combed her fingers through his hair. Her back arched off the mattress. She was turned on, the heady fragrance of her arousal a rich perfume in his nose that arrowed straight to his groin. He palmed her other breast, babying the lovely thing, pinching her nipple until she growled the sweet sexy rumbling purr of a woman on the verge of release. Pressing her breasts together, he feasted on both tender points while his cock rested at the cusp of heaven.

But there Jameson stopped, arching his hips back just enough, not wanting this coming over too quickly.

When he backed off, Maddie's growl turned more needy, more feral. Her hands fluttered down his ribs, then over his ass, where she took two firm handfuls and forced him back to her. Thrilled, he went willingly. The instant she grabbed hold, her touch and the warmth of her fingers, nearly sent him over the edge.

"I love you so much, babe," he murmured, wanting her to feel the depth of his heart before he sank into the warmth of her body.

"Then stop playing around," she whimpered. "I'm dying here."

"Copy that," he grunted, thrusting his hips forward into warm sweet heaven on earth.

"Yesss," she cried, spreading herself wide. She hooked both heels around his waist, granting him more access, giving more of herself. Giving everything.

And he was lost in humility, that a woman like Maddie was willing to risk her heart on him. A blind man.

A wicked, blessed fire took control. Their hands were all over each other. She writhed like a temptress beneath him, her fingernails dug into his shoulders like the sweetest grappling hooks.

He took control of her hips. Honestly, what man needed urging at this point? Taking her mouth, he made love to her tonsils until they were both panting with their imminent releases. *More*, he urged his body, his knees alongside her hips for steady leverage, constant power. *Give her everything.* His heart pounded through his head and every last muscled fiber in his ass until.... His spine curved, hammering home. Finally... home.

"God, come!" he ordered with one last thrusting penetration that shook the bed and blasted him into the stars. Deep into her.

"Yessss! Oh, good grief, I'm… I'm…!" she moaned, whining and writhing and sweating and hissing, "Jameson, Jameson, Jamessssson!"

And once again, they were linked. Two stars joined in the sweetest cataclysmic furnace that had once created mankind. Just that quick. They were one, just one. The perfect one. One her. One him. One brand-new soul with the same shuddering heartbeat. The same heated breath.

He sighed into her face, unintentionally fanning the flames that still flickered at the base of his spine. His arms were shaking, and so was Maddie. He buried his face in the quivering hollow of her neck, so damned content and thrilled, he had to fight his tears.

Since that incident in Iraq, he'd become a damned baby. His mom believed his tender emotions were a side effect, that maybe there was some undiagnosed traumatic brain injury. But his dad explained things differently.

He believed those untapped emotions now releasing at the most inopportune times—like now—were simply Jameson's body and soul acclimating to his new reality. That he was now more aware of the universe around him, which in turn, made him more sensitive to other living things and feelings. Other powers and energies, both good and bad.

Which was true. Jameson did perceive people and his surroundings more acutely than he ever had before the incident. He sensed good intentions, and he felt more deeply. Sometimes his lack of sight provided a virtual kind of insight. The incident had awakened an inner sixth sense that made him, well, more sensitive, damn it. And sometimes that sensitivity leaked out his eyes.

There were moments these past five years when he'd wondered if the trade had been worth it, his vision for this cutting new sensitivity to the universe, with all its pulsating depths and precarious twists. Reclaiming his confidence in his dark new world had taken time. It'd been damned hard. But now? With this panting beauty hot and sweaty in his arms and under his body, Jameson had no more doubts. He didn't need sight to know he'd found all he'd ever wanted.

"I love you," he told her with utmost certainty. "You're mine, Maddie. My heart. My soul. God bless, I hope you know that."

He heard her smile. Really. Smiles glowed with warmth, and Maddie was glowing now. Contentment purred off her like a warm, crackling fire that even the densest man on earth could've heard, if he'd been smart enough to listen.

She brushed her fingertips into his hair. Still purring. Still smiling. Her chest heaved. "I do know that. I didn't hurt you, did I? Are you okay?"

"Yeah, I'm good. No worries," he growled as he wiped the back of a hand over his eyes. "But I've got to warn you. I'm as emotional as a pregnant woman sometimes."

"I like that you're not afraid to tell me something like that. Men aren't usually so—"

"Sensitive? Yeah, that's me. I like fluffy puppies and dark chocolate, too."

Maddie's honest laughter made him smile. "Want to know how I'm sure you love me?"

He dropped his forehead to hers. "How, babe?" he breathed.

Her lips melted against his. "Because I think I've been looking for you for a long time,'" she whispered into his mouth. "You're a keeper."

"Nah, you're the keeper. All mine."

She giggled like the little girl she was in so many confounding ways. "Then let's be keepers together. Let's keep each other, just like this. Forever."

He canted his head to make sure he'd heard right. Was that what it sounded like? Had she just proposed? Or was that her way of accepting his proposal? He tread lightly. "Do you know what went through my mind when the Black Rose exploded today? When I thought I'd never get to hear your voice again, never taste another kiss, never smell the lavender flowers in your hair?"

She stilled beneath him. "What?" she asked, her voice as soft and timid as a child's.

He kissed the end of that perfect nose. "I thought how cruel God was, to send me an angel, then let her die while I stood just inches away, too far away to save her. For Him to take her back after letting me have everything I'd ever wanted for only a couple days. To lie to me and tell me I was finally going to be okay, then break my heart like it was all a joke. A divine dirty trick. That I really was alone in the dark."

"Oh, Jameson…"

He didn't care that he was making a fool of himself. Maddie needed to know. "I don't want to go through life without you. I probably sound like a stalker, but I'm not letting you go. I want every last breath I breathe and every step I take to be with you by my side. I'm willing to wait as long as you need. Mom's still expecting us for dinner this Sunday. I told her before I didn't think we could make it, but we can now. If you'll go with me."

"Can I still leave if I want to?"

He swallowed hard, but asked, "You mean from Mom and Dad's place? Sure. We don't have to go if you'd rather not."

"I meant from here. Your apartment. If we get married, can I still l-leave?"

Ah, she was doing it again. Pulling back into her timid shell. It took all he had to tell her, "You can leave anytime, babe. Any day. You'll have your own key. If you choose to marry me, this'll be your home, not your dungeon." *It'll break my heart, but if you want to leave me—*

"I mean, I'll still need to work and buy groceries and clothes, stuff like that. Not leave, leave. Just..." Her shoulders lifted. Her hips wiggled. "Just do what I want, when I want, then come home. You wouldn't lock me out if I was late or if I missed my bus, would you?"

God, she was asking for permission to be a human being. He dropped his head to her shoulder, understanding her ex and her father a little better, and liking them less and less. Both bastards had instilled fear into this delightful, charming, but oh, so timid woman, enough that she'd misunderstood a simple proposal.

"Maddie, sweetheart," he breathed, his damned eyeballs watering again. "I'm not the boss of you, and there are no rules to falling in love with me. Only give and take. Only total freedom. Lovers are meant to fly together, not drag each other down or hold each other back. Men don't own women in this country. You can move out of state if you decide you want to leave. Do anything, be anything you choose. I just hoped you'd want to be all that with me."

"Why would I do that? Leave you?" she asked, her voice tiny, as her palms settled flat to his cheeks, her thumbs under his chin, forcing his head back up.

She was looking at him. He could tell. Seeing the teary eyes he knew were blank and would forevermore be unreceptive to light or expression. Eyes that could never again convey what was in his soul. Yet he sensed no rejection or pity coming from Maddie. Only love when she planted her lush, warm lips on his mouth and what was left of his battered heart.

"Does that mean you'll stay?" he had to ask.

"Yes, Jameson, I want the same thing as you. Can I live here with you while we're engaged?"

"You can stay as long as you want."

"Forever?"

Hallelujah! "And the day after," he breathed, so damned happy. "And every day after that."

Chapter Twenty-Nine

Amazed at the size of the bonus check that hit his bank account simply for joining The TEAM, Jameson took Maddie house-hunting. It was a week after she'd moved in with him, but his apartment was small, built for a single person. They needed room to play and love and grow together.

But first, he'd insisted they update the twelve-year-old budget sedan she'd bought after she'd graduated night school. His treat. He couldn't wipe the smile off his face when she climbed behind the wheel of her very own sapphire-blue, fresh off the truck SUV and squealed, "Are you sure we can afford this?"

"We…" he purred, loving that grounding, delightful, two-letter word, "can afford low interest and a five-year loan."

"Oh, yeah," she giggled. "Us and the bank, huh?"

He tugged the seatbelt across his chest and fastened himself in. Maddie had been like a kid in a candy store on the car lot. For every practical, cheaper, older model she'd selected, he'd upped the options until he knew for certain he was spoiling her. She'd declined every option, saying she didn't need all-wheel drive, nine speed automatic transmission, or a 3.5-liter V6 engine. But he got them for her all the same. The only thing this woman asked for was the ability to charge her cell phone. She had all that and more now, including a new wireless charger for the cell he had yet to buy her.

Two hundred-eighty horses sprang to life the instant she pressed the ignition button.

"Where are we going?" she asked breathlessly. "We've got another week off. The sky's the limit."

"You're driving. You tell me."

"Okay then," she breathed. "Look out world, here we come!"

Jameson adored the excitement in her tone. Since the morning had gone well so far, he broached a subject that had been on his mind since the first time they'd made love. "Do you see us having kids?"

"Sure. Someday."

Cocking his knee, Jameson turned sideways, facing her. "How many? One? A dozen?"

Judging by the direction change in her voice, she'd glanced at him, then turned away. "To be honest, I've never thought about it. It never felt like something I could do with, you know. Him."

He reached for and found the soft silky curls resting on her shoulder. "And now?"

Her hair brushed over his fingers as she turned her attention to him, then just as quickly back to the traffic on the street. "How many would you like?"

"Two's the national norm, but I was an only child, and so were you, and—"

"You want a big family."

His head canted at the hint of excitement in that statement. "Yes. If that's what you want. It was lonely growing up.

Always an adult, never just a kid. Not sure I want to do that to our child."

"So, we're house hunting for a mansion?"

That made him smile. "Only if you'll help me fill it up, babe."

Once again, he could hear her smiling. The energy between them when Maddie was happy felt warm, like a summer breeze off the Atlantic. A man could get lost inside that breeze.

"I'm not good at numbers," she, the only one in the SUV with the accounting degree, lied blithely, while the vehicle shifted into a slow curve. "How about we practice until we get it right?"

Damned if Jameson's eyes didn't burn with unexpected emotion. Sweet Baby Jesus, this woman was everything he'd wanted. "I can live with that," he murmured, his voice husky and his heart in his throat.

Her fingers reached under his chin. "Two people who love each other can do anything," she whispered. "A very smart man I know taught me that."

Taking hold of that sweet hand, he kissed her palm. "Can't remember what I ever did before you came along."

Her arm lifted with a shrug. "You make me happy. Let's make lots of babies. Lots of little boys who look just like you."

"And dozens of fairy princesses who look like their mom."

Maddie drew her hand back and feigned choking. "Dozens?"

"We'll see," he promised with a grin. "You're the CPA in our family. I'll let you keep track."

They were both laughing, as the SUV maintained a straight away for the next few miles.

Since that first topic went so well, Jameson broached another. "Have you ever wanted to talk with your mother?"

Instant silence. Precisely what he'd expected. He gave Maddie time to absorb that possibility. He'd never force her, but this was one very large stone left unturned in her life. And he had a good feeling in his gut, so...

"No," she admitted, the joy in her tone throttled down to a flat nothing. "Why would I? She left me."

Jameson stretched his long legs, loving the comfort this vehicle offered. "Thought maybe you'd like to hear from her why she left, not just what your dad told you."

They rode in silence for a few long minutes before Maddie admitted, "He did lie a lot. Always made me feel worthless when I was a kid, too. I invited him to my college graduation. Thought that would impress him. Make him finally see that I was good for something after all."

"He didn't show," Jameson said quietly.

"Of course not. I should've known better than to ask. Kids aren't very smart, you know. Their whole life, they think they're the problem, that they're what's wrong. That they're the reason they get slapped or chewed out. They try everything they know how to make their dads and moms love them."

Envisioning the younger, more gullible version of Maddie, Jameson settled his fingers over her forearm. "Kids *are* smart, babe. Their only mistake is they unconditionally love the people who should love them first. That's why abused children cover up for their cruel, intentionally thoughtless parents."

And Rick Bannister was a flaming narcissist. In between getting to know Maddie better and moving her into his apartment, Jameson had investigated the guy, which was why he was certain Bannister only kept Maddie to hurt her mother. Yet, because he was Maddie's father, Jameson gave the bastard the benefit of the doubt. "Things aren't always black and white. Deep down, we're all just kids doing the best we can with what we've got to work with."

She huffed through her nostrils. "You should've gone into child psychology."

"I did. That's my minor. Figured it'd go well with criminal profiling."

A few more moments of silence invaded that great new car smell. "I don't know where she lives," Maddie murmured. "I, umm, guess I just believed my dad. What he said."

"How could you have known any different? She left when you were a baby." He canted his head her way, listening for a telltale sigh or a hard swallow. Maddie was still so much that little deserted girl, searching for her place in the world. Which, until he'd come along, she hadn't yet found. Not with her old man, nor her ex. Jameson couldn't imagine how hard life had to have been for a timid girl without a mother against those odds. "What else did he tell you about her?"

She cleared her throat. "When he was mad at me, he used to say I looked just like her and acted like her, too. That I was just as bad. Just as ugly. I hated when he came home drunk after work. Booze makes him crazy. Loud. Mean."

Jameson pinched his lips to keep his opinion of her father from spilling out. Rick Bannister was not only a narcissist, he was an over-weight, alcoholic asshole, with two felonies to his credit. One for stealing his neighbor's car, the other for nearly beating that neighbor to death after Rick decided he liked the guy's wife. She'd shot him to save her husband, which proved how one-sided Rick's take on reality was. Her husband recovered, which was the only reason Rick hadn't done time for manslaughter. All this went down before he'd sweet talked Krystyna into marrying him. She'd been pregnant by him, trapped into marriage with a charming, but mean-tempered man.

In his quiet investigation, Jameson had also uncovered Krystyna's medical history. Two miscarriages, one live birth, and a frightening number of emergency room visits. Some other important details, too. But none of that mattered if Maddie chose not to investigate her mother further. Some things were better left alone. Jameson just didn't think a woman's mother should be one of those things.

"What would you say if I told you I know where she lives?"

"You do?"

He nodded in lieu of answering. Jameson could feel Maddie's heart racing. She was probably grabbing sharp glances at him. Breathy panic crackled through the air between them. The atmosphere in her car had turned into a sucking black hole.

"Why would you do this to me?" she whispered.

"Because I'm a mama's boy, Maddie. Yeah. Big, tough Navy SEAL here, but I know who's been in my corner every step of my way. I grew up with everything you didn't, and I guess... I believe..." He inhaled deeply, needing a gut full of positivity before he said, "Most moms love their kids more than they love themselves. Like my mom loves me. We don't have to visit Krystyna, honest. We can just leave this in the past and never find out why she left you behind, why she thought she had to. But if you ever decide to meet her, I'll go with you. I've got your six, babe. I'll always be in your corner. Just want you to consider the possibility that she might be in your corner, too."

"You... y-y-you want me to give her a second chance?"

His fingers squeezed her arm tighter. "You gave your dad more second chances than he deserved. Why not your mom?"

A quiet hitch in her breath was all that answered. Miles passed. The tires hummed over smooth pavement.

Jameson took his hand back. By then, he had no idea where they were, except inside Maddie's car. The traffic sounds were the same. Busy. Rushed. A herd of people he'd never see or know rushing by like soldiers off to their private wars. She maneuvered corners, waited for red lights, then smoothly pulled over to a curb. Still not speaking.

At last he asked, "Where are we?"

"Brentwood. Crabby Rocks."

Great. They were parked outside her dad's bar. Her expressionless tone explained more than her words. Maddie was hurting, right back where she'd started, and that was on Jameson. Thank goodness it was too early in the day to go inside for a drink.

"I called him this morning," Jameson admitted. "Your dad. While you were showering after the second time we made love. Before I made breakfast."

She snorted. "How'd that go?"

"He's everything you said he was and less."

"What'd you expect?"

"Honestly?" Jameson turned in the direction where he guessed Maddie was looking. At what he now knew was a two-bit bar in a rundown neighborhood that boasted more murders per capita than most other Washington, DC, neighborhoods. Computers for the visually impaired were a godsend. A guy could find anything if he knew where to look and what to look for. "I wanted his permission to marry you, Maddie. That's why I called your dad. I wanted his blessing. It's what a real man does when he loves a woman. He does the right thing. He respects her enough to man up and ask to meet her dad, so they can talk face-to-face about the woman he intends to take away from that father."

Maddie was staring at Jameson by then. He could feel her eyes on him. "What'd he say?"

Unfastening his seatbelt, Jameson tugged Maddie closer, wishing new cars didn't all come with sturdy consoles between the driver and passenger seats. "He said he didn't know what I was talking about, that he didn't have a daughter. To get lost."

"Th-that's all?"

Jameson nodded as he leaned her under his arm. She was crying, he could tell. Rick Bannister had also told him to fuck off, that he'd beat the shit out of Jameson if he ever showed his face in his bar or at his front door. But Maddie didn't need to know that.

"Have you talked with my m-mom, too?"

"No, babe. But I know where she lives, and I have her phone number if you want it. She's actually not far from here. She lives in Bailey's Crossroads. But that's up to you. I just thought if your dad could so easily deny the beautiful, intelligent, courageous woman that his daughter is, well... Maybe he'd treated his wife the same way, and she's feeling as bad as you. As lost."

"I don't feel bad. Least I didn't until—"

"Until I brought all this crap up, huh?"

She was breathing hard. Swallowing hard, too. Trembling. "My life with Dad *was* crap," she admitted. "So… I've been close to where she lives all this time, huh? Does she, umm, live in a house or on the street, or is she—"

"A house. She lives in the nice residential area. There's an elementary school within walking distance. She teaches fifth grade there."

"Wow, you've been busy…" If Maddie's heart beat any harder, she'd go into cardiac arrest. But for the first time, hope had also whispered through her tone.

"Breathe," Jameson murmured into the side of her head. "We don't have to do anything you don't want to. Just thought you'd feel better knowing you have a mom, and that she still lives nearby. Close enough to visit someday, when you choose. It's all up to you."

Maddie sniffed. He'd made her cry. "Aw, babe, I'm sorry. Damn, I'm an ass. I ruined your new car day. I've spoiled everything."

"No," she whimpered, her face pressed into his neck under his ear, her breath warm and moist on his skin. "When I was a little girl, I used to dream my mom was a queen from another country. That she only left me behind because she was so much more important than me, you know? That her country needed her more than I did. That she'd come back someday to get me."

He held Maddie tight. She was coming apart, and his heart was breaking for having hurt her. "Let's go back to my place. We'll go mansion hunting another day." *And I'll keep my big mouth shut from now on.*

"No. I... I think I'd like to call her." She turned in his arms and smoothed her fingertips into his hair over that same ear. "You went to all this trouble just for me. Maybe I could call her, you know, j-j-just to talk. See if she remembers me. Where's her number?"

Jameson produced his phone and handed it over, tipping his lips to her forehead. "I'll never lie to you, and I only want what's truly best for you. I'm okay if you'd rather not call. But if you do, her name's in my contacts list under B for Bannister."

"She kept her married name? She's not—?"

"Remarried? You won't know until you talk to her."

The tension between them changed from desolate to excited, and in that moment, Jameson wasn't sure what the hell he'd done. This could go so, so bad. Yet he'd relied on his gut, and he had that same feeling now as when he'd first met Maddie. This could also go so, so good.

She was working his phone. Then, "H-hello...? Is Krystyna there? Oh..." Silence. "Well. Umm... okay, well... umm... hi."

Jameson pressed his nose in Maddie's hair, content to breathe the flowery scent of this amazing woman into his soul, while she reached out for the mother who might just need her as much as Krystyna needed her baby girl.

"Umm..." Maddie stalled. She smacked her lips and gulped and breathed too hard until, at last, she whispered, "My name's Maddie—"

"Maddie? Madelyn Bannister?" Krystyna shrieked loud enough Jameson heard her over the connection. "Is this you? Are you my baby girl?! Good grief, tell me it's you! God, please let you be my Maddie! My baby!"

"It's me, M-m-mom," she choked through her tears. "Yes, it's me."

Jameson bowed his head and smiled. He didn't need to see to know they were headed to Bailey's Crossroads next.

Chapter Thirty

Maddie stared at the traditional American Foursquare home at the end of a neatly edged walk in Bailey's Crossroads, Virginia. The walk led straight up a couple steps to a pair of hunter-green doors with frosted windowpanes. A sturdy brass knocker that formed a golden heart. One long, elegant brass handle. Two huge, red geranium plants in terracotta planters, one at each side of those doors. The matching hunter-green runner that started at the edge of a graciously large porch, ended at those doors. White lattice work concealed all lower sides of the porch, and plump Boston ferns in bright red pots hung from chains attached to the ceiling. The house was postcard perfect. Surely a teacher couldn't afford to live here.

Weathervanes decorated every quaint, tidy home in this delightful neighborhood, where wide green lawns stretched like welcome mats from one home to the next. But the proud standard flying high at the steepled peak of this address on Melody Lane was as telling as the woman Maddie hoped she'd find inside. A tremendous, golden, perforated heart, each hole in it another cookie-cutter-shaped heart. Hope in that beautiful weathervane had echoed inside Maddie's chest the moment she'd parked at the curb and turned off the ignition.

That SUV all by itself had made this day one of accomplishment. She'd felt as if she'd arrived when Jameson guided her through the automobile loan process, which hadn't been difficult at all. But doing that with him made everything almost, well, fun. She'd been on top of the world. But now...

Her feet refused to move, and she was afraid she'd pass out. Her lungs had rebelled, refusing her breathing rights. Her poor heart now resided between her tonsils, which might also explain why her stomach felt it needed to climb out of her mouth. Tiny black dots danced at the edge of her peripheral. The only thing holding her steady and upright was the valiant, handsome man at her side, his left hand at her elbow, his white cane stuck out in front of them like a divining rod. Or a spear in case the gentle woman she hoped to encounter ended up being another dragon to vanquish. Like Rick Bannister.

"You'd think she'd be waiting, watching for me," Maddie mumbled more to herself than to Jameson.

"She's probably as anxious about this meeting as you," he confided. "Put yourself in her shoes. She deserted her little girl. What would you say to that baby when she returned to you as an elegant, well-cultured woman?"

"I'm not elegant or cultured."

"Oh, yes, you are." Like the bulwark of strength he always was, Jameson wrapped his strong left arm around her shoulders and breathed into her ear, "One step at a time, Maddie. That's how we get the tough jobs done. You can do this. I have enough faith in you for both of us."

That right there was what made him different from the overbearing men in her life. Jameson offered endless encouragement, never bullying. He'd only ever built her up. Even when he'd been angry with her back at Delaney's warehouse, he'd stayed at her side instead of letting her face Alex alone.

She huffed through her nose. Her poor heart fluttered like a sparrow had gotten trapped in her ribs. It hurt. The risk of this letdown was suddenly too great. Better to hold onto that little girl's dream of a queenly mother, who'd merely stepped out of her daughter's life because she had to rule an entire nation. That fairytale version seemed so much safer than taking another step forward and proving just how little anyone wanted an unlovable—

"Maddie?"

Good grief. There she is. At her door. Krystyna Bannister. My mother. She's blonde. Light blue eyes. Just like me.

"Is that…? Good grief. It is! It is you! I recognize my baby anywhere!" The mother Maddie had been dreaming of all her motherless years ran off that porch and down her walk, and then Maddie was…

Found…

Wanted…

Wrapped up tight in a hug that stole her breath in all the best ways.

"I… I…" There were no words for the wealth of feelings and emotions bubbling up from her poor battered heart. Filling it up. Flooding its darkest fears with something she'd long forgotten. Being treasured by the mother who had only ever loved her. Krystyna's blonde hair was wrapped in a thick braid that hung down her back. But that voice, that sweet caring lullaby of notes from a language of somewhere far away, was why Maddie had dreamed her mother was a queen.

They cried and cried, clinging to each other, their hands warm and possessive.

"My baby girl. My *dziecko anioła*. I hate your father with every feather of my soul," Krystyna cried as she enfolded

Maddie in a vaguely familiar feminine scent of powder and…
Chantilly perfume. That's what it was. It came in a pink box,
and it smelled like cloves and orange blossoms, and it was…
My Mom.

"He's not on my Christmas list, either," Maddie replied,
feeling rather lighthearted and pleased now that she knew her
mother wanted her.

"But I really hate Rick. The day he kicked me out of our
house, I swore I'd come back for you. He said if I ever showed
my face, he'd cut your throat and throw your dead body into
the street at me. And I believed him. He said he'd call
Immigration. I couldn't take the chance of losing you
forever." Krystyna's chin quivered as she cupped Maddie's
cheeks and peppered her face with soft kisses. "I missed you
every day, my sweet lost *dziecko anioła*. Every single second.
He stole everything from me the day he made me leave you
behind."

"He kicked me out, too. I wanted to join the Marines. He
wanted a cook, a maid, and a slave."

Krystyna's elegant fingers knotted into fists against
Maddie's head. "That black-hearted bastard."

"But I went to college, and I graduated, and I have a really
good job now, and I like what I do, and… and… *Mom*…" And
she was doing it again. Talking too fast and saying too much.
But that word… That one word broke her heart and healed it,
all in one breath. "Mom," she cried, the poor heart opened
wide. "Mom. My Mom…"

They stood locked in each other's arms, breathing each
other in, remembering and loving and soaking in all they'd
reclaimed. Maddie had never hurt so much, nor felt so loved.
This was what she'd missed, and she'd never lose it again.

Krystyna pressed a soft kiss to her tear-soaked cheek. "I am so proud of you."

"Why didn't you go to the authorities when he kicked you out?" Jameson asked quietly.

"Good grief!" Maddie came to her senses. "M-m-mom. This is Jameson Tenney. He's the reason I'm here today. This was his idea, to come meet you. I'm so glad I did."

With Maddie safe inside one arm, Krystyna's gaze raked over Jameson, his black hair, the spectacles he hadn't taken off, and the way he'd cocked his head the tiniest bit when he'd been introduced. The way he stood there tall and proud, always listening. Her chin dipped when she noticed the straight white cane he held erect at his centerline.

"Because I was in the country illegally, Mr. Tenney. My student visa expired after I met Maddie's father." Her voice had turned stern, but not once had she remarked about his cane.

"You're Polish," he stated with a genuine smile, and Maddie was so proud of Jameson. He always knew what to say and do.

"Yes, I'm from Poland, but I'm an American citizen now." She looked to Maddie. "By the time I swore my allegiance to America, I'd lost track of you. It took me a while to find you again, but by then, you were in college. I'm sorry, *dziewczynka*. I didn't know what he'd told you about me, and I didn't want you to have to decide between the two of us. I chose to wait for you to find me, instead of me causing you more pain."

Jameson cleared his throat. "*Dziecko anioła* is…?"

"Polish for angel baby," Krystyna replied, her head up and a good strong arm still around Maddie. "And *dziewczynka* means baby girl. What are your intentions for my daughter?"

Maddie couldn't hold back the cheek-cracking smile that stretched from one ear to the other at being named the daughter of this strong woman. "Relax, Mom. Jameson is my hero. He's a former Navy SEAL, and we work together in Alexandria, and we're going to marry in a month or two, and I want you to walk me down the aisle."

"Marry?" Krystyna's voice quavered.

Maddie looked into the sweet faded-blue eyes of the first person she had ever loved. "Yes, Mom. It'll be a small wedding, maybe by a justice of the peace is all. I don't have a lot of family, just—"

"But I do," Jameson announced with unexpected rowdy conviction. "SEAL teams consist of six platoons, Maddie. Each platoon is sixteen SEALs strong. Two officers. One chief. Thirteen enlisted. Trust me. My brothers'll all be there. Then there's Mom's and Dad's brothers and sisters. Two sets of grandparents. All my cousins."

"And I have eleven brothers and sisters, *dziewczynka*. All live in America and all with sons and daughters, cousins you've never met. Your grandparents, Matka and Ojciec, my mom and dad, are still alive. They'll be so thrilled to meet you. I'll have to rent the hall in my church. It might be large enough, but if it isn't…"

Maddie looked to Jameson. He was grinning. Like her. So many words she used were her mother's. She traded Krystyna's embrace for Jameson's, knocking his cane to the ground as she burrowed under his chin.

"Thank you," she told him as she circled her fingers around the back of his neck and pulled his forehead down to hers. "You gave me back my mom."

"I think we should serve lemonade at our reception," he whispered into her mouth. "What do you think?"

"I think I love you, Jameson Tenney. Forever and ever—"

"Amen," he breathed.

Chapter Thirty-One

"Lexie. Whatcha doing, sweetheart?" Alex asked, not sure what his precocious little one was up to. Her bright brown eyes sparkled from the corner of the front room sofa where she sat with Bradley snuggled in her arms. With his face pressed to her—chest?

"I feeding baby, Daddy," she said, the sarcastic "duh!" in her tone obvious, like he shouldn't have asked such a silly question.

"Oh, my, no," Kelsey murmured. She'd barely settled into the nearby rocking chair after making sure Lexie had a good hold on Bradley. Now she was back on her feet. "No, honey. Put your shirt down. Let me get you a baby bottle to feed Bradley."

"No, Mama. I wanna feed him like you do. He likes it this way."

Alex nearly roared with laughter the way Lexie had Bradley's face plastered to her flat, little girl chest, as if she knew better than her mom and dad. Girls. God, he loved them. Never a dull moment at his house.

"Kelsey? This one's all yours."

Her brown eyes laughed back at him. "Just you wait. Bradley's going to give you a run for your money one of these days."

"Plan on it, Mama." Nothing would make Alex happier.

After all was said and done and explained to the satisfaction of the authorities in Boston, he'd brought Mel home and put him to bed. The next day, he moved his old man out of the comfortable bedroom in the basement, upstairs to the bedroom closer to Lexie's, two doors from Alex and Kelsey's.

Since that telling night in Boston, Mel had been semi-faithful about taking his meds, with Alex riding shotgun to make certain he did. Mel had also explained more about his relationship with Pops Delaney and the Irish mob. His claim of being Pops' lieutenant wasn't verifiable, since everyone involved was dead, and, according to Tucker Chase, the FBI had no evidence he'd ever been to Ireland or in Boston. But none of those answers or explanations changed the fact that he'd deserted his family for a life of intrigue and dirty-dealing. That he'd left them as destitute as beggars on his folks' doorstep, then missed most of his only son's life. Not to mention his wife's and parents' deaths and funerals.

If Mel had ever been sharp enough to leave no trace behind, as he claimed, he would've been a completely different person than the father Alex remembered. Which cast doubt on every word out of the old con's mouth. Alex didn't fall for Mel's stories. He was certain they were mostly lies. But Mel *had* gotten them to the Black Rose in time to extricate Maddie from certain death, and he *had* seemed to know details about Lucy Delaney that agreed with Jameson Tenney's more trustworthy observations. Those two truths Mel told were undeniable.

Since that day, he'd also filled in a couple holes in a certain nine-year-old kid's recollections. Not enough for Alex to give him a key to Kelsey's castle, but enough he was willing to listen and hear the old guy out. Which brought peace back to the castle, as well as story time with Gramps for Lexie, whom he now remembered.

Boston authorities had turned Mel over to Alex for safekeeping. Said they didn't send Alzheimer's patients to jail. Which made him Alex's father, once and for all. Mel was finally home and that was okay.

Alex now knew that Mel's lucid moments, which was all that their time together in Boston had been, would occur less frequently from now on. Alzheimer's robbed everything from its victims, and this might be the hardest battle Alex would ever fight. But what else did a person do when their long-lost parent finally came home? For that answer, Alex looked to Lexie.

At the moment, she'd traded Bradley for her Grampa. Mel had her on his knee while she read one of her favorite books to him, a story about a pink ballerina. They were sitting in the dining room, between the stone fireplace and the wide picture window that offered a magnificent view of the Shenandoah Mountains to the West. Whisper, the laziest guard dog in Virginia, and Lexie's faithful shadow, snoozed on his side at their feet, while Smoke sat alert at the window.

Mel would offer an insincere *'aha'* whenever Lexie pointed out something he needed to know about one of her beloved characters. She'd shove the book into his face when he dozed off, scolding him to *'stay awake and listen, Grampa, until I'm through reading.'* That then, only then, could he take a nap. That reading was important; he should try it all by himself sometime.

It was plain to see she adored her Grampa, as much as Alex still adored his Gramps, Patrick Bradley Stewart. Full circle, damn it. Life had come full circle, and Alex was standing back where it all began. With his Gramps, and Lexie's Grampa, and a whole lot of family between the two headstrong Irishmen.

As far as The TEAM went, Mark was still managing assignments and doling out his brand of leadership. The man was a natural. Didn't hurt that Harley was now fully engaged and more single-minded than he'd been in years. Which was saying a lot for a man as beset by post-traumatic stress as he'd been when he'd come home from war. But he'd stepped up as Mark's right hand man now, and didn't that beat all? Alex had two strong leaders on the job, holding The TEAM fort down.

With all well at home for the moment, he planned to go back to work in a couple days. Where he'd once considered ending The TEAM he'd built from the ground up, he knew now that he'd over-reacted. He had an appointment with Jameson Tenney first thing Monday morning. He still needed to have that chat with Mother. But he'd never been more sure. He'd built a damned solid company of snipers, and ended up with the best family a man could ask for. Life was son of a bitchin' good.

"Hey, son. Alex?" Mel interrupted from his cozy seat with Lexie.

As usual, his timing was impeccable. Alex jolted out of his first half-pleasant reverie in days, annoyed. "Yes?"

"You do know Pops was my only sibling, don't you?"

Thank God. "So?"

"Well, err, so… Lucy was his only kid, and you're my only kid, and—"

"And your point is?"

"They're, umm…" Mel placed both hands over Lexie's ears and whispered, "They're both dead. Him and her."

"What are you trying to tell me? Spit it out."

Lexie shook her head, dislodging Mel's hands with a crabby, "Stop it, Grampa. I reading."

"Well, Pops had a will," he told Alex. "Last time I seen it, he left everything to Lucy first. Wanna know who else he named as beneficiary in case something happened to her?"

A pregnant pause filled the lovely stone home, before he begrudgingly muttered, "Not really."

"What's a bena-fishery, Daddy?" Lexie asked, her brows furrowed, and her bottom lip stuck forward in a studious pout.

"It's someone who's related to a person who dies, sweetheart. Like a wife or child," Alex explained. "They inherit whatever that person left behind."

"Is I your bena-fishery?"

"Mama, you, and Bradley," he told his darling daughter.

Her big brown eyes welled with tears. "But I don't want you to die. Neither does baby Bradley or Mommy or… Wah!"

He waved for his strong-willed, soft-hearted daughter to come sit with him. Lexie tossed her book aside and traded Mel for her father's arms. "I'm not going anywhere," Alex promised as he snuggled her in where she belonged. "We've still got to go birthday present shopping for Mommy, remember?"

She nodded, her curly head bumping under his chin as she wiped her face and settled onto his lap. "I love you, Daddy."

He pressed a kiss to the crown of her perfect head. "I love you too, baby girl," he said as he looked over her to his dad. "Mel, explain."

The golden sunset spilling through that huge picture window casting an unearthly, almost heavenly glow on the old codger's craggy features. "You, son. You were always his second beneficiary. Not me. I can almost guarantee his Irish lawyer's gonna be calling you one of these days, just wait and see. I got his card somewhere. When I find it, I'll give it to you. Maybe you oughta call him. Pops never trusted Lucy. Can't tell you how many times he wrote her out of his will, added her back in, then wrote her out again. Might even explain why she left Ireland in a snit and came to New York. She mighta found out she wasn't getting anything. Always was a hateful little thing."

Alex refused to care. It'd be a cold day in hell before he accepted a cent of ill-gotten gains from an uncle he'd never met, much less from an underworld crime boss. A lowlife who hadn't had the balls to stand by his own father, who'd disappointed Patrick Bradley Stewart so deeply, he'd never told his only grandson about that uncle or cousin.

The notoriety of those associations hadn't hit American media outlets yet, thank God. Alex could hardly wait for that shitstorm to reach Alexandria. But it would. Reporters would be climbing all over him, once they knew he'd been related to Pops and Lucy Delaney. Probably other mob bosses, too. They might think he should take over whatever was left of Pops' empire. Like hell. Alex refused to be bullied or coerced by the legacy of any damned thug. He'd deal with the mess his uncle and cousin left, later.

Want to bet Tucker Chase already knew? Alex shook his head at the trouble that ending the Delaney empire might cause him and his TEAM. His family. He might just have to work closely with the FBI before this thing was over. Damn.

"You seen my big bag?" Mel asked suddenly, his blue eyes gone blank, searching the room for some unknown bag he never mentioned when he was lucid. "Says NAVY on it. I was a SEAL, you know."

And here we go again.

"Have you looked in your bedroom?" Alex asked his father tiredly. Didn't matter what he said. Just answering seemed enough to calm his father's angst.

Lexie burrowed deeper inside the crook of her father's arms. "Grampa's not feeling good anymore, Daddy," she murmured. She knew the signs. Also knew story time with Grampa was done for a while.

"He'll be back," Alex assured her quietly. "Grampa forgets things when he's tired, doesn't he?"

"Ah huh and sometimes he's stinky," she whispered behind her fingers.

Alex smiled. Yes, for sure, Mel was now certifiably old and losing his mind. But he was off the streets and safe, and that mattered. Even to Alex. Because, like it or not, want to admit it or not, Mel Stewart was his dad. Just like Patrick Bradley had been Mel's and Pops Delaney's father. Made a man wonder what possessed sons to change their names, deny their birthrights, and their families. Yet Lucy had done the same thing when she'd left Ireland for the lights of NYC. Like father, like daughter.

Alex also wondered if Gram and Gramps had ever known about or met Lucy. If so, had they missed her? Had they grieved for the little granddaughter they surely would've loved? Better question, had she known about them? Probably not. As conniving as Lucy was, she would've used them worse than Mel had, if she'd known where they'd lived. Then, like him, she would've left.

Seemed Pops and Lucy had both wanted to be something they weren't, something different than they'd been born to be. Something greedy and wicked and powerful. Mel had been caught up in that same intrigue, enough that he'd turned his back on his family, too. Which was just plain sad. He'd lost everything. Well, except for that nine-year-old kid who, apparently, was still looking out for his old man.

In the end, life was just a string of decisions followed by consequences. Either people learned by their mistakes, or they didn't. Alex had finally learned how to forgive the old fart sitting across from him and Lexie, the gray-haired man with his head tipped forward, already sound asleep and drooling. Yeah, him.

Because a man took care of his family. All of them.

Even prodigal fathers.

Epilogue

Jameson lay on his back, his eyes open, staring at the ceiling he couldn't see. Not like whether it was spackled or smoothly painted plaster mattered. He didn't care, and seeing it wouldn't enhance its value. Not to him. Blindness had a way of balancing the scales, of forcing a guy to acknowledge what was important in his life and what wasn't.

His mom had called last night, after they'd gotten home from spending the afternoon with Krystyna. Wedding plans were now in full swing. Krystyna was busy ordering invitations and making sure she left no one out. Karen was busy ordering flowers, cakes, and all those things mothers ordered when their only son was getting married.

She'd cried when he'd told her she was going to be a mother-in-law, but not once had she questioned his judgement, the timing, or his choice of the woman who would soon be her daughter-in-law. Which was so like his mom. Jameson couldn't wait for Karen and Jules Tenney to meet Maddie this afternoon. His parent's total trust in him had always been his springboard into whatever he'd set his mind to. They, more than anyone else in his life, were the reason he was the man he was today. He knew, without a doubt, they would love Maddie, too.

Last night, when he and Maddie had finally tumbled into his bed and ravaged each other's bodies, hadn't been about sight as much as his others senses. The palms of his hands, one currently cupping her lush backside, the other splayed over her hand on his chest, completed a circle of him and her. Of two people who'd become something more in the joining. His future was clear. He'd accomplished what he'd set out to do when he'd joined the Navy. He'd made a difference then, and with Maddie by his side, he would make a better, bigger difference, forever more.

Not since the first time he'd made love with her had he felt the sublime level of peace and contentment he felt now. Jameson knew he owed that sensation to the soft, warm body snuggled into his side. The sense of having found his way home again, as if he'd been lost until she'd come along, was real and tangible this morning. It gave him a feeling of wholeness that encompassed them like a blanket.

She lay sound asleep, her breath a warm huff feathering over his skin. Strands of her long hair tickled, entwined like it was in the coarse hairs that extended the length of his arm. There was no zing of feminine stress in the air today, as there had been the first time they'd met, only the sweet, sultry fragrance of lavender and their night of sex.

He pressed his lips to the top of her head, so damned blessed that his eyes watered. He had everything he wanted.

His TEAM cell phone barked softly from its charger on his nightstand. Carefully, so as not to wake Maddie, he released her hand on his chest and reached for the first call of the day. Most phones displayed caller IDs. His chirped different sounds, like ringtones, depending on the caller. Spam callers didn't stand a chance. He'd assigned stone cold silence to them. Maddie's unique ring was a heartbeat. His mom and dad merited the calming flutter of a harp, while Alex was a bugle playing taps. Anyone else from The TEAM was a snare drum. All except Harley. Which was why the phone barked.

"Hey, Harley," Jameson whispered into his cell. "Do you know what time it is?"

"Err, no, man. Did I call too early?"

"Nah," Jameson teased. "I really want to know. What time is it?"

"Oh, ah…" Hi voice faded. He must've leaned away from his cell to check his clock. "Five thirty. Guess it is early. Never mind. Go back to sleep. I'll call later when—"

"It's okay. I was already awake. Whatcha need?"

Harley cleared his throat. "Well, I was wondering. Mind if me and the monsters stop by? Little A has something to give you and Maddie, but mostly, you. He's all excited, which is why I forgot what time it is. But if it's too early—"

"Are you and your boys in your Jeep?" The soft hum of a vehicle over the connection told Jameson company was already in transit.

"Umm, yeah?"

Jameson grinned at that answer/question. He could almost hear Harley ruffling a hand over his head. He did that a lot. "Come on over. I'll put coffee on."

"You're sure? I mean, we can come back later."

Maddie's fingertips fluttered over Jameson's nipple to get his attention. "Tell him I've got chocolate milk and donuts for the boys."

"The last thing these kids need is a sugar high," a female voice murmured over the line.

Jameson moved his hand from Maddie's backside and clapped it over her fingers on his chest. "Good morning, Judy!" he called to the woman he'd only heard about so far.

"Hey, Jameson. Are you sure we're not intruding?"

"Positive. We're both awake." *And one of us is up.*

"Yeah…" Harley drew that word out. "It's me, the boys, and my wife. Geez, I should've called later."

"No, Harley," Maddie spoke up. "Hurry. I can't wait to see Georgie's surprise."

"When do you think you'll be here?" Jameson asked as nonchalantly as he could.

"Ten minutes, maybe fifteen at the most. Boys. Not now. Shhhhh. I'm talking."

"We'll be waiting," Jameson replied over the mayhem from Harley's end of the connection.

"Great. See ya soon."

And the scramble to get dressed and semi-presentable in less than ten minutes was on. Maddie jumped in the shower first. Jameson barged in behind her to save water. Yeah, right. The sudsy slide of his fingers down her belly earned him a half-hearted smack, but not before he urged a moan out of her.

"Harley's twins don't need sex education," she muttered. "We can't play now. Cease. Desist. Oh, heck.." Tipping up on her toes, she wound her arms around his neck. "At least don't get my hair wet."

Jameson filled his hands with the cheeks of her butt. "I definitely want a rain check," he mumbled into her lips.

"Me, too," she breathed, her voice so damned sultry, it was all Jameson could do to tear his hands off of her.

"Hurry," she ordered as she pushed off and shut the shower door in his face.

"Awww…" he groused. "Not fair."

Which made her laugh. And there it was, the tinkle of light-heartedness in his life that elicited the same feeling of contentment here, in his tiled, run-of-the-mill shower, of all places.

"Have I told you yet today how much I love you?" he called out as he shampooed his hair, then rinsed. Just that fast, his shower was done. Man-style.

"No, but you will," she teased from the bathroom sink. "I'm going to get dressed and start a big pot of coffee. Step on it, honey."

"I can't step on it. It's not that long," he teased back as he opened the shower door, ready to show her precisely how long it was. Hello, morning.

She giggled on her way into their bedroom. "Clothes. We need clothes and—"

The doorbell rang.

"Yikes!" was the last thing Maddie squealed.

He closed the bathroom door behind her, just in case the bedroom door was still open.

More giggling, then the bedroom door shut. The entry door opened. Then Maddie's bright, "Hello! Hi, Judy! Hi, boys! My goodness, you've both grown. Little A, your hair gets redder all the time, look at you! Jameson will be right out. Oh, my! Is that the surpr—?"

Several extra-loud "Shhhhhs" hissed from beyond Jameson's bedroom, and didn't that pique his curiosity? Hurriedly, he climbed into a clean pair of jeans and yesterday's t-shirt, then slipped into his comfy leather loafers. His ensemble complete, he stalked out of his bedroom into his too-quiet living room. He cocked his head, gauging the distance between him and his woman.

"Can I?" one of Harley and Judy's boys begged. "Please. It's no fun if he can't see him. I mean us. I mean—"

Jameson's nostrils flared. Dog. He smelled dog, sweaty little boys, and a different feminine fragrance in the room. That had to be Judy. But a dog. That was a hard scent to miss.

A gentle tug on his wrist brought him to one knee. "Uncle Jameson." That had to be Little A, so named because Little Alex had inadvertently created the misnomer, Big Alex. Which just did not work for anyone concerned.

But Jameson would never tire of knowing that, the moment he'd become part of The TEAM, he'd also become an uncle to all the agents' children. Even to Alex and Kelsey's, Lexie Rose and Bradley Patrick.

"Yes, Little A. What are you up to?" As if Jameson didn't know.

The four-legged companion standing with Harley's twin boy whined.

"Well, you see," Little A replied evenly. Of the two boys, he was the calmer, more thoughtful twin. Georgie tended to be high-strung, to bounce off walls when he didn't have anything to keep him occupied. He was more like Harley, full of nervous energy. "Daddy let me breed my dog, and I been really careful to take care of all the pups, and she had eight, but they're getting big now, and one was too little. He's the runt, and I hafta clean up all their poop every day, and make sure they don't chew Mom's shoes, cuz they really like her flipflops, and she gets really mad, and—" The kid finally inhaled a deep breath.

"Just tell him, son," Harley interrupted quietly.

Little A must've turned to his dad because the direction of his voice shifted. "Well, okay, but anyway, here." He took hold of Jameson's right hand and pressed a leather leash into his palm. "You hafta hold on real tight because…" Big breath.

"Daddy say's I can't keep 'em all, so I'm giving you my very best pup. He's the runt, but he's growing now, and he's strong, and he's my best friend, and I really love him, and I hope you really love him, too."

But by then, Little A could barely speak. He was all out crying from that pure declaration of a child's love for his best friend. A friend he was giving away.

Jameson leaned into the furry, wiggling pup at the other end of the leash. "A puppy?" he asked, blinking like a damn sissy. "For me? Are you sure?"

"Ah huh," Little A sobbed. "He's a purebred German Shepherd, Uncle Jameson, and he's sable, and that makes him look like a wolf. But he's really a good dog, and he's just for you, cuz Daddy said maybe you could use someone to help you find your way around the streets and roads and sidewalks, and—" The little guy hiccupped. "He's real good at finding things."

That was the last straw. Jameson opened his arms, and Little A plowed into him, bumping his chin with his head and crying at this very brave, very hard thing he was doing. The pup scrambled up with him, and suddenly, Jameson had two kids in his arms.

"He must be a very good dog," Jameson murmured into Little A's sweaty head, as he corralled the bundle of puppy energy in his other arm.

"He is. He's my bestest favorite, but I want you to have him because he's brave like you, only…" Harley's son took a deep, shuddering breath. "Kin I come and visit him sometime? And you, too?"

By then Jameson could barely speak. Settling the pup to the floor between his shoes, he shifted Little A to his knee, and swallowed hard. He'd purposefully avoided getting a seeing eye dog. His cane was enough of a statement to the world; he hadn't needed another. But now...?

"You bet. Come see him anytime. What's his name?"

"Tank. He was so teeny when he was borned, that we had to keep him in an aquarium tank under a warm light, but..." Little A's voice muffled as he ran an arm under his nose. "You kin call him anything you want because he's your dog now, and he's not mine, and...."

Little A burst into tears, and Jameson was right there with him. He took a covert swipe at his eyes, then wrapped both arms around the sobbing boy on his knee and patted his back. Harley, Judy, Georgie, and Maddie were out there watching, and one of them was sniffling, too. But for now, Jameson's attention was focused on the brave little soldier on his knee. "I like it. Tank's a good, strong name for a dog. It's hard giving your best friend away, isn't it?" he asked quietly.

"Ah huh," Little A grunted, as he wiped his mouth or his nose again. It was hard to tell which. "But I gotta do it, cuz that's why these dogs are borned in the first place. They got important things to do, too. Like Daddy and Mommy. Like you. They gotta amount to something or I'm not a good dog owner, only I am. I took real good care of my pups just so I could give this one to you." Again, the boy's voice rapped higher into a whine by the time he finished.

Jameson lifted his face in the direction where he supposed Harley was standing. Everyone was so quiet, it was hard to know for sure. "You've raised a good man here, Harley. You too, Judy."

Harley coughed. "Yeah, well..." He coughed again. "Judy's the reason these guys turned out as good as they have. I'm just their old man."

"You're a thousand times better than my old man," Maddie murmured from Jameson's right. "You should be proud."

"I am."

"He's the best Daddy in the world," Georgie added from Jameson's right, "cuz he's my dad."

"Mine too," Little A said quietly, "and he's goofy and he's funny, and I love him."

"Aww," Judy whispered.

Harley sounded like he needed a cough drop or someone to smack his back.

"Tank, huh?" Jameson asked Little A. "Will you show me how to feed him? What's he like to eat besides flipflops?"

"He likes his kibble and raw pork bones and fresh cow hoofs and chicken legs and eggs and—"

"And pretty much anything that isn't nailed down," Harley interrupted. "He's teething, so the more chew toys you provide, the longer your furniture's going to last. No leather cowhide and no baked bones, though. The leather crap will twist his gut, and cooked or baked bones splinter. Might tear up his innards."

"I brought his dishes and some puppy pads in case he has to pee before you can talk him for a walk and—"

"Cripes, A, take a breath, will ya?" Georgie grouched.

"I don't hafta," Little A shot back at his brother.

"Do too."

"Do not! I can talk how I want."

"Boys," Judy scolded. "What do we do when you're visiting friends?"

"We hafta be on our best behavior," Little A replied meekly.

Georgie snickered, which earned him a thump on what sounded like his head and a stern "Behave," from Harley.

"Wanna take him for a walk, Uncle Jameson?" Little A asked.

"Come with me?" Jameson asked as he set Little A on his feet, the leash firm in his hand.

"Aw right! Then I kin show you how to do it. See?" He took the leash back. "Tank already knows he has to walk on your left side, cuz that leaves your right hand free. Let's go!"

Jameson looked toward where he knew Maddie was standing. "We'll be right back. Wait for me?"

"Always," she answered, a dreamy tone in her voice. "I'll have breakfast ready by the time you kids get back."

Jameson left the debate over donuts or a healthy breakfast behind as he opened the door and began his new life as an uncle and a dog owner. By the time he and Little A had walked around the block, he knew Tank was trained to sit when they came to a stop, to stay on command, and to be quiet. Little A had insisted Jameson hold the leash once they were on the sidewalk, which was mature for the little guy. He was only six. But Jameson also knew that Little A was afraid of the dark, which was why Harley had given him a dog to begin with. He also knew Georgie was a bit of a bully; he lived to destroy Little A's LEGO creations. Also that Harley and Judy needed to soundproof their bedroom. Kids did say the darnedest things.

When they circled back to the apartment's main entry, Little A asked, "How do you know which place is yours and where you should stop? You don't have your cane, and Daddy says you can't see. How'd you do that?"

"I count steps," Jameson told him easily. "And today, I could tell we were nearly back home because Tank slowed when we turned the last corner. He was looking for his new home."

"You think he already knows he belongs to you and where he lives?"

Jameson tugged the dog's leash to bring Tank to a full stop. When pup dropped his backside to the sidewalk, Jameson took a knee and faced Little A at his level. Man to man. "I think Tank might have been born small, but he's smarter than the average dog. I can tell you've spent a lot of time training him. Would you mind spending his first night away from home with me and Maddie? You know, so he knows you'll always come back, and that you'll always love him no matter where he is?"

"Kin I?"

"Absolutely. You two guys can bunk in the living room tonight. Then tomorrow, you can show me what else Tank knows. We'll go to the park and really put him through his paces, deal?"

"Deal!" Little A exclaimed. "But I gotta ask Mommy and Daddy first."

"Of course," Jameson replied as he set A's feet to the sidewalk and reached for the massive handle on his apartment's double doors. With one click of the smart key fob in his jeans pocket, he ushered Little A inside, while Tank followed.

"I really like you, Uncle Jameson," Little A said, his hand so small and warm inside Jameson's. "Maybe you can come see the rest of my pups someday."

"Good idea." Jameson opened the door to his apartment with a cheery, "Honey, we're home!"

Maddie was instantly at his side. "Just in time. Hot chocolate and breakfast burritos are ready. Donuts for dessert," she announced as she pressed a kiss to his cheek.

He leaned into that kiss, then handed the leash to her. "We have a very smart dog. Next time, you have to come with us."

"Mom! Dad!" Little A called. "Kin I stay here tonight with Tank? Uncle Jameson says it's okay, and I'll be real good. Pleeeease?"

Jameson turned toward the kitchen table where he sensed movement and body heat.

"'S okay with me. Mom, that okay with you?" Harley answered from that location.

"Are you sure?" Judy's quiet voice came from the sofa.

Jameson turned to face Little A's mother. "Positive. I have a lot to learn about dogs and little boys. It'll be fun."

"I'm staying, too!" Georgie announced loudly from somewhere near Judy.

"No, son, you're going home with us," Harley told him.

"But Daddy—"

"That's the rule," Judy replied evenly. "Little A did all the work with his dogs, so he gets the reward."

"Besides," Harley drawled. "Not sure Uncle Jameson and Aunt Maddie are ready for two monsters at the same time. Let's break them in slow."

"Aww…"

"Georgie, enough. Until you accept responsibility and do your chores without being told to, no sleepovers."

"Never?"

"You heard me."

"But I was just playing."

Jameson pulled Maddie into his side as the Mortimer power struggle continued. "That'll be us someday," he murmured into her cheek. "A house full of kids and tests of wills. Late night feedings and diapers, doctor appointments and worries, kindergarten and dogs. Maybe a cat or two. A treehouse for sure. You still game?"

She pressed herself under his arm, her body warm and enticing as hell. "I can't wait."

"I love you," he told his better half.

"I know," she whispered back. "We've got a fur baby. We're parents."

And there it was, his future in sold gold. With Maddie. With Tank and the little boy who loved him. Tears welled in the corners of Jameson Tenney's eyes. His greatest challenge had begun five years ago with two other little boys and a miniature donkey. If not for that frightening, horrible day, he wouldn't be where he was now, a dog leash in one hand, his soon-to-be wife in his other. Jameson bowed his nose to Maddie's hair, wishing Derby and Shakespeare could somehow know that he'd honored them by living. Every. Single. Day.

Because it had worked. He had thrown himself back into the deep end of life. He had learned how to swim all over again. But most of all… Life was great!

The End

Thank you for reading Jameson's story!

You are the key to this book's success.

Please tell other readers why you liked Jameson by leaving an honest review at the retail site where you purchased it.

Recommend him to your friends. Lend him. Most of all, enjoy him!

Irish Winters' best-selling series include:

In the Company of Snipers

Alex

Mark

Zack

Harley

Connor

Rory

Taylor

Gabe

Maverick

Cassidy

Adam

Lee

Ky

Hunter

Eric

Jake

Seth

Beau

Renner

Beckam

Walker

Christmas Hearts

Coming soon:
Tripp

Deuces Wild
King of Hearts
Joker Joker
One-Eyed Jack
Ace

Hearts and Ashes
Smoke
Ash

SOBs Novels
Angel
Assassin
Vaquero
Coming soon:
Kruze Sinclair's story

To keep up with my new releases, giveaways, and actionable intel, sign up for my spam-free newsletter at IrishWinters.com.

Keep reading for a preview of another tasty tidbit.

Preview of Harley's story

In the Company of Snipers, #4

Ambushed!

"Rick! Can you hear me?" US Army Corporal Harley Mortimer bellowed, his voice lost in the grinding noise of battle. "Kent? Snakes? Anyone?"

Rick didn't answer. No one did. Only the roar of the fire came back to him. Acrid fumes poured off his overturned and now obliterated Humvee. Smelled like the whole damned Iraqi oilfield was burning again. He rolled for cover.

The chopper overhead sounded odd for a Blackhawk. Maybe a Cobra? Combat Rescue? Already? No way. He knew better. They'd be here eventually, but not this soon. Had to be one of Saddam's. Even that conclusion felt hollow. USAF owned the sky. Everyone in the world knew that. Saddam's air force was rubble.

Enemy bullets zinged too close, kicking up plugs of dirt and razor sharp bits of stone that perforated his face and arms. Blood filled his ear where his earpiece should have been. The link with his men must have blown clear when the Humvee exploded. Panic climbed up his throat. Blood gushed down the back of his neck. *Damn, I'm cut off and injured too.*

Could things get any worse? He slapped his palms to his chest pockets and thighs. Sure enough, they could. He didn't even have an empty holster where a pistol might have been. No tactical vest, no headgear. No knife. Nothing. *I'm screwed.*

Time to leave. American soldiers alone had better keep moving or face certain capture. Not going to happen. Pumped full of fight or flight, he crept around the front of the MRAP, the Mine Resistant Armored Personnel Vehicle that accompanied his Humvee on this foray into hell. Yeah, right. It didn't look very mine resistant now, not spewing its guts the way it was. Looked worse than his ride, both piles of steaming crap.

Fumes and smoke seared his eyeballs, making it impossible to see. What kind of an IED could have caused this much damage? Scrubbing both hands over his face, he muttered a quick Hail Mary. And then he saw them. All six of them. His men. His friends. Kent. Snakes. Carlton. Robbie. Rick. Garth. Their bodies in pieces and bleeding chunks. He faltered. *Who to run to first? Should I run at all?*

One second he was debating how to rescue body parts; the next he was kneeling at Corporal Rick Cross's side, his body stabbed through with a huge shard of metal. So much blood. Harley ripped the dead man's belt off. Every soldier knows how to wrap a tourniquet. Adrenaline pushed his shaking hands.

"I got you, man. You're gonna be fine. Promise." His mouth would not shut up until his ruthless brain engaged and squashed the hope rolling off his tongue.

There's nothing to tie off.

He backed away, choking at the eerie sensation of déjà vue creeping up the back of his throat. This was not

happening. It wasn't real. Couldn't be. Rick wasn't dead—
again. Was he? A long lost memory invaded what sure felt like
reality.

*I am here, aren't I? Sure smells like Iraq. Sounds like Iraq.
But didn't I already—leave?*

Panic sucked the air from his lungs. Like a stupid frog on
a hot plate, he jumped to Specialist Robbie Smith next. Blood
gurgled from the fist-sized wound in his friend's neck.
Suddenly, Harley was with Corporal Carlton Jenner, still and
lifeless on the ground, his body twisted in an impossible-to-
live-through position. Without walking or running to get
there, Harley crouched over Sergeant Kent Roosevelt, and
then Kent's arm, which until then had been in a black-red pool
of coagulated blood a yard away.

He didn't remember taking a step. Logic failed when he
needed it most. He scrubbed the smoke and dust out of his
stinging eyes. Dazed. Afraid. Scared he'd lost his ever-loving
mind.

Abruptly, Kent's unattached hand jumped from the oil-
covered ground and clutched Harley's sleeve, tugging him
back to his men. "Save us," Kent snarled with the grotesque
lip twitching of the dead.

"What the hell?" Harley crab-scrambled backward,
inhaling disbelief instead of air. The dismembered limb fell,
four fingers tapping the dusty ground as if waiting for an
answer. He shook his head to clear his vision. *No way! I'm
seeing things for sure.*

"You gotta do something." Bloody words gurgled from
the dead man's mouth. Harley lunged back, but Kent persisted
with mercurial eyeballs instead of the once deep browns. His

stare brimmed with unsaid accusation. *You lived, you bastard. I died, but you got to live.*

Just as quickly, Carlton sprang to a ninety-degree angle, his hips twisted in the opposite direction to his shoulders. He cocked his head sideways and taunted. "You gotta save us, man. You got to."

Harley groaned at the frightening quandary of seeing is believing. Kent and Carlton were obviously dead with a capital D, but they were talking?

Rick joined the ghostly moan. Robbie sputtered. Captain Snakes Flynn growled. Then Corporal Garth Schmidt. Their voices rose in an eerie chorus of condemnation, while six pairs of unseeing eyes stared him down for help. For rescue. For anything. "You gotta save us this time. All," they chanted. "All. All. All."

"But you guys are... dead." Harley was sure of his words, not his eyes. "I can't save you. You already... died."

Are you sure? He shook the demon of doubt away. It was lying to him. It had to be. Misgivings prevailed. *Why are you talking to them if they're dead?*

"I don't know," he answered himself.

"Don't leave us behind again," the six-man chorus whined over the hissing fire. Even the twisted carcass of the Humvee groaned in haunting accompaniment. A tire exploded. Hard rubber ripped past his head, leaving stifling fumes and heat in its wake.

He watched the horror show, unable to save the men he loved any more than he could save himself. His dead buddies waited, their tongues flicking over their lips from the same thirst in his mouth. But just in case.... He crawled back to assist.

A veil of fumes descended upon the stage, encompassing wounded and would-be rescuer alike. His windpipe constricted. Harley choked until he could choke no more, spitting to clear his throat. Air would not come. When unconsciousness threatened, he bowed his forehead to the dirt and wished to wake the hell up—or die with his men. Like he should have.

As quickly as it came, the haze lifted. He could breathe, but his friends were gone. Not even limbs remained. No puddled blood. No tapping dismembered fingers. Nothing.

It dawned on him then. The Iraqi's fought dirty. Saddam was a bastard. They'd used nerve gas on him. Either that or his men really spoke to him. No. Nerve gas explained everything. It had to be.

Thunder shook the ground. Shrapnel and bullets pinged too close and personal, pushing him to act. So that's the way it was, under fire and his men had been forced to leave him behind. He was alone. Instinct kicked in. Training took over.

Move it, soldier. Move it. Move it. Move it!

He steeled his jaw, stiffened his spine and secured his belt around his own bleeding leg, padding it with a rag from the dirty ground. The chemicals in the smoke provided an acid eyewash that would not quit. He could barely see to stagger away. His feet would not follow. No matter. He carved a drunkard's path into the desert and away from hell. One more step. Then another. Time and distance. All he needed now. Three things were sure. He wouldn't be taken alive. He'd live to fight another day. And he'd catch up with his men.

Keep moving.

Confusion and guilt ruled the day. It sure looked like his men were dead back there. He was sure they'd begged for help. But then they were gone. That meant they were alive, that they walked away. Didn't it? Parts felt real. Parts did not. Like that detached hand. How could those fingers tap like they were attached to Kent when they weren't?

Harley collapsed against a wall. Scrubbing the pain away, he tried desperately to remember or forget. The puzzle remained. Hadn't he seen this same damned movie before?

Shreds of bizarre nonsense swirled inside his tired skull.

"Nine o'clock team meeting, don't be—"

"Your favorite peppered shrimp—"

"Mark's baby girl... JayJay... looks like—"

"Judy."

The last word, that name tugged at his weary mind for further scrutiny. It meant something. He could tell. It was a pleasant name. Like the piercing beam of a lighthouse cast high above the pitch-black storm in his head, it called to him. *'Look at me. Remember me.'*

Harley sucked in another breath of desert air, his soul whipped and beaten by the war.

Who the hell is Judy?

About the Author

Irish Winters...

...is a best-selling author who, when she isn't writing, dabbles in poetry, grandchildren, and rarely (as in extremely rarely) the kitchen. More prone to be outdoors than in, she grew up the quintessential tomboy on a dairy farm in rural Wisconsin, spent her teen years in the Pacific Northwest, but calls the Wasatch Mountains of Northern Utah, home. For now.

She believes in making every day count for something, and follows the wise admonition of her mother to, *"Look out the window and see something!"*

Connect with Irish online:
On Facebook: https:/www.facebook.com/author.irishwinters
On Twitter: https://twitter.com/irishwinters1
Or at http://www. IrishWinters.com

www.ingramcontent.com/pod-product-compliance
Lightning Source LLC
Chambersburg PA
CBHW021056110726
47900CB00007B/1904